CHRISTMAS EVER AFTER

JAIMIE ADMANS

Boldwood

First published in Great Britain in 2024 by Boldwood Books Ltd.

Copyright © Jaimie Admans, 2024

Cover Design by Alexandra Allden

Cover photography: iStock and Shutterstock

A CIP catalogue record for this book is available from the British Library.

Paperback ISBN 978-1-83561-763-2

Large Print ISBN 978-1-83561-764-9

Hardback ISBN 978-1-83561-762-5

Ebook ISBN 978-1-83561-765-6

Kindle ISBN 978-1-83561-766-3

Audio CD ISBN 978-1-83561-757-1

MP3 CD ISBN 978-1-83561-758-8

Digital audio download ISBN 978-1-83561-759-5

Boldwood Books Ltd
23 Bowerdean Street
London SW6 3TN
www.boldwoodbooks.com

For everyone who still believes their nutcracker will turn into a prince on Christmas Eve!

1

This is it. I'm finally going to kiss him.

I have never loved mistletoe more than I do right at this moment, because mistletoe is about to bring me lip-to-lip with the man I've had a crush on since I opened The Nutcracker Shop four years ago: Jorge, the baker who works at the year-round festive bakery on the corner between Ever After Street and our little festive cul-de-sac, Christmas Ever After. Until now, I've never had the courage to say anything more than some inane comment about the weather when I go into his shop to buy cakes. And I go into his shop to buy cakes a *lot*.

He makes the most perfect mince pies, gingerbread, chocolate orange muffins, stollen buns, and Yule logs, and I *might* spend a not-small amount of time, and money, in there, because with every cake, I think... maybe this is the one. *This* is the cake where he'll look up, meet my eyes across the counter, our fingers will brush as he hands me my change, and he'll suddenly realise that the love of his life has been working right down the street all this time.

He'll pick up my hand and lift it to his mouth. 'How have I never seen you before?' he'll say. Or maybe it'll be something like,

'Did you do something new with your hair? How have I never noticed how beautiful you are until now?'

Okay, beautiful might be pushing it a bit, but daydreams aren't meant to be realistic, are they?

'Cameras ready!' A shout interrupts my reverie. 'Are we in position? Jorge, move a tad to the left, the sun's reflecting off your cheekbones. Franca, stand on tiptoes or the angle will be awkward. We really should've picked someone taller,' Mitch continues. He's the social media manager for Christmas Ever After, self-appointed cameraman, and also one of the Santas who occupy Santa's Grotto every day of the year. I move back to give Jorge more room and the stool I'm standing on wobbles precariously under me.

It's the first day of December and we're hanging the first mistletoe of the season – an event that's streamed live online and photographs from which will be published on our website and sent out with press releases to local news outlets to advertise the festive season on Ever After Street.

Every year, there's a ballot to decide who gets to share the first kiss and be the face of the Christmas Ever After photos for that year. The name of every shopkeeper goes into a barrel, and then one man and one woman are chosen to hang the mistletoe on the arch that marks the entrance to the year-round Christmas end of Ever After Street, and share a kiss underneath it.

And this year, Jorge's name was chosen first, and then, in a twist of festive fate that I didn't see coming because I never win *anything...* so was mine.

'Franca, can you stop moving about like that? Do you need a wee or something? You're practically vibrating, the camera keeps getting a motion blur.'

'Right, sorry.' I swallow hard. I'm nervous. Ridiculously nervous. The man I've fantasised about for so long is going to fall in love with me in just one kiss's time. It's a lot to prepare for. It'll be our first Christmas together, I'll need to get him the perfect present. Will we meet each other's families or will it be too early? No, wait, he can *never* be allowed to meet my family. Crikey, he'll need to be seriously invested in the relationship before that happens because they'll send him running for the hills. My family will have to wait until the wedding, but maybe I could meet *his* family... They might like me and that will further prove to him how perfect we are for each other.

Jorge is ignoring Mitch's fussing. He's ignoring me as well actually, even though I've tried to make conversation a few times since we've been standing here. I've tried a 'good morning' and a 'how funny meeting you here', and then a 'well, this is awkward', and I even lowered myself to a 'so, do you come here often?'

Each one has been answered with either a look or a grunt. Which is fine, because I'm embarrassed enough for myself. It's *hard* to make conversation with someone you fancy this much. A lot is riding on this kiss being absolutely perfect, and not just the marketing success of Christmas Ever After's festive campaign this year. My ex was enough to put anyone off relationships for life, and after a few years of being single, Jorge is the first person who's made me reconsider that. This *has* to go well.

Now he's got a pocket mirror out and is holding it up and doing various model-like poses into it, pursing his lips and tilting his head from one side to the other.

He really is *very* well groomed. Such perfectly shaped facial hair that it looks like it could be painted on. I peer a bit closer. I'm actually not quite convinced that it *isn't* painted on. There are some suspect patches that look like someone's taken a liquid eyeliner pen to them.

'Do you want to borrow a comb?' He says it to the mirror and it takes me a moment to work out if he's talking to me or his reflection.

'Er... no?' I mumble, and then self-consciously try to tidy up my hair. The wind is getting up and blowing it all over the place. Is that his subtle way of telling me I look like a scarecrow?

A comb, though. Does he actually have a comb on him? Who carries a comb around on their person these days? Is he secretly a parent to a small Victorian child whose hair and clothes must be neatly in order at all times?

'And must you really wear that dreadful thing?'

'It's a Santa hat!' My brown hair is mid-back length, but the front is a long, grown-out fringe, and I had it artfully arranged under the Santa hat, tucked to one side and half-covering one eye. I was going for an alluring, sort of Mariah Carey-esque look, but it's windier than I expected, so I've had to tell myself that the look I'm going for is 'relatably windswept' or 'festively dishevelled'. I'm surprised by his comment though. It was very disparaging for someone who's usually so kind, and it's made me feel even more self-conscious than I was feeling anyway. *Was* the Santa hat a bad choice? No, I *like* the Santa hat. It's Christmas. What kind of person objects to a Santa hat at Christmas?

'Smile, you two!' Mitch calls, still perfecting the camera angle. 'You're about to share a kiss under the mistletoe! Jorge, we're not putting together your pouty modelling portfolio for some frightfully posh brand of aftershave that costs more than a small car! Franca, can you hold out a hand to showcase "Christmas Ever After" across the archway, just to make extra sure that people will know where to go.'

Every shop on Ever After Street is themed after a different fairy tale, and Christmas Ever After is its little sister at one end, where every shop is festively themed and where it's Christmas all the time.

I make bespoke nutcrackers at The Nutcracker Shop, and there's the bakery, and a shop solely for Christmas lights, a couple of handmade decoration shops, and All You Need Is Gloves – a winter clothing shop for humans and pets run by Mrs Coombe. There's also Coming Gnome For Christmas – a shop dedicated entirely to Christmas gnomes that the owner, Mrs Bloom, makes herself. And there's All Wrapped Up – a gift-wrapping shop, and a few others, including my favourite, A Very Muggy Christmas – a shop that sells nothing but Christmas mugs. It's impossible to have too many Christmas mugs.

'This is big business for our social media. It's like the launch of the John Lewis Christmas advert. *Everyone* tunes in to see the first mistletoe kiss of the year.'

Mitch might be exaggerating there. It creates a bit of a buzz and people always come out to watch the 'official opening' of the festive season on Christmas Ever After, and there's a photo opportunity for couples to stop for a kiss underneath the archway for the rest of the month, but the John Lewis ad trends on social media and people make parodies of it on YouTube, so I don't think our little corner of Herefordshire is quite at that level yet.

At least, I hope not. Especially when Mitch adds, 'We've already got three hundred viewers and the livestream hasn't started yet.'

My cheeks heat up at the mention of the livestream. The main camera is on a tripod, but there's also a videographer walking around with a camcorder to capture the action from every angle. I smooth down my sparkly red Christmas jumper self-consciously. With the number of mince pies I've eaten lately, some angles are better avoided.

Admittedly, I'd have preferred my first kiss with Jorge not to be *quite* so public. Our fellow shopkeepers are gathered to watch, and shoppers have started to hang around to see what's going on. That's without the photographs, the video recording for TikTok, and being livestreamed on YouTube for all the world to see, but every relationship has to start somewhere. As soon as Jorge kisses me, he's going to know I'm the one for him. He'll see past the inane comments about the weather and that laugh-snort-gurgle thing I do when I'm nervous, and none of the multiple pairs of eyes on us will matter any more.

'Can you two stand a bit closer together and look lovingly into each other's eyes so we're ready when the camera starts rolling?'

Jorge reluctantly puts his little mirror away and turns towards me with a frown that suggests I'm inconveniencing him by being here. He's lovely in the bakery. Friendly and chatty, and he always makes me feel like I'm his best customer, although to be fair, I probably *am* his best customer. But out here, it's like he's been possessed by the narcissistic ghost of a vain catwalk model.

He turns towards me. This is it. The moment I've been waiting for. Nerves flood my body and my knees feel unsteady and shaky, and it's not just because of the wobbly stool I'm balancing on.

I've pictured this moment so many times. I've imagined all the ways our first kiss might go, but I'm still unprepared for the moment to actually arrive. It's going to be perfect. It *has* to be perfect.

He turns towards me and opens his mouth and...

I gag. His breath is bad enough that it makes me take an involuntary step backwards and sway precariously on the stool again. My eyes start watering and it's *not* from the wind chill. 'What the heck did you have for breakfast? Overnight onions? Three-week-old garlic?' The words slip out before I realise I've spoken. I would never usually say something so bold to Jorge, but his breath has catapulted me right out of the fantasy about our perfect first kiss.

'Monster Munch,' he says with a grin. 'Pickled onion and roast beef flavour. I like to mix the two together and play Monster Munch roulette; you never know which one you're going to get!'

'Who eats crisps before 10 a.m.? You're a baker! Don't you bake something delicious and healthy for breakfast?'

'Nah. Living my best life.'

'Monster Munch constitutes your best life?'

After spending the past twenty minutes trying to engage with him, *now* he chooses to grin at me with a nod, clearly not detecting the sarcasm in my question. I fully support most breakfast choices, but... Monster Munch? Really? In all the times and all the ways I imagined my first kiss with Jorge, Monster Munch breath never entered my fantasies.

Nothing has *ever* made someone more unattractive than pickled onion crisp breath and there's no way I'm going through with this. 'I'm not kissing him.'

'What?' Jorge's face has gone red and his pout has turned into a sneer.

'*What?*' Mitch echoes and looks at his watch. 'Franca, it is 09.57 and fifty-five seconds. The livestream is starting in literally *two* minutes! Whatever hang-ups you've got, get over them *now!*'

'I am not kissing someone with breath like that!' I didn't mean it to come out so loudly, but the band are about to start playing and the noise of their instruments tuning up is drowning me out, and I've just accidentally announced it to the entire street. I can see the eyes of our fellow shopkeepers go wide, and the gathered crowd of onlookers start giggling.

I didn't mean to embarrass him, but Jorge's face has gone from red to purple and his hands are curled into fists.

'Yeah, well, as if I'd kiss *you*, Mariah Scary!' He steps off his stool and stalks away, leaving me standing alone under the Christmas Ever After archway, with the camera about to start rolling.

Mitch is shout-whispering furiously at Jorge. 'Get back up there *now!*'

'Hell, no! I'm not going to let Windswept McScruffy insult me like that! Forget it!'

I try to finger-comb my hair. My usual level of self-consciousness is bubbling into overflow because I've just embarrassed my crush in the most public way possible. I should have said it more quietly, although if he'd had the decency to speak to me at any of the other times I tried to initiate conversation, I would have got an earlier whiff and this could've been sorted out with plenty of time to spare.

Mitch has gone from whisper-shouting to not even trying to hide his frustration. 'Well, this is a fine mess, isn't it? What am I supposed to do n—' Before he can finish the 'now', his eyes fall to a figure walking past and light up immediately. 'Raff! The perfect fit!'

I follow his gaze to the dark-haired, hoodie-wearing man on his way to his shop.

No. No, no, no, no, no, *no*. Not Raphael Dardenne. *Anyone* but Raphael Dardenne. Literally, anyone. I would kiss someone with Monster Munch breath over him any day. Hell, I would kiss a *packet* of Monster Munch before I'd kiss him. It would be a privilege to kiss someone who's been eating pickled onion flavour crisps rather than get within a ten-foot range of Raphael Dardenne.

He's the owner of the ridiculous 'matchmaking' snow globe shop, Love Is All A-Round. Peddler of the complete lie that their snow globes magically move if you hold one with your soulmate. A con-artist who makes the rest of us on Christmas Ever After look bad. Raphael Dardenne is the most awkward, annoying, difficult person to ever work on Ever After Street, and he and I are in direct competition with each other this year.

Thankfully, he walks on, ignoring Mitch. There's no way he'd get involved or do anything to help. The only thing Raphael Dardenne is interested in is doing everything he can to mess things up for those of us who will still be here next year, unlike him when he finally gets evicted in January, with a bit of luck.

'I'm sorry,' I say to Jorge, trying to appeal to his better nature. 'Please come back. Christmas Ever After deserves your cheek-bones on its advertising materials.'

At first I think it's working, but then Jorge's eyes flit between Mitch, who is waving frantically to get Raphael's attention, and the man who's steadfastly trying to ignore him, and me. Everyone knows how much Raphael and I hate each other, and I can see the cogs turning in Jorge's mind. The perfect punishment for insulting him. He folds his arms and stands his ground with a petulant nod.

Raphael has ignored Mitch's shouting but, far from being deterred, Mitch has now physically accosted him and hauled him onto the scene, shouting a frantic explanation while trying to drag his hoodie off and make him more presentable. 'Live! One minute! You, up there! Mistletoe! Kiss! Smile!'

If Mitch was young enough to lift Raphael, I think he'd have picked him up and deposited him on the stool next to mine, although after a bit of shoving, cajoling and threatening, before either of us have worked out what's happening, Raphael is standing on the stool opposite mine, wearing a crumpled but festively red T-shirt with mussed-up hair and a confused look on his nefarious face.

He looks around in bewilderment until his eyes fall on me and he recoils so quickly that he wobbles on the stool and nearly falls right back off it. 'You've got to be joking! I'm not kissing *that!*'

I gasp in annoyance. 'I'm not kissing *that* either, you weaselly little con-artist!'

'Shut up!' Mitch suddenly yells. In the four years I've worked here, I've *never* heard Mitch speak at that volume before, but Raphael Dardenne could try the patience of Ol' Saint Nick himself, never mind a man who plays him.

'We've got a situation on our hands! That camera is going to start rolling in thirty seconds. I need two people to kiss under the mistletoe *now*! It can be on the cheek, if you must.'

'God only knows what would happen if those two touched lips,' Mrs Bloom, the owner of Coming Gnome For Christmas, says. 'Something apocalyptic, I wouldn't wonder.'

'I'm not getting involved in this. I don't even know how I got here. I thought Jorge was the man of choice this year.' Raphael looks around until his eyes fall on Jorge, standing at the edge of the crowd, looking satisfied with this turn of events. 'Oh, let me guess, Franca offended him in some way, like she offends everyone else.'

'With good reason!' I snap. Raphael really is the most infuriating person to ever exist. 'I can hang the mistletoe by myself this year, in solidarity with single people everywhere. Not everyone has a handsome man to kiss under the mistletoe and Christmas Ever After should be inclusive to all relationship statuses.'

Mitch interrupts before I can get any further. 'Look, I know you pair are locked in this "war of words, may the best man win" thing, but only one of you is going to be evicted in January, and the rest of us who *aren't* going to be evicted need this to be a Christmas to remember. We all need a good December to survive, and you both owe us that much for putting up with your constant bickering and nitpicking! There are now *four* hundred viewers tuned in, waiting for our livestream to start, which it's going to in' – he checks his watch – 'twenty bloody seconds! All you have to do is hang the mistletoe Mrs Bloom is going to bring over, smile, and give each other a peck on the cheek, and for the love of all things Christmas, be civil to each other for the few minutes it will take to get some decent pictures, or so help me, I will petition the council to have the *pair* of you evicted!'

After his outburst, Mitch starts the countdown like a seasoned film director. He's organised this whole thing every year for the past decade or so, since before anyone had even heard the word 'livestream' and TikTok was nothing but a twinkle in the internet's eye, and it's never gone this wrong before. 'Five hundred viewers now! This is going to be our biggest Christmas yet! And if it isn't, I'm holding you two personally responsible!'

A cymbal clatters and the band strikes up with 'We Wish You a Merry Christmas', and there's the telltale bleep-bleep of the camera recording. I'm shaking with... well, earlier it was nerves, but now it's just annoyance at being shoved together with Raphael Dardenne of all people.

I don't want to get *near* this man, never mind let him kiss my cheek, and no doubt he feels the same about me, but I can tell how agitated Mitch is, and Raphael and I *have* caused everyone some trouble with our constant goading of each other. Surely we can tolerate each other for a few minutes?

I meet his dark eyes and then look away quickly. I know he blames me for the snow-globes-versus-nutcrackers position the council have put us in. We've been pitted against each other for years anyway, but now we are literally pitted against each other. His shop or mine. One of us has to go in January, and it's absolutely *not* going to be me.

And it *is* kind of my fault. At the last council meeting in November, Raphael and I were criticising each other – because that's what we *do* at council meetings. We find something the other has done wrong and we complain about it. We talk *about* each other or *at* each other, but never *to* each other. I delighted in the fact he's got some bad reviews lately. Customers complaining about how his snow globes have lost their 'magic' matchmaking ability and how bad his matches are, and he complained that the giant nutcrackers outside my shop were blocking the display of other shops, and the leader of the local council in charge of Ever After Street lost his rag. He snapped that customers had commented on the rivalry between us, our fellow shopkeepers were fed up with it, and something had to give. He said that Herefordshire Council wouldn't be putting up with another year of our nonsense, and that one of us would have to go. They set a challenge – Raphael has to help five couples find love with his 'magical' snow globes and disprove his terrible reviews, and I have to prove that nutcrackers are still popular by getting five genuine posts on social media from customers who love my nutcrackers, and we both have to do it before Christmas.

Your lack of enthusiasm has been noticed is what Mr Hastings said to me. *We want to see social media engagement and excited customers. No one cares about nutcrackers. In our surveys, no one comes to Christmas Ever After to visit your shop. We need to see customers who are engaged and interested in your products.*

So if I don't get a *lot* of people talking about nutcrackers this month, I may lose. To *him*.

I glance at him again and this time, he looks away like he can tell what I'm thinking. He's annoyingly handsome in the traditional tall and dark-haired way. It should be illegal for a man who is this much of a twit to also be this gorgeous.

Mrs Bloom is acting as Mitch's assistant today. She's dressed in a Mrs-Claus-style red robe with a fluffy white trim. The mistletoe is placed on an antique Christmas tray and she ceremoniously carries it over to us. It's ordered fresh from a small town in Wales where there's a legend that anyone who kisses underneath it will have another year of happiness together. It was cut by the park caretakers and shipped by twenty-four-hour courier, so it will stay fresh until Christmas is over.

The original plan was for me to take the mistletoe and hang it on the arch, smile, and turn to Jorge for my magical Christmas kiss, but no one's had a chance to brief Raphael on that plan, because he reaches for the mistletoe at exactly the same moment as I do, and our hands knock together with a jolt as we both try to pick it up.

He *snatches* it from the tray and holds it to his chest as though he's trying to protect it from me. 'What a surprise. Franca Andrews thinking she should always come first.'

'I was *supposed* to be first, you've come in and ruined that.' I snatch the mistletoe back, and my fingernail catches the edge of his hand and scratches it unintentionally. If it had been intentional, I would have *gouged* it.

'Not out of choice. Besides, no one can ruin anything if you're here. With you involved, it's already ruined.'

I yank the mistletoe out of his reach when he grabs at it again. 'Why, you lousy—'

'Franca!' Mitch hisses, gesticulating furiously at the camera, and I turn towards it and paste a smile over my gritted teeth.

'Make the most of it.' Raphael takes advantage of the shift in my concentration and snatches the mistletoe out of my hand. 'It'll be your last Christmas on Ever After Street, I'll make sure of that!'

'I'm not going to be evicted. You are. Our colleagues are all behind me. Everyone's sick of your bad reviews dragging us all down. You couldn't strike up a match if it was in a box and had a red incendiary head and a striking strip on the side!'

'Hah!' He scoff-laughs, waving the mistletoe around in front of him. 'Who would choose your cheap and nasty nutcrackers that fall apart after a day over my handcrafted snow globes that come with their very own magic? And you're getting bad reviews too! One says your nutcrackers are horrible quality and break easily!'

'My nutcrackers are decorative! That reviewer tried to crack a macadamia with it! Only the hardest nut of them all and then she had the cheek to leave a bad review saying it was poor quality.'

'Yes, imagine the irony of attempting to use a nutcracker to crack a nut.' He rolls his eyes. 'How utterly absurd!'

The mistletoe is looking worse for wear now, which is probably a bad omen for Christmas Ever After, and I try to grab it back but he's annoyingly taller than me and keeps it out of my reach, and I can't lean too far without the stool wobbling. 'At least I'll never be as childish as you are. You made a bogey out of Blu Tack and stuck it so it was hanging from the underside of my giant nutcracker's nose!'

'You have no idea whether that was me or a small child with an exquisite sense of humour.' He does a chef's kiss gesture.

There really is no talking to someone who's so infuriatingly immature. 'Oh, why don't you just sod off? You're going in January anyway, why not make everyone's day better and go now? Let us all enjoy Christmas without your stupid snow globes bringing us all down?'

'Fine,' he growls, but instead of hanging the mistletoe on the arch, he tosses it at me, and I squeak in surprise and throw my hands up because it seems like it's coming straight at my face, and he spins around and steps off his stool, except... he's too near me, and the world goes into slow motion. I see what's going to happen nanoseconds before it does, but there's no time to stop it. Raphael's leg connects with the stool I'm standing on, knocking it from the precarious position it was already in. I scream and flail, trying to keep my balance, but it's no good. The stool is tipping.

I reach out, trying to grab at something, *anything* to keep myself upright and *not* splat onto the pavement, and there's something cool and metal under my hands. The arch! I'm hanging onto the arch! 'Help!'

Someone's screaming. I'm not sure if it's me or Mrs Bloom or possibly both of us. A gasp has gone through the crowd.

'Quick, get the stool under her!' Mitch shouts. He's trying to reach up to me, but he's not tall enough. His hands barely reach my ankles where they're dangling high above the ground. 'Get a ladder!'

My grip is slipping. My hands are sweaty with fear of how I'm going to get out of this. I'm flailing above the cobblestones. My jumper is riding up and my trousers are slipping downwards. I can feel the cold morning air rushing around the bare skin of my not-small belly, and the arch... The arch is bending under my weight. It's designed for hanging bunches of mistletoe and a garland or two, not full-grown shopkeepers who buy too many cakes and spend all day sitting in front of their woodturning lathe making nutcrackers.

All the muscles in my body are screaming from the exertion of trying to hold my weight up, and panic is rising. There seems to be no way out of this without hurting myself. Landing on my bad leg could be disastrous. Mitch has got the stool. He's trying to guide my feet towards it, but it's too far away, there's too much space between me and it, and I can't see. The more I move about, the more I'm slipping.

'Someone's gone for a ladder,' Mitch calls up.

It's too late. The arch is crumpling under my weight.

'Call the fire brigade!' someone cries.

'No need for that!' I yell hastily. The situation is already bad enough as it is. A load of hot men in uniform turning up to rescue me like a cat stuck up a tree would really take the biscuit.

Besides, even if I could hold on for that long, the arch wouldn't.

Mitch is below me again, holding his arms up. 'I'll catch you!'

'It'll never work!' I call back. Mitch is pushing seventy. If I land on top of him, he'll probably be pushing something else before long – up daisies, most likely. 'Get out of the waaaaaaay!'

I try to gesture with my fingers, but at the same moment, the metal of the arch twists in on itself and collapses and I scream as I let go.

I squeeze my eyes shut when I fall, knowing this can only end in immense pain and even more embarrassment. Instinctively, I put my hands out to catch myself, and land with a crash on the cobblestones, my hand crushed underneath me, and a sickening crack that I hear both inside and outside of my body – a crack that echoes through the street.

To add insult to injury, the twisted remains of the arch come plummeting down on top of me and land squarely on my chest, causing another jolt to go through me.

Something's broken, I know that much. My leg was badly broken years ago when I was a ballet dancer and it's a bone-deep pain that you don't forget. Someone lifts the arch off me as I lay there on the ground, trying to assess myself.

'Oh, poor Franca.' Mrs Bloom is on her knees at my side in an instant. 'Are you hurt? Can you sit up?'

'I... um...' The truth is, I haven't worked out how much I'm hurt. That was such an impact and my entire body feels like it's juddering and I don't know which bits are actually injured yet. I try to push myself up with my hand and let out a cry of pain when it immediately reveals which bones made that awful cracking noise.

'My fingers are broken.' I pull my hand out from under me and hold it up limply. I just *know*. The pain is radiating from my hand and although my whole arm is throbbing, I can pinpoint it to the fingers of my right hand.

'Oh nooooooo!' Mrs Bloom wails. 'Raff! Look what you've done!' She looks around, searching for the man – scam-artist – in question. 'Where is he? Oh, that rotten... Don't tell me he's gone!'

She clambers to her feet and stalks around, peering into the crowd, searching for him. 'It was a bump and run!'

Raphael Dardenne is nowhere to be seen. Of course he isn't. As if he'd have the common decency to cause serious injury to a fellow shopkeeper and *then* hang around long enough to make sure she was okay. Raphael wouldn't know the meaning of decency if it hit him in the face.

Speaking of faces, Jorge's appears above me in my hazy vision.

Ooh, maybe this is it. Maybe our moment is finally going to happen. Maybe he'll bend down and lift me easily from the ground, overcome by his feelings at the thought of me being hurt... He'll set me carefully back on my feet and we'll...

'Who ate all the pies? Who ate all the mince pies?' His sing-song voice interrupts the daydream. '*You* ate all the mince pies. You did, you did.' He sounds like a small child, except even a small child wouldn't be that insensitive.

'Jorge!' Mrs Bloom admonishes him, but he continues laughing at me.

'I *knew* it was a mistake to sell you so many cakes! I should have put you on rations for the sake of Ever After Street – there's probably a dent in the road now!'

My eyes are watering. They're not tears – it's from the wind chill and the pain, not from his comments about my weight, although it's hard to tell what hurts more – my hand, my pride, or his unexpected cruelty. Maybe it's deserved payback for the breath comment?

'That's enough, Jorge!' Mitch pushes him away and folds his arms like a bodyguard. 'We can't continue filming. Franca's hurt. That's it, everybody.' He addresses the wider crowd and flaps his hands to disperse them. 'Nothing to see here. Go on with your days.'

Jorge takes one last disparaging look at me, and then, he oinks. Like I'm a stuck pig and this is my own fault because I'm not a size ten. He continues oinking all the way back to the bakery.

'Just ignore him.' Mitch's knees aren't what they used to be so he puts the stool beside me and sits on it, reaching out to help me into a sitting position. 'Are you hurt anywhere else?'

'I don't know.' I've tried to deny it, but I'm openly crying now. It's *not* because of Jorge's callousness, and it's not because of the pain, but maybe it's shock of some kind? That was a *hard* fall and my entire body feels bruised and shaken up. And the longer the tears run down my face, the smaller and more belittled I feel.

Not many people have carried on with their day as Mitch told them to, they're all just milling around, watching me as I sit here sobbing, like a child who's fallen over in the playground and is waiting for a teacher to make it all better. It'll take more than a strip of Elastoplast to sort this one out.

I hold my hand out in front of me. It's shaking, and it's bright red and is already starting to swell up. Mitch rubs my shoulder comfortingly, and Mrs Bloom comes back and kneels down again. 'Raff has got a lot to answer for.'

'It was just an accident. You were *both* winding each other up,' Mitch says. 'And the last thing people want in a situation like this is to be crowded around. He was probably only thinking of Franca.'

'Pfft.' Mrs Bloom's disbelieving snort says enough for both of us. 'He could've at least pretended to care. Look, everyone else has hung around to see if they can do anything.'

I groan when she points out the group of shopkeepers from Ever After Street who are standing to one side, waiting to jump into action if needed. Unlike Raphael Dardenne. It's nice of them to stay, but if there's anything worse than embarrassing yourself, it's a large group of your friends and colleagues *watching* you hurt yourself in the most embarrassing way possible.

I want the ground to swallow me up and spit me back out again ten minutes ago, so I could stop this happening at all. This is the kind of moment that needs a Groundhog Day, where you can live it over as many times as it takes to fix it, and then go about your life with unbroken fingers and uncrushed pride.

Mitch helps me to my feet and wraps an arm around my waist

to hold me steady as I try to ascertain that nothing else will need an X-ray. At least it doesn't feel like I've damaged my leg again. Bones are never the same when they've been broken – my leg is testament to that, and I now have to face the same again with my fingers. Panic pushes at the edges of my mind about what that will mean for making nutcrackers and my shop, but I can't think about it at the moment. I can't think about anything at the moment apart from the pain burning outwards from my hand.

'Did anyone cut the livestream?' Mrs Bloom asks.

'Oh, crikey, no, I didn't.' Mitch slaps a hand to his forehead. 'I'd best go and turn it off.'

He rushes back to his forgotten camera that's been focused on me the whole time, and I sink down onto the stool and drop my head into my one functional hand. 'That just streamed live, didn't it? Me wailing? Me clinging onto the arch? Me hurting myself? Jorge's oinking?'

'It, er...' Mrs Bloom looks over at Mitch. 'Well, it might not have... These things, um, well, it might have run out of batteries, mightn't it? Batteries never last on any of my technology; I'm charging my phone every five minutes, it seems.'

She's trying to make me feel better, of course she is. We both know that the most embarrassing moment of my life has been livestreamed for all the internet to see.

Well, second-most; the other one happened in a very public place too, back when I was a ballet dancer, on stage in front of a large audience, and that one also resulted in a broken bone.

'I'll bring the car round and give you a lift to A&E.' She pats my knee again and makes a hasty retreat. 'Anything you need me to grab for you?'

Just my dignity back. And some sort of internet-wide blackout where all livestreams were magically disrupted. Oh, and some way of making nutcrackers one-handed would be good too. Because

I've got nutcracker orders piling up for December... and as I look at my rapidly swelling hand, I have no idea how I'll manage to fulfil them.

December is *by far* my busiest month. If I can't produce my usual output, The Nutcracker Shop will have no way of staying afloat and certainly no way of beating Raphael Dardenne, and after *that*, I am even more determined to beat him. There is no way that I'm going to let the council evict me and keep his ridiculous 'magical' snow globe shop.

No way.

2

'Maybe they're not broken.' My friend Cleo tilts her head to the side as she sits next to me in the A&E waiting area, looking at my hand hopefully. 'Just a bad sprain? A *really* bad sprain?'

It's a nice thought, but my hand is now so swollen that all of my fingers have merged into one mass with no space between them, and although I had knuckles once, you'd never be able to tell. My whole arm is still shaking, and I know you need to elevate injuries like this, so I'm trying to hold it up above my head, but the pain is throbbing in my hand and seeping into the rest of my body as well.

'I can't believe Raff didn't even apologise, never mind stop to see if you were okay,' Mrs Bloom mutters. I didn't expect her to come in and wait with me, especially when Cleo said she'd come, but she's insisted on staying and driving us home too.

'Don't get me started on *Raff* Dardenne.' I hadn't intended to sound quite so venomous, but far too many of my colleagues are taken in by his amiable nickname and Disney prince smile, and this latest incident just proves how lacking he is in any kind of community spirit. 'Wouldn't surprise me if he did it on purpose just to ensure he wins this contest and the council evict me in January instead of him.'

'He'd never do that!' Cleo says incredulously. 'And this stupid competition between you *was* kind of your suggestion in the first place...'

'And didn't that backfire spectacularly?' I grumble. We've *all* had enough of Raff's bad reviews, but I didn't expect the council to turn my complaint into a head-to-head challenge and to be on the chopping block myself.

Love Is All A-Round and Dardenne Snow Globes are world famous. They've got a cult following online and a few thousand fans in their Facebook group who wholeheartedly believe the story that their snow globes will match you with your soulmate. The business was started by Claude Dardenne, Raff's grandfather, who worked throughout the local counties since the 1970s, before eventually settling on Ever After Street. Claude died two years ago, and for the past eighteen months, Raff has been at the helm of the shop.

Claude Dardenne was known as a magical snow globe matchmaker. People flocked for miles, hoping to be matched with another lonely soul, choose a snow globe, pick it up between them, see something move inside, and live happily ever after. If that sounds like an absolute load of codswallop, that's because it *is*. I know because, many years ago, he was responsible for matching my parents, and his 'magical' snow globe sat on the mantelpiece of my childhood home for years of my young life.

Until my mum threw it at my dad's head during the divorce, anyway.

My mum swore that she saw it move once – just like she swears it was love at first sight when she clapped eyes on my dad in Claude's shop, forty-odd years ago. Back then, he operated his snow globe swindle from a little tucked-away shop in an alleyway off the High Street, and Mum was looking for love. Claude pointed out the lonely man browsing the snow globes and told her he thought they'd make a good couple.

And they did, for a while. Long enough to build a life together and have me. She could never get the snow globe to move again, but it was a romantic story that was told to every visitor who asked why we had a snow globe out when it wasn't Christmas. I used to love that snow globe. I used to shake it and watch the flakes fall down over the scene of a snowy street with a couple kissing under a streetlamp, who bore a surprising resemblance to my mum and dad, despite the fact Claude had never met either of them before that day. I used to believe it was magical and that snow globes really could bring people together and help two lonely souls find each other in this crowded world.

But my parents would have been better off *not* finding each other. Their blissful happiness gave way to rows, arguments, and a healthy dose of seething resentment. And now I'm collateral damage of a messy divorce that ended in many, many tears, and a lot of heartache, and the person responsible for that was Claude Dardenne and his definitely-*not*-mystical snow globes.

'He's always seemed okay to me.' Cleo, who runs The Wonderland Teapot on Ever After Street and has yanked a Christmas jumper on over her blue Alice-style dress, goes back to talking about Raphael. 'He comes into the tearoom sometimes. He's got a very silly sense of humour, so Bram *loves* him.' Bram is Cleo's blue-haired other half in a romantic sense and a co-owner of the Alice-themed tearoom they've been running together since the spring.

'He brings shame on all of us who run genuine, heartfelt businesses, and aren't out to make a mockery of our customers. You've all had enough as well. Last month he matched a twenty-two-year-old male stripper with a partially sighted elderly nun! She was delighted – he was marginally less delighted and made his feelings known in yet another scathing review. *Another* one star for Christmas Ever After as a whole. We are *all* struggling because of his shop.'

'Yeah, but it's not personal to anyone else.'

'It's only personal to me because the council have pitted us against each other. If I can just find out the truth and expose the snow globe con, all this will be over. The council will throw him out and thank me for uncovering the crookedness that's been going on right under our noses.'

'It was Raff's grandfather who matched me and my Reginald, God rest his soul,' Mrs Bloom says. 'Many years ago now. I agree that Raff's making a mockery of it, but the snow globes themselves...' She sighs wistfully. 'They're just magical.'

'They're a con. Snow globes don't move. They're faking it somehow. I just don't know how. My money's on hallucinogenic drugs in the liquid. I've been trying to figure it out for years.'

'Have you thought of just asking him?' Cleo suggests.

'Asking him?' I make a face like it's a foreign concept. 'No, that would involve having a civilised conversation with the dreadful man. And like he's going to admit it. If you're doing something dodgy and underhanded, you're not going to say, "Hello, why yes, I *am* doing something dodgy and underhanded," to the first person who asks, are you? And now this.' I shake my hand where I'm holding it above my head and then groan when it hurts. 'He ruined my chance with Jorge. That could've been our moment. He could have saved me like a dashing knight. As I fell gracefully into his arms, our eyes would've met, and...'

'...his breath would've magically been freshened,' Cleo finishes for me.

I huff as the fantasy falls apart in front of my mind's eye. 'Yeah, well, there is that.'

'And who would stop him oinking?' Mrs Bloom adds, and I huff again. Yeah, there is *that* too.

Being oinked at does suggest it's time for a new crush. I don't think I'll ever be able to think about Jorge again without hearing a sing-song of 'who ate all the mince pies?' If I were to have one of his cakes ever again, I suspect they'd taste of oinks and weight jibes.

'I do feel bad for Raff,' Mrs Bloom muses. 'Losing his grandfather wasn't easy on him. They were very close, and from what I've heard, he didn't intend to take over the shop so soon, but had to step up because there was no one else. Maybe we could have been a little kinder. He's still finding his feet...'

'He's been looking for them for eighteen months,' I mutter.

'He hasn't got anyone to help him though, has he? They say his grandfather only hit his stride when he found love and before that, it was a disaster. Maybe their magic is connected to being in love themselves. We shouldn't hold it against Raff if he hasn't found "the one" yet.'

'The Dardennes don't have magic, they have a very sophisticated scam. There is *something* going on in that shop and it's nothing to do with love, or magic, and everything to do with money-spinning and taking customers for fools, and one day, I am going to find out what it is. You mark my words.'

She goes quiet at my cynicism, and many, many hours pass before a nurse finally comes out. 'Franca Andrews? The doctor will see you now.'

* * *

Three broken fingers.

I keep repeating it in my head in the hopes that I'll suddenly be filled with understanding of what to do.

'But I work with my hands and I'm right-handed,' I say to the nurse as she sizes up my splint after an X-ray has confirmed that the little, ring, and middle fingers on my right hand are all broken.

'Only take this off for washing,' she replies. 'Use the straps to re-adjust the tightness as the inflammation goes down. Take paracetamol for the pain and keep your arm elevated as much as possible to reduce the swelling.'

My three fingers are encased in a rigid fabric wrap that holds them straight, and the splint has got an internal metal bar that runs all the way down my hand to mid-forearm, and does up with three wide Velcro straps.

'Keep it on for at least eight weeks and come back if you have any problems.' She gives me a leaflet about hand exercises I can do when the pain allows and sends me on my way with a sunny smile.

Mrs Bloom gives me and Cleo a lift back to Ever After Street and offers to drive me home, but I refuse. They both offer help with anything and everything, but the biggest problem, the main thing I need help with is the one thing that no one can do but me – fulfil *any* of the orders I've taken online in the past few weeks that need to be ready before Christmas.

What am I going to do? I'm useless with my left hand, and my job literally revolves around being able to use both my hands on my chisels as the wood spins on my lathe. I work alone. There's no one who can help. It's by far my busiest time of year. There might be appeal to a year-round Christmas-themed street, but the most *important* time of year is December.

And then there's the Christmas market at the castle on 21 and 22 December, the last weekend before the big day, and the day of reckoning from the council. How am I going to get social media engagement and excited customers without the ability to make enough nutcrackers to fill my cabin? No one can engage with a product that's not there.

Last year, the Christmas market was incredible. A weekend of festive stalls set up in the castle grounds. Hot chocolate. Hot roasted chestnuts. Mulled wine. Mince pies and various other festive goodies, along with handmade gifts and crafts, and the castle was decorated to look like a twinkling winter wonderland. It was an utterly magical weekend. With the increasing popularity of Christmas markets in recent years, it was the only one in this area, and buyers swarmed the stalls so much that queues for each one got muddled together and people ended up in the wrong queue for the wrong stalls, and then bought things anyway. I earned enough money at the Christmas market last December to cover the costs of running the shop for months. I was relying on it again this year.

Without the market... I don't know how The Nutcracker Shop will survive another year, and that's only if it gets to stay at all.

There's also the small matter of the nutcrackers-versus-snow-globes thing with Raphael. He's just tried, probably inadvertently, to eliminate his competition and I can't let him win. If he manages to match those five couples, and I don't manage to up my social media engagement, then I'll be out, and I'm not going to let that happen.

I lost my career as a ballet dancer due to an injury, and I am *not* going to lose another one. Especially not because of an injury caused by *him*. One of us is going down this year, and it's not going to be me. The gloves are coming off. I look down at my throbbing hand. Well, one glove, singular.

If he thinks this will make it easier for him to win, he's got another thing coming.

3

Of all the things that have happened in the past twenty-four hours, the mouse is the last one I needed.

It's the next morning, and after a struggle of a night where I ended up crying in pain while trying to have a shower, and then snatching a few broken hours of sleep in the living room armchair because it was impossible to get my arm comfortable in bed, I've caught the crowded bus to work and opened the shop, but it's still early and customers have been few and far between. Maybe the council have got a point about customer engagement because things are never usually this quiet in December.

Usually I'd be out the back, carving wood or painting nutcrackers if the shop wasn't busy, but I can't do either of those things, so I'm just sitting at the counter, wishing the next eight weeks away, when the mouse runs across the shop floor.

I shriek and jump up onto my chair, although even that is an extra hard task one-handed. 'Oh, come *on*!' I say to no one in particular. Maybe I'm addressing some god of mice or whoever it is that keeps tormenting me with the little blighters. 'Weren't the three last week enough? How about the four the week before that? Why am I being invaded by mice?'

I shudder. I *hate* mice. I can hear the mouse's little feet scratching on the wooden floor as it putters around between my giant nutcrackers. Where do all these mice keep coming from? I'm getting to be quite an expert at catching them and I reluctantly put my feet back on the floor and grab my cotton bud container from under the counter – a surprisingly effective mouse trap – although God only knows how I'm going to use it one-handed.

I creep across the shop, holding the cardboard container in one hand. Usually I'd have the plastic lid ready in the other hand, but that's a bridge I'm going to have to cross when I come to it, and I've left it on the counter for now. If I can just get the cardboard bit over the mouse, then I can worry about getting it tipped up and the lid put on. I just have to get it out of my shop. I've got enough problems without customers being attacked by invading mice.

It's bold as brass and doesn't even flinch at the sight of me approaching it. And it's got right in between the base boards of the life-size nutcrackers, and there's no way I can get my container over it with them in the way. I'm going to have to wait for it to come out.

I stand there for long minutes. My knees have started to lock up and my thighs are screaming at me. My hand is throbbing, the elbow braced on my thigh as I stand, poised with my cotton bud container, and lie in wait. Well, stand in wait. Finally, finally, whiskers twitch towards me and the mouse scurries out, not close enough, and I lean forwards and bring the container down over it. 'Ah-ha! Gotch—'

I groan as I miss completely and the mouse darts between my legs, but the sudden movement has unbalanced me and I flounder around to keep myself upright, but it's no use. I've got no balance and there's nothing to grab hold of, and I go careening face-first onto the floor with a crash.

Ow. It jars everything, from the broken fingers to the bruising that's started to come out across the rest of my body, and it leaves me winded, gasping for breath on the shop floor, shocked by the unexpectedness of it.

I look up just in time to see the tail of the mouse disappear under a shelving unit on the other side of the shop. It has the audacity to turn around and look back in my direction.

If mice can laugh, this one is cackling at me.

I lie there for a minute, feeling shaky and shocked, and really, *really* hurting. I didn't expect to fall over. I didn't expect to nearly hurt myself so soon after hurting myself.

Tears of patheticness fill my eyes. I struggle to push myself upright, but my elbow slides on the smooth flooring and I slip down again. This is ridiculous. Never mind catching a mouse, I can't even get up off the floor. How am I going to get through the next eight weeks like this? How am I even going to get up? Am I going to be stuck down here forever? Will I be found, weeks from now, when the mouse has started nibbling on my cold, dead corpse? Who will find me? Cleo, maybe. Or Mrs Bloom; she promised to look in on me. Maybe a customer will get fed up with waiting for their order and come to check on its whereabouts and find me, starved to death, eaten by mice, all alone.

I usually work so much that it doesn't give me a chance to think about how alone I am, but the quietness and the lack of work this morning makes it hit home.

I'm completely and utterly alone. My dad emigrated to France with his approximately forty-second wife, and my mum lives in Scotland with her very active social life. After my last relationship that ended both my ballet career and the relationship itself in one awful moment, I well and truly learnt the lesson that I'm always better when I'm alone, but today... Today, I let a flash of weakness creep in. I *really* wish I had someone I could call and ask for help.

Last night, I wished I had someone to put their arm around me and tell me it was going to be okay. I really, really wanted someone, anyone, to care. To worry about me. I've made good friends with Cleo since she opened The Wonderland Teapot, and she texted me last night to see how I was doing, but in the grand scheme of things... I don't matter to anyone.

The thoughts of loneliness are making my tears fall harder, and of course – of bloody course – a customer chooses *that* moment to open the door.

'We're closed!' I yell.

'No, you're not. The door's unlocked.' Raphael Dardenne appears in the doorway. Confusion crosses his face as he looks around the empty shop and then his eyes fall on me. 'Oh God, what are you doing down there? Are you okay?'

I groan out loud. It's almost like a jinx – the moment you think things can't get any worse, Raphael bloody Dardenne turns up.

He's carrying a box and he dumps it on the counter and skids to a halt on his knees at my side. 'What's happened? Are you hurt? Can I help?'

'No!' I snap. 'You've caused enough trouble, thank you!'

His dark eyes land on my face and something flickers in them when he clocks the tears streaming down it. 'What's wrong?'

The kindness in his voice is unsettling. I've never heard Raphael speak so gently before, and when I'm in this much of a mess, it really is preposterously unfair that he can look *that* good.

'Besides the obvious?' I wave my splint in front of him and then gasp when the movement hurts, which I doubt he notices because he's too busy studying my stupid, traitorous, tearful face and burning red cheeks. I'm so embarrassed at having been caught in a moment of weakness while stuck on the floor of my shop, by him of *all* people.

'I'm sor—'

'Just leave me alone, okay?'

He doesn't move so I raise my voice. 'I don't want you here! Go away!'

He looks taken aback by being shouted at and quickly gets to his feet. I manage to pull myself into a sitting position and swipe angrily at my face, trying to ignore the twinge of guilt for yelling. I'm angry at being caught crying, angry for letting myself have a moment of weakness, and for being so feeble. I still have two working feet. I *can* get up. I *will* get up by myself. That was just truly horrific timing on his part.

He walks back over to the counter and picks up the box he brought and goes to leave, but he hesitates before he gets to the door. He looks over at me again and then shakes his head. 'No. No, I'm not going anywhere.'

He puts the box back down on the counter. 'Look, I know I'm probably the last person you want to see, but I can't walk out of here in good conscience and leave you like this.'

'What would you know about good conscience?' I mutter as he comes back over and crouches in front of me, even though I'm reluctant to admit that I'm quite touched. If someone had shouted at me like that, I'd have stormed off without a second thought...

'Can I at least call someone you *would* accept help from?' There's kindness in his voice again and it makes my brain sputter to a halt. I'd expected ridicule. 'A boyfriend, friend, or...?'

'No. There's no one.' I didn't intend to make my wretchedness quite so obvious. 'Call the fire brigade. Maybe they can bring a forklift truck to right me and really put the cherry on the top of this hellish week. And it's only Monday morning.'

He laughs. It starts off as a little chuckle, but it gradually increases until he's full-on belly-laughing. From crouching he moves to sit on his knees because he's laughing too hard to hold the position.

At first, I'm annoyed. *There's* the ridicule I expected, but his laugh is warm and genuine, and I feel like he's laughing *with* me, and I think about what a sight this must be. Me, with one arm in a splint, on the floor of my shop in floods of tears, being rescued by the man responsible for putting me in this predicament in the first place. And a mouse, sitting there, watching us both, and the ridiculousness of it makes me start laughing too.

'Sorry,' he says eventually, trying to catch his breath. 'I didn't mean to laugh, but...'

There are tears streaming down my face too, but they're tears of laughter this time. 'If anyone could see us now...'

'Well, there'll be no forklift trucks on my watch, okay? Look, I'm here, and...' He looks around the empty shop. 'No one else is. And I don't come with flashing blue lights and sirens that would attract the attention of *everyone* on the street. How about you let me help this one time and then we can both wipe it from our memories and go back to our regularly scheduled loathing?'

'You're my arch-nemesis!'

'Am I?' He sits back on his knees and thinks about it. 'That makes me sound like a supervillain in a comic book movie. I know we don't see eye to eye, but I didn't realise I'd ever done anything bad enough to make me an arch-nemesis. An arch-rival, maybe? Especially when it comes to this shop-versus-shop thing, but...'

He trails off, sounding as if he's waiting for me to shout at him again, but I don't, and his face softens. 'What *are* you doing down there anyway?'

'There was a mouse.' I hold up the cotton bud container uselessly.

'And you're going to... poke it into submission with Q-tips?'

'It may once have been a cotton bud container, but it's now a highly sophisticated mouse trap and has been used successfully on many occasions. This was *not* one of them.'

'I'd never have guessed.'

I make a face at his sarcasm. 'Can you please go away? Don't you think I've flailed around on the floor in front of handsome men enough for one week?'

He sits back on his knees again and a smile lights up his face. 'You think I'm handsome?'

'No,' I snap, my face flaring even redder at the unintentional slip-up. He's the personification of tall, dark and handsome, and he *knows* it. 'It was a figure of speech. I think *you* think you're handsome.'

'Can't say I've thought about it, but thanks, I think.'

I sigh. I've never actually had a real conversation with Raphael before, and I'm wishing things had stayed that way. We do a lot of complaining *about* each other, but we've never had a one-to-one chat before. I don't think our fellow shopkeepers have ever trusted us to be alone in each other's company without one or the other of us losing an appendage or two.

'So, you have a mouse problem?' He sounds like he's struggling to keep the amusement out of his tone. He's got the voice of a fairy-tale prince – a voice so deep that I've often wondered if he's putting it on, but talking to him like this makes me realise it's his natural timbre.

'At the moment I have a Raphael Dardenne problem.'

'Many do.' There's a sadness in his voice that piques my interest, but he covers it quickly. 'May I?' Without waiting for an answer, he takes the cardboard half of the pot from my hand, stands up and goes to the counter where he picks up the plastic lid and puts it back on. 'Ahh, so you put this bit over the mouse, then tip it up and put the lid back on, and you've drilled air holes so the mouse doesn't suffocate. That's very sweet.'

I'm struggling to get myself upright, but *everything* is so bruised and every movement hurts, and my wooden floor is shiny and slippery. If I can just turn myself over onto my knees, I can grab a giant nutcracker's leg with my left hand and... I must make a noise because Raff drops the container on the counter and comes back over.

'Okay, no flailing. Come here.' He crouches down next to me again and pats his shoulder. 'Put your arm around my neck.' When I do, he continues. 'Okay if I touch you here and here?' One of his hands touches my knee and the other touches my back, and I nod, secretly quite impressed that he's asked permission even to help me up. A very gentlemanly thing to do.

The scent of his aftershave, dark peppermint and clove with a hint of orange, fills my senses, and the strength of his body surrounds me. I focus on the softness of his hoodie under my fingertips and absolutely *not* on the solid feel of the muscles underneath it as his arm slides under my knees and the other goes around my back, and he lifts me easily to my feet. I appreciate the way he tries to keep his grunting to a minimum. I know I've put on weight since I left the ballet but it's nice not to be made to feel like it for once. And I ignore the little frizzle that goes up my spine as he sets me back right and his hands hover to make sure I've got my balance. That was both hot and surprising – because I never imagined Raphael Dardenne could be so gentlemanly, and so attractive while doing it.

I dust myself down one-handed and try to ignore the embarrassment as the shame of needing help creeps back in. It's so humiliating to be caught in such a vulnerable position by *him* and to be... so grateful that he came along when he did. 'Thank you.'

'You're welcome. See how easy it is to be civil to each other if we both try really hard?'

I square my shoulders and walk back behind the counter like he hasn't just rescued me from almost certain death. 'Now, what did you say about regularly scheduled loathing?'

'Ah, yes, right. I came to apologise. I actually thought...' He spreads his hands open on the counter. 'I thought maybe we could start over. Hi, I'm Raff.'

'I know who you are. We're bitter rivals,' I say, wondering where he's going with this. If there's one person on Christmas Ever After who needs *no* introduction, it's Raphael Dardenne.

'I know, but we've never been properly introduced, have we?' He looks at his hands and then at mine, calculating which is the right one to hold out so he can shake my left hand.

I humour him, both amused and curious about this new approach, trying to ignore the warm feeling as his fingers close carefully around mine.

'And you're Franca, right?'

'You know who I am, Raphael.'

'Raff, please.'

'First name Riff?' I ask sweetly as I pull my hand out of his. I don't know what game he's trying to play here, but he's not going to get anywhere with me.

'How clever you are to come up with such an original, hilarious, and entertaining quip. I've *never* heard that one before. Oh, quick, do lend me a pen so I can write that down, I wouldn't want to forget it.'

I give him a scornful look. 'If you've heard it before, it suggests that *many* other people have had the same thought.'

'If I had a quid for every time I've heard it, I'd be retired and living on my own private island by now. Why *don't* people give you money in return for making you listen to tired old jokes that are nowhere near as funny as they think they are?'

He might have been kind to me so far today, but my patience is wearing thin with his sarcasm. 'What are you trying to achieve by coming here, Raphael?'

'The coolest Ninja Turtle to be named after, I'm sure you'll agree?'

I don't intend to laugh, but it makes me let out a snort. 'I think he *may* have been something else before being immortalised as a Ninja Turtle...'

'One of the archangels, a renaissance painter, a Teenage Mutant Ninja Turtle, and now, a snow globe maker from Herefordshire. A decent legacy, I'm sure you'll agree. But please call me Raff. Raphael always sounds so formal and I'm not a very formal kind of person.'

'So I see,' I mutter, letting my eyes run over him, even though there's something kind of charming about his unkempt hair and unassuming jeans, T-shirt, and hoodie combo.

He's got long-ish and floppy brown hair in a grown-out style that wouldn't be out of place on a nineties boyband member, dark eyes that are almost the exact same colour as his hair, and a straight, sharp nose that makes him look elegant and suave. 'Why are you here, Raff?'

'Apart from to save fair maidens in distress from being savaged by itty-bitty mice?'

I narrow my eyes at him.

'Believe it or not, I came to apologise. I'm sorry about yesterday, Franca.' At least he has the decency to look genuinely remorseful. 'I didn't mean for you to get hurt and I didn't mean to run off. I didn't realise how bad things were at the time, and you were surrounded by everyone else. I didn't think you'd want another person fussing over you. I thought it was better to get out of there. I'm sorry. I feel horrible.'

'Not as bad as I feel.' I wave my splint in front of him again, more carefully this time, and the movement still makes me wince. 'There you go, you've done what you came to do. Off you go.'

He looks taken aback by my sharpness, but I don't know what

else he expected. It's nice that he hasn't made fun of me. He could have ridiculed me when he found me in that state. After yesterday, I can only imagine what Jorge would have done, had *he* walked in at that moment. Raff has been thoroughly decent about it all, but under normal circumstances, I'd have thrown him out long ago. No matter how much his kindness has caught me off guard, he is still a Dardenne, and I can't forget that.

'Can I ask you something?' he says instead of leaving. His hands are still on the counter, and his thumbnail scratches at another nail like he doesn't know where to put them. 'Why do you have such a problem with me?'

'Because you're...' I flounder for an answer. I was unprepared for such a direct question and don't want to get into my whole family history with him, and it doesn't seem like the right moment to repeat any of the accusations I've thrown around at previous council meetings. '...bollocks.'

His laugh says he clearly wasn't expecting *that* answer. 'Because *I'm* bollocks or because of *my* bollocks? Because I don't think my bollocks have ever caused you any trouble, but feel free to correct me if I'm wrong.'

My face flares red yet again. Thinking about Raff's bollocks in this much detail was really not on my to-do list for today. 'Well, why do you have such a problem with me?'

'Because you have such a problem with me!'

'And you have such a problem with me!' I snap back.

'Ah, the vicious circle of life.' He sings it to the tune of the *Lion King* song, and holds the cotton bud container aloft like Rafiki presenting Simba to the rest of the Pride Lands.

I clamp my lips together to stop another laugh-snort escaping. He has no right to be this funny. I was totally unprepared for him having such a silly, human side, and I'm determined not to give him the satisfaction of laughing.

'Seriously, aside from yesterday, I don't know what I've ever done to you, but you bad-mouth my shop at every opportunity and tell people not to come in because my snow globes are a scam to steal people's money!'

'And you tell people that nutcrackers bring bad luck and that I'm selling evil dolls that are possessed and are going to come to life and murder them in the middle of the night!'

'I don't think I've ever used that *exact* phrasing, although now I'm going to remember it for future use.' He gives me a cheeky wink and then looks around at the vast selection of handmade nutcrackers lining the shelves. 'Although to be fair, some of the ones carrying swords *have* got a murderous look in their eyes. I wouldn't be even vaguely surprised if we wake up to a news story about them going on a rampage one day.'

I let out an incensed gasp. How *dare* he insult my handsome nutcrackers? 'Yeah, well, *you* ruined my chances with Jorge!'

'Your chances with Jorge?' He scoffs. 'No one's got a chance with Jorge unless they're his own reflection. I've never met anyone who spends so much time looking at themselves. It's unnatural to be *that* well-groomed.'

'It's not a bad thing to take pride in how you look instead of just throwing on any old thing and finger-combing your hair!' I hold my good hand out, indicating him, although I'm well aware that we both know I'm clutching at straws. After yesterday's oinking antics, Jorge is hardly a gleaming example for all other men to compare themselves to.

'Oh, thank you, you think I go as far as to finger-comb this?' He rustles a hand through his floppy dark hair, deliberately scruffing it up. 'And it's not about being well-groomed but being so vain that he can barely function. He trims his perfectly shaped facial hair in the middle of a working day. People are lucky not to get beard trimmings in their mince pies! He also talks down to people, and apparently, oinks at damsels in distress. You can say a lot of things about me, but I've never oinked at anyone. If you seriously think you have a chance with a guy like that, for God's sake, grow some self-respect because you deserve so much better.'

I take a breath, trying to summon up some indignation, but I think there's a compliment mixed-up in there as well, and the two have got muddled and I'm still trying to figure out if Raff was saying something nice when he puts a finger on his lips and points downwards.

I lean over and see the mouse, puttering around at the edge of the shelf, and I can't contain the silent shudder. Raff takes the lid back off the cotton bud container and we both watch in silence, barely daring to breathe as the mouse starts to make its way across the shop again, and quick as a flash, Raff bends down and plops the cardboard container swiftly over it with a dexterity and adeptness that I could only dream of. I let out a cheer that turns into a cry of pain when the movement hurts my throbbing fingers.

Raff looks at me, guilt crossing his features, and he looks like he wants to say something but thinks better of it. Instead, he picks up the lid and crouches down to negotiate it underneath the container and turn it back upright without hurting the mouse or letting it escape. Eventually he stands back up with the little brown mouse safely enclosed.

'That is a nifty bit of kit. My apologies for ever doubting your mouse-catching methods.'

'Tried and tested many, many times.' I hold my hand out for the container so I can go and release the mouse.

He pulls it further away from me. 'How many times?'

I sigh. It can't get much more embarrassing this morning. I may as well admit that I've got a mouse problem too. If he's looking for ammunition against me, harbouring a gang of mice in my shop will certainly sway the council in his direction. 'Several times lately. At least a few times a week for the past few weeks. The weather's cold and maybe the sawdust from my carving in the back room attracts them – something cosy to nest in.'

His face screws up as though he's trying to work something out. 'And what do you do with them?'

'Take them over to the Full Moon Forest and let them go.' I wave my good hand behind me, in the direction of the wooded area between here and the Ever After Street castle.

I don't expect him to start laughing. 'Oh, Franca, you're not being invaded by mice. It's just the one mouse coming back again and again.'

'It is not!'

'Two miles is the rule of thumb. If a mouse finds somewhere it likes, it will travel a *very* long way to get back there. Two miles is the minimum, but it should be released six miles away to be absolutely certain that it won't come back.'

'That's ridiculous! *I* couldn't walk six miles, never mind a tiny little thing like that! How the heck am I supposed to get it six miles away? It was all I could do to get myself home on the bus last night!'

I reach out for the container again, but he takes a few steps backwards and puts it on a shelf near the door. 'I live about five miles away. I'll take Minnie with me and release her in this little park not far from my house, okay? I almost guarantee that your "mouse problem" will be over.'

'Minnie?' I raise an eyebrow, trying to ignore how stupid I feel. He seems like he knows what he's talking about, and it never even occurred to me that it could be the same mouse with a return ticket.

'I'd have said Mickey, but I didn't want any confusion between the mouse and the red-haired woman who runs The Mermaid's

Treasure Trove. People might be concerned if they think we've got one of our fellow shopkeepers trapped in a cotton bud container.'

My mouth twitches as I try not to giggle again, and when I go to ask him not to tell anyone, he stops me. 'Not that I'm planning on telling anyone, obviously. Your mouse invasion secret is safe with me. I've caused enough trouble for you lately.'

I can't help smiling at the deliberate repetition of what I said to him earlier. 'Why are you being so nice?'

'I'm not being nice – I'm just being myself.' He gives me a wink and wanders over to a nearby shelf and picks up a cream and gold painted nutcracker, turning it over in his hands and running his fingers over it.

Seeing him play with one of my nutcrackers reminds me of the usual hostility between us and makes suspicion prickle again. 'Probably scared I'm going to sue you.'

'For what? It was an accident.'

'I don't know. Stepping off a stool with undue care and attention!'

'Not a crime.' He shrugs and puts the nutcracker back down.

'Well, it should be,' I huff. 'Dangerous walking. Drunk in charge of a vehicle.'

'It was 10 a.m.! I wasn't drunk *or* in charge of a vehicle.' He comes back over to the counter and leans on his elbows, his eyes twinkling at me. 'Could you be clutching at straws again?'

So he *did* realise I had been earlier too. I screw my nose up at him, desperately trying to come up with some witty retort or clever idea that *could* be a crime, but his aftershave, his bravery with the mouse, and his sense of humour have short-circuited my brain.

'It seems like hours ago now, but I did actually come in for a reason. I made you something.' He pushes himself upright again and pulls over the box he brought with him. 'It's stupid, I know. I just felt so awful last night and wanted to do *something* to say sorry.

I don't know anything about you or what you like apart from nutcrackers, so...'

'Why would you make me anything?'

'Because I've caused you a serious injury, Franca, and it's upset me. Not as much as it's upset you, obviously,' he adds before I can jump in, 'but I've never hurt anyone like that before, and honestly, I couldn't sleep last night, and I didn't know what to do with myself. I'm not trying to make it all about me, but I didn't mean for that to happen yesterday, and I feel awful, and I'm sorry, and it's the kind of thing where "sorry" doesn't cover it, but I have no idea what else to say or do. And it had to be *you*. Of all people, it had to be the one who's got it in for me anyway, and in the middle of this stupid thing where we're pitted against each other too.'

The sentence has come out in a garbled rush and he hasn't taken nearly enough breaths to stop the words tripping over each other, and it makes me feel better to know he isn't finding this easy either. I thought he'd be relishing being pitted against me *and* causing me an injury, and it's good to know he isn't.

At first, I think about snapping something in response but I stop myself. He looks genuinely wretched, and his chest is heaving like he didn't mean for all those words to spill out in one go, and I wonder how I'd feel if the roles were reversed. I don't think I've ever caused anyone a serious injury either. It wouldn't be something I could just brush off. I'd feel awful too. Even if it was someone I didn't like. And I like that he openly admitted that. It's good to think that he's human too. Surprising, but good.

'That was really nice of you. I didn't expect you to give it another thought.' I pull the heavy box over with my left hand. I'm quite touched actually.

I lift the lid off the box and gasp. My initial instinct is to be horrified by the fact he's brought me a Dardenne snow globe and there's no way I'm going to accept one of his fraudulent pieces, but it's so beautiful that it stops me in my tracks. Inside the box, on a bed of red satin, is the most beautiful snow globe I've ever seen. In the middle of a landscape of snowy fir trees and tiny mountains, there's a nutcracker soldier and a ballerina, dancing in a clearing. He's dressed in a red and blue uniform and she's wearing an iridescent pink dress and tutu. The detail is astounding, from the ribbons doing up her pink ballet slippers to every individual golden button on the nutcracker's uniform.

I momentarily forget everything I know about Dardenne Snow Globes. It's the most beautiful creation I've ever seen in my life. And *he* made that. *For* me.

'God, Raff, that's…' There aren't any words for how incredible it is.

He's looking around my shop rather than looking at me, almost like he expected me to hate it, and I use my left hand to lift it from the box, but it's heavy and the glass is too smooth for me to get a grip on it one-handed.

'Oh, sorry, let me.' Raff holds it with both hands and lifts it from the box and passes it to me.

The nutcracker prince and the ballerina are covered in a flurry of snowflakes and shimmering glitter that sparkles all around them, making the snow globe even more beautiful.

I go to take it from him with my left hand and use the splinted wrist of my right hand to steady it, and at that exact moment, it moves. The nutcracker prince spins the ballerina around, just once, a perfect pirouette.

No. This is impossible. Snow globes don't *move*. Only gullible people who believe in magic think a Dardenne snow globe would move. And I definitely don't.

I must be seeing things. That's the only explanation. Hallucinating from the pain. Maybe I've overdone it on the painkillers today. Okay, they were only paracetamol and I've only taken two, so

I don't think I've quite reached hallucinogenic levels yet, but what other explanation is there?

It's not like the legend is true, is it? That if you hold a snow globe at the same time as your soulmate, it will move in a way that only you can see.

I look at Raff. He doesn't seem to have seen anything. He's still looking around the shop, his dark eyes flitting from nutcracker to nutcracker, and not concentrating on the snow globe he's helped me get out of the box.

Even if there was any truth in it... I look at him again. It's *Raff* for goodness' sake. It's not like *he* could be my soulmate. We despise each other. And I don't even believe in love, never mind soulmates.

The fact I'm even thinking about it means I've fallen into their trap. Am I a victim of the Dardenne con?

Maybe it didn't move. Of course it didn't bloody move. Come *on*, Franca. Think sensibly. There's no way. Maybe it was a reflection? A refraction of light coming in the window? Raff has let go now it's safely in my good hand, and I shake it again, trying to recreate what just happened. *How*? How did it move, just once, but now it won't?

Exactly like my mum and dad's one. It moved on the day they met and then never again. No matter how many times I shook it as a child, it never moved. My mum swore that when she first picked it up, the couple kissing *spun* around. Just like the nutcracker prince and the ballerina just did. Is there something in that?

Raff is looking at me looking at the globe. 'Do you like it?'

'It's...'

'You hate it. I'm sorry, I should've known it was a mistake. I was stupid to think you'd want—'

'It's beautiful,' I cut him off. 'Did you really make this?'

I could ask him about the movement. I *should* ask him, but it's what I thought about yesterday – if he's doing something dodgy, he's not going to admit it. The last thing I want to do is let him think he's fooled me too. I've made enough of a fool of myself in front of Raff for one day, I'm certainly not going to let him think that this nonsense has taken me in too. He will have a field day if he knows that one of his snow globes has got to me. I've now seen a Dardenne snow globe in action... I just need to figure out *what* that action actually was, because there's no way it was any kind of soul-mate magic.

'It doesn't go any way towards making up for what I've done to you, but...' His cheeks have gone red, and he seems uneasy, like he was genuinely nervous about giving it to me.

'It's beautiful, Raff. You're...' I trail my fingertips over the smooth glass dome, trying to see past everything else, because it's an absolutely outstanding snow globe, even I can't deny that. 'You're incredibly talented.'

'So are you. These nutcrackers... woodturning?' He's wandered away and picked up a pastel pink nutcracker with a cupcake for a hat, and he runs his fingers over the smooth finish.

I nod. 'My lathe is out the back.'

'They're so clever. I can't believe I've never even been in here before.' He puts the nutcracker on the shelf and comes back to the counter. 'Do you think we've entered some parallel universe where you and I say nice things to each other? Maybe I shouldn't point it out in case it breaks the spell. It was nice to meet this version of you that doesn't despise me.'

'Oh, I despise you fully and wholeheartedly,' I assure him, even though it sounds a little less wholehearted than it would have in previous days.

'Because I'm bollocks, right?' He gives me a mischievous grin.

'Yes. You're a bollocks person in general, Raff.'

'I know.' He collects Minnie in her container and winks at me. 'You know that sounds like a compliment, right?'

I make a noise of frustration at the ceiling as he saunters out. Raff Dardenne has got a lot to answer for.

'Hey.' In the middle of my noise, he pops his head back round the door. 'Seriously, if you need any help, with *anything*, give me a shout, okay? Anything at all. From daring rescues from mice-infested buildings to... I don't know, a ride home from work or someone to grab lunch for you, I'll be there.'

He's gone before I have a chance to get out the 'thank you' that's caught in my throat.

I pick the snow globe up again and shake it. The snow falls but it doesn't move.

I don't know if I've just been conned... Or proved wrong in my assumptions about Raphael Dardenne after all these months.

4

Since the moment I started working on Christmas Ever After, I've tried to spend as little time as possible thinking about Love Is All A-Round and Dardenne Snow Globes, but I've spent most of today like a Kylie song – I can't get Raff Dardenne out of my head.

The way he helped me this morning without a second thought. The way he was kind, funny, good-natured. He didn't mock me or try to make me feel stupid. He was even nice to the mouse.

Cleo comes over mid-morning with a cup of tea and a box containing some baked goods she and Bram have made, and Marnie from the Tale As Old As Time bookshop brings me a book she's chosen for me, and Sadie from The Cinderella Shop stops in to see if I need anything, which warms my heart, especially when Mrs Bloom comes in at lunchtime with a sandwich and a cuppa she's made for me.

'Did he apologise?' She shakes a fist at the door in the vague direction of where Love Is All A-Round is up the street. 'I'll give him a piece of my mind if he didn't.'

'How did you...?'

'Nothing gets past me, especially *interesting* comings and goings like that. That boy will have a clip round the ear if he caused you any more trouble.'

I'm thirty-eight and Raff is easily my age, if not older. The thought of him being scolded by Mrs Bloom is too much for me, and I laugh so hard that I have to lean on the counter to stay upright.

She looks at me like she wants to find the paracetamol box and double check that there *isn't* anything stronger lurking in there.

'It was fine,' I say quickly. 'He actually un-caused some trouble. Most days, Raff Dardenne deserves a clip round the ear – today isn't one of them.'

'I knew you'd get on if you actually spoke!'

'We don't—'

'And look at this!' She grabs the snow globe that's still on the counter and shakes it. 'You didn't see it move, did you?'

'As i—'

I don't get as far as an overcompensated 'As if!' before she barrels on. 'The day I met my Reginald, in dear old Claude's shop, the snow globe was a Christmas tree and the moment we picked it up, the Christmas tree turned around, but it never happened again. It still lives on my kitchen windowsill. If my Reginald hadn't seen it too, I'd have thought I'd imagined it.'

'It spun?' I can feel tendrils of my mind reaching out towards that word. Spinning again. It's always spinning. That's three snow globes now that have been seen to spin. There's got to be something in that. I think of the nutcracker prince and the ballerina twirling this morning, and Raff's uncertain but hopeful eyes when he gave it to me, and inevitably, my mind goes to the strength of his muscles underneath that hoodie, and my cheeks have gone involuntarily red before Mrs Bloom speaks again.

'I like to think it was a sign from the universe. The Cupid's arrow of festive decorations.'

I can see why Dardenne Snow Globes have got such a cult following. She's put my snow globe back on the counter and I run my fingers over the glass again. A matchmaking niche. Finding love via the medium of snow globes. I turn it around one-handedly, but I can't make the nutcracker and the ballerina move again. I can't see how they ever *did* move – the snowy ceramic ground they're standing on looks completely solid. So what is Raff doing? Is there some sort of trickery in the figurines themselves, or their landscape, or is it more to do with reflections – holographic particles that catch the light and make it seem like something moves when it doesn't... and why does it only ever happen once? And why did *I* have to see something in there? The last thing I expected was that snow globe to move; it hadn't even crossed my mind that it might...

Mrs Bloom looks alarmed when I make a noise of frustration out loud.

'I feel like a traitor because I have one of these in my shop, and... I don't hate it,' I say by way of explanation. I can *never* let a soul know that I saw this thing move. I will never live it down after everything I've said about Love Is All A-Round.

I didn't hate Raff either. I've never had a problem hating him from afar, but in the face of his kindness this morning, it was pretty impossible to maintain my dislike of him, no matter what jiggery-pokery he's up to in that shop.

'Raff's not so bad,' she ponders. 'And I'm sure he's not entirely to blame for *all* his bad reviews. It's not his fault he matched a young stoner with a seventy-year-old forager, is it? "Interest in mushrooms" is open to interpretation. An easy mistake.'

I laugh, but the elderly forager's derogatory review is one of the many blazing out their singular red stars about Christmas Ever After as a whole, and I wasn't wrong to suggest that his reviews are dragging us all down... no matter how much I didn't hate Raff this morning.

After she leaves, a few customers come and go, but I've only sold two ready-made nutcrackers from the shelves, and when someone enquired about having one made, I faltered because I couldn't fathom how I could ever manage it, and she quickly left with a cheery, 'Maybe next year!'

There won't be a next year if I have to refund the deposits for all the orders I've already got and leave a trail of disappointed customers in my wake. *I* will be getting the bad reviews that I've complained about Raff getting. And I have no idea how to get customer engagement and summon enthusiasm for nutcrackers when I can't make a single one. I've been trying not to let it over-whelm me, but every moment of pain today is increasingly showing me that... I don't know what to do. My business is bespoke nutcrackers. People order them as gifts with aspects that are signif-icant to the loved one they're shopping for. A football-loving nutcracker wearing a certain team's colours for a football-mad friend. A grandfatherly nutcracker with a wooden dog sitting beside him. The customer brings me a photo and I do my best to recreate them out of wood. Favourite colours, activities, custom sizes, custom hair colours, clothing painted to resemble their own favourite item of clothing, faces painted to resemble the person in question, each a one-of-a-kind creation that makes The Nutcracker Shop stand out from other decoration shops.

When I'm not doing orders, I make nutcrackers that customers can buy off-the-shelf, and my shop is packed with all different sizes, from six-foot-tall life-size ones, to tiny ones for hanging on Christmas trees, but it's physically impossible to use a lathe with only one hand, and selling a few pre-made nutcrackers off the shelves is not going to have much of an impact.

Watching an empty shop is something I never do. I keep myself busy all the time, but today has dragged along. Now I'm on the crowded bus home from work, standing room only, clinging onto a pole with my left hand, and trying to hold my right arm above my head so no one bumps into it, and every pothole, every slam of the brakes, and every fellow passenger who shoves past sends so much pain blazing through my hand and down my arm that I feel light-headed.

It's December, the buses are only going to get more crowded from now until this month is over, and I feel small and unnoticed. I don't want to be fussed over by strangers on a bus, but it would be nice if someone just offered me a seat. I'm used to being strong and independent, and I *hate* how vulnerable I feel with only one functional arm and one that's hurting so much I can barely think straight, and I hate how much I much wish that someone, anyone, would notice I'm struggling and show kindness. Apart from the other shopkeepers, the only person who's made me feel like they care lately is the one person who really, *really* cannot.

I've noticed a few curious looks from the driver, and as I make my way to the front of the bus when we approach my stop, he seems to realise where he knows me from. 'It *is* you from the video, isn't it? *You* ate all the mince pies!'

For a moment, I wonder how on earth he knows, and then it hits me. The livestream. The livestream was never cut, was it? It went live to at least five hundred viewers, and he must've been one of them. Did *everyone* hear Jorge's chanting and oinking? Just how bad did the whole incident look on camera?

I rush home to open my laptop and attempt to use it left-handed to scroll to the Ever After Street social media pages and track down the link to the livestream. Surely Mitch will have deleted the video straight away? It's not like it's still going to be there, available for all to see me having one of the most humiliating moments of my life, is it?

Except... it is. And it seems like *all* have seen it. Well, 15,539 people to be exact. How have fifteen-thousand people watched this? Do people have nothing better to do with their lives than watch a stranger get injured?

I press play, and it starts with me and Raff on the stools, and I stop it instantly. I don't want to see it. I don't want to relive the mortification of yesterday yet again. I can't face the thought of seeing what all those people have seen. The petty argument with Raff. My desperate cling onto the archway. My jumper riding up, my trousers slipping down, displaying my oversized, stretch marked belly. No one wants to see that. It's a moment I'll be reliving in my head for many months to come, and I certainly don't need to see the YouTube version too.

I find myself battling that feeling of being totally alone again. No one *cares*.

I pull my phone over and call my mum. No matter how old I get, I still wish I had a loving and supportive family, and in times of crisis, I *still* think my mum will be there for me when I really need her.

'Oh, hello, darling.' She sounds harried when she answers and I can hear the echo as she puts me on speakerphone and the swishing sound of her pulling a coat on. 'Can't talk now, I'm on my way to book club! Everything okay there?'

No. Everything is *far* from okay. But what's the point in saying it? She'll promise to call me back later and then get distracted by all the other things she has do and I'll be even more upset when she forgets to ring.

'It's fine,' I say instead. 'Just wanted to say hello.'

'Well, hello and goodbye, darling. Cheerio.'

The line goes dead before I can even say goodbye in return. She hasn't got time for me. That's the thing about my mum – she'd probably listen if she didn't have knitting class, or yoga class, or a wine tasting, or basket weaving class to get to. After the divorce, she was so eager to fill her life with things to do that she never gave herself time to think about my dad, and as a bonus, her packed social life ensured that, whenever I spoke to him, I would pass on how busy and happy she was without him.

I could phone my dad, although it's been so long since I saw him that I'm not sure he even remembers my name. Neither of my parents approved of my career move from dancing *The Nutcracker* to making nutcrackers, and neither have ever let me forget it. A daughter who was a ballerina was something to be proud of – one who works in a shop, not so much. My parents worked hard to pay for my ballet training when I was younger. When I didn't immediately return to dancing after my accident, they thought I was throwing my life away. It might be the *only* thing my parents have ever agreed on.

I balance the phone on my thigh and use my left hand to type a text to Mitch instead, which takes longer than it should and has more mistakes in it than necessary, even though it still gets across the general gist of my insistence that he take the video down immediately.

Mitch replies instantly.

> Are you kidding? It's gone viral! 15,000 people have now had eyes on Ever After Street who had probably never heard of it before. I've always wanted a viral video. I'm trying to get the news sites to run it! You and Raff are hilarious! This is the best thing to happen to Christmas Ever After in years!

'It's the *worst* thing to happen to me in years,' I say aloud to the empty house with a sigh.

Before long, I get fed up of the self-pity party. This isn't me. I don't expect anything from other people and I push away anyone who expects anything from me. I don't need anyone to comfort me. I'm perfectly capable of getting on with things one-handed. Growing up while being shunted between battling parents made me learn to stand on my own two feet early on. I don't need anyone's help and I don't need anyone to care about me. I don't know why I keep thinking I want that. Life is complicated enough without adding people who care.

I haul myself off the sofa and go to make something for dinner. Cleo offered to make me something to bring home, but I refused. I don't want her thinking I can't manage.

It takes me a while, but even making a sandwich can be accomplished one-handed, and I make a cup of hot chocolate in my favourite Christmas mug.

It's a huge red mug with a hinged lid that keeps the drink warm, but the lid is shaped like a domed swirl of cream with sprinkles and peppermints and a ceramic gingerbread man on top. I got it years ago, at a Christmas market when I was visiting Mum in Scotland, and I only ever use it during December. It's one of those mugs that makes every drink taste better just because they're in it.

But as I lift it off the unit with my left hand and go to carry it across the kitchen, the handle slips from my fingers and the mug crashes onto the kitchen floor tiles. It smashes into a million pieces and covers the kitchen in a wave of boiling chocolate liquid and shards of red china.

'Noooooo!' Not my favourite mug. I can cope with my fingers being broken, but not the mug. Please not the mug. It's been with me for so many years and I've never found another one like it. It's not Christmas until I get that mug out of the cupboard.

I feel helpless as I look around the devastation of my kitchen. The mess. Oh God, the mess. The hot chocolate has sploshed so far that it was surely a bucket full and not just a mug. It's gone *everywhere*, all the way across the floor, it's splashed up the walls, all over the cupboards, up the radiator, all over me, and my mug... My beautiful, special Christmas mug is dead.

Of all the things that have happened since yesterday, it's the last straw, and I let out a wail and sink down onto the floor. Warm hot chocolate seeps through my trousers but I don't care. It's all too much and the misery overwhelms me and the tears fall, and I let every bit of frustration and anger and annoyance and pain be released in a flood.

I know it's just a mug, but I *loved* that mug, and my own inability to do something as simple as carrying a mug across the kitchen presses down on me. I feel utterly useless. Even the most basic of tasks are too much for me. I want to hibernate. It will be the end of January before my fingers will be healed enough to take the splint off – why can't I just sleep until then like a bear or a squirrel? This is the worst December ever and it's only the second day of it. How am I going to get through another two months of this?

Something else becomes clear too – this is the end of The Nutcracker Shop. I can't make nutcrackers in this state. I can't operate my lathe. Even if I could, I can't carve anything with only one hand. And there's no way I can paint left-handed. When I get to work tomorrow, I'll start cancelling the orders and refunding my customers' deposits, and... hand the win to Raff on a silver platter with a neatly arranged sprig of mint. Customers who don't get what they order leave bad reviews. Never mind the costs of running the shop and the money I'll lose – none of that will matter because the council are expecting to see happy customers and people talking about nutcrackers, and what they're going to end up talking about is the nutcrackers they *didn't* get. Raff has inadvertently eliminated his competition. He'll match his five couples easily, but there's no way I can get customer engagement and excitement about nutcrackers when I can't make a single one.

It's over. Love Is All A-Round has won, and I can't see a way to fight back.

5

I'm wearing a knitted hat pulled down to my eyebrows, dark glasses, and a scarf pulled up over my nose when I get the bus to work the next morning, and as I walk down Ever After Street towards the festive cul-de-sac at the end, I can feel eyes burning into me, and not just because I *look* like I'm trying to go incognito. It's a relief to get inside my shop and hide away from curious gazes, and my fear of how many more people have seen the video and might recognise me.

It's just after 10 a.m. when the door opens for the first time, but instead of a customer, Raff pokes his head round it. 'Good morning!'

I glare at him for his cheerfulness. I go to snap that there's nothing good about it, but I can't help the little flutter at seeing him. In an otherwise dark morning, it's like the sun peeks its head out from behind the clouds. Of everything that's happened in the past forty-eight hours, the absolute highlight was laughing with him yesterday, and I realise I was *hoping* he'd come by again today.

'Just came to return your revolutionary mouse-catching gear.' The door closes behind him as he comes in. He's got my cotton bud container in one hand, and a Tale As Old As Time tote bag from Marnie's bookshop over his arm. He might be a con-artist, but at least he's a con-artist who reads.

It's such a bizarre sight that I can't stop myself laughing. 'I never expected to see that again. You could've just thrown it away. I've got another couple at home.'

'Toss out such high-tech innovative equipment? Unthinkable!' He holds it out to me as he comes over to the counter and my fingers brush against his when I take it with my good hand. 'And I thought you might want to know that Minnie is safely released and happily residing in a park six miles away. I found a hollowed-out tree trunk and let her go in there with a handful of peanuts to keep her busy. She'll never darken your doors again.' He's got a playful tone to his voice, like he's poking fun at me, but not in an unkind way.

'Th-Thanks for doing that.' Why is my voice stuttering? Why am I suddenly nervous and... excited? No, definitely not excited. And whatever's going on in my belly, it's *not* butterflies. 'I didn't have you down as someone who would be kind to mice.'

'I don't think you know me well enough to have me down as anything, do you? I mean, what do we know about each other? I know your name and the fact you're scared of mice, and you know... my name. What judgement can either of us form based on that?'

'Well...' When he makes it sound so reasonable and sensible like that, it's hard to come up with an answer. 'My judgement is based on what you do – and what your grandfather did – to customers.'

'What, try to make them happy? Bring a little magic into their lives? Truly unforgivable crimes and heinous offences, yes?'

'Yes!' I snap, wondering why I was glad to see him just now. He has this way of turning things around and making my totally justified hatred of his shop seem utterly irrational.

Instead of replying, he pokes the snow globe he brought me yesterday where it's still on the counter. 'You didn't throw it out.'

'I wouldn't. I might not like what you do there, but your craftsmanship is undeniable.'

He grins. 'Good, because I've bought you another gift.'

From the totebag, he pulls out... a long tunnel made of transparent plastic with a grid on one end and a gate on the other. 'A humane mouse trap. Just in case Minnie makes her way back or her loved ones come looking for her. Put a bit of peanut butter in this end. Mice *love* peanut butter.' He taps the grid and then runs his long fingers along the length of it. 'Mouse goes in, sits here to eat, triggers the gate to close, mouse can't get back out, but has got plenty of room to run around and plenty of food until you're ready to release it, miles away. You'll never have to worry about being mauled by delinquent mice again.' Even his sarcasm sounds so good-natured and teasing that it's impossible to fire anything back at him, and I'm quite touched by his thoughtfulness and dedication to protecting all mice.

'I don't have any—'

'And yes, I bought some peanut butter.' He puts the mouse trap down on the counter and gets a jar out of his bag before I can finish the sentence.

I take the expensive-looking jar he holds out and read the label. 'You bought finest, golden-roasted, organic, crunchy peanut butter for a *mouse*?'

'Mice have discerning taste too, you know. Unless' – from the bag, he produces two plastic spoons in cellophane wrapping and holds them up with a grin – 'you also want to try it? I love peanut butter; there's no way a mouse is getting all of this.'

I don't intend to laugh, but I'm weak in the face of digging a spoon into a jar of peanut butter and I rip the packet open with my teeth. He pops the jar open and stands it on the counter, and keeps hold of it so I can dig my spoon in one-handed.

In an instant, I go from laughing to feeling my eyes well up. It's such a little thing, but he does it instinctively, without any fanfare, and in a few days where *everything* has been so much harder than usual, this thoughtful, considerate little thing to make my life easier touches my heart.

I'm trying to cling onto my hatred of him, but he's making it very, *very* difficult, with his down-to-earthness and his tiny little acts of kindness that feel big when you're struggling.

I dig out an unnecessarily large spoonful and shove the whole thing in my mouth, hoping that stuffing my mouth up will also stuff my brain up from thinking these benevolent thoughts about a man who runs a snow globe empire that I've been determined to bring down since childhood. He's a fraudster who's doing something trickster-y with snow globes, and one day I *am* going to uncover what it is, but for *this* day, he's brought me peanut butter, and that's enough. I dig my spoon in for a second time. 'So you really like mice?'

'I really like peanut butter.' It comes out muffled where his mouth is glued together. 'I have no strong feelings towards *mices* either way. They're no less deserving of their place in this world than we are. Just because we're bigger and have a wider vocabulary and opposable thumbs doesn't mean we have a right to hurt anything smaller than us. Except spiders. They don't count.' He shudders. 'Outside, fine. If they cross the threshold, they sign their own death warrant.'

I *love* that attitude. I've always thought exactly the same, especially the spiders bit. But I can't tell Raphael Dardenne that we agree on something, can I? 'The plural of mouse isn't mices.'

'No, but it's much more fun to say. I don't mind sounding like an idiot if it makes someone smile.'

I was intending to snap something sarcastic, but I can't argue with that perspective either, and for some reason, I find myself smiling.

He takes another spoonful of peanut butter from the jar. 'What have you got against our micey friends?'

'Have you ever read *The Nutcracker*?'

'The original book?' He chews on his spoon thoughtfully. 'I think my mum read it to me when I was young...'

'The description of the mice has haunted me since I was young. The way they're described as watching the main character with small twinkling eyes and the sound of a thousand scampering feet, and the Mouse King himself with fourteen eyes and gnashing teeth and seven heads wearing seven glistening crowns. It's the stuff of nightmares. So thank you for what you did yesterday in being a real nutcracker prince and saving me from Minnie's wrath.'

He laughs. 'I've seen the ballet a couple of times. Isn't it usually the ballerina who saves the nutcracker prince from the Mouse King by thwacking it with her slipper?'

I can't help being surprised that he knows that. 'I haven't been a ballerina for a long time.'

He pushes himself up straighter and looks amazed. 'I didn't know you ever were. Did you ever dance *The Nutcracker*?'

'Yes.' It's a one-word answer that I *really* don't want him to question me on. My career ended during 'Dance of the Sugar Plum Fairy', and now it feels like my second career is on the brink of collapsing too, in no small part because of him. He is not the right person to discuss this with.

He watches me for a few moments, still holding the jar of peanut butter so I can take another spoonful and avoid looking at those soul-searching brown eyes, because I'm certain he can read *everything* that's playing out in my mind. 'You don't do it any more?'

When I glance up at him, he's grimacing, like he knows he's going to get snapped at for asking.

'No. These days I look like I've *eaten* a ballerina.'

His unexpected laugh fills the shop. He laughs so hard that it makes him choke on the peanut butter he's still eating, and it takes him a couple of minutes to recover his composure. When he stands back upright, he's wiping away tears of laughter and his mouth is twitching like he's still trying to hold it back, and I can't help smiling when I meet his eyes.

He taps a hand on the counter. 'Hey, for what it's worth, you look great to me. I'm not exactly a Calvin Klein model, am I?' He prods at his own stomach. 'People underestimate the long hours of sitting on your bum that creative work takes. It's not always easy to find time to hit the gym too, and the gym is *always* my lowest priority. And it's hard to resist the lure of year-round mince pies and those cookies Mrs Coombe makes for us. Jorge was out of line on Sunday – I hope you know that.'

I'm surprised by how vehement he sounds. I did *not* intend to start a discussion about my weight, and I really did not have Raff trying to make me feel good about myself on my bingo card for today.

'I'd rather eat peanut butter straight from the jar than worry about gaining an extra few pounds. Life's too short to count calories.' He holds his spoon out to toast against mine. 'Cheers.'

How many times in one day can I appreciate his attitude? I've despised Raff for the eighteen months since he took over his grandfather's shop, but I have *never* stopped to think about what he might be like. It had *never* crossed my mind that he might be a thoroughly decent gentleman, away from the whole 'conning people to give them money in exchange for magical matchmaking snow globes' thing and being my arch-rival in all senses of the word.

I know I've put on weight in the years since leaving the ballet. It's impossible to go from a hugely disciplined full-time schedule of dancing, performing, hours upon hours of show rehearsals and hours more of practice, to being in a leg cast for months, and stay the same size. It took *years* to regain full strength and be able to walk without a crutch, and then without a limp, and in that time, I've gone up three dress sizes in the shops that size generously, and four in the less-forgiving ones that I feel too frumpy to enter these days. Apart from Jorge, no one on Ever After Street has ever tried to make me feel bad about it, but I'm always surprised by the number of strangers who think it needs pointing out to me, like the extra roll of fat around my belly has slipped past me undetected.

Raff leans his elbows on the counter, rests his chin in his hands, and speaks around the plastic spoon hanging out of his mouth. 'So, how are you?'

His question takes me by surprise. I didn't expect him to sound like he genuinely cares about the answer, and it takes me a few moments to figure out how to reply.

'Fine,' I say warily, feeling a bit guilty for half-expecting him to have an ulterior motive. I suck my spoon clean and put it down. I wasn't sure there was any such thing as too much peanut butter, but I've found the threshold.

'Seriously, Franca. The truth – not the brush-off answer you'd give to anyone else. There's no point in pushing me away because I'm going to keep coming back, and there's no point trying to deny it because I can see how washed-out you look.'

'Thanks,' I mutter, although it's undoubtedly true and I appreciate him not pussyfooting around it.

'This is my fault and being honest with me is only going to

make me feel worse about it, so be honest with me. Make me feel
as bad as possible. You'll enjoy that.'

An unexpected laugh escapes because there's something to be
said for that logic. I've tried to brush off how hard this has hit me
from Cleo and Mrs Bloom and from the other shopkeepers who
have come to check on me because I don't want people to feel
obligated to offer help, but what have I got to lose by telling Raff?
'I've had better weeks, to be fair. Did you know the video has gone
viral?'

'*What?*'

I'm surprised he doesn't know yet as I explain about the
livestream still going out as planned and the ghouls who have
found it funny. Raff gets his phone out and I'm envious of his
nimble fingers that quickly find the offending link and open it.

'Don't watch that!' I snap when the noise of the video starting
comes from his phone. 'I don't need the reminder! I never want to
see that footage, ever!'

To his credit, he stops it immediately and I watch him scroll
down to the comments section and see the way he flinches as he
looks through them. 'Whatever you do, don't read the comments.'

'I glanced at them last night,' I say, feeling stupid and guilty,
like an author who can't stay away from the one-star reviews. 'I
didn't even know there were *that* many pig emojis.'

'I'm going to downvote these. No, wait...' He's frowning as his
fingers fly across the screen. 'I'm reporting every single one of
these, and I'm going to report the video itself to the site and hopefully they'll take it down. And then I'm going to give Mitch a
gigantic piece of my mind.'

'It won't help. He's delighted. Mitch's job is to get social media
interest, and he's just got fifteen thousand pairs of eyes on us.'

Raff grimaces and turns his phone screen around to show me.
'Twenty-three thousand now.'

The number on the screen increases with every second that passes, and I let out a groan. 'Just when you think things can't get any worse.'

He types a complaint to the video site and then drops his phone onto the counter. 'Try not to worry about it. Today's news is tomorrow's fish and chip wrapping.'

'Except it's online for all eternity, and no one wraps fish and chips in newspaper any more, it's horribly unhygienic.'

'Well, tomorrow's digital fish and chip wrapping then,' he says with a laugh and then continues before I have a chance to ask what digital fish and chips are. 'It'll blow over. Give it a hot minute and there'll be some idiot doing something stupid on TikTok and all these people will be watching that instead. It's only getting views at the moment because it's new, and—'

'Because everyone's talking about it? Because Jorge's comments are hilarious if you're *not* on the receiving end of them and people are quoting him? And you and I...' My eyes flick up to his and then look away quickly. I feel silly and disgraced for having such a trivial row with him even when we both *knew* the camera was rolling. Maybe Mitch is right and we *both* deserve to be evicted. '... are petty and stupid and couldn't put our differences aside for even a minute.'

'At least these thousands of viewers think we're good entertainment?' he offers, although his cheeks have reddened too.

'And then with the falling and the hanging on the arch...' I let out a groan. 'I'm a meme on Reddit. Cleo phoned this morning to say someone's made a gif of me on Twitter. A gif, Raff!'

'I'm so sorry about all of this. I never meant for...' He sighs and pushes a hand through his unkempt straight hair, seeming lost for words, and I actually feel bad for him. He looks like he's got a huge weight of responsibility on his shoulders, when really, an accident is an accident. We've *all* been guilty of not looking where we're going from time to time, and we *both* had that argument. We wound each other up, and if we hadn't, if we'd both been mature enough to hold onto our tempers for the good of Christmas Ever After, then none of this would've happened.

He sighs again and looks up at me. 'How are you coping? Are you sleeping? Are you managing to cook and eat and shower and dress and... everything? I fell off a climbing frame and broke my arm when I was seven and I remember my mum having to do *everything* for me. It was a nightmare.'

I wish it was a nightmare, at least I could wake up then. 'Fine, like I said.'

He raises a dark eyebrow, staring me down, wordlessly challenging me to lie to him while looking straight into those deep brown eyes, and goosebumps tingle the back of my neck. There's something in his eyes that's so genuine and there's honest concern etched on his face.

It undoes something inside of me. 'I'm not coping at all. I can't do *anything*. I'm useless. I've already lost one career due to injury and now I'm going to lose another one. I can't make any nutcrackers. I thought I was going to pass out on the bus home last night because the pain was so bad and I desperately wanted to sit down, but no one offered, no one even looked at me until the driver recognised me and laughed, and then... I broke my favourite Christmas mug.'

The mug is my downfall and a big, uncontrollable sob bursts out, and tears I hadn't realised were building up spill down my face.

Within seconds, Raff is behind the counter. He has the forethought to touch my elbow and gently lift my hand out of the way before wrapping me in his arms.

One arm goes around me and his hand rubs my back, and his other hand cups my head, holding me against his chest, surrounding me with his aftershave and the solid strength of his warm body as he squeezes me *so* tightly. 'It's okay, I've got you.'

They're probably the nicest words anyone's ever said to me, and they make me cry even harder, because for the first time in a really long time, I feel like someone truly cares, and for the moment, it doesn't matter that it's *him* of all people.

His hand strokes through my hair, and his chin presses against the top of my head where I fit perfectly against him, and I'm so *tired* of trying to be strong and trying to pretend I'm okay, and he knows I'm not anyway, and I let myself fall apart while he holds me tight enough to keep me together.

'The broken fingers have revealed how many other parts of my life are broken. One spinning plate falls and all the others falter too, like a ripple effect. I didn't realise how much I was barely holding on, and now I can't hold on. Literally.' I wave the splint around over his shoulder, even though the movement hurts deep inside my fingers. 'I hate that it's Christmas. Working here, our entire lives revolve around this month, and now it's guaranteed to be the worst Christmas ever.'

'No, it not,' he murmurs into my hair. 'No one has a bad Christmas on my watch.'

It such a nice thought. As if he could influence the kind of Christmas I'm going to have in any way, but his strength and deep, reassuring voice have the effect of making anything seem possible, and I let my control slip and let everything out. I blub into his chest, and he does nothing but hold me, his hands stroking, soothing me, making me feel safe while I fall apart. I'm not okay. Every year, Christmas seems to get harder and harder, and my family seem to get further and further away, and the loneliness builds with every passing month, but I feel it more during December. I haven't been okay for a while now, and I didn't realise how much I needed someone to know that.

He makes me feel like he's got all the hours in the world, and it takes a long, long time for the tears to dry up and I sniffle my way out of his arms.

'Sorry, I've soaked your top.' I step back and rub my good hand over the wet tear stains on the black long-sleeve top that he's wearing under his hoodie. I look up and our eyes meet, and I have an out-of-body experience where I'm looking down on the shop, and I can see myself standing there, rubbing Raphael Dardenne's chest, and I have *no* idea how I let this happen.

I make a noise of anguish and stumble backwards as I come back to myself. I am going to *have* to stop taking those paraceta-mols. Maybe the hospital *has* muddled up my prescription and given me mind-altering drugs by mistake because there's *no* way this would've happened if I was in my right mind.

'Sorry, I'm a hugger.' He steps back sharply and holds both hands up in a surrendering gesture. 'If I see someone in need of a hug, I can't help myself. Even if they'd probably impale me with a giant nutcracker if they had full use of both hands.'

I laugh a wet laugh and swipe a hand over my face as he leaves the sacred space behind my counter and goes back to stand oppo-site me, and I try to fight the instinct to reach after him and cling on. I can't remember when the last time I had a hug was. Not a proper hug like that from a man who *wanted* to hug me, at least.

'Sorry, Franca, I didn't mean to cross any lines there.' He rubs a hand over his face and pushes his hair back. 'I don't even know you – I had no right to hug you. That was hugely inappropriate.'

'It's okay. It was nic—' I stop myself. I *cannot* tell Raff Dardenne that it was nice to hug him. His family con is responsible for the destruction of my childhood, ripples of which still disrupt my life to this day. It might not have been Raff's fault personally, but *he's* still running the con that started it all.

I don't know what to say. I've just hugged Raff. I've just cried on

Raff. Raff's top is wet from *my* tears. I've just opened up to Raff. I don't open up to anyone, let alone my arch-nemesis. He doesn't know what to say either. We're just blinking at each other in awkward silence.

'What was your favourite Christmas mug like?'

I chuckle at how obvious he is about trying to ease the unseen tension between us. 'Like you really want to know. You don't need to pretend to care, Raff. It's just a mug, it doesn't matter.'

'It does matter. I love Christmas mugs. I buy at least one new one every year. Hot drinks from a Christmas mug are the highlight of December for me... By that I mean yes, my life really is so dull and boring that a new mug is the highlight of it.'

I let out a reluctant laugh, trying really hard not to appreciate the way he's trying to make me feel better. I get my phone out and try to scroll through the gallery one-handed until I find the photos I took of my favourite mug last year.

'I appreciate a dedication to Christmas dining ware, but I've never gone as far as taking photos of my mugs yet...'

'I took it to show Thelma who runs A Very Muggy Christmas. I like mugs and she likes mugs, so I thought I'd show her, and I was hoping she might know where to get a spare one in case I ever broke it.'

He picks up my phone from the counter. 'If I put my contact info in your phone, can I send these to myself?'

I nod with a shrug.

'Even though you'll have an evil Dardenne's number in your phone?'

'I've just cried on you, it can't get any worse than that!'

I watch as he fiddles with my phone. 'This isn't me, Raff. I'm strong and independent. I *never* cry this much, and yet somehow, *you've* caught me crying twice in the past two days.'

'Don't worry about it,' he says without looking up. 'I've been known to cry at Christmas adverts. Crying doesn't make anyone weak. You don't always have to be tough and standoffish. It's okay to need help sometimes, especially when *someone* has caused you an obviously painful injury and—'

He's cut off by the shop phone ringing, and the screen reveals a number I called earlier to cancel an order, but the customer wasn't in so I left a message on her answerphone. 'Sorry, gimme a minute, I have to take this.'

I wedge the landline phone to my ear with my right shoulder and pull my order book out from under the counter with my good hand, rifling through it to find the right page.

'Yes, I'm so sorry,' I say in response to the customer's question about cancelling her nutcracker order. 'I've had an accident and I'm going to be unable to make any nutcrackers for the foreseeable future. It's likely to be March at the earliest before I can work again. I know you wanted it as a Christmas present, but the only thing I can do is cancel I'm afraid.'

I can feel Raff's eyes on me as she expresses her disappointment down the line, and I turn away, wishing he didn't have to hear this. It's bad enough that I have to cancel orders without *him* knowing how bad things are. 'I'm really sorry, I wish there was something I could do. I'll refund your dep—'

'Forgive me for this.' Before I realise what he's doing, he's taken the phone out of my hand and put it to his ear.

'Raff!' I shriek and try to grab the handset back, but he steps away, holding a hand out to stop me getting any closer. 'What do you think you're doing?'

'Excuse me for interrupting. *Hel-lo*,' he says to the customer in a melodic, charming voice, emphasising both syllables. 'You'll have to forgive my colleague. She *has* been in an accident and she's overdone it on the pain medication and isn't thinking clearly. We certainly have no intention of cancelling your order. I'm so sorry for the confusion. You *do* still want the nutcracker you ordered?'

The customer must agree because he nods. 'Then that's no problem at all, you can pick it up on the date you've already arranged...'

'Raff!' I get out from behind the counter and swipe at the phone again, but he sidesteps me easily as the customer speaks on the other end, and I make frantic 'cut' gestures, trying to get him to shut up. What on earth is he playing at?

'At the Christmas market,' he repeats her words. 'Yes, absolutely, it will be ready to collect. That's no problem at all. The Nutcracker Shop will be delighted to see you then. Have the loveliest of days. Thanks for ringing.'

He hangs up and hands the phone back to me, and I *snatch* it out of his hand. 'Raff! What the hell? I can't make her order! I can't make *any* orders! Look at me!' I hold up my splint. 'My dominant hand is out of action for *months*. I've had broken bones before; it takes a *long* time to get your full range of motion back and recover your strength in the affected limb. It's going to be a long time before I can use my lathe again. I worked that out while sitting in a pond of hot chocolate on my kitchen floor last night, crying. Because that's all I do lately – cry and drop things.'

'Are you going to lose the shop?'

'Yes!' I snap in indignation. 'To you! Because you're going to match your couples and I can't get customers interested in nutcrackers when I can't make a single bloody nutcracker so you're going to win, and then...' My mind goes to a million places. I thought I had a pretty good chance when they suggested it. Raff is a *terrible* matchmaker. The bad reviews that his shop gets *are* dragging us all down. Everyone knows it. And customers are still enthusiastic about nutcrackers. The only person who hasn't been very enthusiastic about nutcrackers lately is... well... me.

'I'm not talking about that.' He sighs, sounding drained by this whole thing, and I get the feeling he didn't mean it in that way, and I feel bad for expecting the worst of him. 'I run a festive business too, Franca. I know how it goes. We rely on December to make up for the shortfall during the other months. With a bad December, we're up that well-known creek without a paddle. Christmas Ever After has been quiet lately – everyone has noticed it. Assume for a moment that *I* will be gone in January and *you* will win this council nonsense, if you could call it a win.' He stops to do the air quotes. 'If you don't fulfil your orders, how much trouble is The Nutcracker Shop going to be in?'

He waits for me to answer, but I'm so surprised by his insight and clear dislike of the council's scheme that I'm struggling to come up with something to say. No matter how gorgeously kind he's been today, I have to remember that this man is my nemesis. He slags off my shop at every chance he gets. He tries to persuade customers not to come in here, just like I tell people to avoid Love Is All A-Round at all costs. He would, no doubt, *love* to discover that The Nutcracker Shop is going to struggle to cover the bills next year, even with a good December, and *this* is definitely not going to be a good December.

'Do you think I didn't hear what you said earlier – you've lost one career to an injury and you're about to lose another one?' he prompts, and I go to snap that it's none of his business, but he doesn't let me. 'Honestly. No putting on a front. No pretending. No "that's Raphael Dardenne and *he* couldn't possibly care". Just tell me.'

His brown eyes are so deep that it's hard to look away, and his voice is soft and low. Maybe he genuinely has hypnotised me because every time I think about telling him where to go, I end up telling him everything *but* where to go. 'September to December are our busiest times – you know that. We're lucky to be on the end of Ever After Street and benefit from their year-round interest, but not many people are bothered about buying Christmas decorations in the summer. The "ber" months usually earn enough to cover the costs of staying open the rest of the year, and I was relying on things picking up in December. I've had a tonne of orders for custom nutcrackers in the past few weeks, but now I can't make them. And then there's the Christmas market...' Last year, I took a load of accessories and different options for things the nutcrackers could be holding. I took some different colours of fur for their hair, different button options, and hat choices – it was like Build-A-Bear but with nutcrackers, and it went down a storm. But now, all I have are the nutcrackers on the shelves. I can't even customise them, never mind make new ones. 'I'm going to tell Mitch to give my market cabin to someone else. It's pointl—'

'Teach me.'

'Oh, ha ha, hilarious,' I mutter. I *knew* he'd have a field day with this.

He spreads his arms wide on the counter and bends until he can catch my eyes. 'Teach me. Show me how to do what you do. I'll fulfil your orders.'

'What?' I narrow my eyes at him, waiting for the inevitable punchline. 'It's a skill I've perfected over many, many years, Raff. I inherited my grandfather's lathe when I was in my twenties. It can't be learned in a day or two!'

'I know that, but I'm a craftsman anyway. I work with resin and ceramic mainly, but I've done woodwork here and there. I might pick it up easier than someone who's never done any craftwork before.'

He sounds serious, but he can't *be* serious. 'I care about my work.'

'I care about my work too.'

'You make a joke of your work with your ridiculous love twaddle,' I snap. 'This is the most ludicrous suggestion I've ever heard. You and I are rivals. Only one of us is going to stay in January. Are you seriously suggesting that *you* are going to *help* me to beat... *you*?'

'Call it helping to level the playing field.' His hair is parted to one side and flopped over at the other side and he runs a hand through it again and pushes himself off the counter to pace the floor. 'This is my fault. I'm the reason you can't make the nutcrackers that have been ordered. I don't care if you think I'm your arch-nemesis, but I am *not* letting you lose your business because I was angry and stepped off that stool without looking.'

Every sentence that comes out of his mouth surprises me more than the one before. I expected him to gloat, to be ecstatic that the council's scheme has just become a one-horse race, but I *never* expected him to be so genuinely sorry for one split-second misjudgement of a step, and it's making it almost impossible to remember why I've always hated him. My voice is stuttery when I try to formulate a response, but my brain can't catch up with the implications of what he's suggesting. 'Accidents happen. It was terrible timing, but it's not like you did it on purpose, and there's nothing anyone can do about it n—'

'Yes, there is. There *is* something we can do about it now. Teach me how to make nutcrackers. Teach me how to turn wood and carve and... well, I know how to paint. I spend every day making tiny little figurines and landscapes – I'll pick it up easily enough. Use my hands as your hands. You can boss me around to your heart's content. I won't complain, I'll do everything you tell me without objection. We can even do the "Unchained Melody" pottery scene from *Ghost* if you want, but with more clothing on.'

I laugh, and yet, one look into those dark eyes and I know he *is* serious. He stops pacing and leans his elbows on the counter, his chin in his hands, looking up at me again, and my breath catches in my throat. God, he is *gorgeous*. Before, I've always thought he was annoyingly gorgeous. It was irritating for someone so dastardly to be so good looking, but it suddenly seems like everything about him is as charismatic and charming as his Disney prince outer shell, and it's a fight to get my brain back onto the task at hand and away from thoughts of the forearms under the sleeves of that hoodie and how tempting it is to reach out and touch the lock of brown hair that's fallen over his forehead. 'Why would you help me? It's you *or* me. We're pitted against each other. What about your own work – running *your* shop, making *your* snow globes, matching *your* couples?'

He sighs and scruffs his hand through his hair again, his head bowing. 'My shop's not going to make the cut.'

'What?' It's the kind of honesty that feels like a punch in the gut, and I can't hide the shock at the bluntness of his open admission.

'I can't matchmake five couples before the Christmas market. You know that – that's why *you* suggested it.'

'Well, yeah, but... I didn't mean...' I stutter for the right answer. Yes, it was me who suggested that Raff prove his magical matchmaking snow globe malarkey at the last Ever After Street meeting, but I never expected it to spur the council into making us stand against each other. It was just another trivial way of getting at him. I never thought there was any chance of it leading to either of us actually being evicted. 'I'm sorry. I didn't want...'

What did I want? At that meeting a few weeks ago, I'd have been delighted to see people realising that the snow globes in Love Is All A-Round are a sham, but now Raff is standing opposite me, his brown hair flopping over where his head is bowed, looking broken-hearted, I'm reconsidering everything I've ever thought about him. The inverted quotes he put on the word 'win' earlier suddenly make blisteringly uncomfortable sense. Nothing about this feels like a win.

'It's okay.' He reaches out and slides his hand over my good hand where it's resting on the counter and then quickly pulls it back. 'If it hadn't been you, it would have been someone else. Everyone's had enough of me. I *am* dragging down the whole street. My bad reviews *do* reflect badly on everyone else. My shop's failing. I don't have the knack for matching people that my granddad had. I'm missing the magic. My heart isn't in what Love Is All A-Round is supposed to stand for. There are no hard feelings. I can't save my shop, but I *can* save yours. What do you say?'

I go to speak but my voice catches in my throat because I'm suddenly choked up again, and it's not from his offer. I've always had it in for his shop, but it's always been superficial, almost comedic in a sense, like cartoon enemies – the Road Runner and Wile E. Coyote or Tom and Jerry. I never thought that something *I* said could lead to him really being evicted. I thought he'd get five couples matched and he'd be laughing at me, but he's not laughing. His shoulders are slumped, and his hair has fallen over his face and he hasn't bothered to push it back. He seems weary and tired and like he's given up. Is he not even going to try? Is he really just going to accept eviction in January?

I always thought it would be an exhilarating moment of victory to see Love Is All A-Round being replaced by a different shop, but now I've got to know him even a little bit, seen his kindness, his good-heartedness... thinking about Raff Dardenne being evicted doesn't feel anywhere near as good as I thought it would. In fact, it feels pretty bloody awful.

Before I come up with an answer to his question, he stops me. 'Actually, don't say anything, because if you say no, I'm not going to listen, so save us both the hassle of an argument and agree. Either you teach me or I'll go online and learn from people on YouTube, and I think you value your nutcrackers more than that. Are you busy after work tonight?'

I hold up my arm, a wordless answer.

'Then I'll be over when we close at five and you can show me how everything works, and I'll drive you home afterwards.' He interrupts my protest before I get half a syllable out. 'It'll be too late for a bus by then, and I'm not having any repeats of last night's bus journey because it sounds awful.'

'You don't have to do that. You don't have to do any of this. It's so nice of you...' I look into his eyes again, see the twinkle and the sadness in them reflected in equal measure. 'Nicer than I deserve.'

'I can be nice sometimes, when I'm not busy being an arch-nemesis.'

I laugh and he grins and pushes himself upright. 'See you tonight, yeah?'

I nod because his grin has made something flutter in my stomach, and I find myself watching the closed doorway for a long time after he leaves, fighting an unexpected urge to call after him and steal another one of those hugs.

I shake the snow globe that's still on my counter, watching as snowflakes and glitter swirl around the ballerina and the nutcracker prince, and settle on the mountains and snowy trees surrounding them. I've always thought having Dardenne Snow Globes on this street was the worst thing, but now I wonder if it would be worse to *not* have them, and maybe everything else doesn't matter as much as that.

6

'Safety goggles.'

'Goggles.' Raff takes the pair of clear plastic glasses I hand him.

'Face shield.'

'Shield.' He also takes the plastic face shield I give him to ensure no stray bits of wood fly up into our faces.

'Gloves.'

'Gloves.'

'If you're just going to repeat everything I say, we may as well give up now.'

'If you're just going to—' He bursts out laughing. 'Sorry, Franca, I'm nervous. I get weird when I'm nervous.'

'Why would *you* be nervous? I thought you were "a master craftsman who's going to pick this up in an instant"...'

'Do I really sound that arrogant?' He glances up at me, seeming the opposite of how haughty I've always thought he was. 'I don't want to let you down. Your nutcrackers are amazing, and you're obviously highly skilled. I know I came across as cocky earlier, but I didn't want you to say no, so I put on a bit of bravado, but do I honestly think I can replicate your work with only a couple of days of practice? No, of course not.'

This has been a wholly unexpected week so far, but the realisation that even Raff puts on a front when he's nervous is one of the most unexpected parts of it, and something I really relate to.

When I show him through to the back room that doubles as my workshop, he's like a child let loose in a sweet shop, and I've got to admit that it's *nice* to spend time with someone who loves craft bits and bobs as much as I do. Apart from my lathe, bandsaw, and disc sander machines, my workshop is piled high with *stuff* – from wooden blanks in every imaginable shape and size, to shelves full of paints, and a haberdashery cabinet in one corner, brimming with all sorts of nutcracker accessories, from fake fur for their hair and beards, jewels for their buttons, ribbons and trimmings and bows and bells, and Raff has picked up a bell and started jingling it before I've even got in the door behind him.

He throws his arms out and turns in a circle. 'It's the craft room of dreams!'

It's nice to see someone appreciating it. I haven't lately. I used to love it here; it was the luckiest day of my life to be accepted for a shop on Christmas Ever After that had a backroom worthy of being a workshop, but in recent years, it's felt as lacklustre as everything else in my life.

I love nutcrackers, I've always loved nutcrackers, but these days, like anything else when something creative becomes your main source of income, it can lose its magic and become about nothing but the bottom line. And making nutcrackers is a lonely job, and that isolation has been seeping through my entire life lately. The broken fingers have hammered home how alone I am, and having to take a step back has made me realise that my shop has become like a bit of a nutcracker production line. What I used to love has been replaced by the constant pressure of sales figures, business outgoings, and the fear that customers won't like what I come up with. All of that has combined to sap away the joy, and this is the first time I've been not-busy enough to realise that.

'Oh dear, what happened to him?'

I follow Raff's gaze to the headless, unpainted giant nutcracker that I've hidden behind the door. 'I was in the middle of making him. He's one of the orders I cancelled this morning.'

The wooden soldier is half-made. He was intended to be five-foot tall and has a base, legs, and a torso, but his head, hat and arms were on my schedule for this week.

Raff looks him over. 'Well, if any of them are possessed, it's definitely that one.'

I like how he's able to find something positive in any situation.

'Be a bit hard to murder anyone with no arms.' I stick up for my half-made nutcracker, even though I can't help giggling.

'Hard, but *not* impossible,' he says with a laugh. 'I can try to finish him off. Actually, if I finish him, can I buy him from you? My niece loves nutcrackers and he's bigger than her, she would *love* to find him standing beside the tree on Christmas morning.'

'You can have him as a thank you,' I say, not letting him get a word out when he goes to protest. It's going to be months before *I* can finish that nutcracker, and once upon a time, I was a little girl with a giant nutcracker who meant the world to me. If Raff's got a young niece who would like that one, I can't think of anywhere better for him to go.

The floor is covered in sawdust, and Raff kicks it aside with his foot. He sits on the bench seat in front of the lathe on the workbench, looking eager to learn, so I sit down beside him, desperately wishing I had full use of both hands. I keep going to do things like I'd normally do and knocking my splint against everything and crying out as pain flares through my hand, and yet, I never remember until it's too late.

'Right, this is the lathe.' I pat the machine with my left hand. It consists of a metal bed with a headstock and a tailstock at opposite ends, spurs that hold the wood between them, and a tool rest to hold the chisel steady and do the shaving while the wood spins. 'It rotates the wood, allowing us to use a stationary tool to shape each piece. Every part of a nutcracker starts off as a rectangular wooden block, the lathe spins it, and we use a tool against it while it's in motion to take the sharp edges off, and then gradually shave it down until it becomes a smooth, cylindrical shape.'

I hold up the square-tipped cutting tool that I use for shaping, knowing he knows the basic concept behind woodturning anyway. 'Once it's a perfect cylinder, we use different tools to taper it, shape it, curve it, and create grooves in it. Each chisel has a different shaped tip that produces a different type of groove. The wood keeps spinning and you just keep shaving it down to create the shape you want.'

I move my hands in an hourglass formation, trying not to wince when even that small movement sends pain raging through my hand, and I see the way he bites his lip because I didn't cover it well enough.

'I don't want to overwhelm you all at once. Ready to have a go?'

'Always.' He gives me a wink that was probably meant to be cheeky, but has the unintended side effect of actually being quite sexy too. There's something about him. He's much more easy-going than I've ever given him credit for, and he seems enthusiastic and like he *wants* to be here, and that makes me glad he's here too.

I get up and collect a wooden blank, and motion for him to follow me because I can't load the wood in one-handed. I make sure he knows how to find the centre of the block, point out the spindle on the headstock and show him how to put in the spur on the tailstock so the wood is held safely in place at both ends but can turn freely. I line up the tool rest along one side and show him how to lock it in place. I give him a brief rundown of the different function of each cutting tool, but he's adept enough to know that, like most things, there's only so much you can learn in theory before you actually have to give it a go.

'Right, hold one hand here.' Each chisel has got a flat side that leans on the tool rest, and I take his hand and position it on the long metal part, and then walk round to his other side so I can position his other hand on the handle. 'You always want to keep this parallel to the floor. You don't need to apply too much pressure, but that's something that will become instinctive with practice.'

I take him through the final safety checks, show him the power button, emergency stop, and how to adjust the speed, and make him put his goggles on and pull his face shield down, and I do the same because I'm not planning to go anywhere while he's still learning and we're both going to get covered in wood shavings.

Raff's been scribbling down notes as I've been talking, and he seems genuinely interested and eager to get started, and he's also managed a previously impossible feat – he even looks sexy in goggles and a face shield, and I try to ignore how much the sight of him wearing my gear makes me grin to myself.

'Don't actually try to make anything today,' I tell him. 'Just have a play around. Make shapes. You're good at this sort of thing anyway. Start it on a slow speed and test out how things feel, try out the different chisel tips, and prepare yourself for finding sawdust in places you didn't know you had.'

He laughs, clearly not realising that when he has a shower later, he *will* find sawdust in places he didn't know it was possible for sawdust to get.

I sit beside him and watch as he starts slowly, the wood turning at minimum speed; the way he carefully touches the tip of the chisel to it, sending sawdust spraying out. He gains confidence as he starts shaving it down, and I can see him enjoying the rewarding feeling of watching wood shavings slip off the block, almost like peeling a coat off in one satisfying swoop. Wood shavings twizzle out in tendrils when he switches to a chisel with a sharper tip for parting grooves where you shave the wood down as thin as possible so it can be cut through easily. I *should* be watching what he's doing, but I find that it's impossible to look away from his lower lip, held between his teeth in concentration, and the way the muscles of his forearms move under the light coating of sawdust that's settled over his skin. The skilful movements of his dexterous hands that leave me imagining them sculpting the clay he uses for his delicate snow globe figurines, the nimble fingers and light touch he must have to be able to do that, and my mind drifts to other things he might be able to do with those fingers and the room suddenly feels much warmer than it is.

When he stops, what's left on the lathe is... well, an absolutely mangled bit of wood, but he takes it off, puts on another one and starts again, and I sit and watch.

There's no point in speaking over the noise of the machine, other than to shout the occasional instruction, and I find that I don't mind. It's nice just to *see* how much he's enjoying himself. He's concentrating so hard that he's not even aware of the *huge* smile that's spreading across his face.

I haven't felt like that when making nutcrackers for a while now, but seeing his smile makes me want to smile too. I used to *love* this. I used to love coming in to work, but recently, it's felt like such a chore that I've forgotten I used to love it once.

Raff's resulting creation is... another mangled bit of wood, but I can see him getting the hang of it. He's already picked up how to tilt the chisel, how to press for a deeper groove, why and when you'd change to a chisel with a different shape of tip, his existing expertise at sculpting mini figures coming to the fore. He's obviously used to shaping things, his hands competent at holding chisels and with a seemingly innate understanding of what to do and why.

He's positively elated when he turns the lathe off and releases the second bit of wood, his hands shaking from the vibrations. 'This is the most fun I've had in years. I've always loved nutcrackers. I can't believe you're actually letting me make them. I know I've got a long way to go, but... this is amazing.'

I hold my hand out for the surprisingly smooth mangled bit of wood and run my thumb over it. 'You... like them? Why are you always slagging my shop off then?'

'Because you're always slagging off my shop and you hate snow globes!'

'I love snow globes. I hate the completely false claim you make about finding love over a snow globe.'

'Well, that makes two of us.' He takes his face shield off and pulls the goggles up so they're on his forehead, smooshing his brown hair up.

I'm surprised because it sounds like a sentence he didn't intend to say aloud, and I go to question him, but he doesn't let me get a word in. 'Be careful, you're getting dangerously close to suggesting we have something in common, and it *might* be against the rules of the universe to have anything in common with your arch-nemesis.'

Something in common with Raff Dardenne. A week ago, that would've seemed as unlikely as Daffy Duck landing from a moon-rocket, but now it doesn't seem like such an impossibility after all, nor like such a bad thing.

He takes the mangled wood from me and tosses it between his two hands. 'Can I come again tomorrow?'

'What about your shop?'

'My brother-in-law's just lost his job, he'd be glad of some shifts, and I' – he lets out a fed-up sounding sigh, and when he catches the wood this time, he doesn't toss it again – 'have nothing left to give.'

I blink in surprise, wondering again if he intended to be that honest. I did not expect *that* to be the ending of that sentence.

'Sorry, I don't know why I said that. I mean, I'm... glad of a break? The pressure of the shop is...' He looks over at me and then shakes his head, like he's giving up the front. 'It's sucking the life out of me. I'm sure that makes you very happy to hear.'

'No, it doesn't.' Guilt shoots through me because surely I'm a part of that? If anything has increased pressure on Raff, it's *my* constant complaints about his shop. And I've judged him too. Raff's always charming, always flashing his Disney prince smile. At Ever After Street meetings, he laughs off bad reviews and makes quips and jokes whenever anyone tries to talk to him about his shop. I thought he was self-centred and careless, but it had never occurred to me that it might be a front to cover something much deeper.

Instead, I like the feeling of his upper arm pressing against my upper arm, the scent of his aftershave mixing with the scent of freshly sawn wood filling the workshop, and I really, really like not being alone. 'I'm glad you're here.'

'Me too.' He nudges his shoulder against mine, taking so much care because he's sitting against my right arm, and that soft, gentle, considerate touch makes me chew on my lip.

What a strange week. I've gone from thinking Raff Dardenne was the worst person in the world to wishing I'd not held onto my grudge so tightly and got to know him sooner. It suddenly seems horrendously unfair that if I survive this month, he will be evicted, and if he isn't, then I will be. If only time travel was a thing and I could turn back the clock and undo all of this.

7

'Nice hat.' I can't help smiling when Raff comes in the next morning with a Santa hat on.

'I just got it from All You Need Is Gloves.' He grins. 'It *is* the most wonderful time of the year, after all.'

I push myself up from where I was leaning on the counter and lift my splint at him. 'I was just standing here wishing December away. At least I'd be halfway through my sentence in this torture device then.'

'Oh *noooo*.' He drags the word out. 'Nothing could make me wish December away. The saddest time of year is Boxing Day onwards because Christmas is over and it's so long until the next one.'

'Some of us think it's the most stressful time of the year.'

'It's the most magical time!'

'The most miserable time?' I try in an upbeat tone of voice, and then sing to the tune of the famous song. 'It's the most com-mer-cial time of the yeeeeear.'

He shakes his head, causing the bobble on his Santa hat to swing around. 'Surely it's illegal to utter words like that on

Christmas Ever After, which is why I got you one of these.' From his bag, he produces another Santa hat and leans over to plop it on my head. 'I know you were wearing one the other day but I don't know what happened to it. Mrs Coombe said it had disappeared.'

The back of my neck goes instantly hot at the thought of the other day. To think Jorge thought the Santa hat was the most embarrassing thing that was going to happen that morning. My Santa hat probably shrivelled up and crawled away in embarrassment, like I wish I could have. 'Mrs Coombe was just saying that to make a sale.'

He shrugs. 'I don't mind. It's my personal mission to support any shop with such a good pun in its name.'

I can't help smiling at the cheerful smile on his face. 'How can you be so positive?'

'How can you work on a Christmas-themed street and not love Christmas?'

'I *do* love Christmas.' I adjust the Santa hat, determined to keep it on all day just to prove him wrong, and the bell in the bobble jingles defiantly.

He raises an eyebrow. Raff's eyebrows can say a lot without a word being spoken.

'I *used* to love Christmas,' I relent and decide to answer him honestly. He's got such deep, understanding eyes and it feels like they can see straight through me. 'But these days, it's nothing but stress, work and navigating family politics, which translates as finding believable excuses to avoid my family at all costs. Funnily enough, they don't believe you if you say you can't make it for Christmas because you're hopping aboard the Space Shuttle and going on a festive tour of Jupiter's moons.'

'Family's the best thing about Christmas. Everyone getting together, playing games, watching movies, eating too much.'

'Not everyone has that, Raff.'

'No, they don't.' He blinks in surprise. 'No, you're right, I'm sorry. Sometimes I forget how lucky I am to have a close family. I didn't mean to...' He trails off without finishing the sentence, and then changes tack. 'Christmas is the time of year to remember what we've forgotten and feel like a kid again. You're never closer to your younger self than you are at Christmas. The years melt away and it's okay to be young and silly and believe in magic again.'

'What if you never believed in magic in the first place?'

'I'd say it's never too late to start.'

I don't think he even gets the cheesy upbeatness of the things he says, but it's impossible not to smile in response. A lot of men are macho and Grinchy about Christmas. Most of my customers are women with grouchy husbands hanging back, huffing in annoyance, checking their watches or keeping track of the football scores on their phones, as though showing an interest in Christmas would have the same effect on their manlihood as giving away half a testicle.

It's nice to see someone embrace the season and be a big kid. I always used to wear festive headbands, Christmas jumpers and Santa hats, but in recent years, I've found that I can't be bothered. What does Christmas bring with it these days other than more hours in front of the lathe, more harried customers, and more opportunities for my parents to make me feel bad about myself? As a ballet dancer, they were proud of me. As an overweight nutcracker-maker, Christmas is an occasion for both of them to analyse my life choices. It doesn't make it easy to get into the festive spirit. Last Sunday was the first time I'd dug out my Santa hat in ages. 'Thank you for this.'

'You're welcome.' He grins. 'Sounds like you're suffering with a case of missing Christmas spirit, and do you know what the cure for that is?'

I tilt my head to the side and make a face at him, certain he's about to enlighten me.

'I'll let you know when I think of it, but I'm pretty sure it involves mince pies, gingerbread and Panettone,' he says with a laugh and then looks around like he's hunting for something. 'And Christmas music. Why is there no Christmas music on in this place?'

'Because...' I search for an answer, but the truth is, because I've let it slide, like most other things around here. The passion I once had for all things Christmas has faded, and I don't know how things got to be like this. I love Christmas, I've always loved Christmas, despite the family politics and massive amount of work in December, but meeting someone who loves it as much as Raff does has made me realise how much I've fallen out of love with the festive season.

He holds an arm out in the direction of the back room, silently asking if he can go through, and I make sure the camera is turned on in the shop so I can see anyone coming in without having to worry about hearing the door over the noise of the machinery, and then follow him. My smile reappears when I see he's already donned his safety goggles and has got the face shield on but pushed up over his head, his hair all smooshed up around it, and now he's taken his hoodie off, underneath he's wearing a pair of paint-stained overalls, and he looks so sexy that it makes my mouth go dry. Maybe I've accidentally swallowed a mouthful of sawdust because there's no way I'm thinking *again* about Raphael Dardenne being attractive. Sawdust, that must be it.

His phone is on the workbench, playing Christmas music, and he's singing along to 'I Wish It Could Be Christmas Everyday' even though the noise of the lathe will soon drown it out.

I sent him home with lathe usage instructions, and he must've studied last night, because he marks out the centre of a wooden blank, puts it onto the spindle, and then secures it with the spur on the tailstock.

I love how eager he is to get started. It makes me realise how long it's been since I saw this as anything other than a job. I used to be excited to get to work every morning. I used to sit on the bus, mentally planning out what I was going to make that day, thinking about orders and how to bring customers' nutcracker requests to life. I would have time just to play – to spin the wood and create fancy flourishes for nutcrackers' arms and pretty patterns for their boots, funny torso indentations or quirky hat shapes, and I *loved* every second of it. How long has it been since I did that? How long since I had time to do anything other than fulfil orders and make the same old tried-and-tested shape nutcrackers to fill the shop with stock?

When he's done, I double-check everything and give him an approving nod, and he slides onto the bench and pats the space beside him. He pulls the face shield down, and I slip mine on too and sit next to him.

He positions the tool rest and starts the lathe on a slow speed, nudging his arm against mine when the wood starts turning, and then picks up the gouging chisel and starts shaving it down, removing layer after layer of wood, each one shearing off like the wood is shrugging off a jacket. He hasn't mentioned what he's trying to do, but he seems like a man on a mission, and I'm intrigued by what he's going to come up with.

'You clearly have a vision.' I wait as he stops the machine to inspect the now-cylindrical bit of wood before speaking, and the sound of the Christmas music from his phone filters back to my ears. It's 'Wonderful Christmastime' now. You can't really avoid Christmas music on this street, most shops play it year-round, and I've convinced myself I've had enough of it by now, but I haven't heard this song for ages, and I listen to it as I sit there, tapping my foot to the jolly beat, enjoying the change.

'Yeah. I thought of something last night – something I've made in miniature many times out of clay but would be a great way to practise woodturning too,' he says, before asking me to double-check if the wood is ready to start the more intricate carving.

'A little more off here, it's not quite even. You'll get better at judging it.' I point out the wonky bits as he starts the machine again.

I'm trying not to watch him as he works, but his overall sleeves are rolled up to his elbows and the gloves end at his wrists, so his forearms are covered in the wood dust that's coming off, and it's hard not to gawk. I can imagine those arms with a tan in the summer, can imagine him stripping his shirt off, the solid chest I leant against the other day, with a smattering of dark hair, the strong biceps... Is there something about overalls? They're designed to cover so much that they have the unintentional opposite effect of somehow making you picture the wearer with *fewer* clothes?

It's not just about clothes though. I've never really looked at Raff before, at least, not well enough to see who he is *underneath* the front he puts on. I still haven't got my head around how he's going to all this trouble to help me, and I haven't been able to stop thinking about what he said last night. How disillusioned and resigned he sounded, and how I'm pretty sure that no one knows what's going on behind the wide smile that Raff shows to the other shopkeepers.

'Who's looking after your shop today?' I ask when he stops the machine again, trying to get back onto the topic he unintentionally opened up about last night.

'My brother-in-law, Quentin. My sister's having her second child, so him being made redundant is the worst possible timing for them, and there's not much going in the way of jobs before the Christmas holidays. He'll have a better chance of finding a new job in January, and he's more than happy to cover Love Is All A-Round for me in the meantime.'

'Isn't Love Is All A-Round kind of a daft name? I mean, snow globes aren't really round, are they?'

'No? What would you call them then?'

'Well, they're sort of... er... dome-shaped? Sphere-shaped?'

'Globe-shaped, some might say. The clue tends to be in the name.' His voice is uneven where he's trying to hold back a laugh. 'Love Is All A... Smooth Spherical Shape doesn't have the same ring to it *or* work for a play on the song title though, does it? And what about the world? People don't say they travel around the world in a sphere-shaped fashion, do they? You go *round* the world and, what do you know, the world is also known as a *globe*, hence Love Is All A-*Round*.' He gives up on holding back the laugh and it bursts out, making my cheeks flush for bringing it up in the first place, even though I'm trying not to look at the way his eyes crinkle up at the edges.

Raff changed the shop name when he took over eighteen months ago, before that when his grandfather ran it, it was just known by their company name Dardenne Snow Globes, and it's always aggravated me because now I can't walk past without getting the Wet Wet Wet song stuck in my head.

'How about we take a raincheck on this whole arch-nemesis thing?' He reaches over to pat my knee and leaves a big, sawdusty handprint on my trousers. 'You don't have to pick holes in everything I do any more. I'm going to be here every day for the foreseeable future, so it would be easier on us both if we tolerated each other. And don't worry, if you take leave of your senses and start thinking I'm not that bad after all, I promise I'll do something horrible and morally corrupt to restore the universe to its natural equilibrium.'

I don't intend to laugh, but nothing I do when it comes to Raff has been what I've intended lately. I'm about to scold him when I hear the bell tinkle above the door and spot a customer coming in on the camera feed.

'Don't break anything,' I say instead as I get up and leave him alone with the lathe.

'I assure you, I've broken enough things for one week,' he calls after me, wiggling his fingers and making me laugh despite myself.

'Oh, you poor dear.' The woman who has come into the shop clasps her hands together sympathetically. 'I thought it was you when I saw the video. How embarrassing!'

My cheeks go instantly red at the thought of the video and how many more people have seen it – well over 30,000 now, according to Mrs Bloom – and how many more of them are likely to recognise me.

The bell in my Santa hat jingles as she looks around, comments about wishing she could both afford *and* transport one of the six-foot-tall nutcrackers home, and eventually chooses two nutcrackers from the shelves that she tells me are for her son and daughter. 'I bet I can't ask you to gift-wrap these for me, can I?'

I hold up my splint and wince, and then bend down to get a coupon from under the counter. 'Pop over to All Wrapped Up, they'll wrap anything for you and make it look so perfect that it could be a Christmas movie prop, and any purchases made on Ever After Street are done for 50 per cent off.'

Since Mandy opened her gift-wrap shop, everyone on Ever After Street and Christmas Ever After has joined in the co-op to have everything gift-wrapped there, because quite frankly, she does it better than anyone else and even the most bulky and awkward shaped gifts come out in neat ribbon-tied boxes adorned with bows and frills and sparkly bits.

The customer thanks me and leaves, and I go back to the workshop where Raff is shearing his wooden cylinder into three distinct sections, although I've still got no idea what he's trying to make.

'Nice to see your shop busy.' He stops the lathe as I sit beside him on the bench again, feeling aimless at not being able to do anything.

'Are *you* busy?' I ask, going back to wheedling for more info about his shop because after last night, I'm certain there's something going on there.

'What, in my terribly named shop that must put customers off with its terrible name and suggestion that round things aren't round?' He laughs a sarcastic laugh before answering. 'Not bad. It's quieter than usual, which I've put down to my bad reviews finally catching up with me. I know it reflects badly on the rest of the street and leads to a lower rating for everyone. I don't blame you for complaining.'

'You do have some good reviews.' I lay my phone on my lap and scroll through it, trying not to get frustrated at how long even simple tasks take me left-handed, intending to find some good ones to read out, but it's hard to ignore all the blazing red one stars.

'I had a great one from a husband and wife who were already matched – by my granddad, thirty years ago. They came to see if the magic of the snow globes was still alive, and whatever they saw convinced them it was, but...'

When he trails off, I nudge my shoulder against his and repeat his own words from the other day. 'Please tell me. Honestly. No fronts, no pretending. No "that's Franca Andrews and *she* couldn't possibly care". Just tell me.'

He glances down at me, obviously getting the reference, and a smile tips up his lips. He lets out a sigh and goes to push a hand through his hair, but the face shield is in the way and my hand darts out to wrap around his wrist before he dislodges it. He blinks at my fingers on his skin for a few moments before I pull back quickly.

'Every match I try to make has been a disaster. My granddad had an instinct. He could look at two people and know they'd enrich each other's lives if they met, but I'm missing that. I've tried, so hard, but... I ask people to tell me about themselves, scribble down notes to try to find a match, but the words blur in front of my eyes, and I... don't care. I don't believe in love. Or, at least, I believe in lov*ing*. I love my family. I love what I do. I love Christmas. But the concept of soulmates? The idea that you're going to run into someone one day and your whole world is going to stop and your life is going to turn upside down and magically become better because you've met "the one"? No. That's what my granddad always swore happened to him when he met my grandma. They just *knew*, instantly. I don't believe that happens, and that's what I'm trying to *make* happen in my shop. The love thing is supposed to be our legacy. It's supposed to be what sets us apart. I'm failing because I don't believe in what I'm trying to do.'

'And your granddad did?'

'After he met Granny Biddy, yes. Before then, he was just a struggling snow globe craftsman who couldn't make ends meet. They met over a snow globe – she dropped it and he picked it up for her at the same time as she bent down to retrieve it, and he came up with the idea that snow globes could bring people together. He built his entire business around it. He was hugely successful. His shop was featured on the news. His snow globes have been used as props in Hollywood films. He had a huge following online.'

I can't help noticing that Raff doesn't include himself in those accolades. 'And you?'

He shakes his head. 'I love making snow globes. I was twelve when I made my first one and I haven't stopped since. But my granddad was the matchmaker and I handled the creative side. I got the business on the internet. I planted the stories and gained traction and followers and customers, and it was great, back in the days when I could hide in the workshop and let him send those customers away with their perfect match. But now he's gone and it's just me, and it's become *all* we're known for. No one cares about the craftsmanship of the finished product – only about the legend. It's taken on a life of its own and it's taken over *my* life, but I can never live up to him. He had a unique ability to see what would make people happy, and—'

'No, he didn't!'

'What?' He looks at me and I look away.

I had no intention of telling him, but like most things with Raff, what I intend or don't intend have very little to do with what actually happens, and I hate how hard he's being on himself when I know he's got an idealistic view of his grandfather and is holding himself up to impossibly unrealistic standards. 'Your grandfather was a fraud. He certainly had no matchmaking ability. His only criteria for matches was being single, and any that worked out were surely just coincidences driven by greed.'

His mouth has fallen open in shock and he lifts the face shield up so he can look at me without the plastic barrier between us. 'How can you...?'

'He matched my parents.'

His face lights up. 'Oh my God, that's amaz—'

'*Not* a good thing, Raff.'

'Oh... Oh... Ohh.' He says the word in three different tones until understanding dawns on his face. 'Wait, is that *it*? Is *that* what you've got against me? Is that why you've always had it in for my shop – my granddad matched your parents and, what, it didn't work out?'

'It didn't just "not work out",' I snap. 'It shattered my life. It shattered their lives. It made my childhood an absolute misery, and to be honest, it hasn't done a lot for my adulthood either. They finally divorced when I was nine, after many, many years of fighting and shouting and trying to one-up each other and prove each was the "better" parent and trying to make me pick sides between them. After the divorce, I had to choose which one I wanted to live with, when by that point, the answer was "neither". I stayed with Mum because she was keeping the house and I didn't want to move schools and say goodbye to my friends, and my dad never forgave me for that decision. He thought it meant that she had "won" this unseen battle between them.'

'I'm sorry.' He brushes his gloves off and reaches over to press his palm to my knee again, and this time, he doesn't take it away. 'That's a hugely unfair thing to put on a child.'

'After that, Mum painted herself as the hard-done-by martyr of the piece, abandoned by her selfish husband and bolstered by her ladies-only post-divorce support group, "All Men Are the Spawn of Satan". And for his part, Dad moved as far away as possible and decided to reduce the chances of a repeat divorce by dating approximately half the female population of Britain, and had a new girlfriend every time I saw him. Which was hardly ever because "I'd made my decision and I clearly didn't care about him or want him to be part of my life".'

His hand tightens on my knee and his upper arm presses harder against mine.

'Even now, each one begrudges me having a relationship with the other. My dad has remarried more times than I can remember and now lives in France with his, I don't know, sixty-third wife, and Mum moved to Scotland and filled her life with friendships and social activities because if she stops moving for even a minute, steam comes out of her ears and her face boils red as she starts replaying all the ways he ruined her life. Christmases have been a nightmare since I was nine years old. The first Christmas after the divorce, they intended to put aside their differences and spend it together for my sake, and it lasted until midnight on Christmas Eve when the police had to be called for the third time!' I didn't mean to tell him any of that, and I'm suddenly short of breath from how fast I've been talking and my eyes are damp from reliving the long-buried memories of Christmases gone by.

'I'm sorry,' he repeats. His hand is still on my knee, and now his thigh knocks gently against mine, and he shifts minutely closer. 'But you can't honestly—'

I cut him off because he's obviously about to defend Claude Dardenne. 'Your grandfather was responsible for all of that. He threw two people together with one of his trickery-fuelled snow globes for no reason other than to make a sale. He had no way of telling if they were a match or not. He didn't care. He was quite happy to set up two people who were toxic to each other and put their money in his till without a second thought for what would become of them. My parents should never have met, and a hell of a lot of lives would have been a lot better if they hadn't.'

'That's not fair. He always truly cared about his customers' happiness. There's *no* way he could've known what would happen between your parents.' He takes his hand off my knee and raises one of his dark eyebrows. 'If you were nine when they divorced, they must've had some happy years.'

'Some. Back when Dad could still have a conversation without referring to Mum as "*That* Woman", and she still called him Jim rather than Toerag VIII – that's like Henry the Eighth but with more wives.'

Raff bursts out laughing. 'Oh, Franca, I'm sorry, I really am, but you can't blame any of that on my granddad. At least they were happy for a while. Maybe that's all any of us can hope for? A happy-for-now rather than a happily-ever-after? No one could have predicted how things would turn out. And my granddad's gone now.' He was sounding upbeat but he has to stop and swallow hard on those words. 'You don't have to dislike *me* because of something that happened so many decades ago. And he might have introduced them but he didn't influence how your parents behaved when they were together. That was on them.'

I wrinkle my nose because he kind of has a point. And when he makes it sound so reasonable, I feel a bit daft. *He* had nothing to do with what happened between my parents and I already know I've been a tad irrational in holding my grudge against Raff too, especially in the face of his kindness this week. 'But you're *still* peddling those same fake-moving snow globes.'

'When have you ever seen one of my snow globes move?'

I do something that's a cross between a laugh, a scoff and a snort. 'I haven't. Obviously. Why would I have? That would be ridiculous.'

He raises that all-knowing eyebrow again as I overcompensate.

'You're still promising to help people find love over a snow globe. You *still* say that a snow globe will move if you look into it with the person you're meant to be with,' I say while my face blazes with heat at the memory of the nutcracker prince twirling the ballerina around inside the snow globe when he handed it to me. I feel like I've seen something I shouldn't have, but admitting that to him would be a step too far. 'And people still believe you. But regardless of what happened with my parents, snow globes don't move, Raff, so you're up to *something* that's dodgy and underhanded – I just don't know what it is yet.'

'Yet...' He's smiling at me good-naturedly, indulging me, but he obviously isn't going to be drawn in to any insults about his family legacy. 'Through all this, you're forgetting one vital bit of information.'

'What's that?' I give him the same sweet, indulgent look that he's giving me.

'If your parents hadn't met, you wouldn't exist.'

He's not wrong there, and I mouth at the air, trying to come up with a clever retort, but my mind is frustratingly blank. I've never thought of it from that angle before.

He nudges his shoulder gently against mine. 'And I'm not convinced that wouldn't be a Very Bad Thing.'

I go hot all over. It's one of the nicest things anyone's said to me in years, and it's like I'm in a parallel universe because it's Raff Dardenne saying it, and I can't help but wonder, yet again, quite how wrong I've got this man and just how unreasonable my grudge against Dardenne Snow Globes has been.

8

'How much for the snowman?'

I clutch the snowman Raff made the other day protectively. 'He's not for sale, sorry. Just my Christmas mascot.'

'Shame.' The customer looks at it longingly. 'You could make a killing with those. Mix it up a bit. Nutcrackers get quite samey after a while, don't they?'

I stutter for an answer but the man has gone before I come up with one. Is he right? Is that why business has been so slow lately – because The Nutcracker Shop is a one-trick pony when it comes to selling only nutcrackers? Would people like more choice? Would *I* like to make something else and change things up a little? I run my fingers over the snowman's smooth hat. Maybe it *would* be nice to do something different with the lathe when I can use it again...

It's the third enquiry this week about purchasing the snowman. When Raff came in with something in mind on Wednesday, after our chat about my parents, he came out that afternoon with a beautiful, woodturned snowman. Very simple, very far from perfect, and quite possibly the most touching thing anyone's ever given me. It's got a body, a head, and a top hat, all carved from one piece of wood, with deep grooves separating each rounded section. He's buffed it up by turning it against a handful of sawdust for a smooth finish, and finally glued on a tiny carrot-shaped nose. He's made a few of them as practice pieces and I love that he knew how much he needed to learn before starting on making nutcrackers and I'm both touched and impressed by how much he's throwing himself into this. It's now 6 December, and he's been here every day this week, arriving just after opening time and staying until long after closing time when he insists on driving me home, presumably for no reason other than trying to prevent a repeat of the first bus journey I told him about.

'Do you want to have dinner with me tonight?' Raff appears from the workshop holding two nutcracker legs and goes to one of the shelves to compare it to a pre-made nutcracker, and then looks horrified and quickly backpedals. 'I mean, not in *that* way, just... er... I bet you're not managing to cook much lately and it might make a change from sandwiches at The Wonderland Teapot.'

'I had a bowl of cereal this morning. More milk ended up on the kitchen unit than in my mouth, but still. Baby steps,' I say, despite the fact that an actual baby would probably take less messy steps than me when it comes to eating lately. It is *hard* to do everything with your non-dominant hand, and I have never wished so much that I was ambidextrous.

'You could come back to mine after work, enjoy a nice, hot, home-cooked meal, and I'll run you home afterwards?'

I think about it. On the one hand, eating is not an easy task at the moment and do I really want Raff to pity me even more? But on the other hand, I've been enjoying spending time with him, and I've got to admit that I'm curious about where he lives and it *would* be mildly interesting to see his house... and I feel a bit fluttery that he's asked. We've been spending every day in the workshop, a fact that hasn't gone unnoticed by Mrs Bloom and the other shopkeepers, but the idea that any gossip doesn't bother him and he wants to spend even *more* time together makes me go hot all over. It would be nice to see him outside of work, away from nutcrackers, to talk about something unrelated to Christmas Ever After, and the fact that he wants that too... I can no longer deny that the fluttery feeling inside of me is butterflies. Big, big butterflies.

I've been so lost in thought that he's mistaken my silence for abject horror. 'Sorry, it was a silly idea, I shouldn't have asked.'

'No, actually I'd love to. That would be really nice.'

The size of his smile has no right to be as wide as it is. 'It would.'

I try to ignore the intense fluttering in my belly. I've been spending far too much time with Raff Dardenne lately, and it's hard not to want to spend even more time with him. In the back of my mind, there's a little niggle. In a couple of weeks' time, the council are going to be deciding whether he gets to stay or whether I do. What if this considerate and thoughtful man, who is throwing himself headfirst into making nutcrackers to help me, trying so hard to make up for one misjudged step, is no longer a part of Christmas Ever After – because of me? But then again, what if *I'm* not – because of *him*? Whatever this truce between us is, it's going to come crashing down sooner or later, in one way or another, and I don't want it to. No matter how much I've always hated Dardenne Snow Globes, it's becoming increasingly impossible to hate Raff.

It's 6 p.m. before we finish for the night. The shop is long closed and I've been out the back while Raff uses the lathe. I sit next to him, pass him each wooden blank as he needs them and take the completed ones over to the painting desk, ready for the next step. The only useful thing I've been able to do is bevel the edges of the square base pieces by running them along the disc sander, but everything else is a two-handed job.

As we step out the door and I lock up, the sound of a children's choir reaches our ears.

'The Carollers' Cabin must've been set up,' Raff says.

Every year on Christmas Ever After, they put up an open-fronted shed and invite choirs from nearby schools to sing there to entertain the shoppers and practise for any upcoming carol concerts.

'My niece's school are doing it and she's super excited to be in the choir this year. She hasn't stopped talking about it.'

We both automatically drift closer to the sound of an after-school choir practice. The shed is strung with fairy lights and a few parents are huddled in scarves and coats outside, watching on, as the teacher leads the children through a rendition of 'Silent Night'.

Streetlamps are on, and although the shop windows are darkened now, every building is decorated with twinkling lights, and tinsel sparkles from every lamppost. Above our heads, hanging cascades of icicle lights criss-cross the road, and glowing blue and white snowflakes of different sizes dangle down at seemingly random intervals.

It's one of those perfect December nights where it's dry and cold, the sky is crystal clear and the stars are sparkling, and it feels magical to stand there in the dark, watching the illuminated interior of the shed and listening to the young voices singing carols that I remember singing when I was their age.

I don't know when my eyes closed, but I'm standing close enough to Raff to be almost leaning on him. I can't remember the last time I simply stood and listened. The school choirs come every year, from the first week in December until schools break up, a couple of different ones a day during working hours, and then it's free for after-hours practice sessions, and I used to make a point of going outside to listen, but in recent years... they've barely even registered on my radar. Rather than looking forward to the

Carollers' Cabin arriving, I've not paid any attention to them. It might be Christmas year-round on this part of Ever After Street, but when did I stop noticing when it really *is* Christmas?

'I'll miss this.'

The words are like a punch in the gut. He'll miss this. He really is resigned to losing this competition he's helping me to win. 'It's only early December. There's still time to get those matches made. You don't have to keep helping me every day. Go back to your own shop, do your magical matchmaking thing, and then...' I trail off. *And then* I get evicted instead. It doesn't seem like we're in direct competition with each other, and yet, we *are*, and I don't want either outcome. I don't want to lose my shop, but I don't want him to lose his either.

He doesn't reply, and I bite my tongue because this is all my fault. The other shopkeepers might be getting annoyed with his bad reviews, but I doubt anyone would have suggested evicting him, until I came along with my big mouth and complained very loudly and very publicly to the council bosses, and goaded them into starting this ridiculous scheme.

Thinking about it has replaced the joy of the carollers with a melancholy feeling, and Raff inclines his head towards the car park. 'C'mon, we should go.'

We walk towards the car park, past the mangled wreckage of the Christmas Ever After arch that I brought crashing down. It's been moved aside onto a grassy verge but no one has done anything about it yet, not even had it collected for scrap metal. It's an unwelcome reminder every time I see it, and I can see Raff watching me as I try to avert my eyes while being simultaneously compelled to look at it and relive the humiliation of that day.

Raff's car is small and red and it smells of his aftershave and the dry wood he's been turning, and every time we get in it, he immediately puts a Christmas radio station on. Tonight, rather than driving me home, we go in the opposite direction, and it doesn't take long before he turns off the motorway and pulls into maze-like residential streets, houses twinkling with festive light displays and bright living room windows with their curtains open and their trees on show inside. It reminds me of when I was young and my parents used to drive around just to see the Christmas decorations, before things went so wrong.

'Pretty neighbourhood,' I say as he pulls up outside the prettiest and most festive-looking house of all. It's a large detached property, with garlands everywhere and lights along every eave of the roof and strung around the trees outside, along with glowing reindeer decorations on a small front lawn, and giant light-up candy canes lining the path to the door, which has got an illuminated wreath hanging on it. 'Do you live *here*?'

'Nope, I live there.' He takes a hand off the steering wheel to point to a darkened building on the other side of the driveway that looks like it must be a garage turned into a flat. 'My mum lives here.'

'Your mum? You live on your mum's driveway?'

'I live in a converted garage annexe that's also my workshop and happens to be on the grounds of my mum's property. Totally my own place which is also conveniently close should my family need anything.'

That's actually surprisingly sweet. With a fractured family of my own, I'm just thinking how much I like how family-orientated Raff is when a realisation hits. 'Wait... your mum? We're not having dinner with your mum, are we?'

'Of course not.' The words sound alarmingly sarcastic as he bypasses two other cars in the driveway and stops in a space outside the garage-flat. 'My sister and her family are coming too, by the looks of it.'

'*What*?' Immediate panic sets in. 'I can't go for dinner with your family! I can't hold utensils, Raff! I can't use a knife and fork! I can't eat in public! Dardenne public, at that!'

'Oh, don't worry, we keep our horns and cloven hooves hidden at meal times.' He turns the engine off, unbuckles his seatbelt, and opens the door.

'I didn't mean it in that way.' I scramble out too. 'I meant that I barely know you. I had no intention of meeting your family. Why didn't you tell me?'

He meets my eyes across the car rooftop. 'Because you'd have said no and I wanted you to say yes.'

It makes me feel warm, and I appreciate his honesty, even though I would've appreciated the chance to say no too.

'Look, there's no better way of recovering lost Christmas spirit than meeting my mum. She's Mrs Claus personified. I told her about you, about the accident, and she insisted on meeting you. When my mum insists on something, there's no option in the matter.'

The car beeps as he locks it and walks towards his own flat. 'Come in for a second, I need to strip these overalls off and she'll crucify us if we don't wash our hands.' He glances at my splint. 'Or wash one hand and wet-wipe the other.'

Before we get a chance, there's a hammering behind us, and a little girl is silhouetted in the window of the big house, waving wildly.

Raff waves back. 'That's my niece, Sofia. You'll meet her in a minute.'

I try not to panic. The thought of meeting his family fills me with fear, especially now, when I feel so incompetent and unlike my usual self. The broken fingers have knocked my confidence, as well as my ability to do most things, and I am so utterly unprepared for this. What if they hate me? Two weeks ago, I would have been fine with being hated by Raff's family, but now, it seems vital that we get along.

I don't get enough of a chance to look around Raff's flat. 'No Christmas decorations?'

'My mum has enough Christmas decorations to decorate thirty towns. I spend most of my time over there, it doesn't make sense to put them up in here as well.' He jerks a thumb towards what must be a bedroom. 'Gimme a sec to get out of these. Make yourself at home.' He turns lights on as he goes and leaves me to poke around.

It seems like an annexe built onto a garage and the original garage is still behind it somewhere. There's no upstairs, just a living room and a kitchen, and when I poke my head into a door-less hallway, there's a bathroom, and another door with a big sign in child's crayon writing that reads, 'Uncle Raff's Top-Secret Work-shop. Keep Out!' and has a colourful drawing of a snow globe on it. I feel an almost unfamiliar urge to go and have a prod around and see if I can uncover his snow globe secrets, and I'm almost relieved when Raff returns before I've had a chance to creep down the hallway and at least see if the door is open.

When we've both cleaned ourselves up, he invites me to step outside and places a warm hand on my back, guiding me gently across the driveway and along the path up to the front door.

The outside of the house might look like somewhere Clark Gris-wold decorated, but inside, it's like stepping onto the set of a Hallmark movie. The warmth of the house after being outside wraps around me like a blanket. I've never been able to keep *one* poinsettia alive for longer than a week, but Mrs Dardenne seems to be operating some sort of poinsettia factory because there's one on almost every surface, and none of them have got shrivelled-up leaves or look like they're desperately gasping for water having been forgotten. There are pine garlands arranged along every surface, all wound with twinkling lights and decorated with winter berries, pinecones, and cinnamon sticks. And the smell pervading the whole house is unreal. It's fresh pine, combined with cinnamon, the heat of food being cooked, and an unidentifiable component that's the embodiment of Christmas.

'Uncle Raff's brought a girl home!' a young voice squeals from somewhere inside, and a girl of about seven barrels towards us and throws her arms around Raff's waist.

He bends down to hug her and ruffles her blonde hair. 'This is Sofia,' Raff says to me. 'And this is my friend, Franca. Do you remember I told you I've been working with her because she's got an injury at the moment so we've all got to be extra gentle with her, okay?'

It's an understatement to say I melt at the tenderness in his voice. His whole demeanour softens when he talks to her, and he picks her up and swings her around and she gives me a wave from his arms.

I wave back. 'It's nice to meet you, Sofia. I've heard a lot about you.'

Her face turns red, and she makes Raff put her down and runs to the kitchen, repeating her earlier shout, and I feel like Lumiere and Cogsworth are watching me from somewhere, murmuring in disbelief that there's a girl in the castle.

'This is my sister, Erin.' Raff beckons her over and she gives me a careful one-armed hug, her protecting her pregnant belly and me protecting my hand.

'And you know my brother-in-law, Quentin.'

I wave to the man I met briefly a couple of days ago when he came in looking for Raff after a customer query at Love Is All A-Round.

'And this is my mum.'

The woman who bustles out of the kitchen is... well, if she's not *actually* Mrs Claus, she should definitely be cast to play her in the next Santa movie that gets made. She must be in her early sixties, with brown hair with streaks of grey in it, the same dark eyes as Raff, freckles across her rosy cheeks, and hair that winds over her head in a plait to meet in a bun at the back.

'Thank you for having me, Mrs Dardenne.' I hold my left hand out to shake hers, but she envelopes me in a bear hug that I'm fairly sure must be tighter than an actual bear would give.

'I'm so sorry about my clumsy oaf of a son.' She squeezes me even tighter. 'I gave him a serious talking-to about watching where he's going when I heard what happened. And not a word of this "Mrs Dardenne" nonsense – you call me Trisha, okay? Make yourself at home. Help yourself to anything you want. It's all there for the taking.' She pulls back and her brown eyes meet mine and she squeezes my shoulders with both hands. 'It's a pleasure to have you, Franca. An absolute pleasure.'

My nose burns with the effort of not tearing up at the warmth in her voice and how welcome she's making me feel. Christmases were never like this at home. Even in the good years, there was tension between my parents. Mum wanted things to be perfect and Dad wanted to go to the pub. Visitors weren't welcomed in case they disrupted Mum's carefully prepared plans, and visits to extended family had to be planned with military precision. There was nothing easy-going about it, but here it seems like anyone could turn up on the doorstep and they'd be welcomed warmly.

'What am I, chopped liver? Used wrapping paper, scrumpled up and tossed aside as an afterthought?' A crotchety voice comes from the living room.

'We were saving the best for last, Grandma.' Raff goes down a step into the living room and bends to give her a hug and a kiss on the cheek to save her getting up from the armchair she's sitting in.

When he steps back, the elderly woman is trying to hold onto her frown, but no one is immune to Raff's charm. She takes a sip of her martini and raises the glass to me in a toast.

'This is my grandma, Granny Biddy.'

She wags a scolding finger at Raff. 'Don't you dare use the G word around me, young man. I refuse to be known as anyone's grandmother. People will think I'm *old.*'

She transfers the martini glass into her other hand so she can reach out and shake mine with her curled arthritic fingers. 'I'm an old biddy called Biddy – proving that age is *just* a name. I don't let people think I'm over fifty. Unless it benefits me in getting me out of doing something I don't want to do. "Stand in this long queue, good sir? With *these* hips? Oh, I couldn't possibly, I'm just a poor, feeble old woman."' She coughs for effect and then gives me a toothy smile. 'You don't think I'm old, do you?'

'Not at all. You don't look a day over thirty-three,' I say with a grin. She's clearly well into her nineties.

She squeals with delight and then turns to Raff. 'Ooh, I like this one. You should bring girls like this home more often!'

'As opposed to the hundreds of other girls he brings home?' Erin asks sarcastically.

'Do you bring a lot of girls home?' I raise an eyebrow at him.

'You're the first.'

'We were starting to think there was something wrong with him,' Erin says.

'Starting to? I could start a list of all the things wrong with him.' I pretend to scoff and glance around at them. 'But I won't, because that would be rude when you're being so hospitable and he's been very good to me this week.'

'Well, he's also broken three of your fingers so the bar is set pretty low.' Erin gives her brother a mocking grin and he pokes his tongue out at her and I can't help laughing at them. It would be so easy to forget that this is the Dardenne family, if it wasn't for the snow globes everywhere.

I wander over to the fireplace and the mantelpiece above it, looking at the array of snow globes lined up.

'That's the first one my husband ever made,' Biddy says. 'Many decades ago now.'

'And you've kept it all these years,' I murmur, running the fingers of my good hand along the wooden shelf, being careful not to touch any of the ornaments on it. 'Did he make all of these?'

Erin nods. 'Granddad used to make one for Granny Biddy every Christmas.'

'Will you youngsters stop using the G word? Being anyone's granny only comes in useful on Mother's Day! Unless you're going to buy me a gift, do not refer to me as anything so old!'

'But you're *my* great-grandma, Biddy,' Sofia tells her and she covers her ears, pretending not to hear such a slight against her.

It's impossible not to smile at them, all of them. This is what a family *should* be like.

'That's the first one Raff made on his own,' Biddy says when she sees me looking at a snow globe with a young ballerina holding a nutcracker soldier aloft, exactly like the protagonist does in the ballet. 'That one stays on display year-round.'

It's faded with age. The liquid inside is starting to go cloudy and there's glue around the base that's turned brown. Trisha leans over and gives it a shake, and I watch the little ballerina being enveloped by iridescent glitter.

Everything keeps coming back to nutcrackers. They've always been a big part of my life, from my career as a ballet dancer to opening a shop that specialises in them and spending every day of my life making them. Even so many years ago, he was making them too. A feeling of fate or coincidence or *something* tingles at the back of my neck, but I force myself to ignore it. No matter what, the main thing I should be concerned with is what *else* he puts into those snow globes.

The tree in the living room is such a traditional family Christmas tree. It's six-foot tall with an angel on top, smells of pine, is strung with multi-coloured lights, tinsel, and garlands of popcorn, and adorned with an array of mismatched ornaments, from photographic ones to handmade ones to shop-bought individual ones. It's the sort of tree that you'd see in happy family commercials, but never in reality. In my life of alternating Christmases between parents, Dad would always get a real tree but only a little one and he never had any decorations for it, and Mum always insisted that the faded plastic thing she kept in the loft was perfectly adequate and didn't make any mess, unlike a real one. I've always wished I had a family Christmas tree just like this. It has a red and white striped skirt and already has a few gift-wrapped boxes underneath it with bows and tags on.

'Do you think the tree will grow at midnight on Christmas Eve?' Sofia asks me as I stand and look up at it.

The tree growing is what happens in the ballet when the wooden nutcracker prince comes to life on Christmas Eve. It's always been one of the most magical parts of the show. 'Only if you've got a really special nutcracker who will awaken to defeat the Mouse King.'

'Do your nutcrackers come to life?'

'Franca's shop is *full* of nutcrackers.' Raff comes back in from the kitchen. 'There'd be chaos if they came to life.'

'Have you ever been there on Christmas Eve? Have you ever seen if they do?'

'I have. Sometimes I work on Christmas Eve and disappointingly, none of them have ever turned into a handsome prince.'

'No one should work on Christmas Eve,' Trisha says from the

kitchen, and when Sofia goes to protest, she quickly adds, 'except Santa.'

She turns to me with a motherly look. 'I hope you don't make a habit of that, Franca.'

'No, er, of course not,' I lie. The truth is that in recent years, Christmas and the days around it have become just like any other day. Apart from a phone call to my mum and a video chat with my dad, I appreciate the quietness of the street when every other shop is shut, and after a busy December where I'm constantly trying to work between customers, I like sitting in front of the lathe and knowing I won't be disturbed.

Within minutes, Sofia comes back waving a brightly painted nutcracker at me. 'Did you make this one?'

'No, honey, that one's mass-produced tat.' Raff makes us all laugh with his bluntness. 'I never realised how rubbish the factory-made ones are. Look at the glue around his hair and the gap between his shoe and his leg. No refinement whatsoever.' He reaches over and takes it from her and tilts his head to assess it. 'You haven't *seen* a nutcracker until you've seen one of Franca's nutcrackers. They're really special.'

I meet his eyes and mouth a thank you at him and he smiles, making the cold cavity inside my chest feel as warm and cosy as the rest of me feels in this house, and I look away quickly because I can feel eyes on us.

Trisha's gaze is watchful, and she blinks through a serving hatch from the kitchen with a soft smile on her face, before she shakes herself. 'Right, what everyone needs to do is get themselves sat down at the table. Dinner will be ready in a few minutes.'

Erin helps Sofia get seated, and Raff goes over to help Biddy up and offers her his arm to escort her to the dinner table, one shaky step at a time, until he pulls out the chair at the head of the table for her, and she grips his arm as she lowers herself down into it.

I'm so enamoured with watching the sweet scene that I get lost in it, until he comes back and offers his arm to me too.

I smack at it because I don't need assistance to walk the few steps to the table, but I sense those familiar gazes on us again, so I slip my hand through his arm and my fingers involuntarily give his forearm a squeeze. He's got an old-fashioned gentleman vibe about him that's incredibly charming.

At the table, he pulls out a chair for me too, and when I've sat down, he takes the seat next to me.

He mouths, 'Okay?' and knocks his knee against mine under the table, and I nod in response. I'm apprehensive about attempting to eat in public with only my left hand, but the atmosphere in the house is so relaxed and easy-going that it feels like I'm part of their family even though I'm a stranger to all of them.

I'm sitting directly opposite Sofia and her eyes are on my splint where my arm is resting on the table. 'What happened to your hand?'

'I was standing on a stool to hang some mistletoe and your Uncle Raff and I had a bit of an argument and—'

'Uncle Raff let his petty frustrations get the better of him and stormed off without looking where he was going and accidentally sent her flying.'

I stare at Raff when he takes over the story. I feel terrible about the argument we had, especially live on camera. We both brought shame on Christmas Ever After, but it's the first time I've heard him speak so openly about that day to someone else.

'Does it hurt?'

Sofia's question brings me back from the reverie of staring at Raff. 'It does at the moment, but it'll get better in a few weeks. Unlike my pride, because the whole thing was captured on video and over 40,000 people have seen it now.'

'Can I see?' Without waiting for an answer, she starts digging in her mum's handbag, which is hanging over the back of Erin's chair next to her. She pulls out her mum's phone and starts doing something on it, until Raff reaches across and kindly, but firmly, pushes the phone down onto the table and shakes his head sharply.

'Why not?'

'Because we both embarrassed ourselves and Franca was hurt and it was my fault, and neither of us want to relive that horrible day.'

'Sorry.' Erin puts her phone back into her bag and hooks it over the opposite corner of the chair, away from little hands.

'Uncle Raff tells me you'll be singing at the Carollers' Cabin on Christmas Ever After?' I say because Sofia looks disappointed at having the phone taken away.

'Yes!' she squeals and both Erin and Biddy give her a reproachful look for the whistle-like pitch. 'I've been practising *alllllll* the time!' She rattles off a list of Christmas carols, all the old ones that I remember singing in school assemblies when I was her age.

'And she's been cast as an angel in the school nativity, so we've got constant singing at the moment,' Erin mutters. 'Honestly, if I hear about Good King Wenceslas one more time, I'm going to make him *into* the Feast of Stephen.'

'What's your favourite Christmas song, Franca?' Sofia asks me, oblivious to her mum's grumbling.

I'm stumped. So many possible choices swirl through my head, but I can't think of any I like enough to call a favourite. Is this really what it's come to – that I no longer have a favourite Christmas song? I used to *love* Christmas music. I would start playing it in September – way before it was socially acceptable to play festive songs. As festive music plays year-round on Christmas Ever After, you grow immune to it, but as Raff pointed out the other day, I don't even play it in my shop during December these days. 'I... um... do you know, I like so many that I can't choose between them. What's yours?'

'Taylor Swift!' She starts singing 'Christmas Tree Farm', a song I've heard a million times without ever knowing who sang it.

As she sings and dances around in her seat, I remember a song I used to love from a few years ago. 'Mine's actually a bit of an obscure one. "My Favourite Time of Year" by The Florin Street Band.'

'I don't know that one. Can I play it?' Without waiting for permission, she shouts at their smart speaker to play it, and the first bars come out from a small device standing on the TV unit in the living room, filling the house with the cheerful opening music that makes it impossible not to feel festive.

Trisha and Quentin start serving, and a large bowl of broccoli cheese is put down in front of me, along with a plate full of warm slices of crusty white baguette, and I'm certain it's been done for my benefit.

Raff bangs a teaspoon against his mug of tea and then raises it in a toast. 'Cheers to family, this time of year, and new friends.' He leans across until he can clink his mug against mine and then makes an announcement. 'Right, Franca and I are having a competition where we only eat with our left hands and see who can make the most mess.'

'Can I play?' Sofia asks.

'Anyone can play. The more, the merrier!'

'Let's all play,' Trisha says.

'Sod that.' Biddy has another sip of her martini. 'Sorry, Franca, it's hard enough to eat with *both* hands at my age, but you youngsters enjoy yourselves.'

'Oh, no, please, *none* of you have to do that. That's ridiculous.' I kick Raff's foot under the table and stare at him pointedly.

Sofia grabs a spoon in her left hand and plunges it into her broccoli cheese, and everyone else does the same. Raff picks up a slice of baguette and grins at me, and I look around the table, everyone starting on their food with their left hands only, and the warmth that flooded my chest earlier seeps out and trickles into the rest of my body. I never thought anyone would go to that much trouble just to make me feel more comfortable, and my nose burns with the threat of tears rising up.

I pick up a piece of baguette too and dip it into the melted cheese. 'I warn you, I've had nearly a week of practice, I can beat you all hands down!'

'*Hand* down,' Quentin says, and everyone explodes into laughter, and the room is filled with chatter, and a sense of joy and peacefulness. I'm certain the meal itself was made solely because it's something easy to eat with one hand, just as I'm sure the sliced baguette was chosen because I can't slice my own rolls, at least, not without trying to pin one down with an elbow, which is not something anyone wants to showcase in public. Something I was so self-conscious of has become something fun for everyone to join in, and I find myself looking at Raff, his huge smile, his twinkly brown eyes and dark hair that falls to one side. *He* did that, for me. They've all made this so easy. They've welcomed me and made me feel like I've known them all for years, despite only meeting them tonight. They include me in conversations and ask me about myself and want to know everything about nutcrackers, and seem genuinely interested when I get overenthusiastic and talk about my processes too much. This is what I've always wished my family could be like.

'How's the clumsy oaf doing with your precious nutcrackers, Franca?' Trisha asks me.

'He's amazing.' I look at him and smile. I've spotted one of the snowmen he made the other day on the window ledge and I love that he made one for his mum too, and it's only when I notice they're all looking at me that I realise I've just called him amazing and now I'm staring at him and probably looking like I've got hearts in my eyes, and I hurry to correct myself. 'I mean, as a craftsman, obviously. He knew exactly what to do to practise and get used to the process of woodturning. It's been surprisingly refreshing to watch him work. His enthusiasm has reminded me of things I'd forgotten.'

'Fat lot of good it'll do him if he doesn't pull his socks up,' Biddy grouches.

'We heard about the council's plot,' Erin says and then turns to me. 'It sounds totally uncalled for. No one really wants *either* of you evicted, do they?'

'I don't think anyone will complain when I lose and take my one-star reviews with me,' Raff mutters before I have a chance to answer.

'I'm not flamin' surprised,' Biddy pipes up. 'If you can't find love for yourself, how do you ever expect to find it for anyone else?'

'It doesn't work like that, Grandma,' Raff protests.

She narrows her eyes at him for using the G word again, and then explains to me. 'My Claude's powers didn't come until he met me. He couldn't have matched fish with chips before then, but he always said I was his lucky charm. Cupid himself must've been searching for a predecessor and our love was so powerful that his powers transferred to Claude in a puff of smoke – poof!' She does the sound effect. 'And that's Raff's problem – trying to find love for others when he's never experienced it.'

'Oh, good, it's "let's talk about Raff's love life" time again,' Raff says good-naturedly. 'And we've *only* had this conversation three times so far this week, but God forbid we let Franca leave without the full Dardenne experience.'

Are they really talking about magical powers? I keep expecting them to start laughing or imply they're keeping up the pretence for Sofia's benefit, but they all seem serious. They *all* really believe this.

'Grandpa had magic powers,' Sofia tells me in a serious little voice. 'He was going to teach me one day, but now Uncle Raff will. He's got a workshop where he keeps all the magic he inherited from Grandpa. Absolutely *no one* is allowed in, but I will be when I'm old enough. I'm going to learn how to make snow globes and run the shop just like he does and make people go all gooey in love, like Mummy and Daddy are.'

Erin and Quentin smile at each other. A few days ago, I'd probably have called it sickeningly sweet, but tonight, it seems genuinely sweet. 'Don't tell me Claude matched you two as well?'

'Of course he did.' Erin doesn't realise my question was intended as a joke and I *really* didn't expect that he actually had matched them. 'He phoned and told me to come to his shop one day because there was an emergency, and when I got there, everything was fine, but there was this snow globe lying on the floor. I went to pick it up and at the same moment, he shoved Quentin forwards and he crashed into me, I dropped it again, and then we both picked it up and we saw magic.'

'Soooooo romantic!' Sofia sighs. 'They should be in a Disney movie!'

'He deliberately tried to recreate the moment he and Granny Biddy met, and it worked. Four years later, we got married, and a few years after that, this one came along.' Erin ruffles Sofia's blonde hair.

I glance at Raff beside me. He's got a... cynical look on his face, but he doesn't say anything.

'This is not a family business then?' I ask as I realise what she's implying. I always thought Dardenne Snow Globes included the whole clan. 'The rest of you... you're not involved?'

"I work full-time, and the good-at-crafts gene skipped me completely," Erin says.

'We're so lucky to have Raff continuing the legacy,' Trisha says. 'The business would die without him. Our family name and what my father worked towards his whole life would be wiped out. Thankfully Raff was there to step in when we needed him most.'

I glance at Raff, who is evocatively quiet. What did Mrs Bloom say about him not wanting to take over the shop but not having a choice because there was no one else? He looks uncomfortable and I can't help thinking that his silence says what words can't.

'And one day, the magic will be passed down to the next generation in our grandchildren,' Trisha continues, before glancing at Sofia and then at Raff. 'If *we* ever have any.'

'You've got one and another one on the way,' he replies. 'That's more than enough grandchildren to be going on with!'

'Hear, hear.' Biddy raises her martini glass. 'I cannot abide anyone else making a great-grandmother out of me, I'm far too young!'

I laugh at their cheerful banter as time goes by. Trisha brings out homemade chocolate cake piled high with fresh cream for dessert. After dinner, we all crowd onto the sofas in the living room and Sofia sings some of her choir songs for us, and I feel so peaceful and relaxed here. And absolutely stuffed. That was the best meal I've had for ages, and the *only* meal that hasn't been a grab-and-go sandwich or cooked in a plastic tray in the microwave for a *long* time. Raff is sitting next to me with his feet up on the coffee table, and I'm so comfortable on this huge squashy sofa that I even forget about my hand for a few minutes. For just a little while, everything is right with the world.

'Will you come again, Franca?' Sofia asks me when she finishes a rendition of 'The Twelve Days of Christmas', complete with actions for each of the characters.

'Yes, she *will*,' Trisha answers for me and reaches over to pat my leg. 'If we haven't scared her off tonight, we'll have plenty more opportunities to do so.'

'Yay!' Sofia squeals. 'Will you come and see me in my school nativity? It's the week after next!'

'I'd love to.' I'm so surprised that she's invited me that it's the only possible response. Even after only meeting them tonight, the Dardennes have stolen my heart and made me feel at home here. This is exactly what I always wished Christmas would be like, and they're a perfect family. Flawed, loving, teasing, welcoming, supportive, and apparently, sharing a combined belief in magical powers. And it's had the uncomfortable side effect of making me question everything I've ever thought about them. Being in this house, being welcomed into such a lovely family... the snow globe magic that I've always hated doesn't seem like such a bad thing here. It seems... kind of good? Claude Dardenne obviously had secrets, and so does Raff, but the fact the whole family believes in this legacy...

It kind of makes me wish I did too.

9

'Sorry you had to witness that,' Raff says from the driver's seat as he starts up the car to take me home. 'I should have known it would be the perfect opportunity to bring up the "why aren't you in love, why don't you give me more grandbabies" thing. The existence of a pulse makes you the perfect candidate for my family to embarrass me in front of.'

'Ah, don't worry about it. I'm not in love or interested in giving anyone grandbabies either. The only difference is that my parents are so wrapped up in hating each other that they don't notice.'

'Thanks for not telling them that.' He glances over at me and pulls out onto the road. 'About my granddad, I mean. They'd be devastated if they knew he ever got it wrong.'

'That's okay.' I struggle for the right words. I had no intention of telling them. Claude obviously meant the world to them and it wouldn't have been right to rain on their parade like that. 'They don't know, do they?'

'Know what?'

'They're not part of it?' The rest of the Dardenne clan believing in the magic behind the snow globes has really thrown me and I'm determined to get to the bottom of this in one way or another.

'Part of what?'

'Come on, Raff, the obtuse act is wearing thin. Your whole family wholeheartedly believe that your grandfather had magical powers. They think he was Cupid working via the medium of glass-encased glycerin liquid.'

'You don't know that he wasn't.'

'Yes, I do, and so do you, because magic doesn't exist, so what is it? What's making your snow globes move? You can tell me, you know. It's curiosity more than anything now – I won't tell anyone.'

His knuckles go white on the steering wheel but he doesn't react.

'Something mechanical that causes the base to move when shaken.' I'm clutching at straws again. It can't be that because it would happen every time, not just once. 'A glow stick? Something that catches the light and creates an optical illusion and then... disappears?'

'A glow stick?' His eyebrow pings upwards and he glances at me while his hands are still on the wheel. 'You think I put a magically disappearing glow stick into my snow globes but you don't believe in actual magic?'

'I don't know.' I twist my fingers around the open zip of my coat. I really *am* clutching at every straw going, but I *can't* figure out what his trick is, and the more I get to know him, the more it seems like tricks aren't his style.

He shrugs, keeping his eyes straight ahead. 'Maybe it's because people *expect* them to move...'

I shift in the car seat and fix him with a withering look. 'You're telling me that the entire Dardenne legacy is based on wishful thinking and the power of suggestion? Come off it, Raff!'

'Maybe it really is magic.'

'If there was magic in the world, I think it would find something more obvious to channel itself through than snow globes, don't you?' I look over at him again. '*Do* you know how many relationships have broken up? You must have sales records so you know how many snow globes you've sold, do you have records of all the couples you or your grandfather had matched and whether they're still together?'

'Why would I have data on that? I don't serve people and say, "Here's your magical snow globe that's brought you together – be sure to come back and tell us when you have a horrible and messy break-up!"'

I shouldn't laugh, but I can't help myself. He has no right to be as funny as he is, especially when joking about relationships that have gone wrong.

'It's not only about matching people, you know. Some customers *do* come in solely to buy a snow globe.' His eyes flick over to me again. 'Not enough people, mind. Dardenne Snow Globes has got so tangled up in the whole love thing that it's become all we're known for. It's taboo to come into the shop alone, as a single person, because customers think we *only* want to match people up, and on the other hand, people who are already in relationships think it's no place for them and don't come in at all. I've tried to redirect things since I took over, but our legacy looms large. I'm no longer a snow globe maker – I'm a matchmaker who can't make a match, and that's something I never wanted to be.'

There's such sadness to his words and a real resignation in his voice. I've never considered this angle before – that by trying to gain more customers, he's accidentally ended up alienating some too. And before this week, I'd never considered that Raff himself might be unhappy with how his business is going. I'm probably the wrong person to poke around in this, but I can't stop myself. 'What happens if it's... *not* you who wins in January?'

I hate the thought of this. I would be devastated to lose my shop, but the thought of being responsible for him losing *his* shop is heartbreaking too, and it feels like we're dancing around it, never quite facing it head-on, but sooner or later, we're going to have to accept that we're in direct competition with each other.

'I destroy my family's hearts and crush their souls.'

I chew on my lip because although it was a sarcastic brush-off of a comment, after meeting them, I don't think it's too far from the truth. 'Seriously, Raff. What would you do? Start up elsewhere?'

We stop as a traffic light turns red, even though there's no other traffic on the road, and he rolls his head against the headrest to fully face me. 'Change my last name and emigrate to a new country?'

He's trying to be funny but it doesn't sound like a laughing matter, and I give him a pointed stare until he realises he's going to need to elaborate more than that.

'I don't know,' he says with a sigh. 'I don't want to let my family down, but I don't fit the job that's expected of me since my granddad died. Sometimes I wish I *could* start over. Sell snow globes with no myth or legend attached to them. I used to make custom ones that were so special. People would bring in photos for me to recreate in snow globe form. I'd make globes of dearly loved pets who had crossed the rainbow bridge. I once recreated the scene of a proposal as a wedding gift. Specific spots in specific cities. Things that meant something to people. Now I just make bog-standard scenery that people expect to be magical, and if they don't move—'

He's cut off by a car horn honking behind us. The light has turned green and neither of us has noticed. Raff shakes his head to clear it and drives off quickly, but he stays quiet after the interruption.

'And if they don't move...?' I repeat the end of his last sentence, trying to prompt him into continuing it.

'Then customers are disappointed, and disappointed customers leave bad reviews, and the street I work on wants me evicted, and we end up back at the start of the vicious circle. If I went somewhere else, started up without anyone knowing my name, I could do what we used to do years ago – make snow globes that were magical to people because they meant something, not because of a tacky gimmick.'

A tacky gimmick. If that's what Raff calls it, does it mean that's what it *is*? I could jump on that word, push him for an explanation, but the timing is all wrong. Raff's opening himself up. I doubt there are many people who have heard this before because there's no way he'd risk it getting back to his family. 'Would you do that? Go elsewhere? Leave your family?'

'No. I don't know. Maybe? I wouldn't want to, but...' He glances over at me again. 'I can't see a way forward here. There's so much bad-feeling towards me from the fellow shopkeepers. I *am* dragging you all down with my bad reviews. No one is going to choose me over you. I can't make those five matches, and even if I could, the problem wouldn't go away. I can't do what my granddad did and I can't get away from what people expect when they see my surname attached to a snow globe. The bullet will need to be bitten sooner or later; I may as well bite it now.'

'You could rebrand. Drop the love stuff. Your snow globes are absolutely stunning. They deserve to be seen for what they are, not for some gimmick that even you don't believe in.'

He doesn't reply, and I don't push him any further. I pretend to be fascinated by the road in front of us, but really I keep sneaking glances at him from the corner of my eye. Has he always looked this tired? He's been working extra hours with me, as well as dealing with the running of his own shop alongside Quentin, but

I've never noticed the dark circles under his eyes and the taut lines around his mouth. His smile is always so big and charismatic that it makes it hard to notice what might be hiding behind it, and it's probably a good thing I don't have use of my right hand, because if I did, I'd reach over and rub his thigh in a gesture of reassurance. He's reassured me since the first moment he came into my shop, but tonight, it feels like he needs a bit of support in return. And the sense of guilt comes again. I'm the cause of part of this. I'm the one who constantly draws attention to his bad reviews. I'm the one who finds fault in everything he does on Christmas Ever After. Maybe he needed to be able to sweep his feelings under the rug for a bit longer. Maybe he needed more time to decide what to do, but I've forced the council's hand and pushed it to be something that has to be faced *now*, and more than anything, I wish I'd left well alone.

When we pull up outside my house, he turns the engine off but makes no move to get out. 'Thanks for listening to that. No one else knows. Working on the nutcrackers has reminded me of the joy I used to find in making snow globes, and how much that's gone away in recent months.'

'Funnily enough, watching you work on the nutcrackers has reminded me of how much I joy I used to find in it and how much *that's* gone away in recent months.'

He lets out a snort of solidarity and rolls his head towards me, his dark hair flopping forwards and giving me an unexpected urge to tuck it back. 'Well, don't we make a fine pair of Grinches?'

I laugh, even though I never thought I'd have enough in common with Raff Dardenne to be a pair of anything. 'Thanks for tonight. For inviting me – and for doing the left-handed thing. You didn't have to do that.'

'It was a bit of fun. I didn't mind.'

'Yeah, but you did it solely to make me less self-conscious and that was really thoughtful. Thank you.'

'You're welcome.'

Why does he make me smile so much? His head is leaning sideways against the headrest and his answering smile is Disney-prince-like and so wide that it looks like he's got too many teeth to fit in his mouth, and I know he knows he's winning me over, and I can't find it in myself to care.

'Your family are amazing. You have no idea how lucky you are.'

'Oh, I do, even when I don't, if that makes sense?' He waits for me to meet his eyes and when I do, he scrunches his nose up to make me smile.

Everything is dark outside and the only light is the tiny one in the car roof and we sit there in comfortable silence for an abnormal amount of time, until I force myself to stretch and say goodnight.

'Hold that thought.' He jumps out of the car and jogs around to my side, where he pulls the passenger door open and holds his arm out, giving me something to hold onto while I lever myself out of the car. It's totally unnecessary but it's such a sweet and gentle-manly thing to do, and I slide my left hand through his elbow and let my fingers curl into his forearm as I use his strength to haul myself up.

When I'm on both feet, he settles his hand over mine and walks me to my front door, and when I'm safely inside, he tips an imagi-nary hat in my direction and gives me a wink as he goes back to the car.

I stand inside and watch him pull away, feeling glowy and cared for, because of Raff and the whole Dardenne tribe, and nothing else seems to matter more than that.

10

The workshop is littered with pieces of nutcracker. There are legs and arms and heads and hats and torsos everywhere.

'So the hat goes on the bottom of the left foot, right? And the base goes right here in the middle of the torso?'

'Oh, the hilarity continues.' I smack Raff's arm because he's assembling his first nutcracker from all the pieces he's carved, and he thinks the 'this foot goes on this shoulder' gag is much funnier than it is.

In truth, spending time with him is amusing and easy and he makes nutcrackers fun again, and the deliberately mis-assembled nutcrackers are making me laugh, even when I'm trying not to.

He's put his Christmas music playlist on and the workshop is filled with the sound of 'Mistletoe and Wine', and Raff's warm and wintery aftershave is almost outdoing the scent of freshly sawn wood from the array of cut and sanded nutcracker parts strewn across the workbench in front of us.

'Start assembling from the bottom up. Dowels run through the legs and then they're glued onto the base.'

He's got my hot glue gun plugged in but he's clearly no stranger to using one, because he fits the parts together easily and holds them in place long enough for the glue to bond, humming along to Cliff Richard while waiting.

I've already shown him how to make the mouth lever and cut out the groove in the torso for it to fit in, and the next step is lining it up and drilling all the way through from one shoulder to the other. I point it out with the little finger of my left hand, but I'm pretty sure that Raff is just humouring me and has studied my nutcrackers well enough to have worked out how they fit together.

'Your weeks will pass in a flash,' he says as if he can tell what I'm thinking as I watch him drive the drill bit through the wood with his dexterous *both* hands. 'And I'm not going anywhere. I can come and do *anything* you need help with.'

'Thank you.' I realise I'm leaning so close to him to oversee what he's doing that my chin is practically on his shoulder and I sit back quickly.

He lines up the holes and pushes the pin through to hold the mouth lever in place, bashes it in with a wooden mallet, and then takes the arms, lines them up with the pin sticking out of each shoulder, and glues on one and then the other, and he's quiet while holding them in place.

'Have you really never been in love?' I blurt out because it's been on my mind since Biddy announced it so vociferously on Friday night.

'That's not an odd question *at all*.' We're sitting next to each other and he pulls back far enough to look at me. 'Why'd you ask?'

'I don't know. You seem like someone people would fall in love with.'

He tilts his head to the side. 'That's... a very nice thing to say, I think. Unless there's an insult to follow?'

'No. I mean, you're... very loveable.' Where did that come from? He *is*, but I never intended to say it *to* him. I attempt to dig myself out of this hole... and end up making it ten times deeper. 'What I meant is you're... funny. Sweet. Warm. A great hugger. A gentleman. A total softie when it comes to children, and the most respectful grandson anyone could dream of. Why wouldn't people be in love with you?'

'You think I'm a great hugger?' He leans over, slings his arm around my shoulders and squeezes me into his side. 'And thank you for making me blush. While it's quite possible that there are, indeed, a crowd of women out there somewhere who are head-over-heels in love with me, none of them have made themselves known yet, but more importantly, I just don't... believe in it?' He sounds unsure of his answer. 'No, that's not right. I do *believe* in it because my grandma and granddad had it, so did my mum and dad, and Erin and Quentin, but when it comes to me...' He pushes air out through his nose and drops his arm from around me. 'I've never met anyone special. I've never had that life-changing, all-consuming love, where they make your life better just by existing. I've never met anyone who inspires me. Who makes me want to *be* better. Who's worth fighting for. Don't get me wrong, I've dated, I've been in relationships, but never anything with a spark. Never anyone I could see a future with. A few years ago, I gave in to the family pressure and tried to date – apps, set-ups, et cetera. None of the dates ever made me glad I was out with them rather than curled up at home watching a movie.'

I laugh out loud. That has always been my gauge of a good date too. Would I rather be at home with a box of chocolates and the TV on? If yes, they never got a second date.

'Everyone I met seemed either selfish or desperate. Time is ticking when you're in your thirties and your friends are getting married and having babies. I never felt like anyone *cared* about me. Even after a few dates, it was always a "you'll do" rather than, "you bowl me over and upturn my life", you know? I'd rather be alone than be someone's "good enough".' He sighs again. 'And it's not just that. Love has ruined something I loved. All I do, day-in, day-out, is think about love. I'm trying to find it for other people, trying to spot something that makes people a good match, something that was instinctive to my granddad but isn't to me, and I'm failing. How would I ever be any good at love myself when I have no idea what makes it work and what makes two people fall for each other?'

I can't help noticing the similarity between that and what Biddy said. *If you can't find love for yourself, how do you ever expect to find it for anyone else?* I had no idea how much pressure is on Raff, and how much he's struggling with his shop and the promises his grandfather made.

The nutcracker's arms are secure now, and he picks up the head and glues it on without me having to instruct him, and then takes the hat and glues that on too. 'How about you? You're beautiful, funny, talented, fiercely independent... Why don't I see hordes of nutcracker princes lining up to slay Mouse Kings for you?'

I blush at the compliments but laugh at the analogy. 'I'm better off alone. After a couple of bad relationships over the years – one lacklustre, one that ended horribly, I've finally learnt that lesson now. If I sense my guard dropping and I'm letting someone get too close, I push them away. It isn't easy to let people in when I've seen firsthand how bad things can get when relationships break down.'

Enough time has gone by that the glue has solidified, and Raff checks it over and hands me the finished blank nutcracker to inspect, making me appreciate the value of someone who already knew their way around woodworking and craftwork. 'You've made your first nutcracker, Mr Dardenne.'

I love the way his cheeks redden as our fingers brush when I hand it back to him. 'I've loved every minute of it.'

'So have I.' I find myself looking into his dark eyes again, and they have a way of making everything else feel distant and far away. The corner of his lip twitches, and it's impossible to look away from his mouth. I swallow hard at how dry my tongue has gone... It must be the sawdust again. Of course it must.

'Right, painting station.' I jump up and direct Raff to the desk on the opposite side of the room, away from the machinery and any sawdust that might adhere itself to wet paint.

It's a big oak desk with a shelving unit on top of it full of every kind and colour of paint under the sun. There are brushes, sponges, and mixing palettes because you never know what colour a customer is going to request, and there's another workbench to the right where painted nutcrackers are put to dry.

I don't need to sit and watch him work. He paints tiny ceramic figurines all the time, he doesn't need anyone to teach him how to paint, but I like sitting next to him. It's like I'm absorbing his enthusiasm and beginning to find joy in making nutcrackers again. And it, of course, has *nothing* to do with the scent of his aftershave, the warmth of his body next to mine, the ridiculously sexy forearms, or the way his graceful fingers curl around a tiny brush and somehow still manage to look elegant even while covered in paint.

As this one is just a practice nutcracker, he can paint it any colours he wants, and he goes for traditional festive red with green accents, black faux fur hair, and picks out a tub of flat-backed pearls for the buttons.

'I hate to think my granddad was responsible for that.'

'For what?' I ask and then realise he means my attitude towards love and relationships. 'Oh, it's not just that. I always feel insecure when I know people are close enough to hurt me. You make yourself vulnerable when you let someone in, and I'm not good with being vulnerable and especially not with needing people.'

He nudges his knee gently against my left hand where it's resting on my thigh. 'Don't I know it?'

When I narrow my eyes at him, he goes back to painting the

nutcracker's base green, then uses another brush to give him black boots with a confident light touch, clearly well-practised in avoiding streaks and brushstrokes. 'Have *you* ever been in love?'

'I thought I was, once, but when a relationship ends horribly... it doesn't change the happy years, but it changes the slant you see them through, does that make sense?'

'Very much so.' He's painting the nutcracker's hat a glossy black now too.

'I thought I loved him and I thought he loved me. I'd broken the curse of condemned relationships in my family. Every relationship I'd ever been in had felt doomed, apart from that one, and it was after *years* of friendship and mutual trust before I let him in, and we did have some happy years together, but then he did something that was so malicious and heartless, so how could it really have been love? I never could have imagined he'd do something so thoughtless, but he did, so... did I ever really know him at all? It made me question everything I thought I knew about love, and my own judgement, and made me realise that the only person I can rely on is myself and the one thing I will always be is better off alone.'

Raff knocks his thigh into mine gently. 'I want to know what happened but you don't have to tell me.'

I haven't told many people, apart from Cleo and my mum, who used it as fuel for her 'all men are rotten to the core and what do you expect from trusting one' speech, but I can feel myself opening up to him. I've inadvertently shifted nearer. He's got closer to me than I've let anyone get for years. We've been spending every day together. At the exact moment I really needed someone to lean on, he's been there, and he hasn't made me feel belittled or inferior or laughed at me for being the furthest thing from ambidextrous. It would be so easy to tell him everything about how my career and relationship ended with a crash landing at the same awful moment. He's stopped painting and is patiently watching me, his teeth worrying his lower lip, and he makes it too easy to spill everything out.

'I was the Sugar Plum Fairy, he was the prince, and during the Sugar Plum pas de deux, he dropped me. My leg broke in three places, on stage in front of a theatre full of people. He *said* it was an accident, but it turned out he was cheating on me with my understudy and he wanted her to have her moment in the spotlight. He didn't intend the injury to be as bad as it was – he was hoping I'd just sprain an ankle and be out of action for a week or so. Not *quite* how it turned out.'

'God, that's *unthinkable*. I'm so sorry.'

'It was a long time ago. Five years now, and The Nutcracker Shop rose from the ashes.' I don't want to dig into it any deeper, and I'm sure he understands the abrupt way I try to change the subject. 'Maybe we should talk about your love life instead. Or, more specifically, your shop's.'

'I didn't know my shop had a love life,' he says with a laugh. 'Is it going on dates with the other shops? Is it secretly having an affair with Coming Gnome For Christmas? Because, between you and me, I've always thought it had a thing for pun shop names.'

I feel like he's got an inkling of what I'm about to say and is trying to distract me with humour. 'I've always thought Ali and Imogen would make a lovely couple.'

He pulls back and shifts on the bench to face me, narrowing his eyes.

I blush as I try to explain. 'Ali from the 1001 Nights restaurant on Ever After Street and Imogen who runs Sleeping Beauty's Once Upon A Dream. I think there's a little connection between them. His wife died a few years ago, and she's been divorced for quite a while. He goes out of his way to talk to her at Ever After Street meetings and she's always giving him bath bombs and telling him to have a soak after a long day on his feet in the restaurant. I'm just saying that if you were thinking of trying to match anyone up, those two could be a good place to start.'

'Are you... helping me?' His eyes turn from suspicious to confused.

'You're helping me.'

'It's my fault you're in this position. The least I can do is help out.'

'And it's *my* fault that *you're* in *this* position. The least I can do is help out,' I fire back at him. 'I'm pretty much useless for anything physical for another seven weeks but if I can see matches to be made, why shouldn't I do something about it? Why shouldn't we help each other where we can? Call it levelling the playing field.'

He realises I'm using his own words against him, but the eyebrow he raises is so disbelieving that it feels like something has physically stung me. Why *would* he believe me? He and I have nitpicked about each other's shops since he started here. We've traded insults at Ever After Street meetings, and tried our hardest to deter potential customers from going in, and now, only one of us can stay here. 'I'm sorry I ever said that at the meeting in November. I shouldn't have done that. I'm sorry I've held my parents' relationship against you so hard without ever knowing you.'

'It doesn't matter, Fran.'

Fran. No one's ever shortened my name to that before, it's always Franc. It should probably be insulting. People I've known for years don't shorten my name, but with Raff, it makes something in my chest feel soft and gooey.

'Don't worry about the matches. This is an easy win for you. My shop is dying. It's run its course.'

'So rebrand. Change. Get rid of the gimmick and go back to doing what you love. It *isn't* your grandfather's shop any more – it's yours. Do whatever *you* need to do because the Dardenne legacy *has* to be yours now, not his. And honestly, I'm worried about you, Raff. You seem like you can't go on.'

He looks at me, and the last thing I expect is to watch his eyes well up with tears.

He blinks furiously and turns away, and then swears, trying to swipe the backs of his hands over his face. 'I can't wipe my eyes, I've got wet paint all over me.'

'I haven't.' I use my left hand to urge him to turn back towards me, cup the side of his jaw, and his eyes drift closed, letting me gently wipe away tears with my thumb. I can't help wondering how on earth we ended up in this position. How is it that I've sobbed into Raphael Dardenne's chest, hugged him, loved spending time with him, and now I'm holding his face in my hand, brushing away tears that I've somehow caused? And fighting a really, *really* strong urge to lean in and kiss the cheek that my thumb is rubbing over.

He's always cleanshaven and I can feel his skin heating up under my hand, but he hasn't been brave enough to open his eyes yet. 'Sorry, I did warn you – I'm a hugger and a crier.'

'If only more men were. C'mere.' I let my left hand tangle in his hair and tug his head down to my shoulder, and then rest my cheek against it. 'What's wrong?'

He lets out a long breath. 'It's just... That's exactly it. That's *exactly* how I've been feeling and you're the first person who's ever put it into words. I *love* snow globes but the joy of making them is lost. I can't let my family know. They'd be devastated. I'm supposed to be the strong one, the one who's stepped into our granddad's shoes, and I'm...'

He doesn't finish the sentence, but I can finish it for him. Lost. Floundering. Grieving, maybe. Raff has talked a lot about how much his family miss Claude, but very little about how much *he* does, and yet I know they were close. Instead, I curl my fingers tighter in his hair and try to rub his back with my elbow.

As long minutes pass in silence, it starts to dawn on me why he's so apathetic to the possible eviction in January and why he's so determined to help me. 'Do you *want* to lose the shop?'

'Sometimes.'

I get the feeling it's something he's never said aloud before. 'What about this place? I've always thought that you love Christmas Ever After?'

My fingers automatically card through his straight hair and he pushes out a breath, sounding like he's forcing himself to relax. 'I do. I've made snow globes for my granddad's shop for decades. This place has been a part of my life for as long as I can remember. I love the atmosphere, the community, the support from our fellow shopkeepers. The fact no one thinks it's weird if you're singing Christmas songs in July. I can't think of anywhere better to work. But...' He moves his head against my shoulder to get more comfortable. '...it would be an answer to a question that I don't know how to answer. Because you're right, I *can't* carry on. It would be an excuse to start over, to do something different...'

'Different from making snow globes or different from the gimmicky love aspect?'

'The gimmicky love aspect. I never want to stop making snow globes – I just want people to stop seeing it as a way to find love. I can't live up to my granddad's legacy.'

It's not the first time he's said something similar, but I never realised how deep it ran. 'Good. Your strength *is* that you're not him, Raff. Every shop needs to move with the times and the generation who runs it. If Sofia was to take over from you in however many years' time, would you expect her to do everything exactly as you'd done it, or would you want her to change things to suit her style, her feelings, and her own vision?'

We both know what his answer would be, so instead of replying, he says, 'It strikes me that you're the wrong person to be talking to about this. Wouldn't you love nothing more than to see Love Is All A-Round come to an end?'

I turn until I can rub my chin against his hair. 'I'd like to see the end of whatever it is that puts those dark circles under your eyes and the exhaustion in your voice that has nothing to do with physical tiredness. I never knew how much you were struggling. If I had, I'd like to think I'd have been kinder.'

'And I'd have' – his head moves to look at my splinted hand where it's resting on my thigh – 'looked before I stepped off that stool if I'd realised how much pain it would cause.'

He reaches over and brushes the back of his fingers over the sensitive skin of my inner forearm, above the splint, and his gentleness makes me shiver, and I let my hand drop from his hair, and back to my lap.

He goes to take hold of my hand and then stops himself. 'Sorry, I'm covered in paint.'

'I spend my life with paint all over me. I don't mind.' I slide my hand over his and he immediately tangles our fingers together and squeezes, and then he lifts my hand to his mouth and presses his lips to the back of it, right on the edge, just above my wrist.

I go light-headed for a moment. Another shivery tingle runs through me and his lips shift into a smile against my skin, like he knows exactly the effect that had.

'Let me help, Raff. Let me help you like you're helping me. What if we can save both our shops? If we can *both* meet the requirements and prove to the council that we can be friends now, that there will be no more squabbling and no atmosphere between us, then they'll have to let us both stay, and *then* you can decide where to go from there. If you want to leave, it has to be for the right reasons, not because you don't know what *else* to do.'

Instead of answering, he uses his grip on my hand to tug my arm closer and hooks his elbow over it, holding my arm against his thigh as he lifts his head and stretches.

There's a crick in my neck and my lower back is protesting the position. I can feel his eyes on me as I move, and his gaze makes heat rise up my spine.

'Thank you,' he says when I look at him. 'I didn't know I was going to react like that, but thank you for not ridiculing me.'

'The world needs more men who aren't afraid to show their emotions. I know you're the strong one for your family, but you don't need to put on a front with me. Life isn't easy and it gets really tiring trying to pretend that it is.'

Frank Sinatra's version of 'The Little Drummer Boy' comes on and I decide to lighten the atmosphere. 'And I couldn't possibly think less of you than I did before, so the only way is up.'

His adorable giggle turns into a full-blown guffaw, and somehow, his fingers are still intertwined with mine. 'A surprisingly comforting thought.'

It makes me grin too, until everything goes very still when I meet his eyes and my breath hitches at the intensity in them. His fingers are caressing the back of my hand, and every point where his fingertips touch feels like a sizzling spot of heat that's gradually pooling outwards. His grip tightens, like he's going to pull me to him, and I shift minutely closer, surprised by how much closer I *want* to get, and bowled over by how desperately I want to kiss him.

His dark eyes seem darker with intensity, his breathing has gone shaky, and his teeth have still got his bottom lip held between them, crying out to be released by a touch of my lips.

I can feel the tension rising, the temperature building, and one of us has to do *something*, because I'm going to *burst* if he brushes his thumb across the side of my wrist one more time. The breath he lets out sounds as shuddery as mine is, and I get a little thrill that he's feeling this too, and just when I think he's going to come closer and drop his lips to mine...

He pulls back and gives himself a sharp shake, disentangles our hands, and returns to the long-forgotten job of painting the nutcracker.

I'm glad of something breaking the intimacy, and I think it's best to put some space between us, so I leave him to it and go out for a wander around Christmas Ever After, soaking in the atmosphere. Some shops are closed as it's Sunday, but most stay open seven days a week at this time of year. Working here was a dream come true when I got my shop. After it became obvious that my leg was never going to be able to cope with the ferocity of a ballet career again, I was searching for a new dream, and this place was it. I'd never been anything other than a ballet dancer before. It was all I was. I felt like I didn't exist outside of that, and it was Christmas Ever After that helped me find a new version of myself – a version I liked a lot better.

One of the school choirs is practising in the Carollers' Cabin, and there's vestiges of the carousel music from the end of Ever After Street, and the vendor who sells chestnuts has arrived so the smell of hot roasted nuts is strong in the air, and the twinkling multi-coloured lights brighten up the overcast December after-noon, and I feel like I'm seeing it for the first time again. How have I forgotten how much I love this place? How have I been so busy for the past few Christmases that I haven't popped out to *see* it at Christmas?

I'm drawn towards Love Is All A-Round. The shop is shut today, but the darkened window display is lit by warm-white fairy lights and the illuminated snow globes that Raff makes, the lava-lamp-esque ones with glitter that swirls by itself when plugged in. Love Is All A-Round is down the opposite end of the street from The

Nutcracker Shop, at an angle and facing the road from the curve where the street comes to an end, looking out over all of us. One of the globes is displayed in a circle of a holly leaf garland with red berry lights, and the globe features a miniature version of the Ever After Street castle on a snowy hill, with flakes of snow ready to swirl around it when someone gives it a shake, and I turn around and look up at the real castle behind me. A perfect replica. I've thought a lot of things about Raff in the eighteen months since he took over this shop, but I've never realised how exceptionally talented he is. It takes years and years of dedication to get *this* good at a craft, and if this shop wasn't here – magical love gimmick or not – it would be a huge loss for Christmas Ever After. And the thought of Raff not being here... the thought of getting to know him this well and then never seeing him again... it fills me with a cold chill that seeps inside my bones. If I hadn't pushed so hard, neither of us would be in the position we are now. Raff made one mistake and is trying to make up for it, and now I need to do the same. The Nutcracker Shop *and* Love Is All A-Round need to stay on Christmas Ever After, and I have to do something about it.

11

'Franca! Get out here! You've got to see this!' Mrs Bloom bursts through my shop door and I groan internally. More ominous words have never been spoken. They almost always mean that someone is doing something you don't want to see.

It's been ages since I was inspired when it comes to making nutcrackers, but today, I've had an idea for a new one, and I'm leaning on the counter with a sketchbook open, trying to sketch my vision and I'm glad of the excuse to drop my pencil when she beckons me impatiently from the doorway. Drawing left-handed is as impossible as everything else is, but watching Raff work has reminded me of the times when I couldn't wait to get to work every day, bursting with ideas for new wooden soldiers to fill my shelves, when I couldn't draw fast enough to get the ideas out of my head and onto paper before I forgot them, and now my enthusiasm has returned, but my ability to use my hand is still many more weeks away.

'What's going on?' I ask as I follow her.

'He's fixed it.' When I get outside the door, she grabs hold of my arm and drags me further down the road until the entrance to our street comes into view. 'He's only gone and fixed it.'

My eyes fall on a small gathering of fellow shopkeepers where Mitch's pick-up truck is parked, and Raff is holding steady an unmangled Christmas Ever After archway while Mitch drills in steel plates to secure it to the concrete blocks that keep it safely upright.

Someone's repaired it. A few days ago, I noticed that the wreckage of crumpled metal had been taken away from where it's been lying since the accident, but I assumed that was a health and safety thing and someone had finally had the sense to arrange for it to be collected for scrap metal, but this morning, it's back and being carefully reinstated to its former position. It's been straightened out and bent back into an arch shape, to the point where you'd have to examine it close up to know there was anything wrong with it.

'When do you think he had time to do that?' Mrs Bloom says with waggling eyebrows.

'Who's done it?'

'Oh, come on. The one who knows his way around a...' She thinks for a moment. 'Well, whatever type of tools that would be used to fix that. It definitely wasn't Mitch, look at him, he can barely find that drill with both hands.'

'Raff? Why on earth would Raff...' I trail off when he looks our way and smiles, and butterflies start whizzing around in my chest.

'Hmm. Why, indeed?' Mrs Bloom says under her breath.

I give him a wave and, seeing as his hands are occupied, he dips his head in my direction, and I don't realise how much I'm smiling until Mrs Bloom elbows me hard enough to break a rib.

'Jorge never elicited a smile like that.'

'It turns out that the most attractive thing about any man is being respectful and having good oral hygiene.'

She nods sagely. 'One thing you can say about Raphael Dardenne is that he knows how to clean his teeth.'

I can't help giggling, even though he undeniably does.

'Which, of course, you would know, considering how much time you've been spending together lately...' She would be less obvious about fishing for gossip if she had a fishing rod in one hand and bait in the other.

'He's helping me out, you know that.' I'm determined not to give her anything to get excited about. 'And maybe I'm trying to help him a bit too. You don't know of anyone who wants to be set up do you? Anyone we know who'd make a nice couple? Anyone *you'd* fancy a date with?'

'At my age? No. I loved my Reginald. I could never date again, but I *will* keep my very large ears to the ground about anyone else.' She gives me a conspiring wink. 'It's nice that you're helping him. Unexpected, but nice. That's what Raff needs – someone to help him. He's lonely. Claude Dardenne never found his mojo until he met his wife. Raff can't help anyone find love because he isn't *in* love.' She clears her throat pointedly. 'Or, at least, he *wasn't*. He can barely keep his eyes off you.'

'We're just friends,' I tell her, even though my cheeks flare red at the thought of Raff liking me in *that* way. Are we even friends? We don't know each other well enough to have classified it yet. I can't help glancing at him again, and my knees feel decidedly unstable when he senses my gaze and looks in this direction again with a smile.

Mitch is holding the arch now and Raff is drilling it into place. I've never found power tools sexy before, but Raff is making that drill look *hot*. Or possibly the other way round.

Mrs Bloom is watching me with a knowing look and I'm certain she can tell exactly what I'm thinking. I shake myself. 'And no matter what, he's still a Dardenne. He's still peddling his "magical" snow globes with the intention of extorting money from people gullible enough to believe in them.'

I say something she'll be expecting to hear, but it feels unfairly harsh now. Raff is a lot of things, but he's certainly not a crook, and we've got enough people talking about us with the video and the viewing numbers that have exceeded 70,000 now, we don't need to be the subject of street-wide gossip too.

She sees straight through me. 'People like you?'

'No. Definitely not me. There's no magic in this world, and...' I catch Raff's eyes across the distance again and those butterflies get a speed boost. I think about the moment he handed me the nutcracker snow globe in my shop. The way the tips of his fingers touched mine, and how he steadied it until I could safely take it one-handed. His shy smile and how his dark hair flopped over his forehead. The way he so carefully took Minnie the mouse away. 'I wish I did. It would be nice to think there's a power greater than us, driving us to meet the people we're supposed to meet, but there isn't... even if Raff himself isn't as bad as I thought he was.'

That's probably the nicest thing she's ever heard me say about him, and she knows it means something too, and she mercifully doesn't push me any further.

We watch Raff and Mitch double-check the fixings of the arch and check it for steadiness. When they're happy, Mitch goes to take a photo for social media and then move his truck and Raff makes his way over to where we're standing.

'Good morning.' I can't stop myself smiling as he approaches. There's a breeze today and it blows around his silky chocolate-brown hair, and I tell myself that I *don't* want to reach up and tuck it back.

'So you noticed then?' He grins at me. 'I was hoping to get it back up and reinstalled as a surprise, but it was too heavy to manoeuvre on my own and it ended up being a street-wide job.

Mitch wanted to get a new one but there wasn't enough in the budget for it, so I thought I could fix the existing one.'

'How'd you manage that?'

'It's metal, it just needed heating up with a welding torch and bending back into shape. Trying to make *that* day ancient history as soon as possible.'

'You didn't have to do that. It was my fault. I'm surprised Mitch hasn't been after me to pay for a new one.'

'If it was anyone's fault, it was mine, Fran.'

At the nickname, Mrs Bloom's intake of breath is so loud that people in Scotland probably heard it.

'It was only a bit bent out of shape. I've seen worse.'

'You've repaired many metal archways that have been bent by the weight of a giant—' I was going to compare myself to a humpback whale, but he doesn't let me.

Instead, he reaches out and puts a finger on my lips and shakes his head sharply. 'The arch is decorative. Anyone, of *any* weight, would've had the same effect on it. You're exactly as you should be. Don't let anyone tell you differently.'

Mrs Bloom's face has got the look of a kettle that's about to reach boiling point, and I'm sure she's going to let out a long whistle and release a load of steam at any moment. Meanwhile, I'm melting because you don't hear things like that as an overweight ballet dancer, and before I've thought it through, I've reached up, put my arms around his neck and pulled him down for a hug.

His aftershave wraps around me in the same way that his arms wrap around me. His hands spread open on my back and he pulls me tight to him.

'Oh, look at that, I see a customer!' Mrs Bloom sounds like she can't get away fast enough to share this mouthful of gossip with everyone she comes across, but with Raff's arms around me, I can't bring myself to mind.

'I'd have fixed it last week if I'd known it would get me a hug like this,' he murmurs into my ear. His lips brush across the shell and make me shiver, and he mistakes it for a shiver of chill and his arms hold me even tighter.

'He's a clever one, ain't he?' Mitch appears out of nowhere and claps Raff on the shoulder, making us jump apart with an unexpected squeak. 'That must've taken a lot of time and patience, and I didn't even have to ask. I hope you've matched up some couples because I'm not letting you go in January.'

His gaze flicks to me and he looks awkward. 'And you, Franca, obviously. I don't want to see either of you go. If only you could've been this friendly before, eh?'

All of this is my fault, and I get the feeling that Mitch blames me too, and the thought of Raff leaving replaces the butterflies inside me with giant boulders of anxiety and reinforces the feeling that I have to do something about this. 'You're married, aren't you, Mitch?'

'Happily. Forty years next year.'

'Do you know anyone single?'

His eyes flick between us. 'I didn't know either of you were looking.'

'We're not,' Raff and I say in unison.

'Just trying to repay a favour,' I continue. 'Because I'm not letting him go in January either.'

'I'll give it some thought. My son's not long gone through a bad break-up; he could do with someone to take his mind off it.'

'What are you trying to do?' Raff asks me when Mitch leaves.

'The same as you are. Help out. You're doing what I can't do, so let me do what you can't do too and find some couples to...' I trail off, having run out of words that rhyme. '...glue?'

'You've taken on the tone of a Dr Seuss book. You're going to be going on about the Whos of Whoville in a minute.'

I put a hand on my hip and give him the same stern look he gave me earlier. 'I don't want you to go, Raff.'

'For years, you've wanted to see the back of me.'

'And now, I quite like seeing the front of you.'

'Awwww. That's the sweetest thing anyone's ever said to me.'

'And that' – I nod towards the arch – 'is the sweetest thing anyone's ever done for me, along with everything else you've done since the accident, so let me help, okay?'

I have a renewed purpose. I might not be able to make nutcrackers, but I can help out someone who makes this street better just by being part of it, and maybe it's not too late to undo the situation I caused by not seeing that earlier, and make sure that *both* of us get to stay on Christmas Ever After next year.

* * *

'Are you *helping* Raff Dardenne?' Marnie sounds dubious when I go into A Tale As Old As Time later that morning.

'No,' I protest, trying to pretend I'm distracted by looking around her Beauty and the Beast-themed bookshop, a gorgeous place that you can easily lose hours in.

'Wasn't it your idea to evict him in the first place?'

'No,' I say again. We both know that both 'no's are a lie.

'Isn't it you *or* him?'

'Not if I have anything to do with it.' I tell her a bit about my plan to prove that we can work together and both deserve our places here. 'Anyway, is your new assistant single?'

Marnie laughs. 'Now that's a question I was *not* expecting. Why don't you ask her? Nina?' She beckons her new bookshop assistant over and introduces us. 'Franca's got a question for you.'

'This is going to sound weird, but bear with me. Are you single?'

Nina, who can only be about eighteen or nineteen, nods shyly. She's wearing a blue dress and has got long red hair in plaited bunches, making her resemble Anne Shirley from *Anne of Green Gables*.

'You wouldn't happen to like Joshy from the carousel, would you?' I ask, because I've noticed a few coy glances between her and the lad who took over the carousel earlier this year, when the previous operator went to play the Mad Hatter with Cleo in The Wonderland Teapot.

'He's, um, really sweet. But he's so far out of *my* league. You're not going to tell him I like him, are you?'

'I was hoping you might like to go on a date with him. He's single and I'm convinced he likes you. Raff and I are trying to match a few couples before the Christmas market, and my thinking is that everyone from Ever After Street will be coming anyway, so we should spread a little love around ourselves this year. What do you think?'

'Do you really think Joshy will say yes?' Her cheeks have gone redder than her hair. 'He's so nice. Have you heard the way he sings made-up songs to entertain visitors? He sounds like an opera singer. I could listen to him for ages!'

'And you frequently do,' Marnie interjects with a laugh, making Nina blush even brighter red.

Joshy and Nina are about the same age. I get the impression that they're both quite bookish and a bit shy, and there's something indefinable about them that suggests they'd be a good couple. Trying to help Raff has got me thinking about all the little interactions I see between our fellow shopkeepers, and if anyone deserves a little happiness brought into their lives this Christmas, it's the lovely people who work alongside us on Ever After Street, and I'm certain that the way to find love in the world is nothing to do with magical snow globes and everything to do with quiet observation and noticing the little things that suggest people would have something in common.

Nina isn't convinced by my impassioned plea and is certain that she'll be humiliated when Joshy refuses a date, and she won't agree until I promise to talk to him and furtively find out about his feelings towards her.

Imogen, on the other hand, is all too happy when I nip into Sleeping Beauty's Once Upon A Dream, a shop full of bedtime delights like pyjamas, fancy bedding, blankets, eye masks, candles, and bath bombs. 'Oooh, I've always wanted to try one of the snow globes! Do you think one might match me with Ali?'

I go to protest that I doubt the snow globes *themselves* do much matching, but maybe she thinks there's a sentient one like the Sorting Hat in the Harry Potter books. There are less than two weeks until the Christmas market, so I don't waste time in trying to correct her. 'I've got Ali to agree to come into Love Is All A-Round at two o'clock this afternoon. Are you up for it as well?'

Her beam is brighter than any of the colour-coordinated Christmas lights twinkling in her shop and she gives me a happy nod, and as I walk outside and look around, thinking of the colleagues who work in each shop and who would be a good match for some of them, I can feel the ice inside *my* heart starting to melt.

* * *

'Why am I so nervous? I've done this hundreds of times with people I've never met. I *know* Ali and Imogen are a great match, but what if...' Raff pushes his hair back for the umpteenth time. He, Quentin and I are in Love Is All A-Round, about to match our first couple. 'What if it doesn't work? What if the snow globe doesn't move? What if they hate each other and we have to endure their wrath for the rest of our careers here? What if this is the wrong choice?' He gesticulates to the snow globe he's chosen for them, which is inside a beautiful gift box on the counter, waiting for their arrival.

In the glass dome is a replica of the Christmas Ever After tree, laden with tiny modelled versions of the familiar decorations that stay up all year round. The tree is at the centre of Christmas Ever After, near the Carollers' Cabin, complete with brightly coloured presents made of weatherproof resin and decorations that are all plastic and get replaced every few years when the summer sun fades them beyond recognition. Raff has created a perfect mini imitation, with a streetlamp beside it, a tiny version of the cabin, and a couple standing hand-in-hand and looking up at it. The man is wearing a white bobble hat that could double as Ali's chef's hat, and the woman's got grey streaks running through her dark hair, just like Imogen has. It's so perfect for Ali and Imogen that, if I didn't know better, I'd think Raff made it especially for them.

At that moment, the real Ali goes to come in, realises Imogen is not far behind him, and holds the door open and waits for her to catch up and go through first.

She meets my eyes and fans a hand in front of her face as Raff greets them both.

'Ooh, I do love this place.' Ali wanders around, pointing out his favourite snow globes to Imogen. 'You can sense the magic in the air.'

'It's like it's snowing inside,' she agrees.

The music Raff plays in his shop is instrumental, a twinkling, melodic tune that you could imagine being played during a perfect snowstorm, where the flakes are white and fluffy and your only obligation is going outside to dance around the garden in it, and you don't actually have to do anything practical like travel anywhere and you can ignore the fact that the snow will be nothing more than grey sludge by morning. There are piano bits and gently lilting tings of a triangle that do something to my brain-waves and make me feel like I'm dancing through the Land of Snow in *The Nutcracker* ballet, about to be surrounded by waltzing snowflakes.

'Well, we've got your very own snow globe ready for you here...' Raff has slipped into charming mode, but I can *see* how much his heart is not in this. He's *so* different to how he's been when he's sitting at my lathe. He's found so much joy in the wood-turning, the assembling and then the painting and accessorising of the nutcrackers he's been making. He's always animated and excited, but this... it's like he doesn't care. He *cares* about Ali and Imogen as people, but there's no joy in the snow globes. He couldn't care less if that thing moves or not, and it comes across in everything he does.

Raff positions them carefully, with the corner of the counter between them, and the shop's six-foot Christmas tree, which is laden with mini snow globes as ornaments, is the perfect backdrop for the photograph that Quentin takes.

'For social media,' Raff explains after getting their permission to post it. He takes the lid off the box and moves the snow globe so it's upright in its protective packaging, and the snow settles around the base of the tree, ready for the first shake-up.

'Now, you hold here, Ali.' Raff positions Ali's hands between the glass dome and the base. 'And you here, Imogen.' He reaches across and takes her hands and wraps them around the globe between the glass and the base too, and I can't help noticing the very careful way he's positioning them before he instructs them to pick the snow globe up and give it a shake.

There's a sense of stillness in the shop. We're all holding our breath as they lift the snow globe from the box, and then, just like mine did almost two weeks ago now, the miniature version of the

Christmas Ever After tree rotates, sending the snow and glitter inside spinning and sparkling. The teeny-tiny pinpricks of lights on the tree are painted with something reflective that catches the brightness of the shop's light and makes it look like the tree illuminates for just one flurry of a second, and it makes my breath stop in my throat.

Imogen gasps. 'I saw it!'

'I was too busy looking at Imogen,' Ali says. 'I've never seen her in this light before.'

I glance up at the overhead lights, but I don't think he meant it literally.

I saw it too. I don't know what I expected from this, but I didn't expect to *see* the snow globe move. It feels like magic is swirling in the air, like if I spun around myself, I'd be coated in flakes of glitter too, and they'd settle all around me like they're settling around the feet of the couple in the snow globe.

Is *this* the joy that Claude was always chasing? Is this why he did it? Is this how he felt when he matched my parents, once upon a time? Did he really feel like he'd made a perfect match, and everything that happened afterwards couldn't have been prevented?

It doesn't feel like we matched Ali and Imogen at all – it feels like we gave them permission to acknowledge feelings that were already there. Both Ali and Imogen are in their late-fifties. They've both found love before and lost it. They've known each other as colleagues for years, but neither has ever been brave enough to suggest anything more, until a magical snow globe came along.

I meet Raff's eyes across the shop and he gives me a smile, but it's a muted half-smile. He isn't happy.

Ali carries the snow globe to the counter. 'I'll take this, my friend.'

Raff holds a hand up. 'No charge.'

Ali tries to insist, and I go over and stand next to Raff. 'Just come to the Christmas market and if anyone asks, make sure they know that Love Is All A-Round matched you.'

'And what about you, Franca? How can we help you? I don't want to see this one go.' Ali nods to Raff and then turns back to me. 'But I don't want to see you be evicted either. Shall we go and buy a nutcracker or two?'

'I don't think it would make much difference,' I say as I thank them for offering. My task is less tangible than Raff's match five couples thing. Get customer engagement. Get customers excited about – and talking about – nutcrackers. It's not about sales so much as proving I can do what it takes to pull in visitors, because the council and my fellow shopkeepers had noticed my apathy, even before I had.

I can feel Raff's eyes watching me as I thank them both for trying to help, and I can almost hear the cogs in his mind turning as he thinks it over.

Ali and Imogen make plans to go for dinner on Saturday afternoon, and we watch them as they leave, Ali handing the box containing the snow globe to Imogen as they part with a brief hug.

'One match. Four to go,' Raff mumbles, not sounding very optimistic about it.

I elbow him when Nina timidly puts her head round the door. 'Three.'

'Marnie made me watch when Ali and Imogen came in,' she says when I beckon her inside and introduce her to Raff.

'The carousel is quiet. Let's go now,' Raff says when I've explained about our chat earlier and whisper that when I did a bit of due diligence with Joshy afterwards, he thought that Nina was way out of *his* league and *she'd* never say yes to a date with *him*.

Raff chooses a snow globe with a couple sat on a sofa reading, a

Christmas tree behind them, surrounded by books, and with a cat curled up between them.

'Oh, I have a cat. So does Joshy,' Nina says when she sees it.

He's made a perfect choice again, even though I'm almost positive he had no way of knowing that.

Quentin stays in the shop this time as the three of us go over to the carousel, and Joshy shyly looks at Nina. Between them, they set up a date for next week, and Raff puts the snow globe box down, positions their hands again and takes a quick snap on his phone as they lift it out of the box. This time I don't see it move, although Nina and Joshy's eyes light up like they have.

We leave them chatting and walk back towards the shop. Raff moves to my left side and offers me his arm, and I'm not going to ignore that thoughtfulness so I slip my good hand through his elbow and give his forearm a squeeze.

'You're so good at that. Choosing the snow globes. You instinctively know what will mean something to each person.'

'Years of practice, I guess. I pick up on little things that give away what people might like, just nothing on *who* they might like. In years gone by, we were more like you with your nutcrackers. People would come in to order custom snow globes as gifts, they'd tell me about what the person liked, what their favourite things were, and it was like a little challenge – to design a snow globe perfect for this stranger's loved one who I'd never met. My granddad did his matchmaking, but I was happy doing that. Granddad was genuine, but when I was younger and even more cynical than I am now, I saw it as an opportunity to make money, and now I regret it. It shouldn't ever have become what it has.'

I see exactly what he means. The matchmaking snow globes have become a weird publicity stunt that takes away from what Raff really does – make the most beautiful snow globes and somehow know exactly which one will be perfect for each person.

And that is what Love Is All A-Round *should* be celebrating.

12

'What's this?' I ask, watching in amusement as Raff comes into my shop with a large box under one arm and a Christmas tree over his other shoulder.

'This is a Christmas tree. They're quite common. You may have seen them here and there in December time...' He pats the trunk as he drops the box onto the counter and gives me a sarcastic grin over the top of it. He's out of breath with his hair sticking to his forehead in a way that has *no* right to be that sexy, or make me want to reach over and brush it back *so* much.

He hefts the tree off his shoulder and leans it against the counter too. 'I've been thinking...'

I groan. Sentences that start like that rarely end well.

'It's competition time.'

'You win a prize for guessing it's a Christmas tree?' I fire back at his sarcastic comment and then realise which competition he probably means, and it makes unease settle inside me. 'Wait, between us?'

'No. For you. Because you're making matches for me, but I'm doing nothing to help you.'

I glance towards the workshop out the back. 'You've taught yourself woodturning in less than a fortnight, made over twenty ordered nutcrackers so far, and have got many more on the go. That's not "doing nothing", Raff.'

'Honestly, it's been the greatest privilege. I can't remember the last time I enjoyed anything so much, but it's nothing to do with that. We both have these silly goals to reach. Five couples, five social media posts. The only way we can both win is if we *both* do what the council has asked of us. We must draw even. We have to make it so they *can't* choose between us. You're helping me with matches, and you need social media posts and customers who are invested in your nutcrackers, and no matter how many orders I fulfil, you're still not getting that.'

He's not wrong there, and I know he knows his stuff when it comes to social media. Dardenne Snow Globes have got a huge following, and he's responsible for most of their online presence, and I haven't the foggiest clue where to start. The Nutcracker Shop has social media accounts, but most of the followers are bots or scantily clad women who *really* aren't interested in nutcrackers, and the only person who ever comments is Cleo for moral support.

'We need an amazing prize.' Raff's eyes flit around the shop and he eventually settles on one of my giant nutcrackers and walks towards it with his hand outstretched. 'This one.'

I raise an eyebrow at the six-foot tall sceptre-holding nutcracker he's selected. 'You want to give away one of the most expensive nutcrackers in the shop for free?'

'Nope, but *you* do.' Raff stands next to the nutcracker and slings his arm around its shoulders like it's an old friend. 'It's a bit late in the year, we could've done with more time to build momentum, but there's nothing we can do about it now. It's about customer engagement and getting people talking about you.'

The whole idea makes me uncomfortable. I've tried not to

think about my part in this contest between us, because if I do well, then he fails. 'Have you seen how many viewers the video has had now? Ninety thousand. Enough people are talking about me, thank you.'

'So you're just going to sit back and let me win?' He drops his arm from around the nutcracker and folds them instead, giving me a defiant look. 'Or, like with Ali and Imogen and Nina and Joshy – *help* me win?'

'I don't...' I make a noise of frustration. This is awful. It's unthinkable to have gone from hating Raff so much, to liking him *this* much, to thinking that next week, one or the other of us is going to lose our livelihood.

He sighs and pushes a hand through his hair. 'I know,' he says quietly, his voice full of understanding. 'I don't... either, so let me help.'

That loaded pause makes me feel sick. Neither of us can think of a word for it, but in that pause is the possibility that my plot won't work. What if it's not enough? What if the council stand by their plan, no matter what?

'I'm good at social media, you know that.' The giant nutcracker is heavy and he starts waddling it towards the shop door, one side at a time. 'You don't do anything to encourage people to post about your nutcrackers. People just buy them and that's it. You have an Instagram account but you barely use it, and it's cold and impersonal and you only ever post when you've got a sale on. You never let customers get to know *you* or share anything about the process of making nutcrackers or show what goes into each one. What we need is an "event" to get people talking. Hence, giving away a giant nutcracker.'

'Where *are* you going with him?' I ask as he stops to negotiate the door, and I go over and hold it open for him to manoeuvre the nutcracker through and onto the pavement outside, and he stops to grin at me as his body brushes against mine.

Once the nutcracker is outside, Raff comes back in and heaves the tree onto his shoulder and pulls the box towards us.

'He's going to stand out there, in prime positioning, next to this nicely decorated tree, which we're going to decorate with these.' He plunges a hand into the cardboard lid, pulls out a bow-shaped tag, and holds it up for me to read.

Take a bow to win! Grab a tag, hold it up and take a selfie with the nutcracker! Post it on social media, and follow and tag The Nutcracker Shop to enter!

'Oh wow, that's genius. Forcing people into social media engagement. You're a publicity wizard.'

He blushes and if he didn't have a tree over one shoulder, I'd throw my arms around his neck because I'm so touched that he's even given it a second thought, let alone gone to all this trouble.

I peer into the box and realise it's absolutely packed with the handwritten bow-shaped tags, as well as lights and tinsel for the tree. He must've been up *all* night doing this, and he's already doing two jobs anyway. 'I can't believe you did this. You didn't have to...' The words get choked up as they're coming out. His unwavering support is the last thing I expected, but it's something I've never had before and the thought that he's *this* determined to save my shop reinforces how much I want both of us to stay.

'You're welcome,' he says gently and I'm certain he can tell what I'm thinking. He reaches out and touches my left forearm, like he's trying to think of something else to say. His fingers graze my skin and trail downwards, over my wrist with a feather-light touch, across the back of my hand, and when he reaches my fingers, he slots his fingertips between mine and jiggles them playfully and meets my eyes, and I realise it's been far too many minutes since I last took a breath.

While I claw air into my lungs, he blinks as if he isn't sure what just happened and pulls his hand away quickly and mumbles something about no time to waste in getting it set up. The tree has slid off his shoulder and he hoists it back up and heads for the door, and I follow him out with the box.

There's a tree stand in place on a flat part of the cobblestones, with a chain to a nearby bollard to prevent the nutcracker being stolen. He gets the tree set up and I hold it steady while he secures it into the stand, positioned in the perfect spot between my door and windows, but not blocking either of them.

'Ever tried to decorate a tree one-handed?'

'Nope.' I can't help laughing at his enthusiasm as he takes the box out of my arm and starts pulling strings of lights out of it. 'But there's a first time for everything.'

He grins and hands me a battery pack to hold while he untangles one of the strings of blue star-shaped lights and starts draping them around the tree, and I watch him, well aware that a few of our fellow shopkeepers are looking at us curiously.

'What if it rains?' I glance up at the ominous-looking mid-December sky. 'These nutcrackers aren't designed to stay outdoors. The two by the door are weatherproof, this one isn't.'

'Ahh, you think I haven't thought of that.' He throws one last string of lights onto the tree, and then rifles through the box again. 'And now for the *pièce de résistance...*'

He gets out a festively red umbrella, and when he opens it with fanfare, there's a pattern of green and white tiny nutcrackers all over it.

'Where'd you get that?' I ask, impressed by his ability to think of everything.

'I asked Mrs Coombe in All You Need Is Gloves to source a

nutcracker umbrella for me, and she did.' He lifts the sceptre out of the nutcracker's wooden hand, unscrews the handle of the umbrella, and pokes the shaft through the hole where the sceptre was held, and positions it so the huge umbrella perfectly covers the nutcracker and the tree.

The sight of a giant nutcracker holding a nutcracker umbrella finishes me off, and I get the giggles, and in trying to stop laughing, I realise something else. 'You've been planning this?'

'I wouldn't say planning. I'd say... giving it some thought... for a while now.'

'Raff, you are...' I stop myself because there are so many words that could fit after that pause. Brilliant. Funny. Gorgeous. But the most fitting one is 'lovely', and that feels like too much of an unguarded admission to make out loud.

'I know,' he says with a grin that's nowhere near as confident as it looks. We hold each other's gaze for a moment and I'm sure he knows every possible word that just went through my mind.

Eventually he shakes his head and bends down to get a handful of bow-shaped tags from the box, hands me half the stack, and starts hanging them on the tree branches, and I try not to watch him walking around the tree, or think about the concentration on his face as he chooses the *perfect* branch for each one.

I do the same, listening to the carollers in the cabin, trying to remember the last time I did anything this Christmassy or enjoyed anything so much.

Raff keeps glancing at me and each time I meet his eyes, he smiles but looks away quickly, and I get a little thrill every time as we carry on hanging tags.

'So how long have you hated Christmas for?'

'I don't *hate* Christmas. I love Christmas, but it's...' I let out a sigh. 'It's the time of year for nutcrackers and ballet performances and parents who make digs about my career choices, and every year it gets harder to ignore. Every Christmas feels more difficult than the one before. My mum thought I should have gone into teaching ballet when my dancing career ended. She thought it was criminal to throw away all my years of training to make "wooden toys", and my dad thinks it's just embarrassing, and every year...' I think about it before I carry on because it's the elephant in the room that I never acknowledge, but it's always there, looming in the background. 'I wonder if they're right, I guess. I wonder if I have thrown my life away and if I should be doing something more.'

'Do you want to move on?'

It reminds me of when I asked him if he wanted to lose his shop and he deserves an answer as honest as the one he gave me. 'No, not from here. But the council are right. My shop feels stale. *I* feel stale, like I have nothing left to offer Christmas Ever After, and if they choose you over me, then maybe it's for the best... Maybe it'll be the kick up the bum I need to get out of this rut.'

'Hey.' He waits for me to meet his eyes and then holds his hand out, and when I slip mine into it, his fingers curl around mine and squeeze them emphatically. 'You're the most exceptional person I've ever met. I can't imagine what it's like to be injured so badly and to pull yourself back up and forge on with a totally different career. And I do know that you still struggle. Maybe you think I haven't noticed the limp when you've been on your feet for too long, or the way you absent-mindedly rub your leg, so I know it still hurts from time to time, and now you're dealing with this as well.' He holds up his other hand, indicating my splint. 'And I know you're worried about recovery time, but the only thing that matters is if you're happy with your life. Just *you*. No one else. Are you happy?'

He lets go of my hand and goes back to putting tags on the

branches, like he's trying to ease the pressure of expecting an answer.

'Yes.' I look around the bustle of Christmas Ever After. The school choir singing from the cabin over by the tree. The sparkling tinsel and glittering lights from every shop. The feeling of community and being part of a team, even though I work alone. It's the best place in the world to work.

'I could have gone back to the ballet, but I didn't want to. The company I worked for did offer me a part-time training role, but I was... kind of traumatised? The thought of going back there, watching others do what I could no longer do, and trying to instil the discipline that had taken over my life into younger girls... I couldn't do it. I needed to do something different, and Christmas Ever After was the answer to my dreams. I love getting to do something creative for a living. I love everything about this place...'

'...But you've let other people make you doubt yourself, and that's seeped into everything you do.' He finishes the sentence for me and I can't dispute his answer. He's put into words what I've never been able to verbalise before, and it makes me feel braver in opening up to him.

'It's not just that,' I admit. 'It's the loneliness too. I hadn't realised how lonely this job is until you sat at my lathe and filled the shop with Christmas music and Santa hats, and beautiful wooden snowmen, and nutcrackers that are a bit different, and made me realise how deep my rut is.'

It makes him smile and I can't help watching the way his dark hair blows around in the breeze as he stops hanging tags and turns to look at my shop.

'You ever thought about naming them?'

'The nutcrackers?' I say with a snort. 'You think the answer to loneliness is naming nutcrackers and calling them my friends?'

He laughs. 'Nah, not for you – for customers. You could humanise them.'

'They're wooden soldiers...'

'Yeah, but they all have different personalities, different looks and interests. They're like little wooden Christmas people.'

'Little wooden Christmas people,' I repeat to myself, wondering if he's quite alright. I reach over and fit my hand against his forehead to check his temperature. 'I think you've been working too hard.'

He reaches up and his fingers brush against my skin as he takes hold of my hand again and uses it to tug me back into the shop.

Inside, he lets go and walks over to one of the shelves and points out a nutcracker with furry snow boots on, holding a pair of skis. 'That one, for example, likes going skiing and for long walks in the mountains. His name could be Aspen.' He moves on and points out another nutcracker, this one holding a tray with two wooden cups of hot chocolate on it. 'That one likes warm drinks. But who is the second mug for? Maybe he's lonely and looking for a female nutcracker to share that tray of hot chocolate with? Or maybe he's on his way to a first date with the nutcracker of his dreams and he's nervous... He looks like a Henry, don't you think?'

'I'm not sure if you're a genius or *seriously* sleep-deprived...' I can't help grinning as he bounces between shelves, pointing out nutcrackers and their potential personalities. It's something I have, admittedly, never thought of before, but is actually quite brilliant.

'And this one with his sword, maybe he's a knight, waiting for a princess to protect, and this one with his crown and sceptre... Did he once have a kingdom to rule and someone overthrew him, and now he waits and watches, yearning for the day he'll be able to claw back his throne and return to his nutcracker queen, and... wait... speaking of princesses, queens, and nutcrackers waiting for dates, where *are* all the female nutcrackers?' He looks around the shop again. 'They're *all* men. Why are there no women?'

'Because nutcrackers are traditionally male. The nutcracker prince from the original story was a handsome young man, turned into a nutcracker by a curse when he accidentally stepped on a mouse, and he needed true love to break the spell. Folklore dictates that nutcrackers are male. It's never crossed my mind to make ones of a different gender.'

'The one thing you're good at is breaking tradition. There is way too much wooden testosterone in this shop. You need to get some female nutcrackers in here, fast.'

Wooden testosterone. When I woke up this morning, of all the ways I wondered how today might go, I never imagined that a conversation about wooden testosterone would come into it. But as I look around the shelves of wooden men staring back at me, I see he's got a point. Why have I never made female nutcrackers? It wouldn't be difficult – a little extra flourish on the chest area to represent boobs, a dress instead of a jacket, longer hair, gems for jewellery...

'This is exactly the sort of thing social media would respond to,' Raff encourages me. 'You could make celebrity nutcrackers. Sets of Spice Girls nutcrackers, for example. People would *love* that.'

'It's not the nineties any more, unfortunately.'

'I grew up with an older sister – I'm told the Spice Girls are forever, not just for the nineties. Go for whoever's big now then. Sofia loves Taylor Swift and Beyoncé. Or Disney!' He gets over-excited again. 'You work on Ever After Street! Tie in with the theme! Disney princess nutcrackers. Rapunzel with her long blonde hair. Ariel with a mermaid's tail instead of feet. Belle in a yellow ballgown and carrying a stack of books or a red rose or something. The possibilities are endless.'

'You spend too much time watching movies with your seven-year-old niece,' I say fondly, even though I'm laughing at his eagerness and I can feel myself fizzing with excitement too.

He stops and looks at me like he can feel my eyes on him and his cheeks go red. 'Okay, forgive me for getting a bit carried away, but if you name each nutcracker, give them interests and life stories, and partners, customers will see them with personalities rather than just as Christmas decorations.'

'I think the fumes from your ceramic kiln have scrambled your brain... in the best way possible,' I say, because if there's one thing I *love* about Raff, it's his boundless enthusiasm.

It motivates me too and gets me thinking. 'If I name them, I could attach tags to all of them, couldn't I?'

I've still got a few bow tags in my pocket and I hold one up, thinking over an idea I had a while ago, about encouraging customers to see nutcrackers as more than just Christmas decorations. I could never figure out a way to make it work, but Raff has made it seem feasible. 'This photo idea doesn't just have to be about a giveaway, does it? I could keep something similar going all the time. Every nutcracker could come with one of these...' I spin the tag between my fingers and think up some potential wording to go on one and test it out to Raff. '*Hi, my name is Colin and I enjoy drinking hot chocolate and roasting chestnuts on an open fire, but there's nothing I love more than Christmas. I'm so happy you chose me to be part of your Christmas celebrations. If you want to share the nutcracker love, take a photo and tag me online at The Nutcracker Shop. I'd love my friends to see what I'm getting up to this year!*'

He grins and turns over the nutcracker he's still holding in his hands. 'Sold. I'd buy him in a heartbeat and take photos of him in funny places. Travel with nutcrackers. Where has the nutcracker gone today? You could even do mini giveaways if people guess where they are. You know, give us a like and a follow online and correctly guess where he is. It could be somewhere local or photo-shopped into the spikes on the Statue of Liberty's crown or halfway up the Eiffel Tower...'

'You really are a marketing genius. With scrambled brains from overworking, but still. Thanks, Raff.' I smile at him, and the smile he gives me in return sends those butterflies somersaulting again. 'Thank you for... unlocking whatever it was in me that needed unlocking. It's been so long since I was excited about nutcrackers, and now I can't *wait* to get this splint off so I can jump back into this shop headfirst, and...' I stop myself as that familiar realisation dampens down my excitement. All of this might be for nothing. This time next month, I might not have a shop. And if I do... he won't.

What I'm thinking must show on my face because his Adam's apple bobs as he swallows, and then he pastes on a smile and comes over to drop an arm around my shoulders. 'We'll get through this together, I promise.'

What if we don't? What if our plan fails? What if it really is me or him? I don't know which would be the worst option. Love Is All A-Round deserves its place here, but so do I, and I just hope the council can see that we can work together and make Christmas Ever After better as a whole.

'Yeah, we will,' I echo, but it sounds hollow and I'm unable to hide the apprehension in my voice. 'And next year, I'm going to make a nutcracker holding a snow globe and name him Raphael.'

He bursts out laughing so hard that it shakes me as well. 'Now that, I *have* to witness. You see? It's non-negotiable that The Nutcracker Shop gets to stay, if for nothing more than that.'

I glance up into his expressive brown eyes and snuggle a bit closer into the weight of his arm around me.

Maybe for a few other reasons too.

13

Every time I step inside Love Is All A-Round, I wonder why I stayed away for so long. Apart from the whole arch-nemesis aspect, obviously. Everything's bright and twinkly. Raff's Christmas lights are all dazzling white, his display tables have fake snow piled on their surfaces, along with sprigs of holly and red berries, and twists of cinnamon sticks and pinecones wound around display plinths for each snow globe. One table display has a model train running in circles around each display stand, and each snow globe is themed after a place in Britain and has a tiny vintage travel poster on a stand beside it. The globes displayed on the tables are the bigger, fancier, more expensive ones, and then there are rustic wooden shelves wrapped with twinkling pine garlands and smaller snow globes are lined up along them. The whole shop smells of that Christmassy mix of cinnamon and pine, with a healthy dose of Raff's orangey aftershave and the ever-present slight chemical undertone of the resin he uses in his work.

'Are you sure you don't mind doing this?' Raff asks for the thousandth time. 'Because I can close up for the afternoon, it doesn't—'

I interrupt him before he can finish a sentence he's already said more than once. 'I always cut off in mid-December because there's not time to make any more nutcrackers before Christmas. Any that don't sell from the shelves can be used to stock my stall at the Christmas market, and *you're* doing *me* a massive favour, so it's no problem.'

Quentin is at a pregnancy scan with Erin this afternoon, and earlier on, I had a customer come in to buy one of my five-foot tall nutcrackers and she wanted it to be delivered today. That's a hefty cash payment in the till, but before I could explain about having to get it packed up and collected by a courier, Raff stuck his head out of the workshop and offered to take it to her this afternoon. Between us, we've wrapped the handsome chap in bubble wrap and waddled it out to his car, where he's had to flatten the seats to get it in, and now he's going to deliver it. The least I can do is watch his shop while he's gone.

He's spinning his car keys around on his finger. 'If you see any couples who look like a good match, give 'em a snow globe and tell them to come to the Christmas market, will ya?'

He sounds like he's joking, but there's an undertone to Raff's voice whenever he 'jokes' about Love Is All A-Round that makes it sound like he's really quite worried. 'I'll be as quick as I can.'

'Take your time. You can have the afternoon off if you want, you've been working like a fiend lately.' The dark circles under his eyes are getting darker every day and he's finding it harder to disguise the tiredness in his eyes, even if he thinks his smile covers it.

'Like a little nutcracker-making fiend?' He grins as he walks backwards towards the door and gives me a salute with the car keys as he leaves. Surely a sign of true confidence is taking the chance of walking backwards in a shop full of very, very breakable items.

The truth is that this December, I've been taking it easier than ever before. I can't do a majority of the things I'd usually spend December doing. Usually I work day and night making nutcrackers, and if I'm not doing that, then I'm up until the early hours trying to catch up on online shopping for gifts, wrapping and packing up presents to send to my parents, writing Christmas cards, and ticking things off an endless festive to-do list that seems to get longer every year.

But this year, with Raff doing my usual work and everything else having to be cut out, I'm finding myself with afternoons free to wander around Ever After Street and evenings to spend curled up reading Christmas books that I never usually have time to read, and it's been lovely. A welcome reminder of the Christmases that I used to love, before December became about nothing but work, work, work and stress, stress, stress.

There's a bracing breeze and a nip in the air today, but I go over and hook the door open to let in the sound of the children's choir singing from the Carollers' Cabin and the strains of 'Joy to the World' filter in, making me feel like I'm encased in a Christmas snow globe, and I find myself humming along.

Opening the door doesn't do much for getting shoppers to actually come in though. I see couples coming along, I see them glance up at the shop sign and the quick explanation of what Dardenne Snow Globes do, and they walk on. They *all* walk on. This is what Raff meant about not getting the customers who don't want to be matched up. People think there's nothing here for them except that.

I'm still wandering around the shop when a middle-aged woman comes in. 'Oh, my dear, it *is* you from the video, isn't it? How *are* you?' She clasps her hands together and tries too hard to sound sincere.

I can't escape that video. Wherever I go, one of the *now* over 100,000 viewers will always find me.

'I thought you were the nutcracker lady,' she carries on without waiting for an answer to her previous question.

'I am. I'm just helping out a friend.'

'That awful man who knocked you over?' She clicks her tongue.

Mrs Bloom has told me that Raff and I have both been 'named and shamed' in the comments section of the video, so anyone who didn't already know who we are certainly does now, but still the back of my neck prickles with a sense of privacy invasion and I try to get her off the topic. 'Is there anything in particular you're looking for?'

'I don't want a match,' she says quickly. 'I just wanted to look around. My daughter loves snow globes and I'd love to get a handmade, local one for her, but I'm already married. I saw you on your own in here and thought you might be more approachable than that horrible man.'

'He's quite sweet really,' I say, even as I wonder what parallel universe we've stepped into where someone insults Raphael Dardenne and *I* stick up for him.

Her comment about not wanting a match reinforces what Raff said though. His reputation precedes him, and people *don't* realise that his shop is so much more than just a matchmaking station.

'Is there anything in particular that your daughter likes?' I prompt. Raff has done so much for me, it would be great if I could make a non-romantic sale for him.

'She's a real animal lover.'

'There's a few over, er, here somewhere...' I've definitely seen some animal snow globes since I got here, but the whole place is so full of snow globes that it's impossible to find anything specific when you're unfamiliar with it. 'Look, there are some dogs there.' I spot the spots of a ceramic Dalmatian and direct the woman to a shelf where Raff has got a few snow globes featuring different breeds of dog, and a few cats too, along with a sign saying that they can be custom-made to match photos of customers' own pets.

She shakes her head and I look around. 'Look, there's a "Twelve Days of Christmas" one there.' I point out a large, expensive musical snow globe, which features the avian battalion of the song – multiple swans, geese, three hens wearing French flag scarves, two turtle doves, all gathering around a partridge in a pear tree.

I love Raff's imagination, but she peers at it and shakes her head. 'Bit pricey.'

It's one of the larger globes that's got a £60 price tag on it, but as I understand all too well with nutcrackers, it's not always easy to strike a balance between charging enough to allay the amount of time and work that's gone into it and a price that customers won't baulk at.

She continues walking around the shop, running her fingers over globe after globe, leaving prints on the glass, but I'm not convinced that she really wants to buy anything.

'Ooh, are those reindeer up there?' She eventually points out a snow globe on a high shelf that Raff or Quentin could probably reach but I haven't got a hope in hell.

I scout around for something to stand on and find a step-stool tucked under the counter. I pull it over and clamber up on it, struggling to get my balance and gripping the shelf with my good hand to steady myself.

The globe in question is at the back, behind another row of snow globes. It features two reindeer standing amongst snow-covered trees, and I reach over and pick it up by the glass dome and lift it out, but Raff's snow globes are good quality, heavy ones, and it needs two hands to hold.

I try to steady it with the wrist of my broken hand, but it's no good. As I go to pass it down to the customer, the smooth glass slips out of my grip and it crashes to the floor, shattering into smithereens and spraying the stool, my feet and trouser legs, and her shoes with glycerin liquid and an avalanche of wet glitter.

The woman shrieks and jumps backwards in shock, and then peers at it. 'Oh dear, you wouldn't think they'd make such a nasty mess, would you?'

She suddenly looks up at me in horror and quickly starts backing away. 'That wasn't my fault, was it? I only asked if they were reindeer, I didn't mean for that to happen. I never touched it. You can't blame me!'

'I wouldn't,' I call after her as she runs out of the shop like she was expecting me to start squawking, 'You break it, you buy it.' It was my fault entirely. Of course it was. It wouldn't have crossed my mind to blame her.

I sigh and look down at the chaos around me. The water is slowly running across the laminate flooring, taking rivulets of glitter and iridescent snowflakes with it, the glass has shattered into splinters, and the base has split into pieces and scattered across the shop.

That went exceedingly well, didn't it? Trying to get a non-romantic sale has ended in a broken snow globe and a customer unlikely to ever return. Brilliant.

I keep hold of the shelf while I step down from the stool, trying to avoid the broken glass. What a nightmare. Broken glass is bad enough to handle with two functional hands, never mind one. There's a hazard sign folded up behind the counter so I put that out in case anyone comes in, and run to the back room to find a dustpan and brush, and then I get down on my knees and use my thighs to brace the pan as I one-handedly sweep broken glass into it. Who knew one snow globe could go *so* far?

I'm panting and sweat is beading on my forehead by the time I've got all the glass swept up and as much liquid mopped up as possible. I've got glitter in places I didn't know I had, and the joins between the floorboards are sparkling with the stuff.

The base has cracked into several pieces and skittered across the shop and I crawl around to gather up all the nearby pieces, intending to pull them all into a pile and sweep them up too, but there are so many *bits* scattered around that it couldn't possibly all have come out of that one base... could it?

At first I think it must have been a light-up snow globe or a musical one, but it was on the shelf full of ordinary ones, small ones with a £25 price tag... I pull a piece of cracked resin base over, one that's got wires and a circuit board attached to it. Electrical components? Why are there electrical components in the base of a snow globe? What are all these wires with little thingamabobs on the ends?

And that's a...

I scramble over and pull out a tiny buttoncell battery from where it's rolled underneath a table. Why would there be a battery inside the base of an ordinary snow globe?

Unless...

The floor is damp underneath me as I sit down and scrabble all the parts of the broken base in front of me and try to piece together what I'm seeing. One of the wires with a... whatever the small thingamabob is... on the end of it is clipped onto the inside of the base, and there's a tiny pinprick hole going through from the outside to the thingamabob. That wire is connected to a small circuit board, along with three other wires with thingamabobs on the ends of them too, and a lot of other electrical components, all painstakingly soldered onto the board, and a round metal holder where the battery has popped out.

Is this *it*? Is *this* the secret? It's got to be, hasn't it? I might not know much about electrical bits and pieces, but I know this stuff doesn't belong in the base of an ordinary snow globe. I put the battery back in and wait for it to do something, but it doesn't.

Maybe the fall has damaged it somehow.

I try to piece it back together, which seems like something you'd need an engineering degree to be able to do with both hands, never mind one. I'm bracing the broken parts against my thigh and trying to trace the wires back to where they came from. The broken clips holding them in place are still on the different shards of the base, each one next to a similarly small pinprick of a hole, so tiny I'd never have noticed it if I hadn't smashed the base into pieces and could see light coming through.

My breathing speeds up. I'm uncovering what I've been desperate to uncover about Dardenne Snow Globes for years. This is their secret. This small, perfectly soldered, battery-powered circuit board hidden in the base *has* to be how the snow globes move.

Why did I never think of doing this before? Buying a Dardenne snow globe and dismantling it, and now I've done it inadvertently and...

I stop. I'm not sure if I want to know. All I can think of is Raff. His deep eyes, his smile, his kindness. I *know* his snow globes don't magically move of their own accord, but if I figure out the perfectly sensible and ordinary reason that they do move, will it change everything? Our new-found truce and the undeniable friendship we've struck up over the past couple of weeks? The tingles I get when he looks at me?

I could gather this up and throw it away, and I wouldn't be any the wiser. You can know something without *truly* knowing it.

And yet, I can't stop myself. I have a one-time opportunity to find out the secret behind the snow globe that matched my mum and dad all those years ago. I *have* to know. My younger self, the girl huddled on the stairs listening to raging parents screaming at each other would never forgive me for turning away... *She* would want to find out, regardless of the charming smile of the man running this show; she would need to know the truth.

I try to piece everything back together. The reindeer have been decapitated in the fall, and the trees are in shards, but part of the snowy ground they were standing on has come loose, and I wriggle it around. It's loose because it's not actually joined. With thick glycerin liquid and an abundance of glitter on top, you'd never be able to tell, but in broken pieces right in front of me, with nothing obscuring it, it's not joined... so it can revolve freely.

As I pull it, I can feel something below it, and I shift around on the floor until I can grip the broken base between my thighs and give the loose part a sharp yank, until it comes away, revealing a tiny motor that's wired up to the same circuit board.

We've got a motor, a tiny electrical hub, and a power source, all in the base of the snow globe. So how does he do it? Is it remote controlled? Does he press a button somewhere and the loose part revolves? Surely he would have been caught out by now. And in my shop, when he handed me the globe, both his hands were on it, there's no way he could have had a hidden remote somewhere...

Hands. *That's* what the thingamabobs and pinprick holes are! That's why, on every snow globe I've seen him give so far, he's carefully positioned the hands of the two people holding it. When he handed the nutcracker snow globe to me, there were inadvertently two pairs of hands holding it.

I shift again until I can jigsaw the base into an approximation of what it should look like. Four thingamabobs. Four pinprick holes. Two on each side of the wide base. Absolutely impossible to cover with one pair of hands.

Even though the motor itself has got wet, I lay the motorised part of the base on my leg, and try to grab all the thingamabobs in my left hand, and sure enough, when all four of them are in my grasp, the motor sputters and burns out with a pop.

And it all starts to make sense. Horrible, profiteering, money-grabbing sense.

The thingamabobs are sensors. The pinprick holes, hidden inside the fancy swirls and scrolls and decorations on each base, are hiding motion sensors, so far apart that it's impossible for one person to cover each one at the same time. It's *only* when two pairs of hands hold the snow globe together that the sensors detect the motion, send the signal to the motor, and the motor spins a cleverly disguised section of the scenery inside the globe.

This is why it only ever works once – because how many people ever pick up the snow globe together again? How many couples ever have all four of their hands in the exact same position as the first time? None of them. My mum shook up her snow globe many times, alone. I shook it up when I was little, willing it to show me the magic she'd once seen inside it, but nothing ever happened.

When Raff gave me that nutcracker snow globe, I was never meant to see it move because he never intended to hand it to me.

Because one pair of hands can't cover the sensors that trigger the movement. One pair of hands can't uncover the secret, unless they drop it from a great height onto a hard surface and use their thighs as a substitute hand.

And now, *this* pair of hands has uncovered the secret and...

...and it feels like the sky is falling.

I immediately wish I didn't know.

After all the time I've spent with Raff lately, I *wanted* it to be true. I wanted him to be a magical snow globe maker. I wanted his grandfather to really be the matchmaking guru that his family revere him as. I shouldn't be as surprised as I am. I've always known it was a trick. Everyone knows that magical matchmaking snow globes aren't a real thing, but everything has felt so magical with Raff lately, that I'd kind of hoped... that maybe there really was some kind of enchantment going on here. If there was any magic in the world, *he* would be able to channel it.

And now I have this information in my head, and I don't know what to do with it. A few weeks ago, I'd have taken a photo for proof, dashed from the shop and phoned the local newspaper while simultaneously posting it on *every* social media site. I'd have been over the moon to discredit Dardenne Snow Globes and humiliate them in the most public way possible.

Emotions war in my head as I sit there on the floor, surrounded by bits of broken snow globe. This is exactly what I've wanted since the moment we were pitted against each other. This is a one-way ticket to saving my shop. All I have to do is reveal this information and the council will kick him out immediately. There will be no contest and my nutcrackers will be safe.

But things are different now. The thought of Raff being publicly humiliated makes me want to wrap my arms around him protectively. If this gets out, it will destroy him, and his family. His lovely, warm, kind family, who all genuinely believe their grandfather had magical powers.

The thought of being the one to ruin that spurs me into scrambling to my feet. I sweep the broken bits of base into the dustpan, and when I throw away, I bury it at the bottom of the bin, hidden beneath the other rubbish. The last thing I want is for Raff to know that I know. I don't want him to think I've got something to hold over him. He'll worry that I might tell people. He'll know I've got this ace up my sleeve – that I could reveal this information at any moment and end this competition between us once and for all. A few weeks ago, I'd have been jumping for joy – now, I wish I didn't know. I don't want to win over him – I want us *both* to win, and it would feel horribly wrong to even think about undermining him with this revelation.

I'm still pacing the shop in frustration, wishing I could wring my hands together when Raff comes back.

'I come bearing gifts.' He holds up two steaming paper cups with a mountainous swirl of whipped cream on top of each one from the pop-up hot chocolate bar that's arrived on Christmas Ever After for the month. 'Well, hot chocolate. It would be a pretty rubbish gift, even if it *is* Terry's Chocolate Orange hot chocolate. You okay?'

With one look, he can tell instantly. 'What's wrong?'

'I dropped one. I'm so sorry. I should have known better than to pick up something valuable *and* breakable with one hand. I'll pay for it, obviously.' I had no idea what I was going to say until the words come out. 'And I lost a customer.'

'Dead?'

I snort at the randomness of his response. 'Not that I know of. Splashed shoes and an overwhelming fear of "you break it, you buy it". Are dead customers a regular occurrence?'

'Well, I wondered if you'd dropped it on her head or something because you look like you've spent all afternoon burying a body. C'mere.' He puts the hot chocolates down on the counter and reaches a hand out, and when I step closer, he tucks my hair back and brushes glitter out of it and picks a few snowflakes from the strands. They must have been where I pushed my hair out of the way while cleaning up.

Before I know what he's doing, he's draped an arm around my shoulders and squeezed me into his side. 'Don't worry about it. The living customer or the dead snow globe. These things happen. Why are you so wound up? You can't honestly think I'd hold that against you?'

'I'll pay for—' I go to repeat but he doesn't let me finish the sentence.

'Don't be daft, I won't hear of such a thing. It happens. Why d'you think there's a hazard sign behind the counter? If there's one thing I excel at, it's causing hazards. Don't give it another thought. Are you okay? You didn't hurt yourself, did you?'

I shake my head mutely, struggling to come up with an answer in the face of his compassion.

He drops his arm from around me and nudges one of the hot chocolates towards me instead. 'Here. Guaranteed to make any stressful afternoon better.'

The steaming cup does look tempting. The whipped cream is drizzled with chocolate sauce and has a Chocolate Orange segment sticking out the top. It *would* improve the afternoon, but it would do nothing to change the fact that Raff is faking enchanted snow globes and fudging soulmates, and knowing exactly *how* makes it worse somehow. I suddenly want to put some space between me and these traitorous snow globes because the more time I spend here, the more likely I am to blurt it out, and that feels like a can of worms that's best left unopened.

'Nah, I shouldn't. I should go.' I gesture towards the door and nod decisively. 'I'm going to go.'

A flash of hurt crosses his face and he blinks in surprise. 'Oh, don't, not yet. I've only just got back. Please stay. At least drink this with me?'

He sounds so genuine, and like he really wants me to stay, and it's nice to feel that. And he did buy me a gorgeous-looking hot chocolate, and I'm firmly of the belief that there's rarely a reasonable excuse to turn down hot chocolate.

I thank him instead and pull one of the cups over to me and take a sip through the straw. 'Was the delivery okay?'

'She was thrilled. Her only comment was that if they weren't so expensive, she'd have bought another six... Which would've made for a really disturbing Christmas for her family. I love nutcrackers, but *six* giant nutcrackers watching on while you scoff your turkey...' He does a comedy shudder.

I don't feel like laughing, but his humour cuts through my defences, and I can't help giggling, even though I own a shop full of nutcrackers and don't mind them looking at me while I work. 'Be careful of insulting nutcrackers, you know the ones with swords can go on murderous rampages if the mood catches them right.'

He laughs at the throwback to the day we met. Is it wrong to call it the day we met? Technically, I'd known him for ages, but he was right that day – it *was* the first time we'd really met, and I liked that he recognised that.

And now things are awkward between us. I've never had to *make* conversation with Raff before, but today, I have no idea what to say. If he looks at me with those dark, questioning eyes, he's going to know I *know*.

I take another sip of hot chocolate and look around the shop, but the sheer number of snow globes is unfathomable. 'Did you really make all of these?'

'Not all of them. Some are my granddad's. He enjoyed matching couples up, but first and foremost, he was a snow globe maker. I guess all of his ones will sell eventually and be replaced by mine, and...' He trails off but, but not quickly enough to hide the emotion in his voice.

I know his grandfather meant a lot to him, and I could push and prod, but it doesn't seem like the right moment. 'Do you have a favourite?'

Instead of answering, he gets his keys out and comes behind the counter to open a locked display case. He carefully takes a snow globe from it and goes to hand it to me, but I put both my hands up and take a step backwards. It's going to be a while before I have the courage to pick up a snow globe again, especially one that's special to Raff.

He shakes it and sets it down on the counter, and comes to stand next to me, leaning on his elbows to watch the snow fall inside the glass.

It's a perfect little village scene. A cobblestone street with brightly coloured shops, people outside, and a carousel... 'Wait, it's Ever After Street, isn't it?'

He nods without taking his eyes off it. 'He was intending to make one for every shopkeeper who works here. This was the prototype. It was unfinished when he died, and I completed it. The last one we'll ever work on together, in a roundabout way. I put it on display in case customers recognise it, but it's not for sale.'

The tiny people are carrying shopping bags, and the shopfronts are painted in colours that match each shop's theme – a pastel blue for The Cinderella Shop, yellow and royal blue for A Tale As Old As Time, pink for Rapunzel's hair salon, green for The Mermaid's Treasure Trove... I nudge my arm against his. 'That's so special. And so thoughtful.'

I don't often say nice things about Claude Dardenne. He's been a villain in my mind for years and it's hard to reframe that, but it doesn't feel right to say anything unkind in this moment. 'You've never told me what happened to him...'

'He died.' Raff's eyes flick up to mine and he lets out a sigh. 'We didn't expect him to die. I know that sounds weird because he was ninety-four, but he was fit and healthy. He still went to work every day, even though the whole family told him he didn't have to. He had some old-age medical niggles, but nothing serious. Then there were some anomalies in a routine test, he had more tests, and with waiting for appointments and then results... by the time they came back with a diagnosis, he'd deteriorated so much that there was nothing anyone could do. People think cancer is a long goodbye, but it was so *fast*. Less than five weeks and he was gone.'

'I'm so sorry, Raff.' I reach out so I can squeeze his fingers with my good hand.

'My father died when I was really young – under two. Erin was five, so she remembers him a little, but I don't. My gran and granddad stepped up to help our mum. They bought the house next door and moved across the county to be there for us. He's the only father figure I've ever known. I was *captivated* by his snow globes. Getting to do what he did was all I ever wanted...' He shakes the snow globe up again, and then puts it back in the display case, and picks up another one from a nearby shelf. This one is a more traditional scene of a park in wintertime, with tiny models of families skating on an ice rink, others sitting around a fountain, and streetlamps that actually light up when he presses a button on the base.

'Have you ever done anything else?' I ask as I watch the snow falling on the idealistic little scene.

He shakes his head. 'Never wanted to. I love snow globes and the sense of wonder they bring. They're a perfect escape. You can watch the snow falling and imagine who lives in this perfect little scene and what their lives are like. Nothing exists outside of this. It's a snapshot of an ideal life that most people can only dream of. A world within a world – a perfect world inside the not-perfect real world. You can lose yourself for a few moments while looking into a snow globe. What other Christmas decoration gives you that?'

It's not a question that needs an answer. His passion for what he does shines through in every conversation. He shakes the snow globe again and I find myself gazing into the park scene, wishing that real life was that picture-perfect, and trying not to think of his arm pressed against mine.

'Why nutcrackers?' he murmurs, making me realise the snow

settled in the globe long ago and I've been staring at it, lost in thought.

I blink a few times and glance at him and then look away. 'I've loved the story since I was little. We had one at home, it was about four-foot tall and I thought I was going to marry it one day. When it came out every December, I would give it a kiss on the cheek every night before bed, convinced it would turn into a handsome prince during the night and whisk me away from all the fighting.'

'It didn't?'

'Funnily enough, no. Magic isn't real.' I give him a pointed look, but the significance of it goes completely over his head. 'He was a friend when I needed one most. I couldn't tell anyone at school what was happening at home, but that nutcracker was there with me. Every December, he stood and observed it all. He understood what no one else could. When I was a teenager, he got thrown out and I was happy to see the back of him – he was a reminder of all the childhood disappointments and dreams that weren't real, but then, as an adult, I kept thinking about him. A lot of my so-called ballet friends lost interest in me when my usefulness to them was gone, and I kept thinking of that childhood friend who was *always* there, and I wanted to do that for other people. Nutcrackers are said to bring good luck and keep danger away from the homes they're in, which was something I wished for when I felt so vulnerable. I couldn't walk. I was hobbling around on crutches, but I struggled with them and used a walking frame, which was incredibly humiliating to accept at thirty-three. It felt like the *only* thing I could still do was sit at my grandfather's lathe, and I decided to try to re-make the friend I'd lost.'

My left hand is next to him on the counter, and he wraps both hands around it and pulls it to his mouth. 'That's the loveliest thing I've ever heard.' His lips move against my skin and his clean-shaven jaw rubs the side of my hand, making me feel even more overheated than I was feeling anyway. 'I'm sorry for everything derogatory I've ever said about your shop. I wish I'd got to know you sooner and understood you better.'

'I'm sorry too,' I murmur.

He bows his head, letting his hair fall forward. 'At least you've got plenty of nutcrackers to talk to this time around. And you can always talk to me. I'm slightly less wooden, but I promise not to judge or ridicule, and I can stand in complete silence, grow a beard, and bare my teeth at anyone who walks by, if you want.'

'Crack nuts between your teeth?'

'Can give it a try, but I warn you, I have a phobia of the dentist.'

'Awwww.' The noise has popped out before I'm even aware of it, and I can't help the smile that spreads across my face. It's something that's so real and honest, and Raff's openness makes me grin, and yet, what I *know* twinges in the back of my mind again.

I've always known that the snow globes didn't really move by magic, but actually knowing it changes things somehow. Raff is warm, honest and open, but the images of those wires in the resin base flash into my mind again. When it comes to his work, he's running the trickery that I always knew he was, and the problem with tricks is that they have a tendency to get found out. And I'm surprised by how much I *don't* want that to happen now.

14

It's been decades since I heard 'Little Donkey' and yet, I still know all the words. I don't know how or why I agreed to this when Sofia asked me, but somehow I have joined the Dardenne family at her school nativity. I've also been roped in to going back to the house afterwards for an evening of board games and mince pies. Right now, it's just after 6 p.m. on a damp Wednesday night and we're sitting in the main hall of the local primary school, watching a group of seven-year-olds put on the nativity show.

I'm sat in a row with an empty chair to my right, and Raff's sitting on my left, and the family are filling the rest of the row of hard plastic chairs, apart from Biddy who's in a wheelchair tonight and has been parked on the aisle end, next to Trisha.

Raff's right forearm is resting against mine on the hard chair arms, and he senses my eyes on him and looks over with a smile, and then bends his fingers outwards until the backs of them rub gently against my good hand, and he mouths an: 'Okay?'

I nod and... take leave of my senses, because instead of just letting his fingers stroke my hand, I turn it over until I can slip my last three fingers over his, and his fingers immediately fold around them and he tugs my arm closer, and a tingle goes down my spine.

He catches my eyes as I turn back and his smile grows wider. I can't help returning his smile as I settle back in my seat. I *know* I should pull my hand out of his. My fingers shouldn't be anywhere near his, and yet, the more I tell myself to pull my hand away, the more it seems impossible to do so. It's like my fingers are stuck to Raff's warm hand with the hot glue we were using earlier to put the finishing touches to some nutcrackers, and the tighter he squeezes, the warmer and more relaxed I feel, especially when his thumb starts rubbing up and down my little finger.

And so, we sit through 'Away in a Manger', 'We Three Kings', 'Hark! The Herald Angels Sing', and more. The three wise men who bring gold, myrrh, and 'Frankenstein' to the baby doll that Mary's now holding upside down by a leg, having yanked it a bit too hard from Joseph earlier and pulled an arm out, and not knowing what to do with said disembodied arm, has thrown it to the side of the stage where it's now lying in front of the sheep. The sheep themselves have got confused and started mooing, and the third wise man has started eating whatever was doubling as the myrrh. The shepherds have had a fight and one's yanked the tea towel from the other one's head, and the cardboard star has fallen off the ceiling and is now being held up by a teacher on a stepladder, whose neon pink blouse wasn't the best choice for blending unnoticed into the background.

And I somehow don't let go of Raff's hand until we stand up to applaud after a rousing finale of 'Santa Claus is Coming to Town'.

When it's all over, we pile out into the night and wait for Erin, who's gone to collect Sofia from backstage.

Trisha is pushing Biddy in a wheelchair. 'I don't need it,' she exclaims. 'It's just less work than a Zimmer frame. They're such ungainly things, don't you think? They make one look so *old*.'

Quentin is about to make a witty retort when Sofia rushes at us, squealing in excitement, and throws her arms around Raff. 'Did you like it? Did you think it was brilliant?'

'If it doesn't get nominated for an Oscar next year, I'll eat my Santa hat,' Raff says without missing a beat.

'You're not wearing a hat, Uncle Raff.'

'I left it in Franca's shop.'

'Ooooh-wah!' She squeals like leaving his hat at my shop is some kind of innuendo for something that seven-year-olds are definitely too young to understand.

Sofia grabs my good hand and jiggles it. 'Did you like it, Franca?'

'I thought it was brilliant. The best night I've had in years.' I thought that sentence was going to come out sounding sarcastic, but as I say it, I realise it's true.

This is what families do at Christmas, and it feels like I've been on a family outing with good company and people who care about me. The show itself was unintentionally the funniest thing I've seen in ages, and Sofia is a born performer with a confidence that only children have. The music, the old carols that I used to love when I was young, have been a welcome reminder of childhood Christmases gone by, of happy parents sitting in the audience, being proud of my Very Important Role of playing a tree one year, and the back end of a Highland cow the next. There wasn't traditionally a Highland cow in the nativity but our teachers had the unenviable task of ensuring there was a part for *every* child in the class, hence why, one year, Mary and Joseph went to Bethlehem via three donkeys, two dolphins, and a kangaroo, and shared their stable with two elephants and a rhinoceros.

The school is within walking distance from the house so we start meandering home, and Raff offers me his arm. There's something about his thoughtfulness with the broken hand, how he always stays on my left, always thinks about which is the good side before doing anything, and when he hooks his right elbow towards me, I'm powerless to stop myself slipping my hand through his arm.

Sofia skips on ahead and twirls around, spinning her cardboard-and-feather wings, her tinsel halo glistening under the streetlamps, chattering excitedly the whole way about the rehearsals for tonight's show and funny things that happened backstage, and that feeling of not being alone warms me from the inside out. Being welcomed into this little unit is the nicest thing. Walking in the dark, past the Christmas lights of the neighbourhood houses with Raff's reassuring strength beside me. Going to their home for an evening of more festive fun. Erin's walking nearby, asking me how I'm managing everything one-handed, and it makes me feel like I really matter to them. It's been so many years since I did anything as festive as watching a school's nativity play and even more years since I felt like I wasn't alone.

Sofia twirls back over to us. 'Franca, Mummy says you're the Sugar Plum Fairy. Can I come and see you in the ballet like you've seen me in the nativity?'

It's such an innocent question and I don't realise I'm going to get choked up until I go to answer. 'Aww, I wish, Sofe. I don't do ballet any more. I had a bad accident and had to stop dancing.'

'Did you break your fingers before?'

'No, I broke my leg that time.'

'My teacher says that's called accident-prone. There's a boy in my class who says he's accident-prone but Daddy says some people are just idiots!'

Erin gives her a scolding look, but she ignores it. 'Was your costume pretty? Was it fun playing a fairy?'

'It was. It was my dream role, until it turned into a nightmare when my dance partner dropped me on stage and the entire theatre watched my leg crack in three places.'

'Just like this time with the video.'

'Way more people have seen the video.' I hate thinking about the ever-increasing viewing figures. 'Thankfully no one recorded it and put it on social media last time.'

'That must've been harder than you've ever let on, Fran,' Raff says when Erin has walked on ahead to catch up with Quentin.

Why does it make me melt so much every time he calls me Fran? And that gentle encouraging tone in his voice is melt-worthy too. 'It's okay. I'm happier on Christmas Ever After than I ever was in the ballet. Yeah, it was years of pain and physiotherapy, but it was kind of the intervention I needed too. I wasn't happy. Wasn't healthy. There was so much pressure to stay thin and stay fit. I pushed myself too hard and never ate enough. The doctors were quick to tell me that my leg probably wouldn't have shattered if I'd been healthier. There was a lot of competition. You were pitted against people you thought were your friends. People cheer you on while secretly hoping you fail, and it made me second-guess everything.' It seems natural to tell him the rest too, the things about my previous career that I've never admitted to anyone and not entirely even to myself. 'It was more of a childhood dream than anything else. One of the last times I can remember my parents being happy was when we went to see *The Nutcracker* ballet, and I remember being completely entranced by the Sugar Plum Fairy. She was so pretty, so perfect, it seemed like she'd never had any problems in her life. I thought her life must be perfect, and if I could do that some day, then mine would be too. And I just kept chasing that. No matter how hard it was, no matter how miserable it was making me, I clung on to the thought that if I just got a lead role, all my problems would be solved. My parents would be happy again. I'd be *enough* for them.' I'm struggling to keep the wobble out of my voice, because the only thing that's ever made my parents happy is being apart. Nothing I did was ever going to make a difference, and in a way, I'm only just starting to realise that. I thought getting a lead role would do it, and when it didn't, then I thought bringing down Dardenne Snow Globes would be the answer, but spending time with Raff and seeing how hard he's pushing himself to continue doing things in his grandfather's way rather than the way *he* wants to has made me realise that it's impossible to make other people happy and the best thing you can do for any family is make *yourself* happy. The Dardennes would be so upset if they knew how much Raff is struggling, and deep down, I don't think my parents would have pushed me so hard if they knew how unhappy I was as a dancer.

'If only life was that easy, hmm?' Raff uses his elbow to squeeze my hand against his ribs in gentle, silent support. His voice is deep and shaky, and he sounds like I've touched a nerve for him too.

When we get back to the house and everyone is in the hallway inside the door, taking off coats and shoes and the cardboard wings that Sofia reluctantly removes after being told they're too cumbersome to wear all night, I feel like such a part of the family that I can't help saying something.

'Thank you all for being so kind and welcoming and including me.' I splurt the sentence out, unsure of what I was going to say until I opened my mouth. 'I just wanted you to know how grateful I am. It's been a long while since I felt like part of such a loving family, so thank you for having me and being so lovely.'

'Aren't you a sweetheart?' Trisha comes over and envelops me in a hug, and then pulls back to look into my eyes. 'You're more than welcome, my lovely. It's a pleasure to have you.'

'Pleasure to see a certain someone so happy.' Biddy points at Raff, who has gone in first to help her down the step into the living room.

'Gran – Biddy,' he hastily corrects when she glares at him. 'I'm always happy.'

'No one is happy alone.'

'Raff's literally the happiest person I've ever met.' I stick up for him. 'Nothing fazes him.'

'He *should* be fazed by the possibility of being alone forever,' Biddy grumbles. 'Who would trust him to help with their love lives when he can't even help himself?'

'He does make incredible snow globes. Isn't that how Claude's business started out? It wasn't *all* about love, was it? No one can deny that your grandson is a master craftsman. He's getting pretty good at nutcrackers too.'

I'm distracted by his smile and the way it does funny things to my stomach, until she mutters something and then clicks her fingers towards me as she wheels herself across the living room, careening into tables and sending decorations sprawling as she goes. 'Oi, you can come and help me out of this menace.'

'Once Biddy starts referring to you as "Oi", you know you're part of the family, Franca,' Erin says kindly.

I squeeze through the gathering in the hallway and race after the errant wheelchair. 'I'm not much use for helping anyone at the moment.'

'Oh, I know.' Biddy clamps a hand around my good arm and uses it to haul herself to her feet and shuffle to the armchair. 'I don't need your help, I just wanted an excuse to whisper to you.' She beckons for me to lean in closer. 'He's not always happy, he just pretends he is because he doesn't want us to worry about him.'

I'm surprised by her directness, but also really glad I'm not the only one who can see past Raff's bravado. He isn't as good at putting on a front as he thinks he is. 'I gathered that. I didn't know any of you realised it too.'

'You can't hide anything from a Dardenne. What Raff needs is someone he doesn't have to be strong for. Someone he can be honest with. Raff grew up far too quickly. His father died when he was very young, and that boy took on adult responsibilities when he was just a child. That's why he's such a big kid at Christmas now – he never got to be a kid when he really was one. And since Claude died, he's taken everything onto his shoulders, and now he keeps people at arm's length so no one sees past his walls and forces him to face his own vulnerability.'

He's let me see a vulnerable side. He's strong and fun and protective, and I know he's been extra attentive to me because of the injury, but he's been open too. He hasn't hidden his own struggles or pretended that he doesn't find things hard, and it makes me instantly desperate to give him a hug because, of all the unlikely people in all the world, he's let *me* see past his walls and into his heart.

'He needs someone he doesn't have to keep up pretences with.'

I'm not sure if her eyelid is twitching or if she's trying to wink at me, but I get the feeling this sentence has a double meaning. Does she know something? She was Claude's wife – would he have shared the truth behind the snow globes with her? Has she somehow worked out that I've discovered it too? Maybe you really *can't* hide anything from a Dardenne, not even if you want to.

She's watching me knowingly as I try to formulate a response, but Raff calls over before I have a chance to come up with something.

'Why are my ears burning?'

'Probably allergic to your shampoo,' Biddy shouts, making me giggle. 'Try a different one.'

Raff laughs and comes over to fold down the wheelchair and stash it somewhere, and Erin brings in Biddy's martini and a plate of mince pies.

'What are you doing for Christmas, Franca?' she asks me.

I answer without thinking. 'What I usually do – microwave meal for one and a whole selection box.'

The room goes silent. Everyone's attention is suddenly on me, and every face has got varying degrees of pity on it.

'Sometimes I cook it in the oven to make it extra special,' I offer with a helpless shrug. I should have known how sad my lonely little Christmases would sound to a big family.

'Oh, my dear, don't you see your family?' Trisha comes in from the kitchen.

'Not very often. My parents are separated and live far apart and I'm usually working.' My face is heating up as I try to justify my quiet Christmases to people who clearly spend Christmas together in a happy family bubble that I've always wished I had. 'I send their presents in advance and we always do a phone call or a video chat on the day. And I enjoy the peace and quiet of working on holiday days...'

'Oh, no no no.' Trisha shakes her head. 'I won't hear of it. You must come here and spend the big day with us. I can't abide anyone being alone for Christmas.'

'What if it's what they want?' I suggest.

'No one *wants* to be alone!' Biddy clangs her plate down onto the table for emphasis.

'I can't spend Christmas with you, I barely even know you.' I'm laughing awkwardly because they sound so serious, but who *really* invites a complete stranger to spend Christmas with them?

'I don't see how that's relevant,' Erin says. 'What better way to get to know each other?'

'There's already a present for you under the tree,' Sofia says.

'There is not!'

Sofia bounds across the room to grab my good hand and haul me over to the Christmas tree, where she dives into the pile of wrapped boxes underneath and starts rifling through them until she holds one up to show me a label with my name on it. 'There is, see?'

'One of Santa's elves must've put it there.' Trisha winks at me.

'I'd love you to, if that makes any difference,' Raff says. 'I'll come get you in the morning and drop you home whenever you've had enough of us.'

'Or you could spend Christmas Eve night at his place too. He's got a really comfortable sofa...' Biddy waggles grey eyebrows and then glances at Sofia. 'So they can stay up together and watch for Santa, of course. Two people are much more likely to hear reindeer hooves on the roof.'

'Oh go on.' Erin pats me on the shoulder. 'It'd be great to have you.'

'Pleeeeeeeease,' Sofia says as only a child can.

'We know you're not working this year.' Quentin holds up his right hand and waves it around, indicating my splint.

'And at least we'll know you're not struggling alone one-handed. How would you ever get the cellophane off that microwave meal without both hands?' Trisha smiles at me. 'Let us look after you. You deserve to put your feet up and let someone take care of you given everything you're dealing with at the moment.'

Somehow, Raff knows I'm going to cry before I do because he's wrapped an arm around me and tugged me into his side as tears spill over, and I turn to hide my face in his chest.

It's the feeling of being wanted and the idea of being looked after. I've been taking care of myself for years, I don't need anyone's help, but it's the thought that they *want* to, that they're worried about me... that they *care*...

My cheeks are burning with embarrassment at the uncontrollable tears. I've got my hand covering the part of my face that's not buried in Raff's chest, but rather than drawing attention to me,

Trisha just reaches over to pat my shoulder. 'We'll take that as a yes then,' she says before returning to the kitchen. 'Sofe, mince pies this way! Quentin get down that tin of Quality Street, I can hear it screaming to be opened. Erin, grab the Monopoly!'

Raff's fingers tangle in my hair as he brushes it back, rubbing his chin against the top of my head.

'Your family are turning me into an emotional wreck.'

'They do that. You get used to it.'

Being near Raff has a way of making me feel better, and I sit next to him for the rest of the night as we scoff mince pies and drink hot chocolate, play Monopoly in teams while trying to catch Team Biddy and Sofia out in their cheating, laughing until there are tears streaming down my face in Articulate, and knowing that the sound of the popping dice will haunt my dreams tonight after a few games of Frustration.

And I forget about everything outside of this. I forget about only having one functional hand. I forget about how much every small movement hurts. I get lost in a happy family who have been kind enough to welcome me into their fold and enjoy the fun and laughter and teasing, warm and happy, and relaxed. This is what I always dreamed Christmas would be like. Everyone you love, gathering together to celebrate. No judgements, no arguments, no pressure to be something you're not, and the Dardennes make me feel like I'm enough, just as I am.

It's what every day should feel like, not just Christmas.

15

'It's time to celebrate breaking up from school, work, and taking a step back from our regularly scheduled routine of yelling at daytime telly.' Trisha raises a glass to Sofia, Erin and Biddy in turn.

'All daytime TV competitions are a scam,' Biddy grumbles. 'Sometimes they go from segments on how to avoid scammers to encouraging people to enter their scam competitions! What a joke. And some of the "advice" they give. A dead shrew would be a better problem solver!'

'It's the night of our annual three-legged gingerbread house competition.' Trisha ignores her obviously familiar rant and holds her mug out in a toast to me. 'And in honour of our honorary Dardenne, Franca, instead of a three-legged gingerbread house competition, this year we've decided to have a – break, ho ho ho – from tradition and make it a three-armed competition, so if you'll all get into your pairs – Raff and Franca, Erin and Quentin, and Sofia and I are going to team up, and Biddy will act as the judge of all things gingerbread...'

'I fully support anything where I get to sit here with my lovely drink and eat gingerbread without having to do any work.' She raises her martini glass to me as well. 'Usually these buggers make me join in their three-legged gingerbread house nonsense, but you can take my place this year. I'm far too old for such shenanigans.'

'I thought you were only fifty-three, Grandma,' Sofia says and gets a glare for her use of the G word.

It's 20 December, Raff and I have spent all day preparing for the Christmas market which starts tomorrow, but for tonight, he's invited me to join in the annual event the family does every year – the three-legged gingerbread house competition. A bit like a three-legged race, but instead of racing to a finishing point with one of your legs tied to your partner's, you're attempting to build the best gingerbread house together. As I'm at a disadvantage on the arm front, Trisha has decided to make it fair this year by forcing all three couples to tie their arms together instead of their legs.

'I've never made a gingerbread house before.'

On reflection, I should have known that admission would be greeted by looks of complete shock.

Sofia's mouth falls open. '*How* have you never made a gingerbread house before?'

I glance around at six expectant faces. 'I've never had anyone to make one with. It's pointless when you're on your own, isn't it?'

'You've got *so* much catching up to do on Christmas!' Sofia squeals.

It's a nice thought. This family really knows how to *do* Christmas. And as I'm coming to realise, I don't. I'm terrible at Christmas. I never used to be, I used to go all-out to make up for the rubbish family Christmases when I was young, but it's seemed so pointless in recent years. When it's just me, it's just another day that is better spent working.

'Well, you're not on your own this year.' Trisha appears in front of us with a ribbon. 'Arms!'

Raff's wearing a hoodie over a festive green T-shirt, which he stops to shrug off and throw into the living room, leaving my arm pressed against his warm forearm and sending goosebumps racing across my skin. I gingerly hold my right arm against Raff's and let her weave a ribbon in and out of our forearms, holding our limbs together. She's extra gentle and stops before she reaches the splint, giving us more leeway than she's given Erin and Quentin, but it's still the closest my broken hand has been to another person, and I didn't realise how much I'd have to trust Raff not to make any sharp movements or yank my arm hard enough to hurt.

'I'll be careful,' Raff whispers as Biddy laces up Trisha and Sofia and delights in making the ribbon so tight that it's guaranteed to cut off their circulation. 'I promise your bad arm is safe with my arm.'

It's another one of those moments that requires an audible 'awwwww' noise. I'm once again touched by his thoughtfulness and empathy. For someone who I thought was so heartless, Raff has surprised me in every way, and I can't think of anyone I'd trust more to have my broken hand tied to. Which is quite ironic considering how this injury came about in the first place.

Not that he hasn't done plenty to make up for it. My nutcrackers are selling well. Raff has made all of the nutcracker orders and only packing them is left to be done. The ones on the shelves are dwindling, and the snowmen Raff's made are also dwindling, and I can't wait to be able to use my lathe again because there are so many different things that can be made, from female nutcrackers to Disney-inspired ones and to things that are different altogether. Raff's snowmen flying off the shelves has shown me it's time for The Nutcracker Shop to expand its inventory slightly.

The giant nutcracker giveaway has been wildly popular too. My mentions on social media have exploded with photos of people sending their selfies with the umbrella-holding nutcracker, and in terms of matches, we've made another one this week with Mitch's son Cedric and Mandy from All Wrapped Up, who we matched over an icy penguin snow globe, and they've arranged to do an escape room date together this weekend.

That's three out of five matches on Raff's side, and a hundred or so customers who care about nutcrackers and have interacted with me on social media. I don't know if we've got time to match any more couples before the council meeting at the Christmas market on Sunday afternoon, but I don't think it's going to be important now. This was about me and Raff and the tension between us causing an atmosphere for the other shopkeepers. That's no longer an issue. I'll withdraw my last complaint about him and he'll withdraw his last complaint about me, and they'll forget all about this silly idea and everything will go back to normal. It *has* to.

'Rules are simple,' Trisha announces. 'You've got one hour. Whoever's made the best gingerbread house when the timer runs out is the winner.'

'What do we win?' Sofia asks.

'Honour. Respect. And a box of Maltesers.'

I laugh out loud. I love this family. 'It is a truth universally acknowledged that Maltesers always taste better from a box than from a bag.'

Erin giggles. 'Something we can all agree on. With that attitude, you're one of us alright.'

It shouldn't make me feel as warm and fuzzy as it does.

Sofia instructs the smart speaker to start playing Christmas music and the sound of 'All I Want for Christmas Is You' fills the house. The three teams are stationed at different spots around the kitchen. Each team has four pre-made gingerbread house walls and two roof panels ready to assemble, a cake board for mounting, and the island in the middle of the kitchen is a free-for-all decorating station, piled high with piping bags and tubs of royal icing, along with bags of sweets, gumdrops, chocolate buttons, marshmallows, food colouring, writing icing, wafer decorations, and every type of sprinkle you can imagine.

'Have you read *The Hunger Games*?' Raff whispers into my ear, and I nod. 'It's like the beginning of that where they can all run to the centre point and grab any weapons they can get, except no one gets horribly murdered in this version.' He glances behind us. 'Unless anyone takes that chocolate reindeer. Then all bets are off because that's ours. We need to strategise – royal icing and piping bags first, and that reindeer. If you go for that and I go for the icing, we can reach both in one move.'

'On your marks! Get ready! Go!' Biddy starts the stopwatch in her hand and has a celebratory sip of her martini.

Carnage is the best way to describe it. Erin lets out a battle cry and she and Quentin attack the kitchen island, clawing supplies into their arms. Raff's more restrained, despite his desperation for the chocolate reindeer. 'We can worry about decorations later, *anything* can be a decoration, let's focus on structure first and let them get caught up in gum-drop warfare.'

'I don't know whether to be scared or impressed by how seriously your family takes this.'

'All's fair in love, war, and Maltesers.' He gives me a wink and we make our run for the kitchen island. Raff gathers up royal icing and piping bags with his one hand, while I reach over for the chocolate reindeer and manage to snag a packet of white and milk chocolate buttons because I have a vision of using them for roof tiles.

We take our loot back to our station by the kitchen door and huddle together. Raff uses his teeth to tear into the pack of piping bags, and I hold one while he spoons royal icing into it, twists the end and snips the tip off. Between us we lay out the gingerbread pieces in the order they should be assembled, and I hold the back wall upright while Raff tries to manage the piping bag one-handed, splurging a big spurt of royal icing along one side. He puts the piping bag down and fits the side wall against it, and we both stand there holding it, and I can't stop smiling. We're so close, every time his head turns for a glimpse of what the others are doing, his hair catches against mine, and the heat of his body is pressed against my side, and he can't stop smiling either.

The others are shrieking and squealing at each other, but Raff and I have done a lot together over the past few weeks. We've got into a rhythm of me passing him wooden blanks and taking completed nutcracker parts away. We've got a routine of him painting and me handing him different parts, brushes, or colours, and this is no different. He's so careful that I can tell he's hyper-aware of having my injured arm strapped to his, but we methodically work our way through. I spin the cake board and hold each wall up; Raff keeps the top of the piping bag held between his teeth and uses his hand to guide the icing out, and I stick each wall to the next and hold it while the icing sets hard enough to glue it in place. His head leans against mine as we stand and wait, listening to the shrieks and cries of the other teams.

It's not long before we've got our four gingerbread house walls standing. We've used enough royal icing to prop up the leaning tower of Pisa, never mind a gingerbread house, and our walls stand firm when we attach first one side of the roof, and then the other.

'Back to the island,' Raff declares. 'Every man for himself. Grab anything you can! Have no mercy! Take no prisoners!'

He grabs at flying saucers and candy canes. I spy a bag of Jelly Tots and lunge for them so hard that I nearly yank Raff off his feet and yelp in pain when it pulls my hand, but it was worth it for the Jelly Tots. We go back to our part of the kitchen unit with armfuls of our winnings, mostly chosen because I want to eat them now, not decorate a gingerbread house with them.

'Your shop feels like being in the middle of "Waltz of the

Snowflakes", and this feels like entering the Land of Sweets.' I hold out a bag of strawberry laces with my left hand so he can take hold of the other side with his right hand and between us, we pull it open.

'And you thought you wouldn't be part of *The Nutcracker* ballet this year.'

'A more enjoyable way.' I glance up and catch his eyes, and then pop a flying saucer in my mouth for good measure.

'Good.' He opens his mouth so I can pop one in for him too.

'With a real-life Mouse-King-slaying nutcracker prince,' I say around a mouthful of sherbet.

'Awww.' He holds my gaze with a smile, and it's only when I notice everyone else's eyes on us that I realise we've stopped decorating to grin at each other. With Raff this close and my injured hand literally tied to him, it makes it hard to concentrate on anything else.

'I can see you trying to copy our work!' Raff shouts, making me breathe a sigh of relief at the distraction.

We fill another piping bag with royal icing, and this time, I guide the tip while he squeezes, and we manage to get a neat line of icing along the centre of the roof. We open the Jelly Tots and place the little gummy sweets one by one in a rainbow pattern along the line, and do the same along each eave of the roof until we run out, a situation which is not helped by both of us eating more Jelly Tots than we're using.

'Could do this all night,' he murmurs, his chin rubbing against my forehead.

'Me too. I never knew it was possible to have this much fun building a gingerbread house.'

'Me neither.'

'You do this every year!' I nudge my elbow against his.

'Not with you.'

'Awww.' How many times in one night can one person need to make that noise?

Next we tile the roof. He squiggles royal icing across the gingerbread and we lay out milk and white buttons like roof tiles, and then splodge some more icing around the outer edges of the cake board and stick candy canes into it so they stand up like trees, and with careful cooperation, we manage to run thin lines of icing around the door and window frames, and when Biddy announces there's only a couple of minutes left, Raff sticks the chocolate reindeer on the front, right at the highest point of the roof, like a figurehead on the bow of a ship, and I'm still holding it steady when the stopwatch starts beeping.

Everyone has to turn around and unveil their creations, and it's a joy to behold. Trisha and Sofia's house has collapsed completely and consists of six gingerbread panels lying in a haphazard heap. 'We tried decorating the panels first before we stuck them together. It did not go well. We'd have been all right if a certain member of our team hadn't been too busy eating the decorations!'

'You ate more than I did, Granny!' Sofia cries in indignation.

Raff's laughing so hard that it's shaking both of us, his head leaning against mine as we hold our creation in front of us, one hand on each side of the cake board because we've used so much royal icing that it's surprisingly heavy.

Considering we've managed to make it with only two arms between us, it actually looks quite good. A bit messy, with way too much icing, but like a traditional little gingerbread house with Jelly Tots instead of gumdrops.

'Ours has got a, um, fully intentional skylight.' Quentin points to the section of their effort where half the roof has caved in. 'And we tried to make a working door but it broke off. We deserve extra credit for trying.'

Biddy hobbles around the kitchen to inspect each one, and

stops at ours. 'And you two haven't tried anything clever at all, and look at the results. Simple and traditional. Proof of what happens when two people are enough for each other just as they are.' She gives us a pointed look. 'You're a great team. I declare Franca and Raff the winners!'

'Unfair advantage!' Erin heckles. 'Franca's had too much practise with her left hand!'

'I've never won anything before,' I start like I'm about to give a winner's speech at an awards ceremony. 'This is my proudest achievement.'

Raff reaches over and lifts my good hand in victory and Erin snaps a photo, and then he bends down and presses a loud 'mwah' to my cheek, and he lingers for just a second too long, his clean-shaven jaw against my skin, his nose pressing just under my eye, and for that one moment, there's nothing else in this room apart from him. I'm instantly so hot and bothered that surely someone has just turned the room thermostat up to 100 degrees, and everything gets a bit hazy and blurry as my fingers grasp onto his, trying to hold him nearer and silently tell him to keep doing that.

I lean into him, close my eyes, and force myself to exhale, but all too quickly, he's gone, and he uses my hand to tug me into taking a bow with him, and I feel so unsteady that we nearly bang heads as we stand back up.

'Best fun ever!' Sofia declares as Biddy undoes their ribbon. Once free, Trisha goes over to Erin and Quentin and Sofia comes to us, and I'm touched by how careful she is of my hand as she undoes our ribbon, and when she's done, in one swift movement, she reaches over and grabs our chocolate reindeer and eats it. Raff tackles her and tickles her mercilessly and she squeals and runs away.

Trisha washes her hands, which are almost as covered in royal icing as mine are, and then comes over to present me with the box of Maltesers, complete with a kiss on both cheeks. 'Thank you for adding a new element to our Christmas tradition this year, lovely.'

'I want to do arms again next year instead of legs!' Sofia says and turns to me. 'Will you come every year?'

'I think that might be between Uncle Raff and Franca,' Trisha wisely answers for me and quickly distracts her. 'Never mind next year, it's not even 8 p.m. *tonight* yet. What do you want to do next?'

'Christmas movie marathon!' Sofia declares. 'And popcorn!'

'Haven't you eaten enough?' Erin looks at the quickly diminishing pile of gingerbread on Trisha and Sofia's cake board.

'There's no such thing as enough, Mummy! It's Christmas!'

Something else we can all agree on.

The entire family has traipsed into the living room. Raff flops down in the corner of a sofa and pats the empty space next to him, inviting me to sit there, and I do without hesitation.

After a couple of minutes, he pulls my hair aside, letting it slip through his fingers as he leans forward to whisper in my ear. 'You can relax, you know.'

I realise I'm sort of perched. Raff's reclined and put his feet up on the coffee table. Sofia's still in the kitchen with Trisha, sorting out what popcorn she wants. Quentin has helped Biddy to her armchair and now he and Erin are sharing a three-seater sofa on the other side of the room and Erin's got her feet up and a hand on her ever-growing belly.

I sit back and let myself lean into Raff's warmth, and I'm not sure if I imagine him shifting closer and, for one bizarre moment, I think he's going to put his arm around me, but he doesn't, and I don't know if I'm disappointed or relieved. Raff and I have had more than enough arm-on-arm contact for one night. Neither of us need to be in such close proximity now. I could move. I glance around the room. There's plenty of space for all of us, and yet, the only place I *want* to be is next to Raff.

When Sofia comes in, she's got a huge bowl of popcorn; Trisha has got another one which she hands to Erin, and a smaller one for Biddy, who clearly isn't going to share with anyone.

'I'm going to sit by yoooou!' Sofia throws herself down on my other side and I can't help laughing as my left hand reaches out to catch some of the popcorn that cascades out of the bowl with the movement.

'What are we watching, Sofe?' Trisha settles next to Erin.

She turns to me like this is a great responsibility. 'What Christmas movies do you like, Franca?'

I freeze like I did when she asked me about Christmas songs. I haven't watched any Christmas films for years. I used to love them but lately, on the rare occasions I've tried to watch one, they've seemed schmaltzy and cheesy and I've turned them off after a few minutes, relegating them to the 'things I used to love but don't any more' corner of my brain and telling myself that the time would be better spent working.

'Have you seen *Elf*?' She prompts when I don't answer quickly enough.

I laugh in relief. 'I have, but not for many years.'

She cheers and I grab the handful of popcorn she sends tumbling over the edge of the bowl again. As Sofia takes control of the remote and puts the film on, Raff touches my injured arm, wordlessly telling me to keep it still so we don't clash while he reaches across me and takes a handful of popcorn too, and his thoughtfulness makes me melt yet again. After his one mistake three weeks ago, these days, he doesn't move without thinking it through first.

Raff's taken possession of the Maltesers box and he opens them and puts them on my lap between us, but after a few more hand-fuls of Sofia's popcorn, I give her a nudge and move them to my other side so she can reach them too, and she grins at me and takes some.

'Hey, that's not fair. We earned those!'

'Like you can't reach from there.' Trisha holds both hands up and rams them together, telling Raff to shift nearer to me, and I get the feeling that's exactly what she's trying to encourage. He moves closer, sinking down until his head is millimetres away from my shoulder, and I lift my arm up so he can reach.

His hand snakes across me, takes a couple of Maltesers, and then he doesn't move away. His arm stays across my lap, and I lower my right arm back down to rest against it, and he pushes his chin against my shoulder, silently asking if this is okay, and I turn my head to the side and give him a quick nod. Somehow, a half-snuggle with Raff is absolutely fine by me.

Everything is so lovely. The rainbow-coloured lights on the tree are glowing, and there are enough lit-up garlands around the room to make it twinkle from all angles. Trisha has got LED candles glimmering from every surface and there's a scent warmer melting cranberry-scented wax, and I'm warm and cosy and laughing along with everyone else, and thoroughly enjoying every moment of just sitting here, doing nothing except enjoying a Christmas film. When it finishes, no one even considers getting up, which is just as well because I'm so comfortable that I don't think I could move if I tried. Raff's arm is still across my lap, giving my splinted arm some-thing to rest against, still reaching over to steal handfuls of popcorn or Maltesers occasionally, and he's got unintentionally closer as the film has gone on, so close that his head is on my shoulder now. I would genuinely be so happy if I didn't have to move again until the new year.

Sofia asks me if I've seen *The Muppet Christmas Carol*, which I haven't, so she puts that on next, and I can't help looking around, loving how relaxed everyone is. No phones are out, no one's doing anything except letting themselves enjoy Christmas and just *be* together. I can't remember the last time I did *anything* like this.

As we get further into the film, Sofia gets suspicious when Raff hasn't stolen any popcorn for a while and she sits forward to peer around me. 'Uncle Raff's gone to sleep.'

I love how it doesn't even occur to her to wake him up, make fun of him, or draw on his face with permanent marker. And there's something so lovely about how at ease he is. I can't imagine ever being relaxed enough around *my* family to fall asleep.

I thought he'd gone quiet, and the arm lying across my lap had got heavy. His head is still on my shoulder and his breathing has turned shallow and I shift until I can see his peaceful face.

'Aww.' I let out a breath, scared of moving even a millimetre in case I wake him. I wish I had use of my right hand, solely so I could reach up and tuck his brown hair back where it's fallen over his forehead, and I only realise I said the 'aww' out loud when I notice everyone's staring at me.

'He's tired,' I whisper by way of explanation. 'He's been doing his own job *and* mine to get ready for the Christmas market and try to beat the council at their own game with this competition between us.'

'The position you're in *is* his fault,' Erin says.

'We were both at fault that day. The fingers were an unfortunate accident and he's trying to make up for it by being a gentleman. Obviously raised well.' I deliberately look between Trisha and Biddy, whispering so as not to wake him.

'Aww, we already love you, Franca.' Trisha smiles at me and whispers back. 'You don't have to butter us up even more.'

My cheeks go instantly red. They love me? Really? It's kind of her to say but they don't even know me. It thaws something inside me when she uses that word so freely, especially when love from my own family has always felt so conditional.

Silence falls for the rest of the Muppets film. Sofia turns the volume of the TV down so it doesn't disturb Raff, and when it's over, everyone makes a very quiet move to leave, and he still doesn't stir.

Sofia looks like she wants to hug me goodbye but we just wave instead, and she whispers that she can't wait for the Christmas market tomorrow, and hands me the remote so I can choose what to watch next because I have no intention of moving an inch for a while yet.

Trisha walks with Biddy to her part of the house and comes back after she's helped her get ready for bed. 'He won't mind being woken up if you want to go home, lovely.'

'No,' I whisper. 'We've pushed his trolley up and down that hill to the castle about thirty-thousand times today. He's doing everything he can for me. He deserves to close his eyes without being disturbed for a while.'

'Well, there's an abundance of Christmas films on that box, so watch anything you fancy, and help yourself to anything you want.' She points towards the kitchen, despite the fact I couldn't move without waking Raff.

She looks down at her sleeping son with a soft look on her face. 'I've never seen him so comfortable with anyone. You're a special girl, Franca.'

The words make me feel warm all over as Trisha gets a blanket from the back of the sofa, opens it out, and very gently settles it over us both, and then stands back and bites her lip as she looks down at us. 'He needs you, you know. He's one of the good ones but he needs someone to take care of him for a change. Goodnight, both.' She gives me a wave as she disappears towards her bedroom.

My eyes slide to the side and I fight the urge to stroke through the mass of chocolate-brown hair resting on my shoulder. Different shades catch the Christmas lights, and as much as I want to run my fingers through it, I really don't want to wake him. He's been working *so* hard for my benefit, as well as doing his own job, the least he deserves is to be allowed to sleep when he clearly needs to.

I point the remote at the TV, turn the volume down further, and look through the selection of Christmas movies, choosing one that sounds good and settling in for another watch, and somehow, I can't think of any better way to spend a Friday night.

The film has nearly finished by the time Raff wakes up with a start. 'Where am I?'

'You're fine. On your mum's sofa. Asleep. On my shoulder.'

He blinks for a few moments, then lets out a contented sigh and the arm that's still lying across my lap tightens as he stretches and then snuggles closer. 'A position that has no right to be as comfortable as it is.'

I stroke his arm, letting my fingers trail up and down it underneath the blanket that's covering us, and I can feel him getting his bearings, the way he looks around and realises everyone else has gone, squints at the blanket, trying to work out where it's come from as he wasn't covered last time he was awake, and I pretend to still be focusing on the movie, but all I can really think about is the gorgeous man beside me.

'Why didn't you wake me?' he murmurs eventually, his deep voice even deeper than usual and thick with sleep.

Because you're the most adorable sleeping man I've ever seen. Thankfully I stop myself from saying that out loud. 'Because you're exhausted. You're spending all your days making nutcrackers for me, even more of your days dealing with your own business, and I'm pretty sure you're spending most of your nights making snow globes too. There aren't that many hours *in* a day. I wanted you to have a moment's rest. And I found this great rom-com movie about a woman who's accidentally bought a Christmas tree farm and is falling in love with her grumpy neighbour, and I was quite happy to watch it. You can go back to sleep if you want.'

I reach over with my left hand and tuck his hair back and his eyes drift closed again and he rests his head back on my shoulder. I keep doing it and he makes a little noise of contentment and snuggles in closer, and I can feel the heaviness of his body against mine as he drifts off again.

I turn until I can rub my chin against his hair and press the tiniest kiss to his forehead, but when I let my hand drop, he wakes back up and turns his face further into my shoulder with a long groan. 'Why does nothing feel as good as sleep does when you've got to get up?'

The urge to slip my arms around him and hold him tight is unreal. I'm surprised and kind of honoured that this man, who I considered my arch-nemesis until three weeks ago, is so open and unguarded around me that he'd let himself fall asleep on my shoulder.

'You don't have to get up yet.' I reach over and stroke through his hair again, and he makes that noise of contentment and snuggles in closer again, but only a couple of minutes pass before he forces himself to move.

'Yes, I do, because it's...' He rolls his head off my shoulder and squints up at the clock on the wall. 'It's quarter to twelve and I've gotta drive you home. I've already kept you up past your bedtime when we have the market tomorrow. You need your beauty rest.'

I snort. 'It'll take more than a bit of rest to sort me out.'

'Hey, you're gorgeous.' His hand slides up the left side of my face and turns me towards him, his thumb brushing along my jaw, and my breath catches at the intensity in his eyes and the sudden certainty that he's going to kiss me.

He tilts my head towards him and his lowers towards me, and I close my eyes and my fingers curl into his T-shirt in anticipation because I'm suddenly absolutely *desperate* for his lips to touch mine, and then... he yanks his hand away and pushes himself upright. 'Sorry, ignore me, I think I'm still in dreamland.'

I try not to let myself feel a sting of disappointment. It's been a long while since I wanted anything as badly as I wanted that kiss, but I can't kiss Raff, for goodness' sake. Three weeks ago, this man was my enemy. I shouldn't be getting *this* close to him, let alone stroking his hair and cuddling him, and certainly not wanting to kiss him that much. What am I thinking? What are either of us thinking?

He vaults to his feet and brushes himself down like he's trying to brush off the lingering madness that made kissing me even cross his mind, and paces for a few moments, and everything feels weird and awkward between us, and I decide to do something to break the tension.

I get to my feet and do an impression of Sofia's young voice. 'Best Friday night ever!'

It was just to show that whatever moment of lunacy that was, it's all forgotten and we can carry on as we were, and he laughs and then watches me seriously for a minute, his head tilted to one side. 'Same, because of you. Thank you for coming.'

'Thanks for having me. I've never done Christmassy things like this. I've never known what it's like to have a big family at Christmas. I love how close you are to them. The perfect family.'

'I don't think any family is perfect, but they're *yours*, aren't they? Every family is individual and there's no right or wrong, they just *are*.'

'A nice sentiment.' Really, it makes me want to say 'awwww' again because he's right, isn't he? No matter what your family are like, you only have the one – whether by birth or the one that finds you along the way.

Raff goes around the room to turn all the Christmas lights off, and I stand in front of the huge Christmas tree and look up at it. It's been years since I even bothered to get a Christmas tree and now I wonder why I've stopped making the effort. Is there anything cosier than curling up on a December night with the main light off and just the fairy lights on? Why have I forgotten everything that once made Christmas my favourite time of year?

'Maybe it really is going to grow at midnight on Christmas Eve...' Raff comes to stand at my back, loops both his arms around me from behind, and tugs me against his chest, squeezing me to him.

The rest of the room is dark now, the Christmas tree is the only thing still shining and it makes this hug feel extra magical, and everything I thought just now about not getting close to him goes out of the metaphorical window because nothing is more important than the way his arms feel when they're around me.

'It's a distinct possibility.' I appreciate the way he references *The Nutcracker* at every opportunity. 'And then your home will be invaded by hundreds of vengeful mice which you will have to slay leading your army of toy soldiers and be rescued by a young ballet dancer with a slipper.'

'I might've helped save you from a mouse, but *this* young ballet dancer has helped me more than she knows.'

It's been a while since I was young *or* a ballet dancer, but his words make me melt and my hand slides over his forearm and gives it a squeeze.

'I'd love you to spend Christmas with us.' His chin rubs against my head as he speaks. 'We've spent so much time together this month and the thought of *not* seeing you on Christmas Day isn't a good one. I don't want you to be alone, and I can't imagine spending Christmas without you. Sorry if that sounds weird or forward or pushy or anything else, but... stay with me on Christmas Eve. Erin, Quentin and Sofe all stay here and we do the whole "reindeer hoofprints in the garden and snowy footprints from the hearth to the Christmas tree" thing for Sofia. I don't know how much longer she'll believe in Santa, but Uncle Raff is not going to let that belief die without a fight.'

'I don't remember ever believing in Santa.' I glance up at him. 'I remember hearing my parents have a fight about who got to put the presents under the tree when I was really young.'

'Well, it's never too old to start.'

'Believing in Santa?' I laugh. 'I appreciate the sentiment, but at thirty-eight, I might be a *tad* too old for that.'

'No one is ever too old to believe in magic.'

That 'awww' comes again and I feel his smile against my hair. 'The Christmas tree used to be so wonderful. Endless possibilities of what could be in all those colourfully wrapped boxes waiting to be torn into on Christmas morning. It's not fun when you're an adult. Now it's just the same old toiletry sets that you don't use and chocolate that you don't like.'

'There's chocolate that you *don't* like? I didn't think anyone actively disliked *any* chocolate.'

'If I never see another bar of Toblerone, it will be too soon.'

He laughs again, and when he stops, I answer his earlier question. 'Okay.'

It's the thought of going back to my empty house and thinking of the warmth and kindness of the Dardennes... I already know I'm going to spend Christmas wishing I was here with them, and what I thought I'd never agree to a few days ago, now I can't imagine saying anything *but* yes to.

'Yay!' He presses a kiss to my cheek from behind and then

groans. 'Can you pretend that you didn't just hear a fully grown adult man utter the word "yay"?'

I laugh and tilt my head back until my lips find his jaw and brush against it. 'Trust me, I will *never* forget, but you have my assurance that I will never tell anyone about this oversight in your manhood.'

He laughs but it quickly fades into comfortable silence. He seems lost in thought, and I get the feeling he simply needs a hug, and I let my head rest against his chest and feel his weight leaning on me.

I rub his arms with my left hand and my eyes fall on a snow globe ornament hanging on the tree with a photo of Biddy and Claude inside it and sculpted wording that reads 'Fiftieth Christmas'. I know Raff's handiwork well enough to know who made it.

I let my fingers curl around his and lift his hand until I can touch my lips to the back of it. 'He would be so proud of you.'

We're so close that I feel his sharp intake of breath, but I carry on, knowing he knows who I mean without having to say it. 'You make the most beautiful snow globes. No one could ask for a better way to be remembered than to have passed that talent on to the future generation, and *you* will pass that on to Sofia, or Erin's new arrival, or your own kids one day. Your grandfather will never be forgotten. Not by your family, and not by any of the thousands of people who own a Dardenne snow globe. His work is in people's houses, wrapped away in boxes to be got out every year, shaken up by parents and children who look into the glass and believe in magic. That's such a special thing.'

He lets out a breath against my hair and I feel his weight get heavier where he's leaning on me, and he's quiet for such a long while that I'm not sure he's going to answer at all.

'His legacy was the couples he matched,' he whispers eventually. 'That's what he wanted me to continue. The gift he gave to people was in helping them find each other. People were happy because of him. People *exist* because of him. Literally you, Fran. If he hadn't introduced your parents, *you* would not be here. He always said that after he met Biddy, he could see a spark between people that he'd never been able to see before, but who would've listened to a doddery old man claiming he could find your soulmate? He would have been a joke, but the legend he created gave him a chance to do that.'

'But it's not real, Raff.' I stop short of telling him that I *know* the truth behind the 'magic'. 'Whether he could see a spark between people or not, it isn't authentic, and the one thing you are *is* authentic. Your love of what you do comes across in what *you* do, and you're obviously struggling to do what he did. The best way you can honour him is by being yourself. *You* are his legacy. There's nothing more magical than that.'

'I'm going to have to pretend I didn't hear that, because falling asleep on you is embarrassing enough for one night, I don't need to start bawling on you too.' He lets out a shuddery breath. 'God, I don't know what you're doing to me, but I've never felt like this before. I feel absolutely laid bare tonight. You could ask me anything and I'd answer you honestly.' He hesitates and then says pointedly, '*Anything*, Fran.'

An open invitation.

He's openly saying he'll tell me the truth behind the snow globes if I ask him. It doesn't seem relevant that I already know. The only thing that matters is how open he is. He *is* laid bare, I can feel it. His walls were down where he hadn't quite woken up yet, and talking about his grandfather has struck a nerve. He's hanging onto his emotions by a thread, and the absolute *last* thing I want to do is take advantage of that.

Even if I didn't know, I wouldn't have asked him in this moment. 'Anything? Anything at all?'

'I'm yours. Metaphorically speaking.'

'Okay. I have a very serious question that I want a very serious answer to... Why did it take three broken fingers for me to see how wonderful you are, Raphael Dardenne?'

His laugh sounds emotional and surprised. I know he was expecting to be quizzed, but all I can think of is what Biddy said about him needing someone he doesn't have to keep up pretences with and all I want him to know tonight is that his feelings are safe with me, and so are his secrets.

'Isn't that a song?' He starts humming 'How Wonderful You Are' by Gordon Haskell and pulls away so he can twirl me around and pull me back to him. I slip my left hand onto his shoulder and he touches my right elbow and leads us in a waltz for a few moments before twirling me around again.

'Do you ever miss dancing?'

'Sometimes. I miss the feeling. With the right people around me, it felt like flying when I was up on that stage, but it's so hard to get to that level, it takes so much discipline that, looking back, I don't know how I ever did it, and I never would again. I've gone feral now.'

He laughs at the analogy, and his hands slip down to my waist, and I lift up onto the balls of my feet and twirl around, letting his strength support me. It's impossible to feel elegant with one hand that still feels swollen and angry encased in a splint. I haven't danced in years, but with his hands on my waist, it's easy to go back *en demi-pointe* and pirouette, and for one blissful moment, I feel like a dancing snowflake again. I feel like the person I used to be. I would never want to go back but it's a nice reminder of someone I've forgotten.

When I drop back onto my heels, he carefully lifts my elbow onto his shoulder so my injured hand is out of harm's way, bends until he can slide both arms around my waist and lift me off the floor, holding me tight to him as he spins us both around, and when he sets me down, he does nothing but hold me against his chest, one hand stroking through my hair, the other spread wide on my back, alternating between rubbing his chin against the top of my head and pressing tiny kisses there, and each one makes me melt a little bit more. Never mind not wanting him to be evicted from his shop in January, I never want to step outside of his arms again, ever.

16

The Ever After Street castle is a winter wonderland. When Raff and I walk along the walled stone walkway in daylight the next morning, *Christmas* is shining out at us, inviting us into the grounds like a physical being. The castle itself is open to show the event space and hopefully gain a few more bookings for the owners, Witt and Sadie, but the outside has been given over to the Christmas market.

They've created a circular walk through the grounds, starting at the entrance and winding through the gorgeous gardens, looping around fancy topiary hedges that have been trimmed into festive shapes, passing every stall on the way, and ending up back where you came in.

Raff and I got lucky that our stalls are just to the left of the entranceway. After the festive food and hot mulled wine station, we're the first sellers that customers will reach when they enter, and the gorgeous old stonework of the castle is right behind us, silhouetting our cabins and shielding us from the worst of the December chill.

The market stalls are open-fronted wooden cabins, and

Mitch has very kindly decorated mine for me. Each stall has a matching pre-lit garland stapled in a triangle along the eaves of their cabin, and under it is a ribbon-shaped wooden sign displaying our shop name, and each one has a chair and a counter, and is lit up inside with enough fairy lights to brighten even the darkest day.

There are mini Christmas trees lining the walkway, interspersed with old-fashioned lanterns with wreaths and red ribbons tied around them, and shooting star lights where their tails form an arch fill the space above us, and somewhere further along, there's a Carollers' Cabin because, even at just after nine on Saturday morning, there are the voices of a children's choir singing 'O Holy Night'.

Last year, the Christmas market was occupied only by the traders of Christmas Ever After, so the usual suspects are all here. Mrs Bloom has got a Coming Gnome For Christmas cabin, Thelma has got a variety of mugs displayed all around her A Very Muggy Christmas cabin, and Mrs Coombe at the All You Need Is Gloves stall has got her festive jumpers with matching doggy jumpers displayed on soft toy dogs. Jorge has been relegated to further around the walkway with his freshly baked gingerbread and mince pies, and Imogen is here with her Once Upon A Dream bath bombs and soaps, but this year, it's been thrown open to other local crafters as well. There's an artisanal cheese cabin, gourmet chocolates, a homemade toffee and fudge shop, many handmade decoration stalls selling everything from fused glass keepsakes to hand-painted baubles, along with a candle cabin, and someone who makes little wooden Christmas toys, and there's a Santa's grotto where Mitch and a couple of other gents are alternating shifts of playing Santa, and right near the end, Mandy is offering her gift-wrapping services. I want to go over and ask her how the escape room date with Cedric went last night, but she's concentrating fiercely on whatever she's wrapping and doesn't look like she wants to be disturbed.

I look up at Raff walking beside me. He's wearing dark jeans and a Dardenne Snow Globes branded T-shirt with a red and black flannel shirt over the top of it, the buttons done up so they hide most of the logo. It would have been so easy to kiss him last night, but nothing went any further. It was 1 a.m. when he drove me home and although I lingered in the car for a while, I stopped short of inviting him in, which is probably a good thing. It takes a lot for me to want to get involved with someone because I know firsthand how bad relationships can get, and I'm already fearing how tangled up I've got with Raff. Him helping me out was supposed to be temporary, but when Christmas is over and my hand is healed, I can't imagine him not being in my life in one way or... another.

He stops at the festive coffee booth and gets us a winter spiced latte each, and we mooch along to our own stalls.

One thing I've always loved is shelves full of nutcrackers, so many nutcrackers that people look around in awe, overwhelmed by the sheer number of them. The giant ones are standing like sentries on either side of the cabin, and the shelves inside are crammed with my wooden soldiers. There's a booth to sit at, and behind it are the boxes of carefully packed custom nutcrackers, labelled with order details, ready to be matched to receipts when customers arrive to collect.

Raff's stall is right next to mine – a pitch engineered by Mitch or Mrs Bloom, I'm certain. There are no matches being made at the Love Is All A-Round stall this weekend – it's all about the snow globes themselves at the Christmas market, and Raff seems much happier about it.

Cleo and Bram have got a Wonderland Teapot refreshment

area, and it's late morning when she bounces up, bringing me a cup of her glittery Wonderland tea. 'Got a minute?'

'Oh, I can't, I—'

'Go!' Raff interrupts before I can finish. 'I've got it covered here. Take as long as you like.'

He pulls his stool out and positions it in the gap between our cabins, showing me he can handle both for a few minutes, and it *would* be nice to stretch my legs...

I've got quite close to Cleo since she took over The Wonderland Teapot earlier this year. She's become a friend rather than just a colleague. We spend too much time sending each other funny memes on social media when we should be working, and I've helped her out at the tearoom a few times when she and Bram have been overwhelmed and The Nutcracker Shop has been quiet.

As we wander away, Cleo looks over her shoulder at the market stalls behind us. 'I've never had an arch-nemesis, but I don't think that's *quite* the way you're supposed to look at someone you hate.'

'Things might have changed a little...' I blush at the thought of how many people have noticed the way things are going between me and Raff. Cleo and Mrs Bloom have noticed, and they aren't the only ones.

'Yes, a few of us have been wondering what happened to the "fraudster who's a scourge on our street".'

'I'm not sure I ever called him a scourge,' I say with a huff, although to be fair, I've called Raff a few things over the years and 'scourge' probably was one of them. 'Maybe the snow globe con isn't what I thought it was. It's more Raff going along with something his grandfather started even though his heart isn't in it. I think things will be different now. He's going to change his approach and go in a different direction with Love Is All A-Round. We just have to make sure the council will keep *both* our shops.'

'What if they don't?'

It's a hard question to hear because it's a possibility that I don't want to think about. What *if* they don't? What if everything we've done isn't enough, and at that meeting tomorrow, they only choose one of us?

'I'm backing you all the way,' she continues. 'He hasn't made his five matches, and you've got a tonne of engagement online now. I went to comment on one of your posts the other day and *two* other people had commented before me.'

Two whole people. Wow. The council will be overawed with that. It makes my mind wander to the possibility of tomorrow again, and what will happen if they do only choose one of us, and how I'll feel if it's me – or if it isn't.

'Thanks,' I mumble distractedly. I have so many ideas to move forward with The Nutcracker Shop, and the thought of losing it is unthinkable, but so is the thought of continuing here at the expense of Raff not getting a chance to take Love Is All A-Round in *his* different direction.

'Never mind social media engagement, you've certainly got the shopkeepers and customers' tongues wagging on Ever After Street. Everyone is talking about you because of the video.'

Every mention of the video makes me cringe inside. Last time Mrs Bloom told me, the views had gone well over the 120,000 mark, so it's the sort of thing customers and co-workers *would* be talking about, I suppose...

'There's a Team Nutcracker versus a Team Snow Globe in the YouTube comments. People are placing bets and everything.'

'Oh come on, seriously?' I say in frustration. You can't avoid hearing whispers of gossip working in such a small community, but the thought of *us* being the subject of it makes me almost as uncomfortable as the thought of *so* many people watching me flail about on that arch.

As she says goodbye, it leaves my mind whirring, and not in a good way.

When I get back to my stall, Raff has sold another three nutcrackers and two snow globes in my absence, and one customer has collected their order, but I'm too hung up on what Cleo's just said. 'Have you heard any gossip about us?'

'I'm not a gossipy type, Fran.' He raises an eyebrow. 'Why? Should I have?'

'I don't know. Cleo said people are talking.'

'Well, you know what people think when two members of the opposite gender start spending time together. People can't comprehend that a man and a woman can be just frie—' He cuts the sentence off halfway through the word 'friends' and it makes my heart flutter as I go from disappointment that he only sees us as friends to certainty that he's been feeling something decidedly more-than-friends for me too.

He stutters for a replacement word for a moment and then shakes his head. 'Well, whatever we are, three weeks ago, we weren't on speaking terms and now we've actually spoken, so... on a small, close-knit street like this, people are going to talk, I guess?'

'Yeah, I guess,' I echo with a jovial shrug but Cleo's words stay with me as I take my seat back inside my own cabin. Navigating what's happening with Raff is hard enough without other people having a vested interest in us too.

* * *

If last year's Christmas market was busy, this year's first day is *madness*. Last year was the first time since Witt came back to Ever After Street and offered use of the castle as an event space, and the shopkeepers of Christmas Ever After put their heads together and came up with the idea of a festive market. We'd never done it before and thought maybe a few locals might turn up, but the Ever After Street social media is popular, and it was picked up by various 'best Christmas markets to visit in the UK' articles; a journalist turned up and wrote a whole front page about it, splashed with photos of the castle decorated for Christmas, but most of that publicity only came about while it was happening or afterwards – too late for most visitors. Over the course of the year, I've heard a lot of people say they were definitely going to come this year, but it's still surprising to see just how many that's translated into. People have been flooding in all day.

It's the fun part of Christmas now. The majority of people have probably broken up from work or school this week, and it's close enough to Christmas that most of the shopping is done, most of the presents are wrapped, and people only have one or two things left on their to-do lists, and now it's time to relax and embrace the season.

The Carollers' Cabin is set back in the grounds, so the sound of children's choirs filter through the whole area, making it feel like we're in an all-day carol concert, even though the schools change every hour. Erin brings Sofia by when it's her turn and Mitch minds both our stalls while Raff and I sneak off to watch her class perform 'The First Noel' and 'O Christmas Tree'.

We take turns in going for lunch, which ends up being freshly baked bread and a cheese board selection from the artisan cheesemaker, and the owners of the pop-up hot chocolate bar have 'popped up' at the market as well, and throughout the day, Raff keeps nipping off and returning with first a Maltesers hot chocolate, then a Ferrero Rocher hot chocolate, and finally an After Eight mint hot chocolate.

'Christmas is the time for overindulging,' Raff whispers when I side-eye the leaning tower of cream with crushed mint chocolate sprinkled over the top. 'You can count calories in January.'

'Cheers to that.' I clink my paper cup against his, and he gives me a smile that warms me up more than the hot chocolate itself.

The market stays open until 11 p.m. on both weekend nights, and it's nearly 10 p.m. when Mitch comes over again in full Santa regalia. He stands in the space between our stalls and beckons us both to come nearer, and then glances around to ensure there aren't any customers around to overhear what he's about to say.

'Bit of a problem on the Cedric and Mandy front. They didn't exactly hit it off. Got stuck in the escape room for hours and had to be rescued by a member of staff – probably just in time before one of them murdered the other one. But not to worry, I've bribed them both to come along tomorrow and fake it. I mean, they *were* matched by you, weren't they? There's no reason the stuffy sods at the council need to know that it didn't work out.'

Raff goes to protest but Mitch doesn't let him. Instead, he stands back and looks over both our almost-empty stalls. 'You two have done well.'

'Prime positioning.' Raff gives him a wink. 'Which I think you, sir, are responsible for.'

Mitch denies it but his blush gives him away. 'It was only for selfish reasons. You two are my most famous residents. The council can't possibly let either of you go after this. Do you know how many people have seen the video now? One hundred and thirty thousand, that's how many! Isn't it marvellous?'

Marvellous is not *quite* the word I'd use. In fact, it makes me feel quite ill. Sicker than the three hot chocolates combined have made me feel today.

'Everyone's talking about it. I'm surprised you haven't been asked for your autographs!'

'Fran's right-handed, it'd be a little difficult.'

At the nickname, Mitch's ears prick up like a dog that's just heard the word 'walkies' and he looks just as excitable. 'It's a beautiful night. Why don't you two go off for a little wander before closing time? I'll mind your cabins.'

I go to refuse, but Raff stretches with the groan of someone who's been sitting for too long, and I glance towards the walled walkway leading to the castle. Things are quiet now. It doesn't look like an influx of nutcracker buyers are suddenly going to swarm the gates at this time of night, and it would be nice to move around a bit.

Raff holds his hand out and squeezes my fingers when I let him pull me to my feet. 'Thanks, Mitch, we won't be long. I doubt there's much left to buy now.'

It's not about buying, seeing as most of the sellers are people we work with every day, but I haven't spent much time alone with Raff today, and I haven't left my stall since it was daylight and can only imagine how magical the castle gardens are looking in the dark.

'Do you want a mulled wine?' Raff nods to the stall that's been on the other side of him all day, dishing out hot mulled wine into paper cups, the fruity scent pervading the air all around us. 'It's all I've been able to smell all day and I think I'm already a bit giddy just from the fumes.'

I nod and he goes to get us one each, and when he comes back, he hands me a steaming paper cup with a cinnamon stick poking out of it and an orange slice floating on top, and we start meandering along the route of the market stalls.

It's late and the children's choirs have been replaced by a live band playing instrumental Christmas music now and most of the visitors still around are couples wandering hand in hand.

We walk past Jorge's bakery stall where he's still serving gingerbread and mince pies. I've seen him in passing since 'the incident', but he's never bothered to ask if I'm okay, and I would never purchase another baked good from him if he was the last baked good vendor on earth. I don't intend to acknowledge him as we walk past, but the sound of oinking reaches my ears.

'Want me to go and deck him?'

I laugh, because if I said yes, I think Raff actually would. 'No, thank you, oh manly protector. Just when you think chivalry is dead, a gentleman offers to punch someone's lights out to defend your honour.' I bump my shoulder into his arm. 'But thank you for offering.'

The atmosphere makes it feel like there's magic sparkling in the air tonight. I've been immune to the atmosphere on Christmas Ever After in recent years. I've forgotten *everything* that I used to love about Christmas, and this sparkly festive feeling is what working in The Nutcracker Shop used to feel like. Every day was tingling with the possibility of magic happening, and for the first time in years, I've been feeling that again lately, and it's mostly because of Raff, with his kind, silly soul, his daft sense of humour, and his love of Christmas that's reminded me of how much I love Christmas. Although maybe magic is the wrong thing to be feeling off the back of our match between Mitch's son Cedric and Mandy being such a dismal failure.

It makes me think of Claude Dardenne and his match of my parents. I've always thought he didn't care who he was setting up as long as they put their money in the till, but what if Raff's right in everything he's said? Maybe his grandfather really did care, and my parents were just one of the cases where he got it wrong, like I have with Cedric and Mandy. Was I wrong to think I saw something between them? Was I wrong to have tried? Is it entirely my fault that they had a horrible night or do mistakes just happen sometimes? Sometimes 'perfect on paper' is not always a good match in reality and it's not necessarily anyone's fault if a relationship doesn't work out...

'What are you thinking about?'

I decide to be honest, even though I doubt he wanted the literal answer. 'Your grandfather. My parents. You. Tomorrow.'

'Don't worry about it. Whatever is going to happen is going to happen.'

'*We're* going to make them listen to us. We've both succeeded. I have plenty of social media engagement now, and we've matched three couples – that's enough. They won't need any more proof than that.' I nod definitively, trying to make myself believe it too. I appreciate his laidback attitude, but the closer it ticks to tomorrow, the harder it is not to worry.

Stars are twinkling in a clear sky, competing with the Christmas lights around us. It's freezing but the hot mulled wine is warming me up as we walk. Raff's led us further into the castle gardens, away from the market and off the path visitors are supposed to stay on. There are topiary snowflake shapes illuminated by lights spread throughout the hedges and water features with a spotlight shining on them so it looks like the burbling water is glowing red and green. The paths wind past glass gazebos lit with fairy lights, low brick walls and neatly maintained small garden areas, and every inch is sparkling with festive lights.

The mulled wine is finished in companionable silence, and Raff finds a bin to chuck our empty cups in, and when he returns, instead of offering me his arm, he holds his hand out and I slip my fingers into his and our hands swing between us as we walk.

It's a crisp and chilly night, and the band's Christmas music is faint from so far away. Our pace is gentle, although my head is whirring at ninety miles per hour about everything Raff's just told me not to worry about.

'Why haven't you told anyone?'

The question comes out of the blue, and I glance up at him, confused by the seemingly random query. 'About what?'

'A couple of days after you looked after my shop. I emptied the bins and heard the broken glass jangling. Thought I'd better check which one had been broken. When I said you looked like you'd been burying a body, it was the body of a snow globe, along with the broken innards. I know you know.'

I chew on my lip, my stomach suddenly twisting around on itself. 'Oh.'

'Oh,' he repeats.

'Why are *you* only just saying something? Why did you basically offer to tell me last night if you already knew I knew?'

'I don't know. I thought it might sound better if I explained. And I didn't say anything before because I wanted to see what you were going to do with the information.' His voice sounds... hopeful, like he knows full well that I haven't told anyone because my feelings for him are very different than they were three weeks ago. 'I didn't know if...'

'You didn't know if I was going to announce it very loudly and very publicly?' I say, and then answer my own question. 'That's exactly why I didn't tell you. I didn't want you to think I was going to tell anyone. You and your grandfather have created something special. A legend that blankets Ever After Street. There's magic in your snow globes. Not the kind that magically matches random people, but the kind that can make something so beautiful feel so special. Looking into one is an experience. I've never felt the way I feel when looking into one of your snow globes. It's like escaping from the world for a moment.' I decide to be blisteringly honest. Too honest, probably. 'And I like you, Raff. You've single-handedly saved my business this December. No matter the cause of the accident, neither of us were at our best that day, and you didn't *have* to do everything you've done, but you have because you're the sweetest soul, and you don't deserve to have your reputation ruined because of me being petty. And your family don't deserve to have the myth ruined either. Sofia genuinely thinks you've got a workshop full of magic, and I couldn't bear to be the one to relieve her of that belief. I'm not going to tell anyone, ever. Your secret stays safe with me.'

'I... didn't expect that.' He sounds surprisingly emotional.

I pull his arm closer to me, turning to press my cheek against it. 'I can't work out how no one's ever known before. Surely someone has broken one by accident over the years and figured it out like I did?'

'They have, but I've persuaded them to keep quiet. People want to believe in magic. It's like being an adult who knows Santa doesn't exist, but no one is cruel enough to tell a child that because no one wants to ruin the magic. People are generally good and don't want to spoil nice things for others.'

I love how Raff sees the good in everything and everyone. I've always been cynical and jaded, but he has a sense of childlike joy that makes me look at things in a different way.

'It did start off organically,' he says as we continue walking through the grounds. 'Granddad was never intending to match-make, but he saw these two people in the shop and just *knew* they'd be good together. He told them both to pick up the same snow globe just to engineer a conversation opener, and inside it was a scene of a train running through a forestry, and they both swore they saw the train move along the tracks. I believe that one really was a trick of the light – the shape of the glass made the trees look curved instead of straight, and moving it from one angle to another made the train look like it had moved – but he was right about the match. They got together and they told their friends and other people came looking for the magical moving snow globes and he tried, but he could never recreate the same effect. But people were talking about this magical snow globe and he saw an opportunity to combine two things he loved – his craft, and finding people who he thought belonged together. It was the seventies, and until then, his business had been failing. He was lucky if he sold a handful of snow globes a month, before a national newspaper ran the story of the couple and their magical meeting, and suddenly he had visitors travelling from miles away, wanting his help to find love, and ultimately, he had to give people what they wanted. He *had* to find a way to recreate it. His lifelong dream had been that snow globes would be his full-time job one day, and for the first time ever, they were paying the bills. Who wouldn't have taken an opportunity like that? He came up with the concept in the early years, and I refined it as technology modernised, and between us, we perfected it over the decades, and then he died, and you know the rest. But you've made me want to change things. You've made me realise how much the gimmick has changed my attitude to work, how much I now dread something I loved, and if Love Is All A-Round stays, it's going to be different.'

'Good. Not because of the love nonsense but because of how unhappy you are. You don't need to tell anyone the truth about the snow globes. His legacy and yours can co-exist. You can change direction while still honouring what he did. You want to make more custom-order snow globes, so shift your focus towards that. They don't even have to be festive then. You could do ones with more year-round appeal. Weddings, honeymoons, special places, beloved pets. Things that matter to people.'

'You could do the same with nutcrackers. I know arguably the point of Christmas Ever After is the year-round Christmas thing, but it wouldn't hurt to have seasonal displays and a little spring-summer section as well, would it? Two nutcrackers having a picnic on the beach... A nutcracker bride and groom getting married under a wooden floral arch...'

'That's a great idea for a spring window display. I've never done that before. I've never really created scenes with them, just displayed them in a "the more, the merrier" fashion, but that would be fantastic. If I clear out the front window... I could put a mat of artificial grass in there, or a pile of sand, or autumn leaves. We could have nutcrackers frolicking in patches of daisies or between gorse bushes, or gathering around a cauldron for Halloween...'

'Post every window display on social media,' he adds. 'Ask people what they think. And you can woodturn other things too, right? Tulips, daffodils, Easter eggs, autumn pumpkins... My snowmen have proved there's demand for things other than nutcrackers. Mrs Bloom does seasonal gnomes, I don't know why the rest of us haven't followed her lead before.'

'How about Mitch in his Santa grotto? A Hawaiian shirt and flip-flops during the summer holidays, his reindeer in leis with Hibiscus flowers tucked behind their antlers. Grass skirts. Mrs Claus hula-hooping.'

It makes Raff laugh. 'Oh God. That's a mental image I can't unsee. I think we've gone too far when we're thinking of Mrs Claus hula-hooping.'

He swipes away tears of laughter but the harder he tries to stop laughing, the more he laughs, and seeing him so giggly makes me laugh too.

'Not sure you were joking about being drunk on mulled wine fumes.'

'It's you, you make me forget everything and feel like I've just downed six mulled wines. When I'm with you, I get giddy and unafraid to hide my painfully uncool side, and I'm so excited for what's to come. It's been so long since I felt motivated or positive about the business and now I can't wait to get back into the work-shop, I can't wait for next year, and it's all because of you and your nutcrackers.'

'Me too.' I bite my lip as I look at him. He's right and I feel it too. I'd lost my love for everything Christmas until he came along and reignited it, and sparked off motivation in me, pushed me to think outside the box and look forward to what's next too.

'Thank you for inspiring me, Fran.'

'Thank *you* for inspiring *me*, and for everything you—' I squeak as he interrupts me with a kiss.

It's both completely unexpected and not unexpected at all, because I've been getting increasingly desperate to kiss Raff and a sudden flurry of tingles flood my body at the realisation that he's been feeling the same.

I get lost in the kiss. My left hand curls into the shoulder of his cosy flannel shirt, clinging onto him to stay upright when the force of it makes me wobble on unsteady legs, and it takes a long few moments for the world to come back into focus with the throbbing pain of my hand being trapped between our bodies, and I make a noise of discomfort and pull away.

He jumps back and sobers up instantly. 'Oh God, I'm so sorry. I don't... I mean... I... er...' He scrubs a hand over his face. 'Have I hurt you?'

'No, no, it's fine.' I look up at him and he looks truly distraught. 'It's fine, Raff, my hand just got a bit squashed. I've done worse making a sandwich.'

'I'm so sorry. I didn't mean to do that.' He nods to my hand and then lifts a finger to trail across his lips. 'I... don't think I meant to do *that* either.'

'It would be a shame if you did *that* by accident.' I raise an eyebrow, and when he meets my eyes, his worried lips slowly tip up into a smile as he realises I'm not complaining about the kiss.

'In that case' – he leans down until he can touch his lips to the edge of my jaw – 'I'm not going to do it again until I can be a lot more careful of your hand. I've caused you enough injuries for one month.'

He pulls back and takes my good hand again and we carry on

wandering until we spot another glass gazebo set up in the castle grounds. It's strung with fairy lights and has a bench inside it, and branches of artificial wisteria dangle from the roof, creating a screen of purple flowers that you have to push aside to go in.

Raff sits and tugs me to sit down beside him without letting go of my hand. He leans forward, thinking for a moment before he speaks. 'I didn't mean to do that in a moment of madness. I've been wanting to do it for a while now, but I didn't think you'd want me to, so I've stopped myself. The hardest time was last night because I couldn't hide it.'

'Do you know how hard it was to force myself to get out of the car last night and not snog you until daybreak?'

He lets out a burst of laughter. 'Hopefully as hard as it was for me not to follow you out of the car and snog you on your doorstep until your neighbours started complaining about public indecency.'

I giggle because public indecency is absolutely fine by me when it comes to Raff.

Even though he hasn't let go of my left hand, he holds his other hand out, inviting me to touch him with my fragile, broken hand. Inviting me to trust him enough to not make any sharp movements or do anything to make it worse.

The fingers that are broken are always cold where the tips of them aren't covered by the splint, and my hand is shaking as I touch my freezing fingertips to his warm hand with a feather-light touch. The fingers are a constant dull ache, interspersed with sharp daggers of agony whenever I knock my hand or touch something or forget and go to use it, and this is the closest I've let anyone get to them since the nurse in the hospital.

His lower lip is held between his teeth and he's watching my fingers without blinking. It's a position where, if my hand was okay, he'd curl his fingers around mine and give them a squeeze, but he just holds his hand open, letting me trust him at my own pace, his eyes glued to the spot.

My hand is shaking, not with nerves, but at the implication of this gesture. I never thought I'd trust someone enough to let them get *near* my broken hand, let alone the person who inadvertently caused the injury in the first place, and it feels like a little, significant way of letting me know I'm not alone, which I've felt since the moment he walked into my shop with that snow globe.

Raff dips his head until he can press his lips to my broken fingers. I didn't know it was possible for someone to be so gentle. I can *see* his lips graze my skin but I barely feel a touch at all, and my breath hitches, not daring to breathe in case my hand twitches or the slightest movement makes one of us jump or jerk away.

'I can't wait until the day I can hold both of your hands.' He squeezes the fingers of my left hand, his deep voice so low that it's almost making the bench vibrate, and this closeness is making my stomach do somersaults. Showing this level of trust in him means something. Since my ex, I've never trusted anyone. I've kept everyone at arm's length and never accepted help with anything, even if I've needed it, but Raff never gave me an option, and somewhere along the way, I've let him in and let my guard down, and I've fallen fallen fallen. And not just off that arch. I think I've been falling in a metaphorical way since the moment he walked into my shop, scooped me up off the floor, and treated a delinquent mouse like a queen.

There are tears running down my face and I'm sure he can read every thought that's racing behind my eyes. He carefully takes his hand away from mine and reaches over to brush my tears away, his fingers weaving into my hair as he tucks it back, his hand at the side of my jaw, tilting my head so I can't look away from his beautiful brown eyes, and the reflection of the fairy lights above us make it look like he's got a cartoonish twinkle glinting in them.

'You're going to hate me for saying this, but bumping into you was the best thing I ever did.'

An unexpected laugh escapes but it makes my breath catch too and another wave of emotion rises up. 'While I find it hard to agree completely' – I hold up my right hand – 'I like where you're coming from. It's had some... unexpected... side effects.'

He giggles too, and then turns serious again. 'Can I...?' His eyes move downwards to my lips, leaving me in no doubt about what he wants.

I let my eyes slip closed and nod, my head held in his hand, and he oh-so-gently lowers his lips to mine.

It's soft at first, just a press of lips against lips, and I know he's hyperaware of my hand after our first attempt, but I hadn't realised how much I've thought about kissing Raff until tonight, and that innocent little peck is nowhere near enough.

The fingers of my left hand twist in his shirt again, and I desperately wish I could use my right hand to tangle in his hair and claw him closer. One hand isn't enough to get across how much I need him to kiss me harder, but he gets the message anyway.

His tongue presses gently, and when my hand yanks his shirt with such vigour that there's the definite sound of a stitch popping, he laughs into the kiss and it gets more forceful. We're facing each other on the bench, and I hook one of my legs around his to pull him impossibly closer and he lets out an involuntary moan at how good this feels.

He tastes of the mulled wine we've just finished, and the scent of his spicy peppermint aftershave is more intoxicating than any alcoholic beverage would've been, and I lose track of everything outside of his lips and the feeling of his body at every spot we're touching.

He's laughing softly when he pulls back, his breathing shuddery and his cheeks deep red, and I unfurl my hand from his shirt and reach up to tuck his hair back because it looks so dishevelled, you'd think he'd been snogging in the gardens of a castle on a cold December night. I let my finger trail down his face, brush over his cleanshaven jaw, and then I lean forwards until I can press my lips to his glowing cheek, and his eyes close and he leans into me and lets out a sigh that sounds bare and exposed and like a sound that no one's ever heard before.

He leans over for another kiss, which turns into definitely more than one, and then forces himself to pull away and shift on the bench until he can drop an arm around me and tug me into his side and press his lips against my forehead.

It's cold. Kissing has kept the chill at bay, but now it starts to seep back in and I'm shivering, and so is he, but it doesn't matter because nothing seems as important as sitting here together. I feel like there are a billion butterflies whirling around inside me, and I lean my head on his shoulder and look out at the beautiful castle gardens.

Just one more day, one more challenge of saving our shops, and one more month of wearing the splint, and then we can start a new chapter, and this December will be consigned to history as one of my worst Decembers ever, and strangely, quite possibly the best too.

17

I don't know why I'm so nervous. I've spoken to these people hundreds of times. I wasn't nervous when I was merrily telling them about Raff's wrongdoings, but now my knees are shaking when all I have to do is tell them about his rightdoings and how much things have changed since that meeting in November.

I look around my fellow shopkeepers, but there's tension in the air – we can all feel it. Something doesn't feel right today. I've woken up with a prickly feeling all over me. Is it nerves or have I just used the wrong washing powder?

It's 3 p.m. on Sunday afternoon and Mr Hastings and Mrs Willetts, the co-councillors in charge of the Ever After Street area on behalf of Herefordshire Council, are visiting the market in an official capacity. As this is only about Christmas Ever After, the regular Ever After Street shopkeepers are minding our stalls for half an hour while we've snuck off into the castle and are huddled in the entrance hall for the follow-up to the November meeting and the outcome of the nutcrackers-versus-snow-globes challenge.

Mickey who runs the antique curiosity shop The Mermaid's Treasure Trove is minding my stall, and her best friend Lissa, who runs the Colours of the Wind museum, is looking after the Love Is All A-Round stall. Ali and Imogen are here, so are Nina and Joshy, and Mitch has got a hand on his son Cedric's shoulder, while Mandy stands on his other side, facing away with her arms folded. Mitch never said what he bribed them with, but I hope it was good enough to hold up to the council's questioning, because right now, the hatred between them is palpable.

'Hello, hello, what a lovely festive bunch waiting to greet us,' Mrs Willetts says as she and Mr Hastings come in. 'Nothing formal today, just a quick check-in with our favourite festive traders. How are we all? All ready for Christmas?'

Mr Hastings is the grumpier of the two and doesn't bother with any conversational niceties. 'The market looks splendidly busy and the castle is looking quite delightful. I hope you've booked this space again for next year!'

Mitch assures him we have, and there's a bit about post-Christmas sales advertising, but everything's already winding down for the year, and there's not much else to say. They've only called us all together because of me and Raff, and the deadline they imposed to see which one of us would come out on top.

There's an atmosphere in the vast entranceway. Most of our fellow shopkeepers are standing around. Some have taken seats on the stairs, or the aged furniture, or on the floor, but that unseen tension is bubbling under the surface. Everyone looks festive – most of us have got Christmas jumpers on, or some kind of Santa hat or reindeer antler headband, and a lot of earrings are ones that flash like Christmas lights and people have their hair tied up with tinsel scrunchies, but no one seems happy.

'Miss Andrews, Mr Dardenne.' Mr Hastings looks at me and then at Raff. 'There's a small matter of the events at the last meeting to discuss. We've certainly been following your journey with interest since *the* unfortunate incident, and you both have our thanks for enticing *so* many pairs of eyes to look at Christmas Ever After.'

If I wasn't already feeling totally nauseous, the reminder of the viral video would certainly have done the job.

'Would you both like to tell us how the challenge we set you at the last meeting has been progressing?' Mr Hastings gestures with his hand, inviting us both to stand up.

Somehow I'm not near Raff. Lissa arrived to look after his stall, and Mickey got held up on the way to cover mine, so he came in before me and the bosses arrived before I could make my way over, and now he's standing opposite me as I push myself upright from the wall I was leaning against. He catches my eyes and gives me a smile, and I try to smile back but it comes out more like a grimace. The underlying fear is ever-present. It hasn't dissipated since I realised how wrong I was about him, but today is *it*, and the fear has multiplied ten-fold. What if us being more than friends now isn't enough? This whole thing is my fault. If it hadn't been for my misplaced vendetta against Love Is All A-Round, we'd have got to know each other long ago, and neither of us would be in this position, and now I need to fix it for both of us.

'I made a huge mistake at the November meeting.' It comes out squeaky and only audible to dolphins, so I clear my throat and try again. 'I was wrong to make Love Is All A-Round the target of my long-held grudge. I should have given Raff a chance long ago, and I'm sorry for all the upset that I've caused for this street.'

Mitch starts clapping, which gives Cedric a chance to step even further away from Mandy, and he has to quickly stop clapping and clamp a hand back on his shoulder.

Even so, his encouragement helps me to gain confidence and get into the swing of it. This is important. This is my chance to undo the mistake I made. I got it wrong about Raff, and despite that, he's done everything he could for me. Neither of us deserve to lose our shops. It was my actions that set us on this path, and now I have to stop it.

'All the negative things I've said were said without ever knowing the history behind Love Is All A-Round and without ever speaking to Raff Dardenne. As far too many people know, Raff and I had an... unfortunate encounter.' I hold up the splinted hand. 'And ever since then, I've got to know him and I've come to understand where the "love" in Love Is All A-Round comes from, and how important this magical little shop is to our street. It's about so much more than making matches. Snow globes are a step outside of real life, a momentary escape from the world, and trying to imagine Christmas Ever After without Love Is All A-Round is like trying to imagine a Christmas without mince pies, Bing Crosby, or Brussels sprouts.'

Mr Hastings makes a face. Maybe Brussels sprouts were a step too far.

Raff takes over. 'What Franca's trying to say is that we've both done what you asked of us. Franca's social media engagement is through the roof, people are talking about nutcrackers, and no matter how unfortunate that video is, people are talking about *both* of us. The issues raised at the last meeting were about the conflict between us, but she and I have reached an understanding that we hadn't reached before, and found a new appreciation for each other's talents that we didn't have before.'

I blush because after *that* walk around the castle gardens last night, I've found a new appreciation for quite a few things about Raff that I didn't have before, and I try to stop my mind going to inappropriate places in front of so many people.

'Even so, you were both tasked with proving yourselves.' Mr Hastings' stern voice cuts through the glowy feeling that comes with thinking about last night.

'And we've both done that,' I say with a decisive nod. 'The couples Raff has matched are right here.'

Imogen and Ali are sitting next to each other on chairs that Sadie and Witt have hastily gathered. Imogen's hand is curled around Ali's arm, and they both give Mr Hastings and Mrs Willetts a wave. Nina and Joshy are sitting on the floor nearby and they do the same. Mandy gives a begrudging thumbs-up and Mitch squeezes Cedric's shoulder until he does an affirmative grunt of pain.

'Only three?' Mr Hastings and Mrs Willetts share a look.

'It's not about the numbers,' I start. 'You can't force love in any set timeframe, but it goes some way towards proving that Dardenne Snow Globes aren't a con and they can do what they say they can do.'

'By *not* doing what we asked in November?'

I get a sudden blast of fear at Mr Hastings' sceptical look. What if this goes my way? What if three couples *aren't* enough and they choose me and throw Raff out? I'll feel like I've failed him. I didn't think those two extra couples would matter, but now I wish I'd tried harder to look for them.

'As you so rightly pointed out, Mr Dardenne's reviews are proving that customers are less and less likely to believe in the whimsical fairy tale he's selling. *You* suggested this little task in order to—'

'We're number four!'

I look up at the unexpected interruption, surprised to see Mrs Bloom jump to her feet, pull Jorge up by his ear, and then ram her arm through his, holding on so tightly that he might find himself swiftly de-limbed if he tries to escape.

'You?' Mr Hastings would look less surprised if a kangaroo had just hopped in and kicked him in the nether regions.

'Yes. Why not us? Love can be found in unexpected places, you know. Isn't that right, Jorge?'

'Er...'

She elbows him and hisses something in the ear she's still got twisted in her fingers. From lip reading and the way she inclines her head towards me, I translate it as something along the lines of, 'Play along. You owe her that much.'

'Er, yeah. Shop. Globe things,' Jorge grunts, trying fruitlessly to free both his arm and his ear.

'You're old enough to be his *grandmother*!' Mr Hastings says.

Mrs Bloom takes the Santa hat off her head and uses it to wallop him. 'Mother at the most! Don't you insult me like that, good sir!'

Surely Mrs Bloom is the only person in the room who is both brave enough to assault the council leader with a Santa hat *and* expect anyone to believe that she and Jorge are an item. 'Age is just a number. The snow globes can see what we cannot. It was a surprise to all of us.'

Raff catches my gaze with wide eyes, looking like he's torn between laughter, shock and concern for her sanity.

She lets Jorge go and he looks like he wants to run away, but I'm touched by my friend trying to help in her own unique way, even though Mr Hastings and Mrs Willetts share another look that suggests they're wondering if they've accidentally wandered aboard a flying spaceship.

'And number five?' Mrs Willetts looks around the room, but no one else volunteers like Mrs Bloom just took it upon herself to do.

'Who's the fifth couple?' Mrs Willetts repeats at the sound of silence.

'I am.' I didn't realise I was going to say anything until it pops out, but it's unequivocally true, isn't it? Somehow, somewhere along the way of this crazy December, a snow globe brought me and Raff together. I look over and meet his eyes again. 'We are.'

I didn't intend to make it public in quite such an ostentatious way, but it seems fitting somehow, considering the moment our relationship started has been seen by so many people on the internet. 'Three weeks ago, Raff made me a snow globe and when he handed it to me, I saw it move. The nutcracker prince spun the ballerina around, just once.' I rotate a finger to mimic the movement.

He tilts his head to the side questioningly. He didn't know that. I've never told him about what I saw in the snow globe that day.

'So if you're all wondering how we went from enemies to friends to something more, that's how. I saw the magic with my own eyes. I know what it feels like to be matched by a Dardenne snow globe because I *felt* it myself. Somehow, that snow globe *knew* that Raff should be more than an enemy to me long before I did.'

A collective 'awwwww' goes through the room, and when Raff catches my eyes again, the soppy smile on his face makes butterflies take off inside me.

Mrs Willetts smiles too, but Mr Hastings looks typically unimpressed. 'And you, Miss Andrews? We've been following your social media with interest. It's nice to see the number of followers rising and all those giveaway entries that are being posted. Top job.'

'Yes, right. I would never have thought of that without Raff. I've got two hundred extra followers, people are tagging me all the time, and the shop is busier from people seeing the nutcracker outside and coming in for a browse, and my market stall is nearly empty, so...' I feel proud of what we've achieved this month, and so grateful for Raff's help. I would *never* have come up with any of that without him. Before the accident, I knew I had to do something, but my mind was blank, frozen by the possibility of losing my shop, and I had no idea how to move forwards, until he burst into my life with his twinkly dark eyes and sunny smile and made it feel *worth* saving.

'Even I've had several orders for nutcracker umbrellas because of that one on the giveaway.' Mrs Coombe from All You Need Is Gloves jumps in. 'And customers keep mentioning the video and saying they'd never heard of Christmas Ever After before but are going to come every year from now on. *Both* of these two have helped us all.'

I give her a nod of thanks as a chorus of other voices agree with her. It's lovely to feel that our fellow shopkeepers want us both to stay too. I did wonder if they were so fed up of our quarrelling that they might be glad to see the back of one of us.

'And how long will it be before you're able to work again?' Mr Hastings holds up his arm and wiggles his fingers. 'Because if you're nearly sold out of nutcrackers, then surely there won't be much *to* sell for the foreseeable future, which will undoubtedly lead to a lack of customers and fading interest, lower income, and disengaged followers.'

'There's just over a month until I can take the splint off, and then a while longer to regain strength and range of motion.' My answer is juddery because I can feel my heart beating in my throat and it's a fight to speak around it. Are they really going to use this against me? I hadn't considered the longer-term implications and what being unable to work for the next few weeks would look like to the council, but I have a sudden realisation that this must put me at a serious disadvantage.

'I'll be helping Franca until she's fully recovered,' Raff interjects. 'The injury is my fault – I won't let her business suffer because of it.'

'That's very princely of you, Mr Dardenne, but you're only one person and running yourself ragged between two shops will have a negative impact on both of them as time goes on, and quite frankly, you need to focus your efforts on your own business. We asked you to match five couples because you desperately need some good reviews to bury the bad ones and show customers that the legend behind your shop is something they can believe in.'

I feel awful because matching people we know was my idea. Our colleagues *can't* leave reviews for their own place of work. I knew this was about the reviews – I suggested such an impossible task, because, at the time, I *wanted* him to fail, but over the last few weeks, it's become more about helping people find love, and the practicality of getting reviews has been forgotten.

'This was to prove that Raff *can* and *will* get better reviews. You'd leave good reviews if you could, right?' I know any reviews from our biased friends would be taken down immediately, but I turn to Ali and Imogen and then Nina and Joshy. Best to avoid Cedric and Mandy, they definitely would *not* leave a good review, and as for Mrs Bloom and Jorge... Well, Jorge is still protectively rubbing his arm and has gone back to looking at his phone now – probably searching for injury lawyers. 'The point is that Raff's going to change direction in the new year and focus on his passion, and the reviews will be exemplary.'

'And we have to ensure that the right businesses are on this street, and any that aren't living up to the others in popularity, well, we really are going to have to reconsider their position here. We have many other businesses vying for a spot. Fresh new faces who would bring much-needed custom and publicity to Ever After Street, but space is limited and we can't continue to accommodate shops who fall short of our very strict standards.' Mr Hastings seems to be enjoying this. Cleo has told me that he's got a kinder side when you get to know him, but I've yet to see any hint of it.

My stomach is flip-flopping like I'm on a rollercoaster, with absolutely no idea if it's going to go up, down, or if the carriage is about to fall off the track. Right now, they seem to be erring in my direction, and that makes alarm bells start ringing. I don't want them to sway towards either of us – I want them to get stuck straight down the middle.

'Raff needs to be allowed time to change direction. He needs to find his feet,' I try again, an ironic mirror of what Mrs Bloom said to me in the A&E waiting room all those weeks ago.

'Fran, it's fine.' He shakes his head at me from across the room, but I am *not* letting this go.

'He's done so much for all of us. With a slow December and without a stall at the Christmas market, I'd have been handing in my notice this year anyway. But he took over when I was unable to and single-handedly saved my business. Well, double-handedly, so to speak.' I hold up the splinted hand and my other hand and form an X shape with them. 'But he's done that at the expense of his own shop. If he hadn't spent so much time helping me, he would have had a chance to match actual customers and get those reviews. No one wants to lose Love Is All A-Round from Christmas Ever After. Mrs Bloom, Claude Dardenne matched you and your Reginald, didn't he? Mitch, you wouldn't let Raff go, you said so yourself.'

'That's very true.' Mitch addresses Mr Hastings and Mrs Willetts. 'These two are the best publicity we've had for a long while. Everyone's talking about them. It would *not* be in Ever After Street's best interests to let *either* of them go. Their new-found, er, friendship is elevating all of us.'

I can sense the desperation growing in everyone. Mrs Willetts and Mr Hastings are giving nothing away, but neither seem very moved by our impassioned pleas so far.

For the past couple of weeks, I've been certain that they would be delighted to see us working together, and quite happy to realise they don't *have* to decide between us, but they don't seem quite as delighted by the prospect as I'd hoped.

In fact, they look decidedly awkward as they share a knowing look with each other before looking between me and Raff.

'While it's nice to see you championing each other, especially after the past couple of years of trying to bring each other down, nothing changes the fact that neither of you have managed to do *exactly* what was asked of you. Mr Dardenne, you have not in any way, shape, or form, matched *five* couples.' Mr Hastings looks towards Mrs Bloom and Jorge, and then at Cedric and Mandy, leaving no doubt that he's seen right through that ploy. 'I accept three at most, and you cannot count yourselves, no matter how unexpected this turn of events is. No further reviews have come in to counteract the bad ones, so your slew of one stars are *still* reflecting badly on your colleagues.'

'Maybe it's time to start giving every shop separate review pages,' I suggest.

'We've tried that, but it's too confusing for customers. People don't come to Christmas Ever After to visit just one shop. Once they step under that arch, they're all-in for the year-round festive experience. They visit *every* shop. No customer is going to bother to leave a review for each individual shop, but most will take the time to review their experience as a whole, including the good parts and bad parts. Unfortunately those all get muddled up together.' Mr Hastings scrunches his fingers together like he's kneading bread dough. 'If anyone is not making the cut, they pull us all down with them, as *you* made clear at the November meeting, Miss Andrews.'

He turns his beady eyes to me. 'And although it certainly seems that you're energised and keen again, we tasked you with getting engagement on social media channels. While your idea of giving away a giant nutcracker is a novel one, unfortunately it does nothing for your engagement possibilities in the long-run. Those nutcrackers cost in the region of £500. Trust me, *all* customers are interested when there's the possibility of getting something expensive for nothing, but when that is no longer on offer, customer interest will drop again. As before, absolutely no one will be taking selfies with your nutcrackers if they don't *have* to.'

'I could give away other nutcrackers. I could do something like this every month.'

'And we have other ideas to move forward with in the new year,' Raff adds. 'New ways of encouraging social media engagement and getting customers talking.'

My heart feels warmed by how hard he's trying, but the glacial look on Mr Hastings' face is enough to turn it back into ice. 'If the only way you can get customers interested is by giving them something for nothing, you're missing a key point of running a business. It's unsustainable to run a big giveaway like this every month, and in the long-term, it will have a negative impact as customers wait to see if they've won, and take their chances again the next time rather than actually buying anything. You also have this hindrance.' He returns to the hand issue again.

'That's discrimination!' Raff snaps. 'And temporary. In a matter of weeks, she's going to be back to full strength. And I haven't done what I set out to either. If we've failed, we've failed together. The playing field is level. We've both been here for years. We're no longer against each other. You can't seriously stick to this ridiculous plan. Neither Franca nor I have beaten each other. We've helped each other, and we both deserve a chance to move forward here.'

'Hear, hear!' Mrs Bloom starts a round of applause, but Raff's deep voice is gradually getting higher as his panic rises, and the horrible, sinking feeling in the pit of my stomach feels like it's getting deeper with every passing moment. This really isn't sounding like it's going to go our way.

Or... *my* way? *His* way?

I search for Raff's eyes in the group. He's wearing a black hoodie with the sleeves pulled over his hands, and the hood has fallen forward so it's half up, like he's trying to hide himself. He feels it too, I'm sure he does. Both of us are on the chopping block here, and it feels like neither of us will get out in one piece.

Mr Hastings clears his throat. 'There really is no easy way to say this, but we have a responsibility to Ever After Street and its festive little sister to ensure that every shop is pulling their weight and making for an exciting and engaging shopping trip for customers, and you're both on uneven ground in that respect – you with the bad reviews, Mr Dardenne, and you with the rut you appear to have been stuck in, Miss Andrews. The council have come to the unanimous decision that things on Christmas Ever After are feeling stale and we need to inject some new life, and give some new shops a chance to shine, so with that in mind, we, er...' He glances at Mrs Willetts, who gives him a helpless shrug in response.

'Well, when we issued you two that challenge, we decided that it was actually a very good idea to cut some old deadwood. Wood – nutcrackers, see? Hah hah.'

I've never seen Mr Hastings nervous before. He's the intimidating type of person who makes you think it's an emotion he's unfamiliar with, and that nutcracker wisecrack is more unsettling than anything else that's been said so far today. Is that a hint at what's to come?

Mrs Willetts is the kinder of the two, and even she's avoiding eye contact in a way that people only do when they *really* don't want to tell you something. 'You've both brought a lot to Ever After Street over your years of trading here, and you've made this very awkward for us. Neither of you have quite met the targets we wanted to see, but you've both made a jolly good effort.' She tries to start a round of applause but her attempt goes down like a damp hot air balloon with a rhino in the basket and she awkwardly trails off the clapping when no one else joins in, and one of the suits of armour along one wall even creaks in embarrassment.

I can feel my heartbeat outside of my body, pumping so hard that I'm sure the entire castle is throbbing in unison with it, an all-encompassing pulsing sound, like the wait on a TV talent show before the hosts announce the winner after an excruciatingly long pause. Except this is a no-win situation and instead of a cash prize and a clap on the shoulder from Simon Cowell, this is the end of one of our careers, and such a sense of despair has come over me that I already know who it's going to be.

'I'm sorry, Franca,' Mr Hastings blurts eventually. He's never used my first name before. 'Dardenne Snow Globes have been loyal to Ever After Street for over thirty years. They're a mainstay of Christmas Ever After, and their magical myth still gets people talking and encourages visitors. While your nutcrackers are very nice, you only started here a few short years ago, and—'

'Four years!' Raff interrupts him. I should be glad of him sticking up for me, but I just feel numb. After so long of feeling ambiguous towards The Nutcracker Shop, now I can't *wait* to get back to my lathe when my fingers have healed. I can't wait to make all the nutcrackers that I have ideas for and photograph them for social media, and there's a sense of injustice at being so excited about what's to come, only to be stopped at the final hurdle.

This is the worst feeling I've ever had in my life. Worse than sitting in a physiotherapist's office five years ago and being told I was unlikely ever to dance again. Given how long my leg was taking to heal and how painful every movement was, I'd already reconciled myself with that fact and reached the point where I didn't *want* to do ballet again, but now... Now, I'm still hoping Mr Hastings is about to start laughing and yell, 'Joke!' but he isn't. Of course he isn't.

He looks gravely serious, and so do the many other pairs of eyes that are blinking at me, waiting in trepidation to see what I'm going to do. I glance around the room. Mrs Bloom is dabbing her eyes. Thelma from A Very Muggy Christmas is shaking her head. Mrs Coombe is rubbing at her forehead like she's trying to ease a headache. Ali and Imogen are clutching each other's hands sympathetically. The thought of no longer working with this little team makes a lump form in my throat, and my eyes fall on the only other person still standing while everyone else is sitting.

Oh God, Raff.

Raff's lower lip is taut and white where he's gnawing on it. I meet his eyes and everyone else fades away. It's just me and him.

He looks devastated. I can see the anguish in his eyes. Neither of us expected this. He pushes out a long breath and looks as if he's psyching himself up, and then he gives me an encouraging nod, like he's telling me to get on with something.

My eyebrows furrow in confusion, and he mouths two words at me. 'Tell them.'

Tell them...? I repeat the words in my head for a moment before the meaning dawns on me.

The truth. He's openly inviting me to tell them the truth about the snow globes.

'It's okay,' he whispers across the room, so quietly that I'm lip reading. 'Tell them.'

'Tell them' – two little words with *big* implications. If I tell them about the motor and wires hidden in the bases of his snow globes, my shop will be saved. There's no way they'd continue supporting Dardenne Snow Globes if they knew the truth. Their decision would be reversed immediately, and my shop would get to stay.

And Raff's... wouldn't.

This is what I've wanted for years. A chance to expose the Dardenne Snow Globes fakery to the people who believe in it.

My mouth has gone dry. With one sentence, I can turn this around. It's what I've been waiting for.

I clear my throat.

Mr Hastings and Mrs Willetts are standing in silence, waiting to see if I'm about to cry, storm out, start shrieking like a hungry seagull, or otherwise. They won't be expecting this.

I look over at Raff again. This man who has gone from being my worst enemy to making me wonder why he was ever an enemy in the first place. Without him, I would have lost my shop anyway.

He nods encouragingly again.

I clear my throat once more. It's just a matter of figuring out what to say.

Come on, Franca. Just a few words. *His magical snow globes are powered by batteries and wires.* I count the words. Ten of them. Ten words to put an end to this once and for all.

The legacy that Claude Dardenne left behind will be destroyed, and so will his family's dreams. *Your grandfather wasn't Cupid's earthly assistant, he was a fraud, and your grandson/son/brother/uncle, delete as appropriate, is continuing the false legacy.*

That beautiful family who have made me feel more loved than my own family have ever managed to. Erin and her bump, soon to be a tiny Dardenne, growing up with the magic of mythical snow globes. Sofia with her adorable, hopeful outlook and firm belief that magic is real. Dear old Biddy who has a heart of gold underneath her tough shell. Trisha who has welcomed me with open arms and makes me feel like she's adopted me... The way they've included me and made me feel like I've never *not* been part of their Christmas celebrations.

'I just wanted to say... um...' I start squeakily and have to clear my throat yet again. Everyone is going to think I'm announcing that I've got tonsillitis at this rate. 'Well, um, the thing is... um...'

Am I competing for how many times a person can say 'um' in one sentence? 'There's something you should know...'

My lips have gone numb and my jaw has locked up. This feels horribly, horribly wrong. I *know* Raff isn't happy with how his work has been going. He wants things to be different. Things are *going* to be different now...

My heart is thundering so fast that I can barely breathe. I imagined so many times how euphoric I'd feel if, one day, I got to denounce the Dardenne Snow Globes mystery to the world, but I feel the furthest thing from euphoric. I feel like I'm about to do the most horrible thing I've ever done in my life.

I try to summon up the worst memories of my childhood, the worst arguments I overheard between my parents, to cling on to the vestiges of loathing for the man who was responsible for matching them... When that fails, I think of my nutcrackers, of the sketches I've made Raff draw so I don't forget any of the new ideas by the time I can use my lathe again. The thought of not having anywhere to make them... Of having to take all my machinery home and work alone, with no other shops around me, no friends to check in with throughout the day, no festive feeling and year-round Christmas joy... The thought fills me with anxiety. Making nutcrackers will never be the same again.

I have a chance to make this different. All I need to do is tell them about the day I dropped that snow globe...

But without Love Is All A-Round, Christmas Ever After will never be the same again either. Without Raff, making nutcrackers will lose its magic too, and so will everything else.

I make the mistake of meeting his eyes and he gives me that reassuring nod again, giving me permission to expose something he's kept hidden for a very long time.

I go to speak again, but the words catch in my throat. I don't know how to say it. It will hurt too many people who, somewhere along the way, I've come to really care about.

My pounding heart suddenly slows down and my shaking hand feels steadier, because I *know* I can't do it. This isn't right. It isn't my secret to tell.

'I understand completely.' I turn to Mrs Hastings and Mrs Willetts. 'It's the right decision. This place wouldn't be the same without a bit of dome-shaped Christmas magic.'

'Fran...' Raff says warningly, obviously getting the throwback to our conversation about his shop name.

'It's okay.' My chest feels damp and I realise there are tears pouring down my face and dripping onto my top. 'It's fine. Thank you for all you've done. Without you, I would never have remembered how much I love Christmas, so thank you for reminding me of that.'

The tears are falling so hard that I can barely get a word out. My nose is blocked up, a tension headache is throbbing in my forehead, and I need to get outside and away from all the sympathetic eyes burning into me.

It feels like the moment I fell off the arch all over again, with people gathered around, trying not to crowd me but full of pity. Friends and colleagues wanting to help but drawing a blank on anything that could possibly make this better.

'Can someone tell Mickey to close the shutters of my cabin and go home? I won't be back today.' I stutter the words out in a barely legible sentence because it's not just today, is it? I won't be back ever.

That thought makes me sob even harder, and that's enough to make me turn and run from the castle. I can hear footsteps behind me, Raff's probably, but I don't want to see him, or anyone else.

I can't run for long and high-impact exercise still has to be carefully managed, and my leg forces me to slow to a walk as I lurch along the walled walkway and down the hill, back towards Ever After Street, and fear about the future engulfs me. What on earth am I going to do now? I've only ever been good at two things in my life – ballet and making nutcrackers, and now both of them are tainted. I can't repair the damage to my leg and go back to ballet, and I don't know how I'll ever make another nutcracker without thinking about Raff and all the ways this *should* have ended.

This got so, so messy, as things always do when you start letting people in. I learnt that from my parents – everyone is better off alone in the end. Things only go wrong when you start dreaming of impossible solutions and letting yourself believe in flights of fancy like the possibility that the council were ever going to save *both* our shops. And if I had kept my guard up, this wouldn't hurt the way it does.

Everything would have been so much easier if Raphael Dardenne and I had stayed exactly as we were – two people who hated each other without ever having spoken.

18

'Maybe I deserve it,' I say to Cleo as I pace the floor of The Nutcracker Shop on Monday morning. 'I've spent so much of my time here hung up on hating Dardenne Snow Globes. If I'd spent *as* much time focused on my own shop and on making my nutcrackers something special, it wouldn't be this way.'

'Your nutcrackers *are* something special, Franc,' she says, displaying the patience of a particularly tolerant saint.

'Not special enough to be wanted...' I stop myself as tears threaten to rise again. I cried so much last night, while ignoring Raff's name continually flashing up on my phone screen and pretending not to read the slew of messages he sent. That meeting totally blindsided me yesterday. I didn't expect that to be the outcome, and I have no idea what to say to him.

'Would you have been happier if they'd chosen you and sent him packing?'

'No, of course not,' I huff, because either way, it would still be just as impossible to navigate. 'It's not *his* fault they picked him, but how can we move forwards after this?'

'You'll find a way!' Cleo sounds more confident than I feel. 'It's like Tom Hanks and Meg Ryan at the end of *You've Got Mail*. She loses her job because of him. That still ended happily.'

'Did it? Did it though, really? Meg Ryan wasn't happy. She lost her beloved shop. Just because she found the guy didn't make that any better. Love was a consolation prize. *Sorry, you lost the place you've loved your whole life and have been fighting to save, but here, have a handsome man with a cute dog instead*. I don't want Raff *instead* of my shop. Our whole relationship has been him versus me, and for the past few weeks, it hasn't, and *that* has been wonderful, and that's what I wanted to continue. I wanted it to be both of us.'

It's the day after the Christmas market and we're waiting for Mitch to bring back my stock that wasn't sold from the cabin, but until then, the shelves are empty and it feels lonely in here without Raff. In three short weeks, I've got remarkably accustomed to the company of someone who *isn't* a little wooden man.

'He made this Christmas feel so special. He made me realise everything that's been wrong in my life lately.' I let out a sigh.

'Why *didn't* you tell them?'

'Tell them what?' I cock my head to the side. Cleo works on the main part of Ever After Street so she wasn't at the meeting. If even she knows what Raff said to me, then people have been talking.

'*Everyone* has been talking,' she says, reading my mind. 'You obviously know something – the secret behind his enchanted globes, I wouldn't wonder. Why not throw him to the wolves and save yourself? Three weeks ago, you would've done that without a second thought.'

Now I feel sick *at* the thought. 'Three weeks ago, I would have done a lot of things. Three weeks ago, I held his family personally responsible for destroying my childhood, and it's only falling in—' I stop myself before I mention the L word. Everything is so messed up now that I don't know *what* I'm feeling for Raff, but it's probably best not to say a word like that aloud. I correct myself. 'It's only *meeting* him that's made me realise how wrong I was to blame Claude Dardenne rather than my parents themselves. He didn't make them fight. He didn't make them stay together much longer than they should have. And Raff didn't deserve my misplaced vendetta. I'd never forgive myself for hurting him like that. He puts on a brave face but he hasn't had it easy. He stays strong for his family, but the right word at the right time cuts straight through his walls. He's got struggles that he's never shared with anyone but me – I didn't want to make them worse.'

'Aww,' Cleo starts, but is interrupted by a knock on the door, and I go to answer it without thinking and take a step back in surprise when I pull the door open and see Raff standing there, waiting to come in with a trolley containing a few unsold nutcrackers.

'You were supposed to be Mitch,' I stutter, for lack of something more eloquent to say.

'And you were supposed to answer *any* of my texts, calls and emails. I figured you wouldn't answer the door either if you knew it was me, so I persuaded Mitch to let me bring these back.' He goes to push the trolley through, but I stop him coming in and awkwardly pull at it one-handed until Cleo jumps up and drags it inside, and I move so I'm deliberately blocking the doorway. Having Raff in my shop would feel a bit like having him stomping over my grave at the moment.

I have no idea what to say to him, so I go back to the nutcrackers that have just come back. 'I expected way more.'

'Mickey didn't listen when they passed on the message to put the shutters down. There were still orders left to be collected and she said she was enjoying being part of the market and didn't have anything better to do, so these are all that remain.'

Even in the darkest moments, my fellow shopkeepers lift my spirits, and the thought of leaving makes me feel like a vice has clamped around my body and tightened its grip until I feel positively ill. I love the people I work with on Ever After Street. Most days, it doesn't feel like work at all. Christmas Ever After gave me a new start when I needed it most. I had no idea what to do with my post-ballet life until I stumbled across this place and spotted the little shop with the 'for rent' sign outside. I was still limping and couldn't stay on my feet too long, and it was Mitch and the others – Mickey, Lissa, Mrs Bloom – who helped me to set up the workshop, and carry in all the nutcrackers I'd made in preparation for opening.

I'd forgotten how much I love it here – until Raff reminded me.

'Where does this leave us?' There's a waver in his voice that suggests he knows the answer as well as I do.

'I don't know,' I say, because I *don't* know. My career is over, and his will continue thriving here. How can we have a relationship when, every morning, he'll be going to work here, and I won't? How will he ever be able to tell me about his day, or share stories of his colleagues and fellow shopkeepers, without being hyperaware of upsetting me?

No matter what, there will always be this huge wedge between us.

'Why didn't you tell them? You weren't supposed to let me win like that.'

'And you think it would've felt like winning to throw you under the bus, do you? I don't want to keep my shop at the expense of your reputation and your family's belief in magic, Raff.' I can hear Cleo unloading the nutcrackers inside, and I'm well aware we're having this conversation in the doorway and are probably attracting gossipy attention, but I feel like I need to keep this emotional wall between us. I've already let down too many walls when it comes to Raff. 'We should never have helped each other. We should have stayed enemies. That's the thing about you versus me. I should have known that one day it would come down to you *or* me, and I wasn't prepared for how devastated I'd be if it wasn't me.'

He goes to speak but I stop him. 'Or *you*, for that matter. How would you feel in my position? If they had chosen me instead? If you'd been told to pack off in January, and I hadn't?'

'I don't know,' he says honestly. 'I didn't want this. I thought we both had a chance.'

'So did I.'

I look into his brown eyes and tears threaten again, and if I cry in front of him, he's going to hug me, and look where that led last time, so I let my teeth shred the inside of my cheek, trying to stem the emotions.

In the awkward silence, Cleo shuffles up beside me to push the empty trolley back out to Raff, and he stands aside and runs a hand through his hair, and I try not to think about how desolate he looks as she goes back inside.

'You can't just give up. We can fight this. We don't have to take it lying down. This December feels like the first time I *haven't* been struggling, even though I've been working harder than ever. People have always said that I need to find someone who inspires me, and that was you, and... that's worth fighting for.'

'No. This is a sign,' I say with a shaky vehemence in my voice. 'This is the end of the line for me. Everything about The Nutcracker Shop has felt like a fight in recent years. Ironically, the only thing that's given my days any meaning is fighting with you, and the only time it stopped feeling like that is when we actually had a big public fight, and that's just too much fighting for one shop. I can't do this any more.'

'You don't believe that.'

We both know it would be a lie if I tried to deny it, so he doesn't give me a chance to respond. 'There's got to be something I can do to change things.'

'Try time travel, Raff,' I snap, because we both need to move on from this, and the last thing I want is him feeling guilty or like he owes me something. He's already done more than enough in his attempts to save my shop. 'Go back in time to that November meeting and stop us picking at each other. Stop the contest. Or, better still, go back years and stop me being so bitter. This is no one's fault but mine, so get on with your life and forget about *all* of this.'

I know he's about to protest, so I close the door sharply and lean against it, trying to get my ragged breathing back under control.

The nutcrackers Cleo has unloaded are on the counter, next to the nutcracker prince and ballerina snow globe. There's no point in even putting them back on the shelves now. They're all ones Raff made. Snowmen. Nutcrackers with ski boots and snowboards. Even one holding a snow globe. I stop and trail my fingers over it, and then have to turn away and bite the inside of my cheek to stop my eyes filling up again. 'I should phone my mum. I could do with a sensible kick up the backside when it comes to giving your heart away, and her advice too. Maybe it's finally time to take up that teaching role the ballet company offered me...'

Mum was always incredibly keen for me to stay involved with dancing in some way. She thought I was throwing my life's work away when I turned my back on it entirely. It's something I never thought I'd agree with, and the mere thought fills me with dread, but I don't know what my other options are.

'You do *not* want to do that!' Cleo doesn't even attempt to hide the horror on her face. 'Franc, of all the things you've told me about your ballet career, not one of them has ever been good!'

'I know, but what good is a year-round Christmas shop

without any other Christmas shops nearby? If I was to rent another shop, somewhere else, to sell nutcrackers, I'd be on my own. Visitors come to Christmas Ever After as a whole, no matter the time of year, because it's an experience. And it's hard enough to stay afloat here. In the blazing hot summer sun, no one would bother coming into a nutcracker shop by itself. They'd walk right past and I'd be back to square one again of not earning enough to cover the outgoings.' My voice is shaking as I say it, but it's a truth that has to be faced. On Christmas Ever After, we all lift each other up, and every shop supports the other shops just by existing, and the thought of starting again, alone, without the little community of Ever After Street is unbearable. 'It's time to move on. Away from nutcrackers, Christmas, and any kind of magic.'

'You never believed in magic anyway.'

My lip wobbles and my voice breaks. 'I did when I was with him. I believed in everything. Enchanted snow globes. The magic of Christmas. Santa.'

'You believed in Santa?' She raises an unconvinced eyebrow.

'Well, no, but I felt like I *could* believe in Santa, and that definitely suggests it's time for a reality check, because no matter what Raff says, some people will always be too old to believe in magic.'

No matter how old I get, when things are going wrong, I still wish I had a supportive family to turn to. I wish I could go to my mum for a hug instead of a rant about the evils of men, and I wish I could go to my dad for a dose of fatherly advice instead of an invite to his latest wedding and thinly veiled digs about my career choices.

When I get home from work, I give Mum a ring, ready for her to dish out her 'slow and painful castration to all men' battle cry.

It's well past time I listened to her manifesto. If you never get involved with anyone, you don't end up in situations like this.

'Oh, hello darling, I wasn't expecting you to call, I've just this second come in from a friend's Christmas macramé class. Hang on while I take my coat off. How are you, Franca? Still making those nutcrackers?'

'Not at the moment. I've got three broken fingers.'

'Oh no!' She gasps in surprise and I feel guilty that it's been over three weeks and I haven't even told her. Raff's family and their love for each other has made me realise that I should make more effort with my own family. 'How did that happen?'

'There was some mistletoe and this guy, and this other guy came along, and...' I burst into tears and hear Mum bustling about in the background.

'I'm just putting the kettle on so we can have a nice chat. Wish we were near enough for me to make you one too!'

I sniffle and go to make my own and then come back to the phone, and it feels strangely nice to be having a cuppa and a chat with my mum, even though there are many miles between us. I spill out the whole sorry story from the council's contest between me and Raff until yesterday afternoon's events and everything in between. 'There's something else you need to know,' I add, expecting a mum-shaped explosion when I mention his surname. 'The man I've been seeing... It's Raphael Dardenne.'

'Who's that?'

'Dardenne,' I say pointedly, and repeat it when it's met by silence. 'Come on, Mum. *Dardenne.*'

I can hear her pondering the name. 'Wasn't that the name of that silly old snow globe company? The one who matched me and your father?'

'Yes! The one who upturned our lives! The one I've resented for years because of their ridiculous matchmaking myth!'

'Upturned our lives,' she repeats, laughing to herself. 'Oh, you are dramatic sometimes. Your father and I had some wonderful years together, and *you* came out of it. I wouldn't change that for all the chocolate in the world.'

'Really?' Her reaction surprises me. I've never heard her say that before. She's always said my dad was the worst thing that ever happened to her, and I've always felt like that unintentionally included me as well, because I am an eternal reminder of that relationship. I thought she'd be a seething ball of animosity towards Claude Dardenne, but she barely even recalls the name, let alone feels any ill will towards him. It makes me think again about how wrong I've been to hold such a grudge against Raff. Maybe it's not him who needs a time machine – maybe it's me.

Mum makes a noise of confirmation, and I explain further. 'I work on the same street as where the Dardenne shop is nowadays. Claude Dardenne, the old guy who matched you, opened there decades ago. Now his grandson, Raff, runs it. We have a... Well, we *had* a complicated relationship. I couldn't abide him and what his grandfather did to our family with that stupid snow globe.'

'Oh, Franca, he didn't *do* anything to our family. Your father and I were adults. We were not skilled at managing conflict, and we never improved, despite the vast amount of conflict we had. He was a manchild with a propensity for shouting instead of listening, and I didn't exactly cover myself in glory with my commitment to taking the moral high ground when I acted just as immaturely as he did. We should have split up long before we did, and we should have done a better job of keeping our struggles from you. I'm so sorry.'

I'm getting teary again. It's the first time Mum has talked openly about her relationship with my dad, and the first time she's ever taken part of the blame, or acknowledged that their constant fighting affected me as well, and a strange sense of relief washes through me. I've always wondered if I was to blame. If I had been different, would they have been happier? Was there something I could have done to make things better?

'We had a wonderful time when we first met; we were young and carefree with no responsibilities, but we weren't suited to each other long term. We knew that, but then I got pregnant, and we thought we owed it to you to stay together. It took too many years to realise that we were *all* better off apart, including you, but the only people you can hold responsible for that is me and your dad. Please don't push people away because of the scars *we* left you with. Heck, even I've been open to finding love again lately.'

'You want to find love again?' I choke on my own tongue. '*You*? The person who has waged a one-woman war on the opposite sex for decades? You, who thinks "all men are evil and should be castrated and fed their own testicles" in a really disturbing feeding ritual, and that's a direct quote!'

'Well, I didn't like to tell you, but I've actually been sort of... seeing someone.' I can hear her doing her nervous habit of wringing her hands together on the other end of the line. 'He's a neighbour. He was divorced a while ago too. We met while taking the bins out, of all things. I ran over his foot with my wheelie bin and broke his toe! At first I was going to tell him that it served him right for having such oversized manly feet, but he really couldn't walk, the poor chap, and I didn't feel right leaving him hopping about like that, so I ran him to A&E and we got chatting as we sat there waiting for hours, and afterwards, I felt terribly guilty and found myself popping round to check on him as often as I could. I eventually had to admit that I quite liked him, and actually, a bit of male company wouldn't go amiss, and do you know, it's been a breath of fresh air. I never thought I'd want to open myself up again, not after your father, but sometimes these things find us when we least expect it. He'd been living two doors down for years and we'd never even met.'

I'm beyond surprised. Mum was arguably the most hurt by the divorce of all of us. She shut the world out, tarnished all men with the same brush, and thought everyone deserved the misery they got when a relationship inevitably ended in tears, but if even she can let love in again...

'You could come up to visit. I'd like to introduce you. And bring this Raff fellow, I'd like to meet him too.'

'I can't bring Raff. We're...' I sigh in frustration. 'I don't know *what* we are. I don't know what we can be when he's got his shop and I'm left contemplating the thought of calling the ballet company and asking if that teaching role is still available...'

'You are not!'

'I'm not over the hill yet, Mum,' I say, assuming she means my age. 'Those who can't do, teach.'

'You would be the worst ballet teacher in existence – not because of your experience, but because you don't *want* to do it. I could never support you going back to something that made you so miserable!'

'But... you...' I had no idea she'd ever realised that I *was* miserable, let alone that she wasn't waiting for the day I'd come to my senses and forge ahead with a dance teaching career. 'I thought you thought I was throwing my life away to make nutcrackers.'

'I did at first, darling. It was a surprise after that terrible accident. What I really wanted was for you to get back into your pointe shoes and show your ex that he couldn't bring you down that easily. But that was *my* bitterness and resentment. What you did was rise above it and move on. Every time I've visited you, I've seen your lovely little shop and how happy you are, and the only thing any parent ever *really* wants is for their children to be happy. And if you *are* happy, then you go back and fight for your place there.' She takes a sip of tea to fuel herself. 'You're never too old for motherly advice. Find someone who makes you feel like a Christmas tree when the lights have just been plugged in, and when you do, hold onto him tight, and when things get difficult, you bloody well fight for him too.'

I let out a wet half-snort half-sniffle. I had no idea my mum felt like that. Maybe if I had known, our relationship would have been easier than it has been over the years.

'I've decided to give men a second chance,' she says. 'Maybe your Raff deserves one too...'

The thought of him being 'my' Raff makes my breath catch in my throat, because of how desperately I want that. Nutcrackers or no nutcrackers, I *still* wish he was 'my' anything.

And having Mum's support makes me realise she's right. I *am* happy on Christmas Ever After, and I *deserve* to stay there, and so does Love Is All A-Round. My shop *and* Raff are worth fighting for. And I don't have to hand my keys in until January...

Maybe it's not too late for a bit of Christmas magic after all?

19

It's Christmas Eve and the doors are locked to customers. I'm pacing the workshop. What I want to do is make a nutcracker. One with dark brown eyes and chocolate-brown floppy hair, holding a snow globe, but my hand is still too painful to even contemplate using my lathe, and the only other person capable of it is Raff himself, which would somewhat defeat the object.

I shouldn't have sent him away yesterday, and with what Mum said ringing in my ears, I've come back to Christmas Ever After to fight for what matters. My shop *and* the man I've fallen in love with. The Nutcracker Shop has so much more to give, and it was my own misplaced bitterness that led to it being in trouble in the first place. I was wrong to have judged Raff like I have for the past couple of years, and Claude before him too. I was a child, desperately looking for someone to blame for the implosion of my parents' marriage, and I should have grown out of that rather than carry it with me for so many years. If I'd behaved differently, maybe Raff and I would have met years ago. Maybe we'd have become friends. Maybe we'd never have found ourselves in the position we found ourselves in this December, and now I have to do something about it.

We *both* deserve to stay on this street. We both proved we can do what was asked of us. We were on equal footing, and then the council moved the goalposts, and I am not going to take it lying down. I've never been good at asking for help, but now I'm going to ask *everyone* for help. Customers, strangers, friends, colleagues. Christmas wouldn't be Christmas without nutcrackers *and* snow globes.

Just as I'm contemplating who to ask to sign my petition first, there's a knock on the shop door and I grumble to myself about customers being relentless. Does anyone *really* need a nutcracker on Christmas Eve? Although I'd rather it be a customer than someone who's seen my light on and come to get the inside scoop of gossip after Sunday's calamity of a meeting.

When I open the door, there's no one there. Instead, there are... gnomes.

A *lot* of gnomes. One is standing right in front of the door with his hand raised, like he was the one who just knocked.

I glance towards Coming Gnome For Christmas, because I'm *almost* positive that resin gnomes can't knock on doors of their own accord. The gnomes form a circle around a Dardenne Snow Globes box, which is on the pavement outside my door, and then a line of gnomes trail off, disappearing around the curve in the road between here and the main part of Ever After Street.

It fills me with a tingling fizziness. *Something* is going on here, and whatever it is, Raff – and presumably Mrs Bloom – must be involved in it.

I crouch down and slip the lid off the box and part the tissue paper to reveal the most incredible, detailed snow globe. I lift it out carefully, holding it with my good hand and trying to support it with the thumb of my splinted hand, terrified of dropping it. The snow inside whirls around a tiny archway. It's the Christmas Ever After arch, the ceramic inside so intricate that the words are readable. There are the snowy grey cobblestones of the street along the bottom, and underneath the arch are two people kissing. The woman has long brown hair, just like mine, and the man has dark hair flopped over at one side like Raff's, and there's a sprig of green mistletoe with white berries hanging by a red ribbon on the arch above them. They're both wearing Santa hats.

My heart speeds up and thuds harder as I shake the globe up again and watch the snow falling over the tiny versions of us.

This snow globe has a small and solid base. There are no micro-holes and no place to stash hidden parts. This is a *real* snow globe, the kind Raff wants to get back to making, and that makes it even more special somehow.

The first gnome is pointing forwards, towards the other gnomes, which must be a hint, so I put the snow globe carefully back in the box and take it with me as I follow the line of gnomes, wondering how anyone has managed to set all these out, especially without me hearing a thing. Who would go to this much trouble? It's the sort of thing that has Raff written all over it...

As soon as I round the curve in the road, a brass band starts playing 'We Wish You a Merry Christmas', and the scene that greets me is... reminiscent of a day, a few weeks ago, that will be etched in my mind forever. Our fellow shopkeepers are gathered to one side, and a few last-minute customers have stopped to see what's happening. Mitch has got a camera set up and trained on the Christmas Ever After arch, and under the arch, there are two stools, and standing on one of them, holding a bundle of mistletoe, is Raff.

When the line of gnomes comes to an end, Mrs Bloom appears at my side, dressed as Mrs Claus, just like she was before. She gently extracts the box from my hand. 'Let me take that, just in

case you find something more interesting to use that hand for...'
Her waggling eyebrows leave no doubt about what that something
might be. She nudges me forwards, closer to the arch, to where
Raff is waiting.

'What are you doing?' I look up at him and lift my splinted
hand to shade my eyes from the low winter sun.

I hadn't seen her until now, but before he can answer, Mrs
Willetts steps forward from the crowd of gathered shopkeepers
and says, 'Righting a wrong, and reversing a decision that it was
wrong of us to make.'

My heart starts pounding at the thought that she might mean
what I think she means.

'Despite the fact we're closed for the holidays, Raphael asked to
see us this morning. He told us everything, including the secret
behind the snow globes and the fact that you didn't reveal the
information when you could have done. He delivered a petition
signed by every shopkeeper on Ever After Street and as many
customers as he could find, which was quite a few in the run-up to
Christmas, and don't get me started on the momentum that's
building online from his social media accounts. You must have
thousands of mentions today from the many, many people
demanding your shop be reinstated immediately.'

My eyes well up without my permission. The thought of Raff
forcing the councillors into work on Christmas Eve, and pounding
the streets canvassing for signatures on my behalf... I'd just been
thinking about starting a petition, and he's already gone and delivered one, and used his own following to boost the signal too.

'He also handed me his keys and forfeited his place here.'

'*What*?' The shock cuts through all the warm fuzzy feelings and
the tears stop instantly to make way for sheer horror instead. I look
up at him, but his poker face gives nothing away. 'No, he wouldn—'

She holds a hand up. 'Don't worry, we didn't let him. Nor did we much fancy the idea of every other shopkeeper going on strike, as they've all assured me they will do if we don't make this right.'

I look over at the group of my colleagues, who are all grinning, whooping, and victory punching the air, and it makes my heart swell so much that it feels like it's going to explode all over the cobblestones.

'Mr Hastings and I have decided that if your shop can elicit such a frenzied response to the threat of eviction, then you must be doing something right,' Mrs Willetts continues. 'So maybe you'd like to keep doing it? We'd be delighted to have The Nutcracker Shop stay on Christmas Ever After, along with Love Is All A-Round, of course. Raphael tells me that you *both* have plans to inject some much-needed new life into our beloved little street.'

'We do...' I was intending to give her a big speech about the different directions we both want to take our shops in, but the lump in my throat is bigger now and the words catch, so she just shakes my hand and steps back, leaving me looking up at Raff again.

'What are you doing?' I repeat.

He looks down from the stool he's standing on and flashes me that Disney prince smile. 'Time travel.'

My face must show nothing but confusion, because he clarifies. 'I asked you what I could do to change things, and you told me – time travel. And I thought... Well, that's not impossible, so here we are.'

'Pretty sure time travel *is* impossible, Raff...' Even as I say it, I can't help smiling at his cocky grin as he beams down at me. Only Raff could hear a sarcastic, flippant comment like the one I made yesterday and take it literally.

'I make magical snow globes, and you make nutcrackers that almost definitely come to life at night. Nothing's impossible.' With that, he steps off the stool he's standing on and walks towards me, the bunch of mistletoe in his hand. 'I thought we'd have a do-over of December the first. The original video will be deleted and this one will take its place. Mitch was... delightfully overjoyed... to agree to getting rid of his viral video.'

I glance at Mitch. 'Delightfully overjoyed' is not *quite* the description I'd use for the scowl on his face.

'What happened on Sunday was wrong, and you're sorely mistaken if you think I'm going to let you go that easily.' He fiddles with the mistletoe as he talks, belying that despite his wide smile and confident stride, he's actually quite nervous, and it makes me want to hug him. 'I've just realised that sounded vaguely threatening, which wasn't my intention at all. A lot of things haven't been my intention lately, Fran. I didn't intend to hurt you on that first day of December, but other things have happened in the past few weeks that I didn't intend to happen either...' His eyes drop pointedly to my lips, making a tingle fizzle up my spine with the memory of the other night in the castle gardens. 'If I *could* go back in time, I would, but with the tedious confines of reality, this was the closest thing I could come up with.'

'How did you get everyone involved in this?' I look around the scene, which is set up as much like the first time round as it can possibly be.

Cleo waves from where she's standing with the other shopkeepers, along with Bram, and Marnie and Nina, Ali and Imogen, Mandy, and Mrs Coombe. Even Jorge is there, and someone's cajoled him into wearing a Santa hat.

'Everyone loves you and wanted to support my nonsense.' He looks over at the gathering of our fellow shopkeepers and friends. 'Apart from the band. I paid them a vast sum of money, assured them of a link to their website on the video, and promised them a spot at next year's Christmas market. Mitch is *delighted* with me.'

I glance at Mitch again. He's screwing a fist into his opposite palm, and has a look on his face that suggests, were it not for the Santa outfit he's wearing and the possibility of children being nearby, he'd be shouting a string of obscenities too.

'See? He's positively bubbling over with Christmas joy. Never has there been a happier Santa.'

When I look back at Raff, his fingers are shredding one of the mistletoe leaves, and I force myself to ask him about what Mrs Willetts has just said. 'Why would you do that, you fool? Offer to give up your shop for me?'

'Because when you said that about it being you versus me, I realised I'd rather it be you *than* me. I've been thinking of moving on for a while and you haven't. You deserve this space. You deserve to give your nutcrackers a fighting chance, and honestly, Christmas Ever After deserves a set of Spice Girls nutcrackers on sale next year. *That* is the gift that keeps on giving.' His eyes flick up to mine but he quickly looks downwards again. 'And I'm the one who screwed everything up. We both had that fight, but I let my frustration get the better of me and stormed off without looking where I was going, and...' He shakes his head like he can't think of a way to finish the sentence.

'It's okay.' I reach over and still his hands before he minces every sprig of mistletoe in the bunch. 'You don't need to apologise again.'

'Oh. Good, because I'm not apologising. I'm not sorry.'

I raise an eyebrow, but he sticks with it. 'I meant what I said on Saturday – bumping into you was the best thing I ever did. I'm sorry – ridiculously sorry – that you were hurt, but I will never, ever regret doing something that brought you into my life.'

I can't help the 'awww' that pops out. I wondered where he was going with that sentence, but he finds the sweetest way to save it.

'Three weeks ago, I didn't believe in love. I didn't think it was possible to feel the way about someone that my gran and granddad felt about each other. I didn't believe that, one day, I'd run into someone and my whole world would stop and my life would turn upside down and magically become better, but then... it did. Because I bumped into you – literally and metaphorically. So yes, I'm sorry for *this*.' He reaches out to touch my elbow, lifting it while carefully avoiding the splint. 'But I am *not* sorry for anything else because it brought us together, and who knows if we'd ever have spoken a civilised word to each other if it hadn't happened, and that would be unthinkable.'

I've been trying to suppress a smile while he talks, but it breaks loose, and I'm having to blink fast in an attempt to stop myself welling up yet again. 'It's okay, Raff. I'm sorry too. I'm sorry for holding such a grudge against you for so long, and I'm sorry for the way I reacted on Sunday. I was overwhelmed and didn't know *how* to react, but over the past couple of days, I haven't stopped thinking about you. When that gnome knocked on my door just now, I was plotting to start up a petition to save my shop, and trying to pluck up the courage to come and apologise to you.'

He's grinning at me and he looks like he wants to say something, but he lets me carry on without interrupting.

'When you came into my shop and cockily announced that no one would have a bad Christmas on your watch, it felt impossible, but you've turned this month around from the worst possible start to the best Christmas I can remember. You've made me forget about my hand, you've made me reconsider everything I thought I knew about falling in love, and about Christmas and working here, and even though I didn't intend to either, I think you're pretty special, Raphael Dardenne, and I accept your non-apology and your non-moving snow globe, and—'

He cuts me off with a kiss that takes me by surprise in the best way possible, and my hand grips onto his arm even though it's nothing more than a peck. We pull back when a cheer goes up from the crowd of our fellow shopkeepers, and I'm blushing too hard to keep kissing him, even though I want to.

And on the plus side, Raff smells of his usual peppermint after-shave and there's not a hint of Monster Munch anywhere.

He steps round to my left side and holds his arm out to me. 'Shall we?'

When I slip my arm through his, he signals to Mitch, and I hear the beep of the camera recording as we walk towards the Christmas Ever After arch.

The two stools that are set up underneath look a *lot* more steady than the ones we stood on so many weeks ago, but even so, I'm not ready for that yet. 'Forget those things. There's a do-over and there's jinxing it.'

'Really? Because Jorge has offered to come by and knock me off just for the full do-over effect. If I break anything, can you learn to make snow globes for the next couple of months?'

'Don't make me smack you with my one hand, because I will.' I hold my palm out threateningly. 'We don't need that faithful a re-enactment.'

He laughs, getting all giggly as my protective side comes out. I make him keep hold of my hand for support as he steps up onto a stool to hang the mistletoe and steps back down without incident, and then he moves them aside so we're standing underneath the mistletoe in the archway. He smiles, his eyes asking silent permission to kiss me, and I give him an almost imperceptible nod, and he lowers his lips to mine.

Last time I was hyperaware of the camera, but this time, Raff has taken over every last one of my senses. His aftershave, the touch of his mouth, and the absolute silence that has fallen over the street. Everything has gone so quiet that it's like we're covered by a blanket of snow, and I'm not sure if it's actually gone that quiet or if kissing Raff has simply blocked out everything else. The street under me has melted away and the only thing I can feel is his hands, one on my lower back, his fingertips smouldering through my jumper, one at the back of my neck, my hair gathered in his hand as his thumb brushes my skin, making time drift away.

At least one of us has retained our awareness of the camera because he pulls back much faster than I wanted him to, but thankfully, just before we were on the cusp of slipping into public indecency.

He's panting for breath, his chest heaving where my hand is resting over his heart and he drops his forehead to lean against mine, a sappy smile playing on his kiss-reddened lips.

'Happy December the first, Fran,' he murmurs.

'Happy Christmas Eve, Raff,' I murmur in reply, making him laugh.

'And cut!' Everyone cheers at Mitch's shout, probably because no one's ended up in A&E this time.

'He knows that absolutely no one is going to want to watch a video that ends happily, right?' I say to Raff.

'It's Christmas, anything is possible.'

Somehow, he makes me believe that, and he makes me feel like I'm living *in* a snow globe – happy, perfect, and with an idealistic little village to call my own where you're never sure that something won't come out of nowhere, shake your life up, and cause a snowstorm.

20

'It's Christmaaaaaaaaas!' Sofia is too young to know who Noddy Holder is, never mind be doing impressions of him, but she flings the door open in her fleecy Christmas pyjamas the next morning with a perfect rendition of the opening line of the Slade song.

'Santa's been!' She dashes off, singing 'Deck the Halls' and a trail of fa-la-la-la-la-ing follows her into the house.

It's 10 a.m., and I slept on Raff's couch last night, although between us, and Erin and Quentin, we spent a good chunk of the night creating sparkly hoofprints on the lawn, big fake-snow foot-prints going from the hearth to the tree, and a piece of red fabric left behind where Santa snagged his suit on the branches. I grated the end off two carrots to make them look chewed by reindeer, and Raff ate half the mince pies Sofia had left out for Santa, and it reminded me of everything I used to love about Christmas, and how you're never too old for a touch of magic. Afterwards, Erin and Quentin crept back in here, and Raff and I went back to his place; he made us a hot chocolate and we snuggled down on the couch, and the next thing I knew, it was morning and his arms were still around me. He'd managed to pull a blanket over us in the night, and Biddy was right about his couch being very comfortable indeed.

Everyone greets us both with a hug and a 'Merry Christmas', except Biddy who growls something about no one having got her a martini yet, and Raff obliges as I lean down to hug her. She squeezes my hand and says, 'Well done, Franca. You've managed to turn our non-believer into a loved-up puddle. I saw the new video, you know. I've never seen him so happy.'

'Never seen who so happy?' Raff returns with her glass, knowing full well who she's talking about.

'You, of course. Have you seen the soppy smile on your face? If I didn't know you were up all night doing' – she looks around to make sure Sofia's not in earshot – 'Santa stuff, I'd think you were up all night doing something a lot naughtier!'

I blush even though we were both too knackered to do anything more risqué than fall asleep on the sofa last night.

'Mum says we can all have one present now!' Sofia races into the living room, runs around the sofa, and races back out again.

Erin's sitting at the table with her feet up, and Trisha and Quentin were in the kitchen preparing to cook the dinner, but Sofia drags them in and chooses a present for everyone from under the tree. She throws something big and squashy onto my lap, wrapped in red pudding-print paper, and hurls a similar looking one at Raff, and then chooses one for herself, which was impossible to disguise. It's the finished version of the half-completed nutcracker that Raff got from me on the day I showed him my workshop. Between us, we wrapped it up last night. Unfortunately it's pretty impossible to disguise a five-foot nutcracker and Sofia's clearly known what it is since the moment she clapped eyes on it standing beside the Christmas tree this morning.

'Oh my God, I love him!' she squeals as she tears the paper off and pushes herself onto tiptoes so she can plant a kiss on the nutcracker's wooden red cheek. 'I'm going to marry him one day!'

'Don't give your heart away just yet, Sofe,' Biddy tells her.

'Maybe one day you'll find a nutcracker prince in real life,' I add. My eyes are on Raff and his little smile makes my heart soar.

'Open yours!' Sofia spins around, holding the stationary nutcracker's arm like she's waltzing with it.

I pin my present down with an elbow and tear through the paper to reveal a huge, red and green tartan snuggle hoodie that's oversized, soft and cosy, and when Raff tears his present open, he finds the same thing but in blue and brown.

'His and hers so you can snuggle together!' Sofia shouts.

I slip it on immediately. It's the softest, snuggliest thing I've ever worn, like wearing a duvet, and I'm beyond touched that they've all gone to such an effort to include me.

After everyone's opened one present each, Trisha and Quentin return to the kitchen, and although I ask repeatedly if I can do anything to help, Trisha stops me. 'Next year, when you've got two hands. Until then, put your feet up and let us take care of you.'

It makes me feel warm and cherished as Raff flops down beside me and leans over until his head is resting against mine. I stroke the sleeve of his snuggle hoodie and he tangles our fingers together and squeezes my hand.

'You wouldn't want to meet my mum sometime soon, would you?' It's been on my mind since I spoke to her, but I didn't know I was actually going to suggest it to Raff.

'I would love to. Even if she's going to castrate me on sight.'

I laugh, but I get the feeling Mum has mellowed in her older age. 'I was thinking of going to visit her.'

'This week? We're both off work and I'd be more than happy to drive up there.'

'She lives in Scotland, Raff. That's a long drive.'

'Or it's a few uninterrupted hours I get to spend with you in the car, and I would *love* to meet your family.'

'Awwww.' I can't stop myself leaning up to press a kiss to his cheek and snuggle in closer, wondering how I got so lucky.

The Christmas dinner is a full-house affair, and once again, Trisha has thought of *everything*, all the subtle things that make it easy for me to eat one-handed, but she doesn't make a big deal out of it, and after we're all stuffed and Sofia's made everyone pull at least one cracker and we've all got paper party hats on, everyone migrates back to the living room for presents.

I didn't expect to be involved in this part at all, but sure enough, there are presents under the Dardenne tree for me, all marked as 'from Santa' – the sweetest, most thoughtful things. Hand warmers in case my fingers feel the cold when the splint comes off. A jar opener in case I struggle to open jars while my fingers are still healing. A fleece blanket with nutcrackers all over it. Fluffy socks. Chocolate. Not a Toblerone in sight, thankfully.

'I've got one for Fran.' Raff, who's been sitting next to me with presents piled all around us, slides off the sofa onto his knees and leans over until he can grab a box from underneath the tree.

When he places the heavy box carefully onto my lap, I'm certain it's going to be another snow globe, but as I go to undo the ribbon, he covers my hand with his. 'It's not the same, but maybe that's a good metaphor because a lot of things aren't quite the same this year. I hope it's okay.'

I'm confused by what he means until I lift the lid off the box, and nestled in a bed of white tissue paper is... my favourite Christmas mug. The one I broke weeks ago. The one I've missed a truly ridiculous amount this month.

I burst instantly into tears. I never intended to kiss him in front of his family but it's physically impossible to stop myself reaching out, letting my hand slide along his jaw and pulling his lips to mine.

It's only a brief peck, and the sound of everyone cheering makes me let him go much quicker than I want to.

'How did you do that?' I whisper without pulling back.

'I work with ceramics every day. I studied the photos, got some advice on shaping from Thelma in A Very Muggy Christmas, and made a *lot* of practice pieces that weren't quite right. And some that were downright embarrassing.'

It seems like forever ago, that day in my shop when I told him about breaking my favourite Christmas mug and he sent the photos to himself. I didn't even know him then and he must've already been planning on doing this.

'He gets it from his grandfather,' Biddy says. 'My Claude's spirit lives on through him.'

It makes me feel uneasy for a moment, but she quickly adds, 'Even if he's not going to make those ridiculous snow globes any more.'

So they know. Biddy's descriptive word suggests she really does know the truth behind them, but more importantly, he's told his family about the change in direction and they're obviously supporting him in it.

'We should thank you for that,' Biddy continues. 'Without your influence, I don't know how long he'd have carried on trying to be someone he's not. The only thing Claude wanted was for Raff to bring his own touch to the shop. The magic of Dardenne Snow Globes has only ever been about the love that goes in to making them.'

Raff's sitting on the floor in front of my legs and I hear his breath catch. I can't help leaning forward and hugging him from behind, made somewhat less intimate by the fact that both of us have got on the equivalent of wearable duvets, and the rest of the day passes in a haze of hugs, gifts, bad cracker jokes, and way too much chocolate.

Exactly as I've always dreamed Christmas Day would be.

* * *

It's later in the evening and darkness has fallen when I slip outside for a moment of alone time and to send a quick message to my dad, and to ask Mum if we really could come up to visit this week.

I've been sitting on the little wall in front of the house for about ten minutes when Raff pokes his head round the door. 'Can I come out or do you need a bit more space?'

'Come out.' I beckon him over. 'It wasn't *just* an excuse to talk to my parents.'

'It's okay. I get it.' He sits down on the wall beside me. 'My family are a *lot* to get to grips with, especially at Christmas.'

'A lot, but in a good way.' I glance up at the dark sky. There's a heaviness to it and an icy chill in the air that makes me think it might be about to start snowing. 'They're exactly what a family should be, and today has been perfect. I feel loved, wanted, and like I may never eat again.'

'Mum's just got the tub of Roses out and Sofia's saving the best ones for you, and you should know that she doesn't usually let *anyone* get a look-in at the strawberry crèmes.'

I laugh out loud. 'Okay, maybe I could be persuaded to eat again shortly.'

He leans down to press a kiss to my shoulder. 'And you are.'

'What?'

'Wanted. And loved.'

'So are you.' I reach over and tuck his hair back, and even in the darkness I can see his cheeks redden, and it's impossible *not* to kiss him.

He shifts nearer and strokes down the side of my face and pulls me to him, and I let myself sink into the kiss, basking in a warm glow that feels like it's coming from inside of me.

We only pull back when the first snowflakes start to land all over us, making us both giggle. I didn't think this Christmas could get any better, but somehow, some power in the universe has just made it so.

And I kiss him again, surrounded by twinkling Christmas lights and falling snow, and I feel like I'm *in* a pretty little village scene inside a snow globe, and nothing has ever felt more perfect.

When we pull back this time, Raff takes my hand and looks up at the sky. 'There's something I need to tell you.'

That sort of sentence always elicits a shot of dread, but one glance at his face and I know it's not going to be anything bad.

He takes a deep breath. 'The snow globe I gave you wasn't a moving one.'

'Oh, very funny.' I give his hand a playful tug. 'Of course it was.'

'It really wasn't. Do you honestly think I'd be stupid enough to give a "smoking gun" to the one person who'd been trying to discredit me for years?'

'But... I saw it...' I stare at him. 'The nutcracker prince twirled the ballerina around.'

'It had a solid foundation. An empty base. There was no trickery in that one. If it moved, it wasn't because of anything I did.'

He could be winding me up, but somehow, I believe him. I find myself believing in a lot of things lately that, until a few weeks ago, I'd have sworn were fairy stories or sparks of imagination. 'Well, what do you know, maybe there is some magic in those snow globes after all.'

'Maybe.' He lifts my left hand and presses his lips against my unbroken fingers and I feel that little flutter inside again.

Sometimes Christmas comes at exactly the right moment and gives you exactly what you didn't know you needed, but you suddenly can't imagine your life without it, and if one thing is for certain, there has definitely been magic in the air this December.

ACKNOWLEDGEMENTS

Thank you, Mum. Always my first and most important reader! I'm eternally grateful for your constant patience, support, encouragement, and belief in me. Thank you for always being there for me – I don't know what I'd do without you. Love you lots!

Marie Landry, my best friend and, forever and always, the most spectacular nut to ever exist! Thank you for being my biggest supporter and loudest cheerleader, and for making me smile every single day! I love you to pieces and I'm so grateful that I get to call you my best friend! A huge thank you also to Nancy Landry for the constant love and support, even from half a world away!

An extra special thank you to Bev for always being so caring and supportive, and this time around, also for the genius invention of 'the cotton bud container mouse trap', which I had great fun using in a scene in this book! And a big thank you to Mrs Mouser herself, Cee Cee, as well!

Thank you to Bill, and Toby and Cathie for your continued love and enthusiasm. Thank you to Jayne Lloyd and Charlotte McFall for being such wonderful friends, and an extra special thank you to Sue Baker for doing so much to champion authors and for throwing the best publication day parties ever and making each book feel truly special!

I want to say a massive thank you to everyone who I chat to on social media, who I've connected with thanks to books, and to all of you who show me so much support and kindness on a daily basis. A big shoutout to some Facebook groups who support me tirelessly and are an absolute pleasure to be part of. A huge and heartfelt thank you to all the members and admins of Vintage Vibes and Riveting Reads, The Friendly Book Community, The Spirituality Café, Chick Lit and Prosecco, Book Swap Central, and Fiction Addicts at Socially Distanced Book Club. If you're a booklover looking for somewhere to brighten your day, lift your spirits, and make you feel like you've found a group of people who understand why we always buy more books even though we need scaffolding to hold up our current to-read pile, please find your way to these groups! You will be glad you did – although your to-read list may not!

Thank you to my fantastic agent, Amanda Preston, and my brilliant editor Emily Ruston, along with the rest of the wonderful and hardworking Boldwood team and the lovely Boldwood authors! It's a total joy to belong to Team Boldwood!

And finally, thank *you* for reading! I hope you enjoyed feeling the magic of Christmas through Franca's nutcrackers and Raff's snow globes. As a lover of both nutcrackers and snow globes myself, I loved writing this one! I hope you'll join me again for the next book where we'll be hanging out with Mickey in her curiosity shop The Mermaid's Treasure Trove! There are always many more happily ever afters to come!

ABOUT THE AUTHOR

Jaimie Admans is the bestselling author of several romantic comedies. She lives in South Wales.

Sign up to Jaimie Adman's mailing list for news, competitions and updates on future books.

Visit Jaimie's website: https://jaimieadmans.com/

Follow Jaimie on social media:

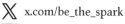 x.com/be_the_spark

 facebook.com/jaimieadmansbooks

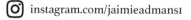 instagram.com/jaimieadmans1

ALSO BY JAIMIE ADMANS

Standalones

The Gingerbread House in Mistletoe Gardens

The Ever After Street Series

A Midnight Kiss on Ever After Street

An Enchanted Moment on Ever After Street

A Wonderland Wish on Ever After Street

Christmas Ever After

WHERE ALL YOUR ROMANCE
DREAMS COME TRUE!

THE HOME OF BESTSELLING
ROMANCE AND WOMEN'S
FICTION

 WARNING:
MAY CONTAIN SPICE

SIGN UP TO OUR
NEWSLETTER

https://bit.ly/Lovenotesnews

Boldwœd

Boldwood Books is an award-winning fiction publishing company seeking out the best stories from around the world.

Find out more at www.boldwoodbooks.com

Join our reader community for brilliant books, competitions and offers!

Follow us
@BoldwoodBooks
@TheBoldBookClub

Sign up to our weekly deals newsletter

https://bit.ly/BoldwoodBNewsletter